W9-DFG-814

SOLD TO A LAIRD

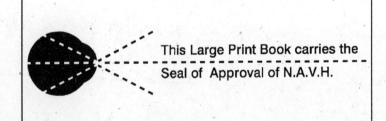

This Large Print Book carries the
Seal of Approval of N.A.V.H.

SOLD TO A LAIRD

KAREN RANNEY

THORNDIKE PRESS
A part of Gale, Cengage Learning

GALE
CENGAGE Learning™

Detroit • New York • San Francisco • New Haven, Conn • Waterville, Maine • London

GALE
CENGAGE Learning

LIBRARY OF CONGRESS CATALOGING-IN-PUBLICATION DATA

Ranney, Karen.
    Sold to a laird / by Karen Ranney. — Large print ed.
      p. cm. — (Thorndike press large print romance)
    ISBN-13: 978-1-4104-2612-3
    ISBN-10: 1-4104-2612-2
    1. Arranged marriage—Fiction. 2. Large type books. I. Title.
PS3618.A648S65 2010
813'.6—dc22   2010005031

Published in 2010 by arrangement with Avon, an imprint of HarperCollins Publishers.

Printed in the United States of America
1 2 3 4 5 6 7 14 13 12 11 10

To my readers

CHAPTER 1

Late spring, 1860
London, England

"Good afternoon, Simons," she said, pulling off her gloves. "Is my father at home?"

"I shall inquire of His Grace, Lady Sarah," the majordomo said, taking her gloves as well as the bonnet she removed. He placed them on a table she recognized only too well. Two months ago, it had been in the Winter Parlor at Chavensworth.

Lady Sarah surveyed herself in the mirror. She was presentable.

"Never mind, Simons," she said. "You know as well as I that my father will probably refuse to see me."

The majordomo didn't respond. Simons was, if nothing else, exquisitely tactful.

Without waiting for him to precede her, she strode down the corridor. Her father was partial to emerald green, and it was obvious here in the dark carpet and the wallpaper. She felt as if she were in a lush cave made of leaves, the smell not unlike that of forest undergrowth, dank and dark. No doubt the result of the tobacco he smoked in his study.

"Lady Sarah," Simons whispered, following her.

Deliberately ignoring the rest of what the man was saying, she halted in front of the study door, then resolutely grabbed the latch and opened it.

"If you send Mother to Scotland, she will die," she said, entering the room.

A second later, she halted, stunned into silence by the presence of the man seated on the other side of her father's desk, a man even now rising from his chair. A look of surprise marred his features. The expression was infinitely preferable to the frightening look on her father's face.

The words needed to be said, and even though they'd exploded from her with none of the tact or grace she'd been taught, they were the truth.

"She is dying," she said, ignoring the stranger in favor of her father who, unlike the man opposite him, still remained seated. His square face was florid, his blue eyes narrowed as they stared at her without a glint of recognition. "She won't survive the journey."

He didn't say a word, merely inclined his head, a gesture that inspired Simons to put his hand on her arm. She shook it off, determined not to be moved from the room.

"Why Scotland? Why now?" If she was going to be punished, she might as well truly deserve it.

The stranger glanced at her father, then over at her. She deliberately didn't look in his direction. What on earth would she do if there was pity in his glance? She'd dissolve into tears, pleasing her father and shaming herself. So she did what she always did in her father's presence, blocked out the emotions she was feeling. Instead, she concentrated on the reason she was here, in London, in her least favorite place on earth — her father's home.

"She's weaker each day. Why send her away?"

Nothing altered his expression — not sorrow, or regret, or any type of remorse. If anything, his expression steadied and solidified, human flesh taking on the impression of stone.

He looked down at the papers in front of him, suddenly pushing them away with one finger.

"You say you need investors, Eston?" he asked, addressing the man standing in front of him. "But you believe this invention of yours to be profitable?"

Was she being dismissed? With no word at all?

Sarah forced herself to remain in place, hands clenched together in front of her. Simons stood behind her, implacable and silent.

"Yes, Your Grace."

Her father stared down at the blotter, picking something up between two fingers and stretching them toward the stranger. The other man extended his hand, palm up, to receive something small and glittering in the afternoon light.

"You can replicate it, then? And make them larger?"

"Yes, Your Grace."

Her father glanced at her then, and Sarah realized he'd not forgotten her presence at all.

"You've asked for a great amount of money, Eston."

"Not for the return, Your Grace."

She took a few steps forward, toward her father's desk. Did she imagine that the older man tensed the closer she came? She could not relent. None of her letters had been answered. Nor had her father deigned to answer any of the handwritten messages she'd sent with a footman. All she had left was this, a personal appeal. If he wanted her to beg, she would. Her mother was dying; what was a little humiliation?

Her father held up his hand as if to forestall her advance. She halted, ever conscious of her father's temper. She'd learned several lessons when dealing with her father, lessons that she'd never forgotten. Don't incite his anger. Never insist or demand. Never tell him he's wrong.

Today, she was flouting all those lessons.

She remained where she was, determined that he would not discover that she clasped her hands in front of her to still their trembling. Or that her lips were clamped firmly shut for the same reason.

Her fear always seemed to please him in some horrid way.

He turned to the man who still stood in front of the desk. Not a supplicant, merely someone who looked, strangely enough, like her father's equal. The Duke of Herridge was a formidable figure, yet the man who faced him was as tall and as commanding in his own way.

If she hadn't been so worried about her mother, Sarah would have been more curious about him.

"How desperate are you for funds, Eston?" her father asked.

"Not desperate at all, Your Grace. If you decide not to invest, there are other men who have made overtures. You're the first I've met."

"I have not said that I refuse to invest in your invention. Instead, I propose that our venture be a more permanent one."

"And what permanent venture would you propose?" the stranger asked.

Her father glanced over at her. "I have a daughter who insists on remaining unmarried. Two very expensive seasons have proven what I've always known. No one else can abide her. I will enter into a bargain with you, Eston, but instead of money, I'll give you my daughter." His eyes narrowed. "You aren't married, are you?"

"No, Your Grace," the stranger said.

"Then take her as your bride."

Sarah was gripping her hands together so tightly she could feel each separate bone. She was bruising herself, no doubt. Was this to be her punishment, then? For daring to challenge the Duke of Herridge's cruelty she was to be sold to a stranger?

"I believe a special license takes a few days, but no more than that," her father said. "If you need somewhere to work, use Chavensworth. In fact, I would prefer it, in order to have some idea of your progress." He sat back in his chair and regarded the stranger with some equanimity.

"You cannot be serious," Sarah said, carefully not looking in the stranger's direction.

She'd never been in any doubt as to her father's feelings for her. He'd made his disdain for her perfectly clear. It was one thing to know that he didn't like her, quite another to share this moment with someone to whom she'd not even been introduced.

The Duke of Herridge folded his arms across his chest and looked impassively at the stranger. "Well, Eston? What's your answer?"

Eston glanced over at her again, and this time she forced herself to meet his gaze. He was absurdly handsome. His hair was black, his features perfect, and his mouth reminded her of the statues in the Greek Garden at home. His nose was a bit too long perhaps, and his chin too bluntly squared. But it was his eyes that drew her attention more than the arrangement of his features. His eyes were greenish blue, the color of a dawn sky.

What was a man doing with such eyes?

She wanted to tell him not to regard her

with such assiduousness. His intensity made her even more uncomfortable than her father's words.

Was he actually giving credence to her father's improbable suggestion? It wasn't the first time her father had said something shocking in public regarding her. He seemed to choose a crowded ballroom, a highly attended dinner party, a foyer filled with partygoers waiting for their carriages to arrive in which to criticize her, illuminate her shortcomings. She'd grown accustomed to his remarks and quite prepared for them.

Nothing could have prepared her for today, however.

"Very well," Eston said. "I'll take your daughter, Your Grace."

"I would say that you've made a good bargain for yourself, but I've no wish to lie to you, Eston. She'll be a chain of rocks around your neck. Still and all, being my son-in-law cannot help but do you some good in the world."

He was serious. He was actually serious. And so was Eston, if the considering glance he gave her was to be believed.

"The arrangement will suit me as well," the Duke of Herridge said. "If your discovery is a good as you claim, you'll make me a rich man. Not to mention ridding me of a nuisance."

"Have you lost your mind, Father?" Sarah said. "You cannot be serious."

He ignored her and spoke to Simons, still standing silently behind her.

"I am ignorant of the procedure for obtaining a special license. See that it's done." He glanced at Eston. "I'm certain you will do what you need in that regard, Eston."

"What makes you think I shall accede to this preposterous plan of yours, Father?"

"If you do not, I'll have your mother packed up for Scotland in less than a day." A smug, triumphant smile curved his lips. "It's your choice. Marriage or Scotland?"

For the first time, Eston spoke to her directly. "What is your name?" he asked.

"My name?" She turned her head and regarded him, wondering why she was suddenly incapable of answering that simple question. She did know her name, did she not?

"If we are to be wed, then I think we should perhaps begin with names."

"Sarah," she finally said.

He placed his right hand against his midriff and bowed slowly from the waist. Not deferential enough to be servile.

"Douglas Eston."

Her father appeared amused. She stiffened

her shoulders and inclined her head.

Not one word came to mind to convince him to change his mind. All her father had to do was simply wave his hands in the air, and she was married, dismissed, and banished with no more effort than it took to dismiss an untrustworthy servant.

The Duke of Herridge turned his attention to Eston again. "Her mother's family lives in Scotland. If she becomes a burden, I suggest you send her there. I should've done the same with her mother years ago."

Sarah turned to leave.

"Where are you going?" the duke asked.

She glanced at him over her shoulder. "Back to Chavensworth," she said. "Mother needs me."

"She'll have to do without you," her father said. "I'm not letting you out of my sight until you're well and truly wed."

Douglas didn't need the Duke of Herridge's money, and he certainly didn't need to be married. But something, an emotion he couldn't quite name, held him rooted to the spot.

Sarah looked terrified, and he couldn't help but wonder if her father was astute enough — or cared enough — to notice. He'd had his own experience with fear and attempting to suppress it. He saw the same in Sarah now. Her hands were clenched tightly in front of her — to hide their trembling? Her eyes were downcast — to mask the fear in them? Her lips were pressed tightly together, either to still their quivering or to hide the fact that they were suddenly bloodless.

Douglas wanted to stand in front of her, to protect her from the Duke of Herridge's cruelty. Or dispatch the man from the room altogether. If they were alone, he might ask her if she loathed the idea of marriage so very much. Or he might even press his suit, a thought that nearly had him fleeing from the room.

He hadn't known her fifteen minutes ago, hadn't seen her or dreamed of her, or envisioned her being part of the world in which he lived. He had not once thought to know a woman named Sarah, with her demeanor, with temper fleshing in her eyes at the same time as fear.

That was the insanity of this meeting. Not the Duke of Herridge's obvious greed and just as apparent cruelty. Not Sarah's aversion to her father. Not even the bargain Douglas was willing to make — a bargain that ridiculously included marriage — but the fact that if Sarah slipped away now, before he'd spoken to her, before he had known her, Douglas knew he would regret it for the whole of his life.

"I shall see about getting a special license," Douglas said.

The duke simply waved his hand at him, as if to speed him on his way.

One last look at Sarah, and he was reluctantly gone.

CHAPTER 2

The town house Douglas had purchased on his arrival in London was not as large as that belonging to the Duke of Herridge, but it was in a fashionable area. The rest of the houses on the square were occupied by peers, a fact he'd already been told. The same person who kept him apprised of his neighbors also harangued him on a daily basis about purchasing the furniture needed to at least equal their standards.

He left his carriage, the equal to any owned by his neighbors. It, too, had been recently purchased, as had the horses, and for an amount that he'd once thought exorbitant.

The young man opening the door was a stranger, but Douglas had given Alano leave to hire a new staff.

"Where is Alano?" Douglas asked.

"And just who would be asking?"

How like Alano to have found the most

annoying young man in London. Douglas bit back his irritation, and answered, "Your employer."

"Sir," the young man said, his attitude shifting immediately, "I am Paulson, and I believe Mr. Alano is in the wine cellar."

Mr. Alano? Douglas shook his head as he entered the house, veered to the right, and angled himself between two stacks of crates.

"Have we any footmen?" he asked. "Or stableboys, for that matter?"

"Two men were hired today, sir," the young man replied. "I do not believe they begin work until tomorrow."

"Then you will do, Paulson," Douglas said, pointing to a long crate beside the door, "I need this crate moved to one of the wagons in the stable. Be mindful of it. There are a variety of flasks and beakers from Italy inside. I would hate for them to be broken."

"You wish me to carry this to a wagon, sir?"

"I do," Douglas said. He looked around the room, now more a storeroom than a parlor. He was looking for one crate in particular, and he finally found it, and made his way to the other side of the room.

"Sir, I was hired for my knowledge of how a gentleman's household should be run, not for general labor."

Douglas moved out from behind a stack of crates.

"I'm not certain what Mr. Alano told you," he said, "but this is not a large establishment. Each member of the staff will be expected to turn a hand to anything that needs doing. I cannot abide laziness, Paulson. Nor will I pay for it."

"Sir."

Paulson didn't look happy, but Douglas was satisfied that he would do as told. He directed the young man to six more crates.

"Move these as well," he said, ignoring Paulson's petulant expression. "And use the same caution, please."

Douglas found the wine cellar simply by following the noise. Above the hammering sounds, Alano was swearing, and there was nothing quite as colorful as his friend's torrent of profanity uttered in a dozen languages.

He leaned against the railing at the bottom of the steps, amused by the spectacle in front of him. Arrayed in a circle were the dozen or so casks of wine Douglas had purchased in Spain. Two or three candles were stuck in empty bottles and served as illumination. In the center of the casks, seated on a stool with a curious contraption strapped to his knee, was Alano. Despite the fact that his hair was white, his dark-complexioned face was curiously unlined. His teeth, on those occasions when he deigned to smile, were as white as his hair. The clue to Alano's temperament lay in his brown eyes, however, eyes that flashed with emotion more often than not.

"Well, lad," Alano said, in a thick Spanish accent, an oddity given that his name was McDonough. His great-grandfather had emigrated to Spain, and begun a dynasty that had prospered. "How did it go? Did the duke agree?"

"I have an investment of sorts," Douglas said, moving through the barrels. "Not money, but marriage."

Alano's look held equal parts disbelief and surprise.

"Marriage?"

"To the daughter of a man who has little liking for Scotland or its inhabitants. It seems that my intended bride's mother is Scottish, and he seems to dislike all of us."

"Start from the beginning, lad. I've the feeling you've left out a great deal."

Douglas began from the moment he'd entered the Duke of Herridge's home, up until he'd been escorted to the door by Simons, the majordomo.

"You can't think to go through with it,"

Alano said, when he'd finished. "There are many other men who've expressed an interest in your discovery, lad. I doubt any of them will force marriage on you."

Douglas sat down on one of the barrels. "Perhaps it's time I married."

Alano put the bottle down and stared at Douglas. "Is she all that rich?"

Douglas smiled. "I have an idea that the Duke of Herridge doesn't have five farthings to rub together. This marriage is his way of saving face and still acquiring an interest in my discovery."

"Is she all that beautiful, then?"

He could see Sarah before him as if she'd stepped into the room. "She *is* lovely," he said, unaware that his voice had softened. "She has black hair and soft gray eyes, and a full mouth. But there's something more to her than just being beautiful. She's brave, and loyal, and loving. Her mother is ill, and you can hear the heartbreak in her voice when she speaks of her. She's frightened of her father; she flinched every time he moved, but she still stood there and defied him."

"So, it's love at first sight, is it?" Alano asked.

Douglas glanced at him, surprised. "Is there such a thing?"

"I've not enough fingers to list the girls I thought I loved, lad. But I've never gone and married one."

Douglas shook his head, either negating Alano's words or his own actions — he wasn't sure which.

"Is this something you're set on doing, then?"

Douglas smiled. "I think I am, yes."

"Are you going to tell him, or her, that you're a Scot as well? Or are you going to leave that a secret?"

"He's the one with the antipathy. Perhaps Sarah, being half-Scottish, will not mind a husband from Scotland."

Alano shook his head.

"You were nervous enough about meeting a real duke. How are you going to feel being married to the daughter of one?"

It was just like his old friend to bring a little realism into the day.

"I've managed up 'til now well enough," Douglas said. "What have you always told me? Something about feeling the part, and looking the part, and soon you'll be acting the part. The Duke of Herridge saw me as a gentleman."

Alano nodded. "You look and act the part, lad," he said. "But I noticed you're still carrying that notebook around with you, as if you're afraid to make a mistake."

Douglas looked away. "It's the other side of the world, Alano," he said. "From where I've come from to where I want to go. It's not that far in distance, but everything else is different."

"You've come all this way on your own, lad. Nobody gave it to you. You didn't inherit it. Every penny you have is a penny you earned. Don't you ever forget it. Those fops in their fine homes cannot measure up to what you've done. The Duke of Herridge got his title and his money from his father, and his father before that, and his father before that. He didn't make it all on his own, like you."

Douglas smiled. "I thought you said that nobles looked down at those in trade."

Alano snorted and reached for the bottle he was corking. "To their detriment. They'd make their own way if they knew what was good for them," he said. "Instead, they marry for money or live in genteel starvation. Not like you, lad. You were destined for great things from the moment I met you."

Douglas picked up a bottle already corked. Despite the number of servants he hired, Alano would always perform this chore himself, convinced that no one else, including Douglas, could do the job competently enough.

"You've always believed in me, Alano. All these years. Why?" He'd always wondered, but today seemed like the day to ask.

Alano looked surprised. "Why?" he asked, his eyebrows rising. "Because you were the most obnoxious boy I'd ever met. And you've grown into a man with the same stubborn streak. You get an idea in your head, and you won't let go of it until you see it through. As a boy, you just needed direction, lad, that was all."

"And as a man?" Douglas asked with a smile. "What do I need?"

"A swift kick, I'm thinking."

After that comment, Alano ignored him for a few minutes. He held an empty bottle below the cask, released the stopper, and watched as the wine filled the bottle. When the level was just below the neck of the bottle, he replaced the stopper, placed the bottle inside the curious leather cradle strapped to his knee, before grabbing a cork from the press beside him. He made a great show of concentrating his attention on hammering the cork into the bottle.

Finally, Alano turned to Douglas. "Does she know that you've just come to London? Does she know this place will be all topsy-turvy when she gets here? I've not yet had time to get the furniture for the front hall, let alone the dining room."

He reached for another bottle, but his expression was so thunderous that Douglas wondered if Alano would rather toss it in his direction instead.

"She has a house," Douglas said.

"And what am I supposed to be doing with this one?"

They'd known each other for two decades, had encountered hurricanes together, not to mention floods, earthquakes, and on one unforgettable occasion, a village filled with angry pygmies. In all that time, Douglas had never felt as flummoxed as he did now, when faced with a domestic crisis.

"Are you going to be like the peerage, then, since you're wedding into it? Keep this place for when you come to London?" Alano looked up, his sudden smile robbing the words of their sting.

"It sounds like a reasonable solution," Douglas said. "There's no need to sell it right away."

Alano nodded, intent on rubbing the dark green bottle in his hands with a rag. "I'll put it to rights, then. I'll settle myself here. I find London to my liking."

There was nothing more to be said. When

Alano made a decision, it was rare that he changed his mind. Besides, he wasn't an employee. Alano had his own fortune. One that, while not the equal of what Douglas had amassed, was certainly enough to enable him to live comfortably.

"You're hiring staff, at least. What made you choose Paulson?"

Alano didn't look happy about that question. "Stupidity," he said. "A mistake on my part. Maybe something about him reminded me of you."

He stared at Douglas, and the look reminded him of the first time he'd seen Alano. He'd been picking his pocket, and Alano had caught him at it, even though he considered himself an expert at the skill. Alano had only grabbed his wrist, twisted it behind his back, and proceeded to swear at him for a good fifteen minutes in Spanish. After that, he'd taken Douglas to a small establishment and fed him.

Alano placed another completed bottle on the barrel and turned to him. "If you're certain you want to go through with this, lad, then I'm behind you. Let me give you a spot of advice, though."

"As if I could stop you," Douglas said, smiling.

Alano ignored him, and continued. "Tell

this woman the truth about yourself, lad. Then you've nothing to fear."

"And if she moves heaven and earth to prevent a marriage between us, Alano?"

"Because you're not good enough for her?" Alano's mouth twisted into a grimace. "Then *she's* not good enough for you now, is she?"

The special license Douglas obtained had cost him dearly, but he'd been able to acquire one because of his extended stay abroad, the reasoning being that he had no home parish. Also, using the Duke of Herridge's name assisted the process.

Instead of returning home, however, he returned to the duke's home midmorning. According to Alano, *morning* calls were not made until afternoon. But this was not a social call as much as one of conscience.

First of all, he wanted to ensure that Sarah was not being mistreated by her father. He hadn't liked what he'd seen of the Duke of Herridge and wouldn't put it past the man to be a bully. Secondly, he wanted to speak to Sarah alone. She deserved to know the truth; he was as far from a gentleman as she was from the alleys of Perth.

Simons, however, refused to admit him when he knocked.

29

"I'm sorry, sir, but Lady Sarah is not at home to callers."

A statement Douglas correctly interpreted, thanks to Alano's tutelage, as being within but unwilling to see him.

"It's important that I speak with her, Simons," he said. "Is the Duke at home?"

"His Grace is not, sir."

Simons dismissed a lingering footman with a gesture of his hand and opened the door a little wider.

"You'll be doing her no favors by attempting to see her, sir," Simons said softly. "In fact, you may well be harming her."

Douglas looked at the man, surprised. "How?"

"The duke would not hesitate to punish her further, sir, if he were annoyed. At least now he's giving her food and water."

"What do you mean, now? Has he done this before?"

Simons looked torn between reticence and revelation.

"Sir, the duke does not like rebellion," he finally said. "Especially from those he considers beneath him."

"His daughter?"

"Quite so, sir. Or his wife." Simons looked toward the back of the house and the stables, as if afraid the duke would return at any moment. "He is like to do anything, and has. At the end of her last season, Lady Sarah did not wish to attend a certain function. His Grace beat her in front of the entire staff for her refusal. He has not hesitated to do what he wished whenever he wished."

When Douglas didn't respond, the major-domo smiled thinly. "It may be the very best thing for Lady Sarah, sir, that she is to marry you. The very best thing."

Douglas took a step back. For all his upbringing — orphaned at eight, running wild through the alleys of Perth — he'd never abused the weak or the defenseless.

"I'm beginning to think that you're correct, Simons," he said. "Tell His Grace that I shall be here at the appointed time tomorrow."

Douglas turned, descended the steps, and entered his carriage, conscious that Simons was still watching him. Once seated in the vehicle, he glanced up to see a female hand gripping the edge of a curtain on the second floor. Perhaps the hand belonged to a maid, industriously dusting. Or was it Lady Sarah?

He'd come to reassure himself of her safety only to discover that she was in more peril than he'd realized.

Tomorrow he would rescue her by marrying her.

Would she see it as such?

CHAPTER 3

Two days later, Sarah was well and truly wed, to a man she didn't know, a man who'd been whisked from her father's home five minutes after they'd met.

"Escort my daughter upstairs," her father had said, and just like that, she was led away, to quite a lovely chamber, if she could ignore the noxious shades of peach. She'd stayed there during her last disastrous season, and there were no good memories in attendance.

As she walked into the room, the door was closed behind her, and a key turned in the lock. She didn't bother pounding on the door or shouting for Simons. Her father's servants were, if not fanatically loyal, then at least afraid of him to the extent they would not release her.

That night, a note delivered with her dinner tray only emphasized her father's intent. Either she married, or he would send her mother to Scotland. Neither fate seemed palatable, but she didn't have the right to choose her own well-being over that of her ailing mother. She sent him a note in reply, asking for his guarantee that he would leave her mother at Chavensworth if she agreed to the marriage.

He didn't respond.

There was no choice, after all, but it was with some irritation that she greeted her bridegroom at the bottom of the stairs two days later.

Douglas Eston didn't look the least disturbed by the fact that she was being forced to wed him or the fact that it was barely a few hours past dawn, a time that few society weddings occurred. Nor did he appear disconcerted that she was frowning fiercely at him. He continued to regard her with a half smile, those strange-colored eyes of his impossible to read.

"You had to be complicit in this," she said, refusing to take his arm when he offered it. "A special license must be procured by the groom."

He didn't answer.

"I shan't be a good wife," she warned him. "I have a solitary nature, one that is not amenable to other people. I'm bookish, I've been told. I have too many flaws. I like to study the stars."

At that, he glanced down at her. Another irritant, that he was so much taller than she. He was rather large, too, with shoulders that blocked her view of the room.

She looked away rather than be mesmerized by those eyes of his.

"How do you study the stars? Have you a telescope?"

She glanced up at him. She was not going to tell him that he was the first person ever to ask her that question. Nor was she going to tell him that his question elicited the first bit of curiosity about him. No, it was best if they remained as they were, strangers who were about to wed because of her father's cruelty.

He led her into the parlor, where a minister stood, chatting away with her father, both of them wearing smiles as if this morning had been blessed by God himself.

Did the minister think that she was with child and this furtive wedding performed to protect her father's reputation?

She didn't say a word to disabuse him of that notion. In fact, it gave her a little thrill to think that the good man might be a gossipy sort, willing to trade a few rumors with a friend. Good, let him pass along the news that the Duke of Herridge's daughter was loose. Her father prided himself on his good name. All her life she'd been counseled on how to act, how to behave in public so as not to shame her father.

Her mother would always chastise her with a whisper. "Think of your father, Sarah."

The minute she left London, she had no intention of thinking of her father ever again. In fact, there should be no occasion whatsoever for her even to see the man.

Two servants served as additional witnesses to her marriage, a young maid she didn't recognize and Simons, who couldn't quite look her in the eyes. If nothing else, she was grateful for him sending a young maid to help her with her hair this morning.

The girl had apologized profusely and endlessly for her ineptitude.

"It's not your fault," Sarah had said. "You were not hired to do my hair. Nevertheless, I appreciate your attempts to assist me. Besides, no one shall be looking at my hair," she added. "They will be stunned into silence by my dress."

She glanced down at herself. The modiste hired by her father had been enamored of stripes. Every dress made for her second season had either had a striped skirt or a striped bodice or a striped leghorn sleeves. This ghastly garment had all three, and when she'd found it in the armoire, she'd sighed inwardly, remembering the loathing she'd felt for it and why, exactly, she'd left it behind in London.

Now it didn't seem to matter since she had no one to impress, and all that truly mattered was the fact she was clean and presentable. Well, hardly presentable with all these pink, brown, and white stripes, but she was clean.

She heard the minister's words and forced herself to pay attention. She'd been to her share of society weddings, and she'd been amazed at the expense necessary to marry off a daughter properly. Giving her a proper wedding would have cost her father a fortune. But she doubted that he'd spent more on this ceremony than the stipend it took to lure the minister to his house.

Even a wedding breakfast was dispensed with in favor of summoning a carriage. She didn't demur, being as eager to leave London as her father was to send her away.

"Thank God that's over," her bridegroom said as he entered the carriage and sat opposite her, his back to the horses. "My commiseration, Sarah."

She glanced at him curiously. "For what?

This disaster of a marriage?"

"Your childhood. Your father cannot have been pleasant to deal with."

"And your own childhood? Was it so pleasant?"

"Yes." A moment later, he began to smile. "I had a very enjoyable childhood. In fact, I've had a very enjoyable life. You might say that I've been enormously blessed."

"Not the least of which is finding yourself married to the Duke of Herridge's daughter."

"Do you always refer to yourself as the Duke of Herridge's daughter? Are you never simply Sarah? What a disappointment for you, if that's the case, to marry a simple mister."

"I didn't come to this marriage because of anything you offered me, Mr. Eston. On the contrary, I married you to give my mother a few more months of life. Being sent to Scotland could not improve her health. In fact, it would have done the opposite."

"So I can consider myself an object of expediency."

"Am I not the same?" She regarded him with what she hoped was a calm expression. Beneath it, however, she was growing irritated. "You wanted my father to invest in something evidently, and he did so. Not only did he invest, but he granted you a daughter and the use of a house, if you can consider Chavensworth simply a house. I cannot see anything any more expeditious than that, can you?"

"You looked unbearably sad."

Startled, she stared at him. "You pitied me? Is that why you married me?"

She turned her head again, concentrated on the view outside the window. She refused to believe him. He was a means to an end and the method by which to dispose of a troublesome daughter.

A daughter her father didn't like very much.

"Perhaps I felt a measure of compassion for you. Perhaps that sweetened the match your father proposed."

"He didn't propose anything," she said. "He imposed it. What would you call my being locked in a room for two days?"

He didn't say anything for a moment, and when enough time had elapsed that she grew curious, she glanced over at him. He appeared as annoyed as she felt at the moment, but whether his irritation was directed at her or her father, Sarah was uncertain. Nor was she about to ask him.

What good would it do to discover that her new husband was incensed with her?

She was who she was, good or ill, and she didn't want to begin this marriage with the pretense of being someone she was not. She wasn't appreciably delicate — she'd never had the luxury of pretending to have the vapors. Everyone around her seemed to be weaker than she, so consequently she'd always been forced to be the one with the level head, a cogent plan, some sense.

Unbearably sad, indeed. He said that only to soften her heart toward him. He felt nothing for her, and even if he did, she didn't want it to be pity. Let him be annoyed, then. Let him be as genuinely troubled as she felt.

"I'm not going to allow you into my chamber tonight."

She clasped her hands together and waited for him to offer up a protest. She was fully anticipating for him to be even more annoyed. He would say something like, "I am your husband. You will submit." Like blazes she would.

Instead, when she glanced at him it was to discover him smiling.

"I have no intention of coming to your bedchamber tonight," he said.

The velvet of the seat was smooth against her fingertips, tiny fingers of fabric reaching out to brush against her skin in welcome.

"We're strangers," each said, exactly at the same time. With anyone else, she would've smiled at the coincidence. But not with this man.

His wife sat opposite him, elbows tucked against her sides, feet properly together, chin lowered — so rigid she appeared almost brittle.

Her black hair was falling loose on one side, but he wasn't about to embarrass her by mentioning it. Nor would he comment on the fact that her dress — her wedding dress — would forever remain in his memory as the most egregious example of dressmaking he'd ever witnessed.

The sarongs of the Polynesians were infinitely preferable to what she was wearing now. In fact, she would probably have appeared attractive in a sarong. Add a smile, and Lady Sarah, now Mrs. Eston, would be lovely.

She wasn't about to smile, however. Instead, she leveled a fulminating look on him from time to time, obviously blaming him for this marriage.

He gave some thought to teasing her from her mood, but he didn't know enough about her to gauge her sense of humor or what she considered amusing. All he knew for certain was that the Duke of Herridge was a cruel and overbearing tyrant, and she carried so much pain in her eyes that when he'd first looked at her, he'd felt some of it.

He studied the documents from his case, finding himself quickly wrapped up in the formulas he'd written the night before. His new carriage was remarkably smooth riding, and he didn't experience the usual disconcerting dizziness when trying to read. To this day, however, he couldn't read aboard ship. The rolling waves made him ill, and since he'd spent a decade traveling the world, his illness was a remarkable waste of time.

For those journeys, he'd employed a secretary, the young man's main task to transcribe Douglas's thoughts and musings so time itself wasn't lost. Not that everything he thought was a gem of wisdom. However, substantial progress had been made on a new astrolabe, the advancement resulting from a single question he'd posed after dinner one night.

He glanced over at Sarah. She studied the stars. Was that an idle boast? She hadn't spoken of a telescope. Did she even know what a telescope was? He decided he wouldn't test her knowledge. If she'd been boasting, he didn't want to embarrass her.

The ceremony linking him to the Duke of Herridge's daughter had been mercifully brief. He knew, however, that if he pressed his memory, he could recall the words, just as he could remember the listless sound of Sarah's voice repeating the vows.

Sarah. A commonplace enough name, and one that garnered little attention. Not unlike his bride. Still, there was something about her that intrigued him. Not wholly, but slightly, as if it were a whisper of sound beneath a greater quietness. Some difference that incited him to watch her without seeming to do so.

Was she given to long silences? Or did she, when freed of her father's influence, laugh with abandon? He doubted the latter because her mouth fell naturally into somber lines. Yet there were faint lines at the corners of her eyes tempting him to believe she was amused often.

"Shall I commission a sculpture of me?" she suddenly asked. "Doing so will allow you to study my features with greater freedom. You needn't be pressed to pretend otherwise."

He smiled. "Why should I want to study a statue? Stone can't reveal what flesh does, either in character or mood."

She turned her head and looked directly

at him. He abandoned the pretense and studied her openly.

"Very well, what have you gauged of my character and my mood?"

"I wouldn't presume to discuss either," he said, burying his smile. "I do not know you well enough. However, I do anticipate the journey of acquaintanceship."

She looked as if she wanted to say something but then thought better of it.

"What were you about to say?"

She raised one eyebrow but didn't answer.

"Have you always been so imperious?" he continued.

The second eyebrow joined the first.

"Have you always been so . . . direct?" she asked.

"Do you think so?" He leaned back against the seat, his papers forgotten. "Is it direct to want to know what my wife is thinking?"

She looked away, her attention on the landscape. "A ceremony occurred, Mr. Eston. It may convey the title of wife upon me, but it doesn't mean that I've accepted it."

"A month?" he asked. "A year? Or less? When do you think you might be able to accept it? Or will you be able to at any time, given that you're a duke's daughter, and I'm a mister?"

"I am not disdainful of others," she said.

He didn't reply.

She turned her head and regarded him with a frown.

"My antipathy to this situation is not personal, Mr. Eston. I do not dislike you. I do not *know* you. I dislike being pressured to marry, but my main concern is not suddenly having a husband. My thoughts are with my mother. It has been three days since I've seen her, and I frankly do not know if she has survived in the interim."

"Forgive me," he said, a moment later. "I allowed my sentiments to overcome the facts of the situation."

Her frown deepened, but she didn't respond.

He returned to his papers but discovered that the formulas written there didn't capture his attention as much as they should have. He flipped open the curtain over the window and studied the passing scenery instead.

"Good God," he said, staring off into the distance. "What is that?"

He wanted to tell the driver to halt, to allow him to study the surprising view. Instead, he remained silent as the carriage climbed the top of the next rise. Here, the scene was even more improbable. An arched bridge reminding him of structures in Italy spanned a roaring river. Behind it, as if protected by the river itself, sat a house. No, a castle. No, perhaps a combination of the two. Three stories tall, of pale yellow stone, it was dominated by a white marble pediment stretching up to a roof surrounded by a railing and adorned with a series of statues.

"What is that?" he asked, even though he already knew the answer.

"That, Mr. Eston, is Chavensworth."

"It's the size of a mountain," he said. A two-story wing sprouted both on the left and the right of the larger section of Chavensworth, each wing disappearing into the forest of trees forming the house's back-drop.

"Hardly a mountain, Mr. Eston." A small smile formed on her lips. "Chavensworth has always been one of the most famous of the stately homes of England," she said, her tone back to being that of a duke's daughter. "Thomas Archer worked on the plans, and the waterworks in the gardens have survived two hundred years. The north front, the public entrance, of Chavensworth dates from the fourteenth century, when Sir Mat-thew de Baines was given license to crenel-late."

"And you cannot bear to be parted from it."

She turned her head and regarded him again. Surprise rounded her gray eyes, but what was the reason for the sudden blush on her cheeks?

"It's my home," she said simply.

"People deserve that type of love, Sarah. Not structures."

There was that look again, the one that prompted him to lean forward and place his hand on her knee. She flinched, but he didn't relent.

"Right this moment, tell me what you're thinking. It doesn't matter what it is. Tell me."

"You haven't the power to command me to speak, Mr. Eston."

"That's a start, Sarah."

"I have been in your presence exactly one hour, Mr. Eston. Bits of minutes gathered up together that probably totals one hour. Add this journey, and it's two, perhaps nearly three. You have no knowledge of me."

Nor would he, if she had anything to say about it.

The carriage rolled through the gates of Chavensworth.

Tall bushes and feathery trees sat amidst a

closely cropped lawn sloping down to the river in the front of the house. In the rear, a road led to the rest of the buildings of the estate, and the stables. Chavensworth was set among prosperous farms and dominated the countryside like the regal house it was. The placement of the many windows and large doorway always made it appear as if the house were smiling, and anticipating her return.

Sarah concentrated on the approach. The winter had been one of ice storms, and the road was pocked badly, necessitating that the gravel be replaced. The paint on the shutters needed to be retouched, and the landscapers needed to finish smoothing out the winter mulch and removing the muslin from the smaller of the rosebushes. The change of seasons always resulted in a myriad of chores, and by the time all the tasks were done, the seasons were changing again.

She made a mental list of things needing to be done as the weather warmed, not simply to take her mind from the man still watching her too closely but to keep her from thinking of her mother. Still, a prayer crept into her thoughts. Please, dear God, let her be well. Let her have wakened. Let her be eating again. Let her recognize me.

She wished she'd thought to have hay spread across the gravel, but then, she hadn't known how loud the wheels would sound.

The carriage rolled to a stop, and she took a deep breath.

Her husband was quite chivalrous, exiting the carriage before her and turning to hold his hand out to assist her down the folded steps. She took his hand and schooled her features so no one could see how much she feared the approaching moments.

After fluffing her skirts, and surreptitiously arranging her hoops, she straightened her shoulders and began to walk up the broad steps toward Chavenworth's front door, praying as she went.

CHAPTER 4

Thomas, anticipatory as always, opened the door just as she put her foot on the last step. For a second, his smile of welcome faded as he glanced at the man on the steps behind her. His face smoothed into an effortless expression, and he bowed from the waist.

"Lady Sarah," he said. "Welcome home."

Sarah began to remove her gloves one finger at a time, sliding the silk from knuckle to nail slowly, a task requiring so much concentration that she'd needn't look at Mr. Eston.

"And my mother, Thomas? Is she well?"

She counted ten agonizing beats of her heart before he answered. Ten, in which she wondered if he was going to hang his head low and murmur the words she so dreaded to hear: Your mother, Lady Sarah, is dead.

Twelve more beats, and Eston moved to stand closer.

"She has not awakened, Lady Sarah,"

Thomas finally said.

"She has not rallied?"

"No, Lady Sarah."

"Or eaten anything?" she asked.

He shook his head.

Hope was the one emotion she found difficult to quell entirely. Every morning upon awakening, she wondered if a miracle had transpired. And perhaps it had, simply because her mother had survived the night.

"I regret, Lady Sarah, that there has been no change."

She nodded. The news was not unexpected. "At least we will not be traveling to Scotland, Thomas," she said.

The underbutler studied the floor with great precision, as if to measure the flagstone squares. His hands were clasped at his back, and he rocked back and forth on his toes. When he looked back at her, his eyes were watery.

"The duke has reconsidered, then?"

"Yes," she said.

She looked up at Eston, wishing she could banish him from Chavensworth. There were too many tasks for her to accomplish, too many duties that required her attention. Who had time for a husband?

He only smiled at her.

Eston was too large for the space. His

51

shoulders were a bit too broad to be average, his height too great to be normal as well. His clothes were quite well tailored, the fabric of his suit a fine twill. His waistcoat was a bit on the plain side, merely black silk. A rather somber garment altogether, as if he'd been observing a period of mourning.

Had he? She knew his name, and the fact that he was an inventor of sorts, and that he'd sought her father out as an investor. He'd had a good childhood. Beyond that, she knew absolutely nothing about the man to whom law had linked her.

"What is it you've invented?" she asked abruptly. "Was it worth giving up your life?"

"Are you saying that our marriage is going to end in my death?"

Thomas made no effort to suppress his look of surprise.

She shouldn't have spoken to Eston at all. She bit back her sigh, and said, "Mr. Eston is my husband, Thomas. You'll please accord him all courtesy."

"Of course, Lady Sarah," he said.

"I would appreciate it if you would keep the knowledge to yourself, at least until I have the opportunity to speak to Hester and Margaret."

"Of course, Lady Sarah," he said, before

turning to her husband. "A wagon arrived this morning, sir. Are those your belongings?"

"If they're piled high with crates from Italy, they are," Eston said.

Thomas glanced at her. "We thought the duke might have sent them, Lady Sarah. Shall I have the crates unpacked, sir?"

"I would prefer that you didn't," Eston said. "I shall attend to the chore soon enough."

She'd learned more in the last minute than she had in the entire journey from London. Perhaps she should use Thomas as an interpreter of sorts. What would the poor man do if she turned to him, and said, "Would you ask him, Thomas, exactly what he expects from this marriage? Does he realize I have no intention, whatsoever, of being intimate with a man I do not know?"

But, of course, she wouldn't. She was, if nothing else, a proper and well-reared lady.

She turned and walked down the hall to what had once been the Summer Parlor. In the last year, when climbing stairs had become too difficult for her mother, Sarah had had the room converted to a sitting room and bedchamber. She slid the pocket doors apart slowly.

Hester, her mother's day nurse, pressed a

finger against her lips, then gestured with her other hand for Sarah to enter.

Sarah came into the room quietly, closing the doors softly behind her.

Her heart sank when she looked at her mother.

"Thomas said she's not awakened in all the time I was gone." Even her whisper sounded too loud.

"No, my lady, she hasn't. And Margaret tells me the nights are the same."

Hester was an older woman of indeterminate years. Her hair, once vibrantly red, had faded to a rust color. Wrinkles ravaged her skin, and age had grayed the whites of her eyes. Despite her age — or perhaps because of it — there was a calm implacability about Hester. But the true reason Sarah had hired Hester was the look in the older woman's eyes, a warmth revealing her caring nature. Hester granted her affection without reservation. She'd never met a stranger, she was fond of saying, and it was for that quality more than any other that Sarah had made her the duchess's nurse.

Sarah sat on the straight-backed chair kept beside the bed for just such visits as these.

Her mother had not been well for years. In the last six months, however, the Duchess of Herridge had become so frail she was a mere shadow of herself. Her complexion was pale, almost waxy, and her lips had a bluish tinge. The hands resting on the top of the coverlet were so white and thin that Sarah could see the tracery of veins beneath the skin. Her rings had long since been placed in the duchess's jewelry casket for safekeeping.

Lowering her head, Sarah kissed the back of her mother's hand, wishing she could warm her in some way. Wishing, too, that her father was at his wife's bedside, if not to say a final farewell, then at least to pretend to care.

Her mother's breathing was labored. At the end of each struggling breath, Sarah found herself inhaling deeply, as if to infuse her mother's lungs with air.

"What can I do?" she whispered. The question was addressed to God, to her mother, to Fate itself, but Hester answered.

"Go on as you have," Hester said kindly. "God gives us trials and tribulations to test us, Lady Sarah."

Just how many trials and tribulations did one life deserve? Her mother loved a man who didn't care about her affection. She'd lost four children before they'd drawn breath.

The door opened suddenly, surprising her.

She glanced over her shoulder to see Eston standing there, accompanied by Thomas.

Would he not give her any privacy, even here?

Hester stood, but Eston waved her back in her chair.

He didn't speak, merely entered the room softly, to take a stance behind Sarah. He placed his hand on her shoulder, and she flinched from his touch, even as she realized it was a gesture of support. Despite her rebuff, however, his hand remained, and she gradually relaxed, feeling the warmth from his palm permeate the fabric of her dress.

"What is wrong with her?" he asked softly.

"The physicians do not know," she said. "One of them said it was a depression of the spirit. Another thought it might be a tumor of the inner organs. Or a deficiency of the heart."

"Is there nothing that can be done?"

"If there is, I do not know it," she said. "I've consulted with physicians, and wise-women, and even a woman who read cards. All I have left is to find a witch."

A moment passed before he spoke again.

"My parents died when I was a boy. Cholera. I've never thought about it before, but I don't know what's worse, not being prepared for the loss or watching as death happens in measures in front of you."

She was startled by his candor. If she'd known him better, she would have answered him with the same honesty and told him that watching her mother die slowly was unbearable. She felt as if her heart were being torn out of her chest every day.

"You sit with her a great deal, I warrant."

She nodded. "Wouldn't you?"

"Yes," he said softly. "I would."

"At least she will not be sent to Scotland."

"Would your father really have done such a thing?"

"Yes," she said. "He would really have done such a thing."

She took a deep breath, stood, and faced him.

"But she will not be moved. Nor disturbed. She will be treated with love and care until the moment she takes her last breath. On this I swear, Eston." Her look defied him to argue with her.

"I have no intention of moving your mother anywhere, Sarah. Nor in disturbing her one whit. On the contrary, whatever she needs, you have but to ask, and I'll ensure it's done."

She nodded, unable to speak.

Finally, she turned, taking up her post beside the bed again. She would not cry.

Not now. Not in front of him. Not in her mother's room. But it took moments for her to regain a semblance of composure.

"When I think of my childhood, I don't think of my father," she said softly, remembering the comment he'd made in the carriage. "I think of my mother, instead. Whatever I learned from my governess, she augmented. She had a wonderful imagination. She and I took long, fantastic trips to Istanbul, Russia, China, and America, even though we never left Chavensworth. I learned to speak French, so that when we imagined Paris, I could converse along with her. There was no happier child than I was. Nor spoiled, perhaps."

"I doubt you were spoiled," he said.

He didn't look at her but continued to study her mother. Finally, he turned to leave the room, glancing back at her. "My name is Douglas," he said. "What shall I call you? Lady Sarah? Even though you've lost your title on marrying me?"

"I haven't," she said. From the look on his face, she'd surprised him. "I've merely changed it. I'm Lady Sarah Eston now."

"A duke's daughter."

"Yes. An accident of birth, if you will, Mr. Eston. Am I to deny it?"

"I wouldn't ask it of you," he said.

She was grateful for his smile. It tripped her annoyance and kept her from tears.

"Call me whatever you wish."

He looked as if he would like to say something but changed his mind. She allowed him the privacy of his thoughts. She would not pull and push as he'd done to her. She didn't want to know what he was thinking.

She looked beyond him to where Thomas still stood. He and Hester were certainly getting an earful. Thank heavens neither was the type to gossip.

"Please prepare the Red Room, for Mr. Eston," she said to Thomas. There, far enough away from her own chamber that he would not be a bother. If she tried, she could even ignore the fact that her husband was living under the same roof.

Eston merely smiled, but instead of correcting her, turned to Thomas. "Ready the Duke's Suite for me. I presume Chavensworth has one?"

"Yes, sir."

"And move my wife's things into it as well."

The fact that she was in her mother's sickroom kept her mute, but nothing could push back her anger or the fear following on its heels.

"I told you I would not come to your chamber."

"And I told you I would not come to yours," he said, still smiling. "Fate has decreed that we have a chamber large enough to share. Or are you telling me that what I imagine is not true? Is the Duke's Suite a cramped closet?"

Hardly, since it occupied nearly half of the second floor. She remained silent, however, not divulging any information.

"Besides, I have always believed in beginning a task with the outlook in mind."

"The outlook?"

"Being a married couple. Acting as man and wife."

She hadn't actually thought beyond getting home. Perhaps she'd believed that once she was inside Chavensworth, the situation would magically rearrange itself, and he would disappear. Perhaps she'd thought that her mother would be well and would banish him with her tinkling smile and a look that dared him to complain. Perhaps she even thought that he would see the error of his ways and feel only shame for having taken advantage of the situation.

Instead, he was saying things like acting as man and wife.

"Are you insane?"

He didn't look mad. In fact, he looked positively pleased. Dear heavens, what on earth did she do now?

He didn't respond to her goad, and she wondered what he would do if she simply stood and walked from the room. Would he demand her return? Worse, would he make a scene in front of the servants?

She gave him a small smile, the same kind of smile she would offer to the upstairs maid when she finished a rather deplorable piece of mending of Chavenworth's linen sheets. The effort was to be commended even though the result was not acceptable.

"Will your valet be joining you?"

"I haven't a valet," he said, his smile appearing to be a more genuine effort than hers. "I have no personal servants. I can cope quite well without people helping me tie my shoes."

Had she just been insulted?

She might have asked him if her new husband hadn't suddenly left the room, leaving her to stare after him.

CHAPTER 5

The sad fact was that, despite her annoyance, misgivings, and general reluctance, Sarah was Mr. Eston's wife. As Mr. Eston's wife, she was subject to his rules, and one of those rules, however much she disliked it, was that they were to sleep in the Duke's Suite.

Since her father never came to Chavensworth, and since it was the largest chamber at the estate, Mr. Eston's proposition made some sense. However, Sarah gave orders to have a cot moved into the room. Just because Mr. Eston insisted they sleep in the same room did not mean she agreed they should sleep in the same bed.

She requested a tray to be served in her sitting room, thereby removing from the staff any temptation to prepare a bridal dinner, or an intimate meal for her and her new husband. She didn't fool herself that they had been kept ignorant of Mr. Eston's presence or role.

"Have you served Mr. Eston?" she asked the footman when he delivered her meal.

The young maid behind him tittered in response. When she glanced at the girl, she bobbed a curtsy and flushed, both accomplished at exactly the same time.

"Begging your pardon, Lady Sarah. Mr. Eston thanked us kindly."

Why did the girl find it necessary to giggle when making that statement?

She dismissed them both, concentrating on her meal. In actuality, she had little appetite, but she managed a few greens and something Cook had prepared, no doubt of a celebratory nature. The beverage consisted of a measure of white wine, currants, and grated ginger, sweetened with sugar and topped off with a sprinkling of lemon rind. She liked it so much that she considered ringing for more but reasoned that it was not the wisest course.

Being a reluctant bride should not be compounded by being a tipsy one as well.

Once she was finished with her meal, she withdrew her journal from its spot on her secretary and spent several moments in earnest writing. Only then did she summon Florie to help her prepare for bed.

"I am married, Florie," she said, when the

girl arrived. "I am married, and I do not wish to discuss it. Not now, not tomorrow, not next month."

Florie said nothing, but it was clear, from her open-mouthed expression, how surprised she was.

Nearly as surprised as Sarah.

None of Sarah's sleeping garments were outlandish or revealing, but she still felt conspicuously uncovered in her linen nightgown and matching wrapper. Of white linen, with pink piping, it was perfectly proper. Unless, of course, one was going to a bedchamber occupied by a man one had only recently met — and married.

Once Florie left the room, Sarah surveyed her reflection in the pier glass. If she stood in front of the light, the shape of her limbs was visible. Since she had no other garments of a sturdier nature, there was nothing more to be done. She would simply have to remain covered at all times.

She left her chamber and walked down the corridor, with shoulders squared and head held high.

Mr. Eston opened the door to the Duke's Suite at her knock and silently stood aside.

"Your cot has arrived," he said.

What a very strange voice he had. Not simply the inflection of his words but the tone of it as well.

"Do you sing, Mr. Eston?"

He looked at her as if she'd lost her wits.

"I was asking because of your voice. You have a very deep voice. We have a great many baritones in our Christmas choir. You might consider joining it."

He shook his head, and she had the impression that he considered her odd, perhaps eccentric.

"It's a very *good* choir, Mr. Eston," she said, frowning at him.

"I'm quite certain it is, but I don't sing."

She was left with nothing to say, which meant that she had no choice but to enter the Duke's Suite.

Indigo draperies, the same shade as the coverlet, covered the many floor-to-ceiling windows. The four-poster bed, sitting on its dais, was swathed in the same material.

The round carpet covering the mahogany floorboards was woven with a deep border in indigo and lavender chains. Lavender, honoring the first crop ever to be planted at Chavensworth, was also replicated on the pillows of the upholstered chairs beside the window and the embroidery on the coverlet.

On the far wall was the defining feature of the room, a series of cupboards with gold-leaf fronts. Each cabinet bore a scene from

Chavenworth's history, from the planting of the first lavender beds to the building of the house itself. The gilt required constant maintenance and delicate handling, so that it didn't flake and peel from the wood.

"Do you really intend to spend the night on a flimsy cot?" he asked from behind her.

"Unless you give me leave to return to my room," she answered quite amiably.

"Do you need my leave?"

He was, like it or not, her husband. But this union would not be dictated solely by his rules but also by her wishes. That, she'd decided in the two days she'd been locked in her room. If he did not like it, Mr. Eston could simply go away, leaving her in the not-unwanted state of being married with no husband in sight.

However, it was one thing to make such a decision in her own room and quite another to do so in his presence.

"I think it would be best if we began this marriage in the traditional way," he said.

She clasped her hands together, making a fist of the two of them. How very cold she was.

"I will not bed you," she said.

Would it become a contest of more than wills between them? He was a very large man, and although she was taller than most of her acquaintances, she could not best him in strength. Would he force her? Surely not. He had seemed like a gentleman upon their first meeting. And he had been kind and polite enough in the carriage. But did his surface veneer rub off in the bedroom? Would he expose himself as a vicious and horrid man?

"In New South Wales," he said, striding across the room, "the aborigines do not sleep together for at least three nights."

She frowned at him. She didn't know whether to satisfy her curiosity or drop the subject entirely. Talking to him, however, kept her attention from what he was doing, and what he was doing was undressing in front of her. He didn't even take the precaution of stepping behind the screen erected in the corner for just such a purpose. No, Douglas Eston was above such sensibilities or beyond them. He was removing his waistcoat, then his shirt, divesting himself of his clothing with such an insouciant attitude that she suspected he had done so many times before.

"You're very comfortable undressing in front of strange females, aren't you?"

"You are my wife. I believe you should become accustomed to it."

Well, she was very much *not* going to

become accustomed to it, regardless of what he said. She deliberately turned and stared at the opposite wall.

"What are aborigines?"

"The native people of New South Wales. It's located on the other side of the world."

"I know where New South Wales is," she said. "I'm very well-read. I've just never heard the term *aborigine*."

"Their habits are no odder than this union of ours, Your Ladyship."

"I'm not to be addressed in that fashion," she said. "It's Lady Sarah. Or my Lady."

"I would prefer Sarah," he said. "Despite the fact that you're the daughter of a duke."

"I had absolutely nothing to do with the circumstances of my birth," she said.

"And if you had? Would you have changed anything? Or would you have preferred, instead, to have been born at a different time? A handmaiden to Cleopatra, perhaps?"

"Why couldn't I have been Cleopatra herself?" she asked, staring into the maw of the fireplace.

"Do you see yourself as royalty?"

She considered the question for some seconds before she answered him. "There is a great deal of responsibility to being royal," she said. "For that matter, there is a great deal of responsibility to being the daughter of a duke."

"Especially the Duke of Herridge."

She merely inclined her head in agreement.

The silence stretched between them for a few moments. She heard sounds like fabric rubbing together and wondered if he was taking off his trousers. The sound of a shoe dropping was loud enough that she jumped, startled, before admonishing herself sternly to remain motionless.

Then there was nothing. No sound at all, unless she counted her own breathing. But in the bathing room, there was water splashing, then the gurgle of the drain.

Was she going to stand here like a ninny for the entire time it took for him to ready himself for bed?

He emerged from the bathing chamber and she nearly turned around before remembering that he would be naked, of course. He should be attired in a nightgown, as was proper, but somehow she doubted he would be.

"Will you not share the bed with me, Lady Sarah? It looks comfortable, at least, and certainly large enough. You can occupy one half, and I shall occupy the other."

"I shall be quite happy on my cot," she

said. Her voice sounded perfectly normal and without a betraying quiver to it. Years of standing before her father and hiding her true emotions had made her quite adept at managing fear.

"A pity, then," he said.

She heard him plump up the pillows, then the squeak of the mattress straps as he sat on the bed.

"Do you want me to leave the light on?"

"That is not necessary," she said. "I can settle myself perfectly well in the dark. There is nothing in the dark that wasn't there in the night."

She was startled to hear him chuckle.

"Do you think this situation amusing, Mr. Eston?"

"I think you are vastly amusing," he said. "More than you could ever imagine."

She didn't know whether to be affronted or relieved. Surely a man who was amused by a woman could not be intent upon ravishing her?

Perhaps she should be like Scheherazade and tell him a tale to entertain him. And unfortunately, the only tales she knew were of Chavensworth. No doubt her life here was boring to him.

"Have you traveled a great deal?" she asked.

"I have, in the past," he said. "Of my future, I can't speak. It has a great deal to do with you."

"I shouldn't think that I would be an object of consideration, Mr. Eston," she said.

She turned to face him, relieved that he was covered by the sheets and the coverlet. His shoulders were bare. The rest of him must be bare as well.

She looked away again.

"Chavensworth may keep you here, Mr. Eston. It's beautiful, is it not?"

"It's a building, Lady Sarah. As a building, it's to be admired. I wouldn't call it beautiful, however."

"Are you that prideful a man that you will not admit to admiring anything? Not a structure, not God's handiwork, nothing that you yourself did not build or cause to be constructed?"

"In other words, am I like the Duke of Herridge?" he asked. "No doubt your father's arrogance has colored your opinion of all men. I am not like your father."

She had no rejoinder for him. Only time, and perhaps familiarity, would tell exactly who he was. But at this moment, she wasn't about to say that. Instead, she only nodded.

A moment later, the lamp was extinguished, and they were in darkness.

"I can smell you," he said. "Do you think that's entirely fair?"

"I beg your pardon?" She navigated to her cot and sat down on the edge of it, staring up at the bed on its dais. He was a shadow in the darkness, but she could tell well enough that he was sitting up and looking at her. She wouldn't have been surprised to see his eyes gleam like a cat's.

Intentionally ignoring him, she lay down on the cot, grabbing the edge of the sheet with both fists and pulling it up to her chin.

"You smell of roses. Here I am, a celibate bridegroom, and my bride lies in her solitary cot smelling of roses and moonlight."

"You cannot smell of moonlight," she said. "Moonlight has no scent."

"You have evidently never smelled a summer night in Borneo."

"I have never left Chavensworth," she admitted. "Other than to London, of course. But the world comes to London. Why should we ever leave?"

"If you have to ask that question, then the answer isn't important."

Now she was affronted. She stared up at the darkened ceiling, wondering how she should respond. "I have always been a person who loved knowledge," she said.

"Some people do not like to travel," he said. "It's enough for them to remain in their homes for all of their lives."

"Are you berating them because that's a choice they made? Perhaps they don't have the funds to venture far from home."

"Which is your excuse? Is it a choice? Or simply because you've never been given the opportunity? What faraway land would you see if you had the funds and the time?"

"I could spare the funds from Chavensworth," she said, lying and disliking that fact intensely. "Up until our marriage, Mr. Eston, I was a single woman. Single women do not travel although it's encouraged for single men. Besides, I have had other duties to occupy me."

He didn't challenge that statement, possibly remembering her mother's condition. But neither did he ease her mind by saying something conciliatory, a politeness anyone else might utter. But he was not anyone else, and these were not the usual circumstances either, were they? There was nothing in any of the books or periodicals she'd read addressing a marriage like this.

"Shall I sleep on a cot for the rest of my days?" she asked, giving voice to an earlier thought. "Will you aid me in rising as my joints stiffen?"

"Can you see yourself being stubborn until you're an old woman?"

"Stubborn? Is that what you call it? I call it not being a harlot. I don't know you, Mr. Eston. Bedding you would be tantamount to acting the part of a loose woman."

"And you would never act in such a way, would you?"

The question was strange, but not because it was intrusive. She had come to expect that from her new husband. No, it was the way in which he had spoken it, almost kindly, pityingly.

"It has been impressed upon me from a very early age," she said softly, "that I am the Duke of Herridge's daughter, and as such, there is a standard of behavior for me."

"But not for anyone else?"

"Of course there is. Everybody, regardless of his role in life, has a set of standards. The groom is not to polish the silver. The footman is not to curry the horse."

"And the duke's daughter is not to feel passion, is that it?"

She sat up and stared at him. "I really do insist that you don't use that kind of language in front of me, Mr. Eston."

"Passion?"

"Exactly. I am not a woman of the streets. I do not doubt that you are unaccustomed to associating with my type of woman."

"And what type of woman would that be? Narrow-minded? Terrified? Tell me, Lady Sarah, do you wear a corset to bed?"

"I have no intention of discussing my undergarments with you, Mr. Eston. Not now, not ever."

"Do you know that the women in Fiji wear nothing at all but a grass skirt? Their breasts are allowed to hang unbound. They're quite lovely."

She lay back on the cot, her arms at her sides, her eyes scrunched shut, and her mind deliberately focusing on something other than his comments.

"I should like to see your breasts unbound, Lady Sarah. I imagine they're quite large. Are your nipples coral? Or are they the most delicate pink?"

She drew the sheet up over her head, ignoring the fact doing so left her feet bare. Let him comment upon her naked toes, anything other than her breasts. She had never even called them breasts to herself. It was her chest, simply put. She was a woman, and that was one of the things God had granted women. They had chests. But he was calling attention to the fact that it wasn't simply a chest. She had breasts, two of them.

If he didn't cease, she would never be able to sleep. She would lie there in a bright red stew of humiliation long after he had fallen into his dreams, no doubt of a libidinous nature.

"I imagine they're exquisitely sensitive. Never having seen the light of day, so to speak. Do you allow yourself to bathe them? Or is it done with a far-off gaze, an admonition to feel nothing from your body?"

She drew the sheet down below her eyes. He really must cease now. To speculate on how she bathed was too much, especially since he was excessively close to the mark.

"I imagine your shoulders are beautiful as well. I should like to see you in an evening gown, something frothy and totally unlike you. Something overly feminine, perhaps."

She was excessively feminine. Who was he to say such a thing to her? Their acquaintance had lasted a matter of hours. What did he know of her?

She shut her eyes and prayed for sleep. Let her be able to ignore him. Let everything he said be nothing more than the drone of an insect, or the sound of water like one of the fountains in the garden. She would simply treat his words like the trickle of water and pay no attention to the meaning.

"Breasts are vastly underrated, Lady Sarah. They are a source of great pleasure for a woman. Did you know that? It is not simply a place for a babe to suckle. A grown man likes to suckle as well."

Water dripping over the stones, that was all his words were. In the water garden, there was a tiny little piper, Pan, standing atop a curling leaf, water pouring from his flute. Or there was a larger statue of Poseidon, the God of the Sea, roaring up from the curved bowl of a large fountain, balancing three voluptuous mermaids on his shoulders.

They were bare-chested as well.

"Cease, Mr. Eston."

"Douglas."

"I really must insist," she said.

"Douglas."

"I really must insist. Douglas."

"Sleep well, Lady Sarah."

She turned her head and frowned toward the bed. Had that been his intent all along? To get her to call him Douglas? Could he be that Machiavellian, that cunning?

She was sleeping on a cot that was anything but comfortable, staring up at her husband, who was a little more than a stranger. Sarah had the distinct feeling that she'd been bested, and that Douglas Eston

might be a bit more complicated than she'd
once believed.

CHAPTER 6

An hour past dawn, Douglas found Chavensworth's library.

Evidently, the Duke of Herridge had not been able to make his mark on this room to the degree he had his town house in London. There was no clutter here, no ostentation. The floors were whitewashed, the bookcases painted white, and the ceiling the same pleasant pale green as new grass. Scattered throughout the room were pedestals topped with marble busts of philosophers, Romans, and no doubt past Dukes of Herridge. At one end of the library were two heavily embroidered chairs with tall backs and deeply carved arms. Above them hung a portrait of a man, and beside him the painting of a woman, both dressed in outdated clothing. The first Duke of Herridge and his duchess?

Chavensworth's library boasted two levels, one accessible from the main corridor on the ground floor and the second only gained through a circular iron staircase in the middle of the room. He found himself exploring the books, amazed at the number of them.

Someone had gone to a great deal of effort to catalog all the volumes. Each bookcase was labeled by subject matter, and the books in the fiction section had been shelved by author.

I am a woman who strives to be knowledgeable. Lady Sarah's words. Was this library so perfect because of her efforts? Or had she hired someone to care for Chavensworth's volumes? Either way, she evidently thought highly enough of the room to devote some attention to it.

Douglas made his way to the windows on the other side of the room. In front of them rested an enormous mahogany desk. He sat back in the chair, pulled his notebook from inside his jacket, and opened it, beginning to write what he'd learned the night before: How Sarah was to be addressed, and the fact that the daughter of a duke never loses her title — she simply changed her last name. When he was finished, he put the leather notebook back into the pocket of his jacket and stood, leaving the library and almost colliding with Thomas.

He'd evidently disturbed Thomas in his early-morning routine, because the young man wasn't as sartorially perfect as he had been the day before. Instead, he wore a leather apron and smelled of something pungent and unpleasant.

"Cleaning the privies?" Douglas asked.

"Demonstrating how to make copper polish, sir," Thomas said. "It's Lady Sarah's recipe, but I didn't want to disturb her."

Douglas tucked that knowledge away for later.

"Is there anything I can do for you, sir?"

"Nothing," Douglas said. "I wake early as a habit."

Thomas nodded and left him, but Douglas could see it was with some reluctance. Did the young man think he was about to steal the silver? Once, he might have considered it. Now, however, he could have purchased a dozen Chavensworths. Perhaps he simply looked disreputable, the shadow of the alleys of Perth still clinging to him.

He brushed that thought aside and continued his exploration.

When Sarah awoke in the morning, it was to find that her husband had already left the Duke's Suite.

She sat up on the edge of the cot with

some difficulty, given that every muscle in her body had stiffened. She missed the clinging softness of her feather bed, with its sweet smell of lavender and heavenly smooth sheets.

It had taken her ages to fall asleep last night, and as tired as she felt right at the moment, she might not have slept at all.

Very well, if this was to be her married life, then she would make the very best of it. She would have Chavensworth's carpenter construct her a bed frame, and the second-floor maids could stitch together a mattress, slightly smaller in dimension than her own feather bed. Nonetheless, it would be vastly more comfortable than the military cot on which she'd slept last night.

Mr. Eston — Douglas — had probably slept like a baby. That thought immediately conjured up an image of a baby's head against her bosom, his mouth against her breast. She pressed both hands to her chest as if to ward off the image itself. She was left with the sound of his voice echoing in the chamber as if he had just spoken those shocking words. *It is not simply a place for a babe to suckle. A grown man likes to suckle as well.*

She was too smart a woman to believe in conjurers' tales or superstitions of any kind, but if she were given to such things, she would have thought that he had the power of magic in his voice. The sound of his voice, the low timbre of it, the way he had of enunciating certain words, almost as if English wasn't his native language, was fascinating. Where had he been born? Only one of a dozen — or a hundred — questions she had about the man who was now her husband.

Sarah stood and walked to the dais, wrapping her arms around one of the four posts, staring at the rumpled bedclothes. She could almost see him lying there, naked and abandoned, his arm thrown over the extra pillow, his hand stretched out, fingers splayed and reaching for her.

She blinked the image away before turning and stepping down from the dais. Moments later she was in her own chamber. She dressed before Florie arrived, choosing one of a dozen day dresses she'd had sewn for her by the seamstresses employed at Chavensworth. The design was one of her own making, and together with her corset, which could be laced from the front, allowed her to dress without having to wait on a servant. She had saved endless hours with such garments. Today, however, she waited for Florie for one reason only. She needed help with her hair.

"It's an odd sign of vanity," she said, watching as Florie brushed each tress before pinning it carefully into a curl at the back of her head. "It's only hair. We should not care so very much about what our hair looks like."

Florie's gaze met hers in the mirror as she removed the hairpin from between her lips and spoke. "Why should we not, Lady Sarah? You would care if your dress was spotted. You would care if your gloves were soiled. Why would you not care about the state of your hair? Women are supposed to care about such things. If we did not, God might as well have labeled us men."

"Oh, but then we should have so much more power," Sarah said. "We could stomp around like roosters, crow to our hearts' content, and say and do almost anything we pleased."

Florie did not comment to that observation, which was just as well.

Why had she spoken so intimately to her maid? Perhaps it was because her only confidante, her mother, could no longer converse. Perhaps it was simply that she was lonely.

How utterly absurd. She didn't have time to be lonely. She especially didn't have time to be lonely this morning. After having been gone from Chavensworth for three days, there were more than enough tasks to occupy her.

She thanked Florie and left the room armed with her journal and her pencil. At the top of the stairs, she grabbed the banister with her right hand and slowly descended. Her fingers registered that there was not sufficient wax on the wood to make the surface feel slippery and warm, and she made a mental note to discuss this with the housekeeper. Dust had been allowed to accumulate on a few of the portrait frames on the wall above her, and she observed that as well.

There were so many places of beauty throughout Chavensworth, so many wondrous things to stop and admire during the day. Her family's history hung around her, was saved in the china cabinets, revealed in the linen-press. The legacy she'd been born to was there in each successive portrait, in the pressed flowers, in the books arrayed in the library.

Sarah nodded to a young maid industriously brushing the treads at the bottom of the stairs.

"Good morning, Abigail. How is that tooth?"

The girl smiled, showing a gap where the offending tooth had been only a few days earlier. "The blacksmith, he took it out, Lady Sarah. It still hurts some, but not as much."

She patted the girl on the shoulder. "See Mrs. Williams today, and tell her I said to give you some Oil of Cloves. Put that on your gums both morning and night, and you'll soon feel better."

The girl nodded and continued with her work.

Sarah entered the Yellow Dining Room, the small family room where she always ate breakfast, and nodded to one of Cook's helpers. The girl bobbed a curtsy, entered the kitchen, and returned a moment later with a hot kettle that she put on the sideboard.

Arrayed before her, just as her mother had always decreed, was breakfast the way breakfast should be presented at Chavensworth.

A cloth, heavily embroidered in shades of purple — to complement the fields of lavender visible from the window, was draped across the sideboard. Atop it, arranged in a pleasing pattern, was a sufficiency of knives, forks, saltcellars, butter dishes, and egg cups. Twin pitchers held milk and cream.

Three chafing dishes warmed sausages and other meat selections. Toast, rolls, and breads laced with cinnamon were arrayed in a basket near the kettle.

How very odd that she wasn't hungry.

She wanted to ask if anyone had seen her husband, but that was not a question she would venture to her servants.

She took a piece of toast and poured herself some tea before walking to the table arranged before the window. This view had always epitomized the beauty of Chavensworth, the majesty of the estate. Below her, in sloping fields that seemed to go on forever, were sixty acres of lavender. Beyond them were the home woods, a thickly bearded forest now green with spring growth.

She should try to locate her husband. It was only too easy to get lost in Chavensworth's two hundred rooms. Perhaps Mr. Eston — Douglas — was hungry. Her duties as a hostess, as the chatelaine of Chavensworth, supplanted any irritation she might feel with him.

A few nibbles of her toast, and she was done. She nodded to the footman stationed outside the dining room, a sign that she had completed her meal, and walked toward her mother's room.

In the foyer, she straightened her bodice and adjusted her collar before pressing both hands against the front of her skirt in order to inspect her shoes. Even though her mother had not awakened from her unnatural sleep, it would not do to appear in her presence slovenly. The Duchess of Herridge was very conscious of appearances.

Slowly, Sarah pushed open the door, scanning the shadowy room for Hester.

Instead of Hester, however, her husband sat on a chair at the side of her mother's bed. Her husband. Nor was he engaged in respectful silence. Instead, he was conversing with her mother as if they had been properly introduced.

". . . didn't speak a word for hours. I would think her shy, but the glint in her eyes makes me think that assumption is incorrect."

"It isn't at all proper for you to be at an invalid's bedside," Sarah said, entering the room and sliding the door closed quietly behind her. "Especially my mother's."

"It was proper enough when I came yesterday," he said as if unsurprised at her sudden appearance. Did the man have eyes in the back of his head? "Why is it not today?"

She decided to ignore that question and

ask one of her own. "What were you talking about?"

"I was telling your mother about our wedding."

"She is not to be told," she said hastily. "It would only disturb her."

"You're her only child," he said, glancing at her. "She would want to know anything that happened to you. Good or ill."

"She will not hear you," Sarah said, arranging herself on Hester's chair at the end of the bed.

"Perhaps she will. Perhaps she's smiling in her sleep."

She glanced at her mother, wondering if he were jesting. But there was no change. Yet neither was there a smile on Douglas Eston's face, only a look of intensity that made her wonder at his thoughts.

"I do not know what I shall do without her," Sarah said, a bit of honesty she'd not intended to reveal.

He didn't respond.

For long moments they sat silent together. Ten minutes later, she stood, walked to the other side of the bed, and bent down to kiss her mother's cool cheek.

"I will be back at noon, Mother," she said in a low voice, just in case her mother could indeed hear her. She glanced at Douglas. "I have chores waiting."

"Of course," he said. A quite amiable answer, but one that didn't quite match the expression in his eyes.

Was he irritated at her? Annoyed? Or simply curious? How very odd that she couldn't decipher his mood. She was very good at reading people, but he remained annoyingly mysterious.

She took refuge in silence, leaving the room with undue haste, grateful that it was a sickroom after all, and that he couldn't call after her.

Douglas sat with the duchess for another quarter hour, feeling a sense of peace in the dim room.

There were some of life's blows that took a person unawares, some that were too difficult to survive alone. When those times came, as they would to each person, they were easier to endure when standing shoulder to shoulder with another human being.

He'd been eight when his parents had died of cholera, fourteen when Alano had rescued him. A callow boy, not yet a man, but certainly believing himself one. Sarah would have him to lean on, but would she accept him? Or would she ignore his pres-

ence as much as she did the fact that her
mother was dying?

CHAPTER 7

Despite the fact that there were numerous tasks to be done during the day, Sarah discouraged the servants from being about their duties before half past six. Anything earlier was an unnecessary waste of coals and candles. The only exception was Thomas, as underbutler, who was balanced between positions in the household. At times he served as butler, and at others, he was head footman, whichever was more necessary to the smooth order of Chavensworth.

The first-floor maids had already opened the shutters and windows of all the lower rooms. Two of the younger maids were in the process of blacking the fireplace in the Chinese Parlor. She nodded in satisfaction when the younger girl — Mary — spread open a cloth over the carpet in front of the fireplace and placed her housemaid's box upon it, withdrawing the supplies that had been issued to her on the beginning of her employment only two weeks earlier: two small squares of leather for polishing the brass andirons, a selection of brushes for applying black lead as well as the lead itself, emery paper, and a japanned cinder pail containing a sieve and a fitted cover. Once the grate was cleaned, the two maids would spread the lead over the bricks, buffing it with the brushes provided.

Sarah began her morning as she did every day, by meeting with Mrs. Williams. She found the housekeeper in the butler's pantry and watched approvingly as the woman mixed together the ingredients for Chavensworth's furniture polish. Linseed oil, turpentine, vinegar, and spirits of wine were applied with a soft flannel rag, then buffed with a clean duster. Every month they made furniture paste together, a concoction of beeswax, soap, turpentine, and boiled water, allowed to steep for two days until it was ready to use. The paste was saved for the most valuable of Chavensworth's furnishings, such as the inlaid chest in the Garden Room, or the French tables in the Chinese Parlor.

She would have to speak to the carpenter this morning if she intended to spend another night in the Duke's Suite.

A week's supply of tea leaves, dried, had been saved in a glass jar, to be used to sprinkle over the rugs on the first floor, then brushed away. Each week a different floor was similarly treated, a rotating method used with most of the chores at Chavensworth. As it was, the estate employed over fifty people, but only fifteen in the house. The cleaning never ceased. Nor was it ever completely done.

"If you don't mind," she said to Mrs. Williams now, "we'll discuss the menus this afternoon, between two and three."

Mrs. Williams nodded. She was a woman of few words but excessive energy, a point in her favor as far as Sarah was concerned.

"I am certain you know by now, Mrs. Williams, that I have wed."

To her credit, the woman didn't look the least discomfited by that news. She merely stopped what she was doing and turned to face Sarah.

Mrs. Williams always seemed to have the temperament of a well-contented cat, easily set to purring, and rarely annoyed. Her round face was dusted with a permanent rosy blush on her cheeks and the tip of her nose. Divots framed her mouth as if directing a watcher's attention to her pale blue eyes. Those eyes rarely seemed irritated, and for that reason she was looked upon with great fondness by the staff of Chavensworth.

"I had heard, Lady Sarah."

All in all, there wasn't much more to be said, was there? She had a husband. He was in residence. Beyond that, what could she possibly say?

"Congratulations, Lady Sarah, on the occasion of your nuptials. Will you be celebrating?"

She blinked at Mrs. Williams for a matter of seconds, long enough that the time seemed absurdly elongated.

"Will I be celebrating?" she repeated stupidly before latching onto an excuse. "No, Mrs. Williams, given my mother's health, that won't be appropriate."

"Very well, Lady Sarah."

And that, it seemed, was that.

A few minutes later, she left the housekeeper, walking through the kitchen, nodding to Cook and her helpers, past the scullery, and into the area where cleaning supplies were stored.

Every week, she took inventory of this area. Cloths, brushes, and knives for cleaning candlesticks and lamps were kept on the second wooden shelf. A bucket filled with tallow grease scraped from candlestick holders sat on the floor. A set of knives used strictly for lamp trimming rested on the bottom shelf. The tradesman who supplied the oil visited Chavensworth every week and aided in teaching the maids how to keep the lamps in perfect order.

On a second set of shelves were the hard whisk brushes made of coconut fiber and used to brush the carpets in the dining and sitting rooms.

He wanted to see her breasts.

Her fingers rested against the raw wood of the shelf as she stared, unseeing, at the stacks of brushes made from goose wings.

This morning he'd been caring and attentive of her mother, and all during that time, she'd thought of what he'd said. He'd imagined her breasts.

She looked down at herself.

Had she laced her corset as tightly as decorum dictated? Had she been as proper as she should? Or had she secretly allowed the lacing to slip between her fingers so that it wasn't quite as tight as usual?

Nonsense.

The maids would be airing out the Duke's Suite. The housemaids knew she liked her bed to slope from head to feet, but the cot on which she slept had no feathers. Would they inquire of Douglas? How did he like his mattress shaped? Swelling slightly, perfectly flat, or did he prefer his mattress with a discernible dip in the middle? The housemaids would beat, shake, and turn the mattress to his preference.

Another mystery about her husband.

The maids would dust the rooms, wipe the ledges, polish the mirrors, and sweep the floor. If it was time for it, they would polish the furniture, then dust the wall of gilt cupboards, before scrubbing the floor with a mixture of very little soap and soda so as not to discolor the floorboards.

Would they wonder why she'd not slept with her husband?

For that matter, would they wonder about her husband?

She couldn't say anything to them at all. She would never divulge anything personal to the servants. Doing so was a breakdown in hierarchy, and Chavensworth ran so smoothly for reason alone. Everyone had his place. Everyone was expected to behave in a certain manner, in a certain way.

Without order, there was chaos, even at Chavensworth.

Thomas escorted him half the way and was dissuaded from accompanying him to the kitchens only after Douglas assured him he was capable of following directions. The underbutler laid out a series of turns that Douglas unerringly followed to the family dining room.

There was no need for defense at Chavensworth — the estate would simply absorb any intruder and cause him to become inexorably lost.

He breakfasted on oatmeal and kippers, both excellent. He pushed open the door of the kitchen to tell the cook exactly that.

She was a large woman, a testament to her talent in the kitchen. A bright red apron was tied snugly around her waist, topping a dress the shade of summer squash. Her blond hair was arranged in a ringlet of curls and perched atop her head like a cap.

"I thank you, sir," she said, her plump face blushing an unbecoming red.

"Is that the accent of Scotland I hear?" he asked, smiling at her.

"It is, sir. Glasgow was my home for twenty years."

Cook's helpers were scattered through the large room, and each one of them seemed to cock her head, ears twitching to hear his answer.

"I knew it had to be a Scottish cook with a fine hand at the oats," he said.

"You're the first to say, sir," she said, blushing even redder than before.

He left the kitchen, not bothering to ask for directions. Sometimes, the greatest adventures are those for which there are no guideposts.

Douglas found himself in a room that would have been considered a Great Hall in any castle. Life-size paintings dominated the walls, stretching up to where the ceiling arched upward even higher. Three crystal chandeliers stretched from one end of the room to the other. For all its dimensions, however, the room struck Douglas as being one of the coziest at Chavensworth.

Throughout the room were scattered groupings of chairs and sofas and lamps as if to urge a visitor to stop and rest for a moment. The walls were covered in a gold-patterned damask, the ceiling painted in a matching shade and embellished with plaster curlicues highlighted in dark brown.

The windows, stretching easily twenty feet high, made up one entire wall and were covered in heavy gold velvet draperies, tied back with gold rope ending in tassels larger than his hand. Ebony Chinese screens blocked off the doors at the far end of the room, more of an inducement to remain in this lofty room and simply contemplate the silence.

In front of a marble fireplace so large that

he could stand upright inside it, were two flanking sofas. Between them was a low table almost as wide as his bed, and on each side of the sofa was a circular table adjoining a blue overstuffed chair.

A hundred people could easily be accommodated in this room, and yet two would find it a comfortable retreat.

Chavensworth was filled with sitting rooms, parlors, and rooms devoted to individual occupations such as music and cards. A large ballroom on the third floor looked empty, desolate, and rarely used. There was, in addition to the large library, a room that looked as if it were devoted to records. A series of ledgers was stacked in large bookcases along the walls.

Where did Lady Sarah disappear to during the day?

He didn't bother opening any of the doors on the second floor, deciding that they were probably bedrooms or guest rooms.

Instead, he found himself at the rear of Chavensworth, heading toward the stables. A curious convergence of odors struck him then: the lavender from the fields to his left and the pungent aroma from the stables farther away. He began to smile, feeling in that instant that he had truly come home. This was not some province in India, or some tiny Asian country where people who looked like him were rare. No, this was nearly home with the sound of English in his ear and the promise of a certain sobriety of purpose and regulation of his days.

The air was warm, accompanied by a mischievous breeze that flattened the material of his jacket against him as it flirted with his collar. The sky was intently blue, not a cloud in sight to mar the purity of the day.

How many times in his lifetime had he wished to be exactly where he was right now, walking down a country lane, en route to an uncertain destination, only knowing that he was filled with contentment. He needn't fear for his life. Nor was he going to be attacked for the discoveries he had made. Here at Chavensworth, he felt a sense of safety and security he'd not felt in a very long time.

He was nearly at the stables if the sounds ahead of him were any indication: the striking of an anvil, the whinny of horses, the call of one man to another. He ignored all of them, suddenly transfixed by the sight atop a small knoll. He left the lane, veered to his right, following a well-worn path in the grass. Someone had thought to lay boulders down into the dirt, to create a toehold. He made his way up the knoll, and stopped, as fascinated up close as he had been in the lane.

The structure that faced him was hexagon-shaped, topped with a domed copper roof now gone to verdigris. He recalled Sarah's words — *I like to study the stars.*

How long had it been since she'd come here? Evidently some time, since he couldn't open the door. He pressed his shoulder against it, and when that didn't result in any success, he bent and excavated the dirt from around the base of the door.

The interior was damp and dark, the dirt floor giving off a sour, musty smell. A telescope was still affixed to a pulley, but when Douglas focused the lens, all he could see was a blur. He lowered the telescope and tied off the pulley so the instrument was held flat against the wall and out of the way. Turning in a slow circle, he measured the room mentally, wondering if it would give him the space he needed. Shelves ringed the room, and a stool was tucked beneath one. A series of grates covered the dirt floor. The domed ceiling could be sealed so that rain would not ruin his work. In the winter, the building would have to be warmed somehow, but he had months before having to worry about the cold weather.

He ticked off the assets of the observatory: It was well away from other people and structures, thereby ensuring that the chemicals he used would not catch another building on fire, or produce a gas dangerous to other individuals. But the greatest asset of the observatory was its isolation. He could have the privacy he needed, no, required.

He was changing the world, and the less the world knew about it, the better.

CHAPTER 8

She should be ecstatic. She should be overjoyed. Her husband had disappeared, and not one person at Chavensworth had seen him since breakfast. Not one. Thomas claimed no knowledge of his whereabouts, and when Sarah went to visit her mother at noon, Douglas was not there.

Truly, she did not have time for this. If the silly man had gotten into some kind of danger, she would have to find him.

She sent one of the footmen to the stables to see if he had been spotted there. Perhaps he'd taken one of the horses to ride in the countryside. Hopefully, the stable master had the good sense to tell the man to remain on the main lanes. There were rabbit holes and burrows aplenty in the fields. A horse could lose its footing all too easily, not to mention break a leg. She also had Thomas send another footman to the river, to see if

Douglas might have wandered to the boathouses.

There were other duties to take her time. She didn't have any free hours to worry about Mr. Eston. In addition, sparing her staff to look for him meant that other chores were not being done.

Although the housekeeper was diligent in her duties, Sarah also inspected the work of the maids and footmen. In her absence, all the tasks necessary to maintain Chavensworth had been done, but never as thoroughly as when she was present to supervise. Yet her thoughts kept coming back to Mr. Eston. Douglas.

What if Douglas had somehow wandered off the lane and into one of the traps placed by the farm steward? She would never forgive him. It was one thing to agree to marry her but quite another to disrupt her entire schedule by sheer stupidity.

"Lady Sarah?"

She turned to find Thomas standing there, his face marred by a frown.

"What is it? My mother?" Her heart seemed to beat slower, as if wishing to stop in that moment.

He shook his head quickly. "No, Lady Sarah. Mr. Eston."

Her heart began beating swiftly again.

"Has he hurt himself?"

"No." Thomas hesitated and she began to tap her toe impatiently.

"Well?" she finally asked. "What has happened to him?"

"The stable master says he came and took the wagon that arrived for him. He gave no indication where he was taking it, but he returned the horses a few hours later."

She blinked at Thomas. His words weren't any easier to understand the longer she stared at him.

"Where is he now?"

"The stable master doesn't know."

One presupposed worry when one cared for another. Why should she worry? She had no connection to the man save that of a legal nature.

I would like to see your breasts bared.

Dear God, what was she thinking?

"Very well," she said. Life at Chavensworth would hardly change without him. He was a raindrop in a storm.

She finished her tasks by six, straightened her hair, washed her hands and face, and went to sit with her mother.

"Has she shown any change?" she asked.

Hester shook her head, her gaze on the duchess.

If anything, her mother looked even more

diminished today than yesterday. Would she simply waste away? If she didn't wake, at least to take water, there was every possibility that's exactly what would happen.

"What shall we do?" she asked, but Hester didn't answer. The older woman had slipped from the room unobtrusively.

Sarah moved the chair closer to the bed, placing one hand on her mother's wrist and the other on her hand. Her skin felt so very cold, as if the grave had already claimed her.

Perhaps if Sarah spoke to her mother, she would hear. Would she come back to life? Would she open her eyes?

"The tablecloth was washed today, the one with the wine stain. It's the fourth time I've had the laundress rewash it, and I think the stains will come out in one or two more washings. I also gave notice that the stable should be painted, and it's time for the hedges to be measured and trimmed. I know you don't like them to grow too high," she said, speaking of the ornamental garden her mother so prized.

"I think the youngest scullery maid is with child," she said, sighing. "I don't know how to broach the subject with her. I have hinted broadly enough that I was receptive to any confidences she might care to make. I think she would come to talk to you, Mother, more so than me." She smiled. "That's an incentive for you to get well," she said. "Chavensworth needs you."

She sat silent for a few moments before beginning to speak again. "I am so accustomed to seeking your counsel, but I don't know what to do when you don't answer me. I think I know what you would suggest, and I use my own judgment as you've taught me. Sometimes, however, it's important to have your thoughts validated."

She picked up her mother's hand and kissed the back of it softly. "I do wish you would wake. I hope you can hear me." She laid her forehead against her mother's hand and breathed in the smell of lavender used to scent the mattress.

A moment later, she forced herself to continue, lifting her head and smiling at her mother.

"The Ladies' Guild has requested the Rose Garden for their annual tea. I've approved the date, but I've also suggested that we limit the attendance to fifty. Last year was just too crowded, and some of the older roses were damaged."

She ticked off the other items in her mind, topics that might interest her mother, activities she'd performed today.

"I gave Thomas the duty of inspecting all the footmen's livery," she said. "I sincerely hope that we don't have to incur expense there. But it's better to be prepared than to be surprised." An adage her mother had instilled in her from childhood.

"The north wing has some damage to the roof. It's not major," she said, trying to recall the steward's exact words, "but I need to ensure that repairs are made before the next big storm."

The Duchess of Herridge did not respond.

"What shall I do without you?" Sarah asked in the silence of the room. "Who will give me advice? Or share her stories with me? Who will make me laugh?"

There was no answer, just the barest sound of the duchess's breathing. Even her breath seemed shallower than the day before.

Sarah bent her head, wishing she could think of a prayer, the perfect prayer, the very one to attract the attention of the Almighty. If she phrased the words in just the correct manner, would God be merciful? Would He stop whatever He was doing and pay attention?

A wall blocked her tears. A tall and thick wall that hid the rising tide of her grief from view. One day, perhaps soon, the level of her tears would reach the top of the wall, and her tears would splash over and be revealed to the world. For now, she was composed. Her servants no doubt saw her dry-eyed and calm, and perhaps they wondered at the coldness of her temperament. This grief, however, this loss, was not for anyone else to wonder at or whisper about. This pain was for the quiet of her chamber, muffled by the sound of her pillow.

She spread her fingers, stroking her mother's skin, wishing she could warm it somehow.

How strange that she was fixed on this moment, unable to summon a single joyous memory or happy moment. She could not move her hand from her mother's, and she could not budge her mind.

"I've finished Monday's and Tuesday's tasks," she said, gently stroking her mother's wrist. "I'm only one day behind," she added. "But we shall make up for it tomorrow."

She lowered her voice until it was just a whisper. "I haven't mentioned my marriage, have I?" She paused for a moment, as if giving her mother time to answer.

"He's quite attractive, Mother. You can almost see him as a knight in armor, holding his helm under one arm. He is very commanding in his way, but he doesn't seem that way at first. I've noticed that he seems to study a situation with some intensity before deciding what to do. Then, once he's decided, he acts with a great deal of forcefulness. He isn't arrogant. He isn't rude. He's just there, like a boulder, or an oak. You know he will not be moved."

Sarah traced a pattern on the sheet with one finger. There were so many questions she wished she could ask her mother, but it was not Morna's illness that precluded her from doing so as much as her own embarrassment. There were so many things she didn't know. Not about how humans copulated — Chavensworth was a large estate with prosperous farms. She had seen her share of animals in rut, even though she was supposed to have ignored any such behavior and pretended it didn't exist.

No, the questions she wanted to ask were of a somewhat different nature. Could a woman be curious about the physical aspects of marriage even if she didn't know the man very well? Could she be interested in copulation, or was even such an interest considered an act of harlotry?

And if a woman happened to find herself lying naked near a sinfully attractive man, should she allow herself to be seduced?

Especially if that sinfully attractive man was her husband?

There was no one to ask, and she was left floundering in her own ignorance. She sighed heavily.

"He is very handsome," she said, lowering her voice again. "But one does not seem to remember that about him. He leaves an impression," she added. "A very definite impression."

One of having been close to lightning.

What would her mother think of Douglas Eston? Would she be charmed by him? Her mother had a way of looking for the best in each person, a trait that Sarah knew she hadn't inherited. She'd begun that way, of course, wanting to believe that every person with whom she came in contact was kind and industrious. She wanted to believe that people had more than their own interests at heart, that they actually genuinely cared for others.

As long as her mother was awake and counseling her, it had been easier to believe in such things. Perhaps there was too much of her father's cynicism about her.

What would she think of Douglas Eston if she were possessed of her mother's optimistic attitude?

Unfortunately, she wouldn't think any differently of him at all, simply because she didn't know the man. She could only go by his actions, and having been in his company exactly one whole day, there wasn't much to judge. He had insisted that she sleep in the same room, which wasn't onerous after all, because he hadn't touched her. He didn't insist upon her sharing a marital bed. Nor did he ravage her in any way, except verbally, perhaps.

He didn't demand that she report to him, that she alter her life in any way. Of course, she hadn't given him the opportunity to do so. Nor would she. Her life at Chavensworth would go on in the same pattern as it had before. No inopportune husband would have the ability to alter her existence.

Was that too stubborn a thought?

He had been very kind to sit with her mother this morning and talk with her. What had he said? Sarah was her daughter, and she would have been interested in anything that concerned her.

What an odd time to begin to weep. Not that anyone could tell. The tears simply rolled from her eyes without volition. She angrily brushed them away with the back of one hand before bowing her head once more.

Very well, he hadn't been difficult at all.

113

But then, he'd simply disappeared. What was she to make of that?

She sat with her mother for another hour, without, thankfully, dwelling on Douglas Eston to any great degree. Finally, she stood and bent over the bed, placing a kiss on her mother's forehead and pressing her cheek against her mother's.

"Please, God," she whispered.

She didn't know what else to ask for. *Thy will be done* seemed to be the four most difficult words in any language. What did God choose, in this instance? *Please, God* seemed as good a prayer as any.

Sometime in the last hour, Hester had regained her chair at the end of the bed. As Sarah rounded the bed, she placed her hand on the older woman's shoulder. Would Hester understand that the gesture meant so very much, conveying words Sarah didn't have the strength to say?

Please take care of her. Care for her as if she were your own beloved. All she could say as she left the room was a whispered, "Let me know if there's a change, Hester."

The older woman nodded.

CHAPTER 9

Sarah went first to her own bedchamber and gathered up those belongings she needed for the night. Then she walked down the hall to the Duke's Suite, opened the door, and closed it behind her. Instead of going into the bedchamber, she walked into the bathing room.

Her grandfather had built this addition to Chavensworth. Long fascinated by all things medieval, her grandfather had raided a French castle, appropriating from it a bathtub that had been hewn from solid rock. He'd brought it back to Chavensworth and had it erected in this room, on a wide platform atop a series of steps.

She lit a few beeswax candles, brought three of them into the bathing chamber, and stood for a moment marveling at the faint, almost indiscernible scent. The flickering light from each candle, such a small yet perfect illumination, caused the stone to glow golden.

This small thing, lighting a few beeswax candles, reminded her that she did not often spare touches of luxury for herself.

The bathtub was massive, a rectangular shape heavily carved around the edges with a pattern that had always reminded her of a Grecian key. She turned the tap to allow cold water to pour into the tub. Her father's house in London had hot-water taps, but here at Chavensworth there had never been enough money to install a boiler. When the tub was half-filled, she left the chamber, glancing at the clock on the mantel as she walked to the door. Just as she had ordered, two footmen stood there, each bearing a hot water urn in each hand.

"Good evening, Lady Sarah," the taller one said.

"Very punctual, Jamison."

He smiled, which wasn't an approved response, but she didn't chastise him for it. Instead, she stood by the door as the two young men deposited the urns in the bathing chamber and returned. She closed the door after them and returned to the side of the bath, where she emptied three of the urns into the tub. Only then did she undress, taking care to place her clothes in a tidy little pile on the pediment beside the steps.

Naked, she mounted the steps and put first one foot into the tub, then the other, sinking down into the warm water, wishing she had some scented bath salts. Another touch of luxury, but one she could not afford. She laid her head back against the hard stone, wondering as she did each time she bathed in this room about the inhabitants of that faraway French castle. Who had they been? Who had used the stone tub before? Had they only taken pleasure in a luxury of being clean? Or had they mulled over their lives as she was doing right now?

She sat up and bathed her face, reaching for the dish of soap. After soaping her feet and ankles, she made her way up her body with diligence and precision. Habits were a reassurance.

She wrapped her arms around herself and bent forward and laid her cheek against the top of her knees. When she wept, when she allowed herself to do so, it was often here, where no one could see her tears or hear the sound of her sobs. No maids would interrupt her solitude. No servants would think to enter the Duke's Suite without express permission.

Tears, however, would not come tonight.

They were pushed aside by annoyance and perhaps just a tiny bit of curiosity.

She had not wished for a husband. What did she care that he'd abandoned her so quickly? Perhaps he was not returning after all. Perhaps he had gone straight back to London, to tell her father that the bargain was not well-done. He did not want to spend the rest of his life with someone like her.

Where was her husband? And just how long was she not to worry?

She lathered her hands and began to wash her shoulders. Her right hand slid down her left arm to her wrist, then back up again. Her muscles hurt from lifting the heavy feather beds, but the work was healing. She didn't have time to think or to worry during the day. Only at night, when her activities ceased, did the thoughts cascade into her mind.

Her left hand soaped her right arm. After lathering her hands again, she began cleaning her breasts. He wanted to see her bare breasts, did he? Was that why he'd left her? Because she'd not played the harlot?

They were quite nice-looking breasts, if she had to judge. A little on the large side, perhaps, but they didn't droop. The nipples were pink more than coral, and tended to point upward, like now. She brushed soap on one experimentally, then smoothed it over the crest of her breast.

Was she supposed to feel wicked?

Her chest was simply part of her, like her nose or her ears. She didn't feel anything unusual when she placed her finger on the tip of her nose. Was she supposed to feel something different when touching her chest? Well, she didn't.

Would she feel something different if *he* touched her? As if she would let him. Good heavens, did he want to suckle her? What on earth would she do if he did? Why on earth was her heart racing?

She stared at the far wall. Perhaps it was a good thing her husband had left. Better he abandon her than she abandon her good sense.

Sarah hadn't had time to visit with the carpenter today, so when she finished her bath and returned to the bedchamber, she looked at the cot in resignation.

Her husband was not here. For that matter, she had no idea if he was going to return. Why should she sleep on that uncomfortable cot? Why should she even sleep in the Duke's Suite at all? She could be just as happy in her own chamber.

She told herself that, but her feet did not

make the journey to the door. She'd learned early in her childhood not to disobey. Still, who was Douglas Eston to order her about? The answer came swiftly enough: her husband, legally acquired, if not morally so.

Very well, she wouldn't return to her own chamber. But she wasn't about to sleep on that miserable cot, either. Instead, she would be the one to sleep in the ducal bed tonight.

Sarah walked to the door and took the precaution of engaging the latch, just in case her husband did return. He would find the door barred against him, an indication of her displeasure, if nothing else.

She removed her dressing gown and arranged the folds of her nightgown so that when she sat on the edge of the bed, it wasn't twisted around her legs. In truth, there were times when a nightgown seemed almost a strangling garment. Once or twice, she'd even thought of what it might be like to sleep entirely naked, without clothes of any kind. Now, that would truly be decadent, and decidedly wanton. Still, it was a thought, a temptation to which she'd almost surrendered once or twice. At the last moment, however, reason always returned. What if Margaret summoned her to her mother's bedside in the middle of the night?

It would not do for Lady Sarah to be thought of as immodest and abandoned.

She sat on the edge of the bed and dangled her feet. A moment later, she leaned over and extinguished the lamp on the bedside table.

In the gap between the curtains, she could see the pale moonlight. She slid from the bed and opened the curtains wider until the room was bathed in a bluish white glow. She bent and opened the windows, not believing the night air noxious. The lavender fields perfumed Chavensworth's air even in spring, and the early-blooming roses added a note of fragrance of their own.

Chavensworth was silent tonight. She wished she could hear something, anything, other than this unearthly quiet. Even the owls' calls seemed muted, and she couldn't hear the sound of the foxes in the nearby woods. Birds were normally silent at this time of night, but she found herself straining to hear them nonetheless.

Nor were there any sounds from inside the house. Normally, she could hear a snatch of conversation as a footman would pass another in the hall or the faint, far-off, sound of laughter.

Sarah returned to the bed, sliding her feet beneath the covers. She laid her head on the pillow Douglas had used the night before. Even though the sheets had been changed — there were sufficient linens in the press that she'd given the order that sheets were to be changed each day — she could smell him.

He was not here, but somehow it felt as if he occupied half the bed. Annoyed with herself, she rolled over and stretched her hand across the expanse of sheet until she felt the edge of the mattress. There was no one there. Not even the ghost of Douglas Eston, wherever he was.

Did he chafe under the restrictions of marriage? Was there someone in his life whom he loved? He'd married Sarah simply for expediency's sake, and had come close to admitting that to her. Did he regret it now, enough to leave her?

How very odd that he seemed to have a presence even when he was gone. Once more, she found herself wondering where he was.

She lay flat on her back and stared up at the tester above her head, now only a dark shadow. She knew that her family coat of arms was embroidered there, but she couldn't see the delicate needlework in the darkness.

It was time for her prayers, time to implore

the Almighty to look after her mother, to bless Chavensworth, to grant Sarah the wisdom to adjudicate those disputes falling to her, and to help her care for those within her keeping. Her prayers done, she closed her eyes and willed herself to sleep.

Five minutes later, she sat up, punched the pillow into shape, and lay back down again.

Tomorrow was going to be another busy day; she needed her rest.

Why was the mantel clock so loud?

She rolled to her side, bunched up the sheet beneath her chin, and stared into the darkness. As a child she'd always loved the dark. It seemed exotic, somehow, an exciting land only as far away as extinguishing her lamp. She had never been frightened of the idea of monsters. There was, actually, nothing quite as frightening as the Duke of Herridge when he was angry. Any other monster simply paled in comparison.

In the dark, almost anything could happen. Chavensworth could become an enchanted fairy castle. She could be its princess. Or it might be a foreign land, someplace she'd only read about in books, or heard of in stories her mother told. The dark always seemed to be safe, surrounding her like a warm, soft, woolen blanket.

Sounds were more entrancing in the night. Scents seemed stronger, more powerful.

She'd never before considered that emotions might be heightened in the darkness as well. She was never lonely, never had an occasion to be lonely. Then why did she feel adrift now? She did not feel so much connected to Chavensworth as simply within it.

Very well, she was lonely. Even more disconcerting was the fact that it felt almost painful.

Was this what marriage had brought her? The sensation of being truly lonely, the experience of feeling abandoned?

Ever since her two disastrous seasons, she'd given no thought to marriage. Oh, when she'd first gone to London, yes. She'd entertained romantic notions of suitors. More than one handsome lord had attracted her attention, but all for naught, as it turned out. None of them were acceptable to her father. Not one. They didn't have enough money, and the one man who'd been wealthy enough to be acceptable to the Duke of Herridge ended up offering for another. And so, she'd been put back on the shelf, until the following season, at which time she was dusted off, dragged away from Chavensworth, and paraded among London's elite once more.

Thank heavens her father had refused to pay for another season. Nor had she allowed herself to think about a potential husband since that announcement. Instead, she'd busied herself with those tasks that occupied her days. There were always things to do, chores to accomplish. Each day had its purpose. She'd filled her life, given it meaning, one day after another. She had no need to dream of the future or to wonder about it. What she did today would need to be replicated for ten years or twenty years or even thirty. Nothing would essentially change, and in her routine, there'd been contentment.

Douglas Eston had ruined that.

Instead of contentment, now she felt only uncertainty and this curious loneliness that she'd never before experienced. She didn't know the man, and there was no certainty that she would even like him once she became acquainted with him. Yet irrationally, unbelievably, she found herself thinking about him. Where was he? What was he doing? Why was he doing it? Was he safe?

Why did she care?

What if he came back while she slept? What if, somehow, he unlocked the door and came to the bed? Would he touch her? Would he place his hands on her, divest her of her twisting nightgown? Would he disrobe her in silence, expose her to the cool night air?

Would he be able to see in the dark? Would his eyes have been so accustomed to the shadows of night that he could discern her shape? Or would he touch her with his hands, his fingers, sliding over the curves of her shoulders, down her arms to rest at her wrists? Would he press his fingertips against her breasts and cup his hands to measure their fullness? And through it all, would he whisper decadent things, shocking things to her?

Or would this perusal of her be done in silence, as if the darkness demanded it?

It was all his fault, of course, that she couldn't sleep. Not only was he not there, and he should very much be there since he'd married her, but he'd set into motion all these thoughts by saying what he had last night. Dear heavens, was it just last night?

I want to see your breasts.

Oh. He had said nothing about touching her. Those had been her thoughts alone. Now, that wouldn't do.

She sat up again, punched her pillow once more, then flounced back on the bed, drawing the sheets up to her chin. She closed her eyes, determined to fall asleep and dream of pleasant things, and not of Douglas Eston.

CHAPTER 10

Sarah was awakened by a warm breath on her eyelids. In her dream, she was being cuddled by a fox, his tail whisking back and forth over her face. She drew back, blinked open her eyes reluctantly, and realized that she was face-to-face with her husband.

Douglas smiled at her, his expression clearly visible by the lamp he'd lit. The wick was trimmed low, so the glow was barely visible beyond the bed, but she could see him quite clearly.

Her eyes widened, and her breathing quickened. Her heart was beating so rapidly in her chest that it felt like a trapped bird.

"You've returned," she said, gathering up the sheets in front of her. They were no protection at all, but the barrier made her feel marginally better.

"I have."

How utterly polite they were being, especially since she didn't feel the least bit amiable toward him at the moment.

"Where did you go?"

"I was unpacking my crates," he said.

She frowned at him. "Why?"

"To make sure my equipment was undamaged."

Of all the things he could have said, that was the one guaranteed to render her silent. She had thought that he might have gone to see her father, to complain about her behavior, perhaps. Or to see an old love.

"You were unpacking your equipment," she said softly. Repeating it aloud didn't make any more sense.

"If you'll recall," he said, smiling, "it's the reason for our marriage. Your father expects me to fulfill my part of the bargain."

"You might have told me," she said.

"Were you worried? I should have told you not to worry."

"Do you have the power to command emotions?" she asked. "If I had wished to worry, I would have, and I doubt anything you might say to the contrary would have stopped me from doing so."

"Did you?"

"I did not," she said. "In fact, I barely noticed you were gone."

And she wouldn't notice that he was here now, except for the fact that he had rolled off the bed and was beginning to remove his clothes.

With his eyes still on her, he slowly unfastened the row of buttons on his shirt. She looked away, down at the floor, across the bed, before returning her gaze to him.

Was it considered proper for a wife to watch her husband disrobe? She didn't think so, but despite herself, her gaze returned to him again and again.

He was a well-made man. Quite a spectacular specimen of manhood, as a matter of fact. A statue of a young man in the Greek Garden was equally as fine, but after her mentally comparing the two, Douglas was the clear winner. Perhaps it was because he was human, and the statue was only marble. More likely it was because God's handiwork was superior to anything that man could attempt to render.

There, she'd managed to think of God, and in doing so she had turned her thoughts from a naked man.

"I won't undress in front of you if it disturbs you," he said softly.

"I think you do so to put me at a disadvantage, Mr. Eston."

Without warning her, he turned, giving her a picture of his back. Quite a handsome back it was, too, with those sinewy muscles and broad shoulders. There were two scars on his back that made her wish to reach out her hand and touch them, so odd were they. The first was a small line near his right shoulder. The second almost a circular scar near the left part of his back.

He had been an adventurer, an explorer — of course he would have scars all over his body. His life had probably been one exciting event after another. Chavensworth was going to prove excessively tedious for him.

When he walked from the bed, she had a fine view of tight buttocks. For a moment, she considered closing her eyes again. But who would know if she studied him?

"Is this the first time you've ever seen a naked man, Lady Sarah?"

Her gaze flew to the back of his head. How did he know?

He glanced over his shoulder at her and smiled.

She really wished he wouldn't smile, especially as he was still naked. Nor had he made any attempt to cover himself. Except for a quick flash of a glance, she had determinedly kept her gaze on his face. How very odd that night seemed to suit him. He was most attractive with his shadow of the beard. Almost wicked-looking.

She shut her eyes before she was tempted to look lower than his chin.

"Of course it's the first time I've ever seen a man without clothes," she said, refusing to be humiliated.

"Do you care to reciprocate in kind?"

She opened her eyes again, but this time she kept her gaze on the tester above her head.

"I would venture to guess that you've seen a naked woman before, Mr. Eston."

"Ah, but I haven't seen you."

She reached over and extinguished the lamp, then sat on the edge of the bed with her back to him before beginning to don her wrapper.

"What are you doing?"

"I only occupied the bed because you were not here, Mr. Eston. Now that you are, I shall return to my cot."

"A pity," he said. "It's a very large bed, and I'm very tired."

She glanced at him over her shoulder.

"Go back to sleep, Sarah," he said softly. "I'll not bother you."

She wanted to ask him, irrationally and pedantically, if he would promise on his honor to leave her alone, but instead, she remained mute, removed her wrapper, and slid her legs below the counterpane. She lay back on the pillow, her arms at her side.

When he lay beside her, his bare arm brushed against hers. Pulling away would have seemed rude, almost a rebuff. Instead, her skin warmed where they touched. Her little finger was beside his, and she didn't doubt that if she moved her foot a little to the left, it would brush his leg.

"Do you not sleep in a nightshirt?"

"I do not. Nor have I ever. Nor will I ever."

"I locked the door," she said.

"I noticed."

Did he unlock it? Or did he force the lock? Had he damaged the door? She certainly didn't want word of *that* getting around Chavensworth. She could just imagine the gossip below stairs.

She wasn't about to ask him. Nor could she get up and check herself. Not with him lying there naked.

Moonlight shone into the room, too bright for her peace of mind.

"Isn't it odd," she said. "I was so tired earlier, and now I don't seem to be at all sleepy."

He didn't respond.

Had he already fallen asleep? If so, she envied him.

Finally, he spoke. "Tell me what growing up at Chavensworth was like," he said.

"Busy," she said, so quickly that it startled her. Nor had she envisioned telling him the truth, so starkly and unadorned. "I was very busy," she added quickly. "Between my lessons from my governess and my lessons about Chavensworth, I had very few free hours."

He didn't respond. No one had ever asked her about her childhood before now. No one had ever been interested.

"And your childhood?" she asked politely.

"I had few free hours as well," he said.

There was a tone in his voice that she wanted to examine, but before she could say a word, his hand reached out and covered hers. She was so surprised by the gesture that she didn't know what to say.

A few minutes later, she thought of a question. "Tell me about your adventures all over the world," she said.

"Tales of a foolish young man?"

"Were you?"

"At first," he admitted. "I had to learn quickly, else I doubt I would have survived. I was all for seeing the world, for learning as much as I could about as many things as I could. I've always had a healthy curiosity."

She moved away, slid from beneath the sheets, and sat on the edge of the bed.

"What's the matter, Sarah?" he asked,

leaning up on his elbow and looking over at her.

"Nothing," she said.

He placed his hand on the small of her back. It was the first time he'd ever done so, the first time he'd ever touched her while she was so flimsily dressed. Only one small layer of clothing separated his bare palm from her bare back. Her body knew instantly, sending a shiver up her spine, tightening her nipples.

"Tell me," he said.

"You always want to know what I'm thinking," she said, twisting to look at him. "What does it matter?"

"You're my wife."

"I am the Duke of Herridge's daughter. The Duchess of Herridge's daughter. Your wife. Can someone not once belong to me instead of me forever belonging to someone?"

"So you would have me be Lady Sarah's husband?"

She knew only too well that she wasn't being entirely rational. The moonlit night with its heady mix of warm, lavender-perfumed air seemed to call for strong emotion.

"Is that why you wanted to see my breasts?" she asked. "Because of your healthy curiosity?"

She spoke to the other side of the room, knowing that if she turned to face him, she probably wouldn't have the courage to continue.

"Why?" He laughed, a sound she hadn't expected. "Sarah, I want to see your breasts so I can at least dream of how it will be to touch you."

"Oh."

"We're strangers to each other, and it's too soon to take you as my wife."

Were all bridegrooms as considerate?

"Besides, you're a beautiful woman, and I'm a man who appreciates beauty. Especially beautiful breasts. But you needn't worry, I've never yet ravaged a woman."

Women probably threw themselves at his feet, like roses wishing to shed their petals.

Several moments passed.

"Even if you weren't my wife," he said softly, "I would be taken by the striking color of your eyes, your black hair. Or perhaps it's your bearing that entices me, your habit of looking at people intently, one eyebrow raised, as if you are waiting for them to prove themselves to you."

"I don't do that," she said, taken aback.

"Yes, you do, and if you doubt me, I suggest you ask anyone at Chavensworth what it's like to be stared down by Lady Sarah."

She faced forward, staring in the darkness, the moonlight adding shadows to the shape of the bureau. "Am I that frightening, truly?"

"Not frightening it all," he said. "Merely arresting."

He thought her eyes striking. Did he think the color of her hair was attractive? And her figure? He hadn't said anything about her figure. Did he think her ugly and was just too kind to say?

If she had any courage at all, she would confront him on that point. But she discovered that she wasn't as brave as she thought herself to be, at least not in regard to her own appearance. Nor did she like facing the fact that she wanted him to consider her pretty, or if not pretty, then certainly acceptable.

A word or two of flattery would not be amiss from time to time.

Were men ever as uncertain about their own appearance? She had never heard that they were, and had it not been for her two seasons in London, she wouldn't have known that other women felt the same way.

Her mother had never spoken of her appearance, had never seemed concerned by it. She never spoke about her green eyes or mentioned her curling auburn hair. They were simply part of her, like her legs or her arms. Her mother seemed not to give a whit about her appearance and, until Sarah went to London, it hadn't been her focus, either. Once there, however, she'd felt ugly, ungainly, and too tall.

She didn't have the blond locks and pale blue eyes that were all the rage. Her coloring was too stark, and different. Her figure was too odd, her breasts were too large in comparison to her waist, which was relatively small. She was used to her body, comfortable within it, understanding it, but until she went to London, she had never judged it.

He pushed gently on her shoulder until she was lying flat on her back. She kept her attention determinedly on the ceiling, but it was difficult when he was leaning over her, so close she could feel his breath on her cheek.

His hand went to the placket of her nightgown, and to her shock, he began to unbutton it.

"What are you doing?" she asked, as her hand went to cover the next button.

"I want to see your breasts," he said. "By moonlight."

"No."

"Pretend it's a dream," he said. "I am a mischief-maker in your dream, a brownie come to entice you to dance naked in the meadow."

"Absolutely not."

His fingers pushed her hand away, unbuttoned one more button.

"I shall not ask that you light a lamp. Nor will I touch you, unless you ask."

"Why would I ask?" she said.

Her hand rested against yet another button, and when he would've pushed it away, she would not let him. The opening in her nightgown, however, was enough that he could slide his hand inside if he wished.

"Have you never felt the anticipation of desire, Lady Sarah? Have you never wanted something so much that you could almost feel it, even before it happened?"

It seemed he didn't need an answer for that question because he bent his head close to her pillow as if inhaling her scent.

"Sometimes the anticipation is too great for caution. Sometimes, you do something rash in order to relieve the tension."

"Are you going to do something rash?"

"I want to rip the nightgown from you," he said. "Is that rash enough?"

Suddenly, she could barely breathe. "Yes."

She sat up then, partly to distance herself

from him and partly to ease the tension in her own body. She wanted to move, needed to do something almost as reckless as what he had proposed.

She unfastened the buttons in the front of her nightgown until it was open to her waist. Slowly, but without thinking about it, she withdrew one arm from the long sleeve of her nightgown, then her other arm, until she was sitting with the garment pooled around her hips and her breasts bared to the moonlight.

Douglas sat up, the sheet falling to below his waist, and began to unbraid her hair.

There was no fire in the grate, and the night was a temperate one, leaning toward cool. Why, then, was she so warm?

Because he was threading his fingers through her hair, pulling her head back. Because he was suddenly so close she could see his eyes gleaming in the moonlight. Because his breath was coming as harsh and as fast as hers.

He spread her hair over her shoulders, draped it over her breasts, sitting back to admire his handiwork.

With a gentle touch, he pushed back her hair so that her breast was exposed, pale white and creamy in the light of the moon.

One finger smoothed across the pebbled nipple.

"You said you wouldn't touch me unless I asked," she said, surprised to find the words nearly impossible to speak. Her heart was pounding so loudly it was all she could hear, and her body ached.

"The anticipation was too much," he said, and smiled.

The night was not responsible for her wantonness. Nor was it the naked man beside her. Something within her decreed that she be wild and abandoned. She was suddenly and soberingly ashamed of herself.

"Shall I seduce you with words, Sarah? Tell you how utterly beautiful you look sitting there, a goddess of moonlight?"

"You needn't lie," she said stiffly.

"Oh, it wouldn't be a lie," he said. "In fact, it might be closer to the pure truth than anything I've ever said. I think, perhaps, that you don't know your own strength, your own power. If you did, you would smile at me, coax me a little closer, promise me satisfaction with a glance or a sigh, then when I was just at the knife-edge of anticipation, you'd press your fingers against my lips and tell me no."

"That sounds excessively cruel," she said.

"What would you do, Lady Sarah, if you

were a goddess of moonlight? If you had all the power of beauty and lust at your disposal? How would you use it?"

She should tell him to leave her alone, to go to sleep, to allow her to return to her cot, to her own chamber. Instead, she reached out and cupped his cheek with her left hand, and with the fingers of her right hand traced the outline of his lips. When that exploration was done, she allowed her fingers to trail up to his temple, then descend to his neck. He had a very strong, masculine-looking neck.

Her breasts felt heated, the nipple he touched bereft because he'd moved his fingers.

She leaned close to him and pressed her cheek against his. In this position, her lips were close to his ear. She could whisper to him and no one else in the entire world would hear or know.

What would she say?

For the longest moment, he didn't move. His hands remained on top of the counterpane between them. With an acute sensitivity she'd never experienced, she seemed to know exactly when he began to move, exactly where his hands were, and exactly where she wanted them to be.

She expected him to place his hands on

her breasts to cover her nipples with his palms, to trail his fingers over the swell and curve of each breast. Instead, his hands went to her shoulders and he pulled her back, staring into her face.

It was his turn to cup her face with his hands, and he did so gently, so slowly that she almost implored him to quicken his pace.

He lowered his mouth to hers, and for the first time, kissed her. Her mouth opened in a gasp of surprise. At first, the kiss was tender, as soft and delicate as the petals of a newborn rose. Then, startlingly, it grew heated until she was almost dizzy from it. Finally, the kiss was done, and she leaned against his shoulder, breathing quickly. His breath was as harsh as hers, the pulse beat at his throat so rapid that her fingers smoothed over his skin in an effort to calm him.

He leaned back and studied her. She sat up, her back straight, her chin raised, her attention directed on the far wall. Let him look his fill. She was not cowed by such behavior. She would not be intimidated by his earthiness.

"Perhaps it's good you don't know how exquisite you are," he said softly. His hand cupped the heaviness of a breast, a thumb pressing delicately against a nipple that had grown shockingly sensitive to his touch. "You would have led the men in London a pretty chase, Lady Sarah."

Even if she'd wanted to comment, Sarah doubted she had the capacity to speak the words. Her world was heated; her blood felt as if it were on fire.

With deft fingers, he smoothed her hair back over her shoulder until it tumbled down her back.

"What glorious hair you have," he said. "Why do you insist on braiding it?"

"Because it would take me two hours to brush it free of tangles in the morning if I didn't," she said, grateful that her voice sounded nearly normal.

"But then I would have the pleasure of watching you brush your hair. Do you ever do so naked?"

She turned her head to look at him. "Of course not."

"I'd like to see you in that pose," he said.

"Now?" she asked, astonished.

"Why not? You can't sleep, and after seeing you half-naked, I doubt I'll be able to either."

He lit the lamp on the bedside table.

She bent her head, surreptitiously spreading her hair over her breasts.

"Must I truly do this?"

"Do you not wish to?"

Part of her wanted to slide back time itself to the moment she'd known he was in the bed. Another part, dormant until now, was very interested in what he proposed. Too interested, as a matter of fact, and almost excited.

She stood, keeping her left arm across her breasts, and with her right hand, gathered up the folds of her nightgown, keeping them at her waist.

"Come sit here," he said, indicating the end of the bed.

She sat and looked up at him.

"What do you want me to do?" she asked.

Her heart was beating so furiously she felt out of breath. Her lips felt full, almost swollen, and her skin so sensitive that the touch of her hair across her shoulders was almost painful.

"Brush your hair as you would every morning."

She shook her head. "I haven't my brush."

He moved to the bureau and returned with a silver-handled brush that fit into the palm of his hand.

"My maid assists me," she said.

"Shall I be your maid?" he asked.

"No," she said, reaching for his brush.

Slowly, she began to pull the brush through her hair, beginning at her temple and continuing until she reached the end.

As she brushed, Douglas reached over and clasped her left wrist, gently pulling it away from its shielding position. She glanced up at him, but he only smiled and shook his head. A message, then, without a word: It was pointless to ask him for a little modesty.

Her left hand flattened against the coverlet, and she closed her eyes, tilted her head back, and concentrated on brushing her hair. She attempted to ignore him, but that was made more difficult when he spoke.

"When you raise your arm, your breasts rise, almost as if they were soliciting praise. Or a kiss."

She slowed the pass of the brush through her hair, kept her eyes closed by force of will, all the while wondering if he was going to kiss her.

Would he put his mouth on her breasts?

If he did, what would she do?

"Arch your back a little," he said, and she did, knowing that the pose made her breasts stand out even more.

Was that his breath she felt?

"Your back is beautiful as well, Lady Sarah. Such a fine line, such a sweeping curve. I can barely keep my hands from you."

Dear Heavens.

"Stand up."

She opened her eyes.

"Please, Sarah. Stand up."

She did, gripping her nightgown with her left hand, the brush in her right. She kept her gaze on the far wall, but out of the corner of her eye, she could see how close he was.

Slowly, as if giving her time to acquaint herself with the idea of it, he reached out and gripped her hand, gently forcing her fingers to loosen their grip on her nightgown.

"Do you want me naked, Mr. Eston?" she asked, frantically reaching for the falling garment.

"Most assuredly," he said.

She stopped in the act of bending over. "You do?"

"What sort of idiot do you take me for, Lady Sarah? It is my earnest desire to have you naked before me, second only to having you naked beneath me."

She was naked in front of a man. She'd never been naked in front of anyone. A screen always remained between her and Florie when she bathed or removed her underclothes. Now, she was standing naked in front of Douglas Eston, and he was smiling. Smiling.

"Turn around," he said.

"No."

His smile was crooked as his gaze traveled to her face. "No?"

"No," she repeated, bending to grab her nightgown. This must stop right this minute. She had allowed herself to go beyond the boundaries of proper behavior, and it really must cease this moment.

Besides, if he continued, he would want to bed her, and she wasn't the least bit prepared for *that*.

"You have a magnificent derriere, Lady Sarah."

Sarah held the nightgown in front of her, well aware that it was a specious covering at best. Still, she kept her back stiff and straight as she walked to the cot and settled herself beneath the sheet.

Only when the light was extinguished did she allow herself to imagine what bedding Douglas would be like.

CHAPTER 11

Sarah met with the home steward the next day. Since it was an even year, the crops had been rotated according to the schedule put into effect by her grandfather. The eleventh Duke of Herridge had made Chavensworth famous for more than its lavender fields. Thanks to him, the farms that had begun as an experiment were now successful. If it could be grown in England, it was grown at Chavensworth.

Jeremy Beecher was her home steward, a post he'd held since she was a little girl. His face was long and narrow, his nose thin. His eyes looked too close together, and when she looked at him straight on, it always seemed that he was slightly cross-eyed. For that reason, she always sat at his side at the table in his office. He was a man of advancing years, and frail for his age, if the stooped shoulders beneath the loose-fitting jacket were any indication. Wispy white hair ringed

149

a bald head mottled with freckles and liver spots. Loose skin hung from his jowls, as if he'd once weighed considerably more.

She never pointed out that his shirt cuffs were frayed and ink-stained or that his hair needed trimming. Such personal details did not detract from Mr. Beecher's abilities or his loyalty to Chavensworth.

Today, he presented the monthly budget to her. She reviewed the columns of figures, her eyes widening at the cost of the livery.

According to custom, the estate paid for everything a footman wore — his work clothes for morning chores, as well as the more expensive livery and party jackets. After six months, if a footman left their employ, he must surrender his livery; but he was free to take all the other clothing with him. All that a footman must provide were his shoes and underclothes.

"Have we had that much turnover?" she asked, distressed by the figures. The amounts were a full fifteen percent higher than last year's.

"No, Lady Sarah. Actually, you haven't had any turnover at all. Young Thomas was elevated to the position of underbutler, so we took one of the stable lads and moved him to footman. In addition, there are three footmen who seem to be growing out of everything. I attribute it to Cook's meals. Perhaps we shouldn't hire them so young."

He knew very well that if she didn't employ some of the young men from the neighboring village, they might well starve. Chavensworth was the only true source of employment for miles around. Either the able-bodied men worked on the farms, or within the house itself.

More than one young man had left Chavensworth and gone on to more profitable employment in London, but some of the people who worked at the estate had done so for a lifetime. More than one family had two or three members employed here, and it was a common occurrence for a father or a mother to come to her and ask if she could find room for a child to go into service.

"It's also time for the Gift, Lady Sarah," Mr. Beecher said.

Sarah bit back a sigh. The sinking feeling was harder to prevent.

Once a year, all the servants were evaluated, not only for the state of their uniforms and whether they needed to be replaced, but personally as well. Which tasks had they not mastered? Which new tasks should be given to them to learn? Another reason to judge their performances was to measure each employee against the greater whole. Had their performances for the prior year been superlative? Should any or all be rewarded with the Henley Gift, a small stipend named after her great-grandfather who began the tradition.

For the last three years, there hadn't been any money for the Henley Gift. Sarah had done what she could to compensate by giving the best employees a full extra day off in each of the twelve following months. She knew, only too well, however, that the staff would much rather have had the money.

Chavensworth managed to support itself, but only barely. She could never expect any funds from her father to support the estate. Instead, the Duke of Herridge swooped down on Chavensworth from time to time to take those furnishings that were not part of the entailed estate and sell them. She knew better than to argue with him. All she could do was stand by helplessly as he had wagons loaded with anything valuable. As it was, the ballroom was left unlit; the chandeliers had been taken years earlier. The windows were unadorned since the gilded drapery rods had been removed a few months ago. None of the guest chambers in the south or north wings were furnished and hadn't been for longer than she could remember.

"Very well," she said. "I will need the ledger book with all the employee names. Please leave word with Mrs. Williams that I will meet with her and evaluate the house-maids first. Then Cook's staff, the stables, the farmhands, and leave the dairymaids for last."

Mr. Beecher began writing furiously as she spoke. "As for the livery, we shall have to do with what we have. We no longer entertain, so party jackets are not necessary for most of the footmen. As far as ribbons, I absolutely refuse to order new ribbons."

Mr. Beecher smiled.

Even though Sarah had gone to pains to reiterate to all of the staff that they were part of the Chavensworth estate, people had a way of creating hierarchies for themselves. The second-floor housemaids were no more talented than the third-floor maids. Nor did they have more responsibilities. It was simply that they wanted to be different, and she had finally given in, allowing the second-floor girls to wear blue ribbons in their hair, and being totally unsurprised when the third-floor wanted to wear green.

At least the stableboys and the farmhands hadn't demanded their own ribbons.

"When do you wish to inventory the farm

tools and implements?" he asked.

Inventory was a chore she dreaded. In the kitchen, it was done once a week. An estate the size of Chavensworth, especially with the number of people employed, could go through enormous amounts of food. The linen was counted once a month and other essentials every three months.

"As soon as the evaluations are finished," she said.

Somehow, she would have to find the time to do everything that needed to be done.

She stood, and the steward did as well, looking at her with a kind, almost fatherly, expression. If he had not been of a good disposition, she doubted she would have been able to work so closely with him.

At half past noon, she entered her mother's room, nodded to Hester, and took her place on the chair.

An approaching storm shrouded the room. Hester had lit a lamp on the far table, but the light only served to accentuate the shadows stretching out like fingers from the corners, pointing at the bed. Or perhaps they were reaching for the Duchess of Herridge, to pull her toward Death itself.

"Has there been any change?" Sarah asked.

"Not since you saw her this morning,

Lady Sarah."

There was more in Hester's eyes, but Sarah looked away. Kindness was not what she wanted. She needed strength, the ability to carry on, to do as she must regardless of the circumstances. Her ancestors had done so — she needed that ability as well.

"Go eat, Hester. I'll stay with her."

"What about your own meal, Lady Sarah?"

"I'll have Cook prepare a tray."

"When will you eat?"

She glanced at Hester. Her features were frozen in an implacable look of resolve. Hester was excessively nurturing, but she was also excessively stubborn.

"I'll eat, I promise," she said.

Hester left, murmuring something about people making promises they had no intention of keeping. Sarah ignored her, intent on her mother's face.

The faint light made Morna's face appear gaunt, older than her years. For a moment, Sarah couldn't see the woman she knew in the face illness had created. She closed her eyes and recalled earlier days, when her mother's laughter had sparkled throughout Chavensworth.

In that instant of time, she became nine years old again, swinging a picnic basket in her left hand, overjoyed with the thought of being able to eat her lunch beneath a tall oak tree on the hill overlooking the lavender fields. Never mind that it was only a few minutes from Chavensworth proper; her mother could make the hour or so an enchanted time. She would tell stories of her forbears, of a castle named Kilmarin, of pixies, brownies, and the Hag of Winter.

"Will you never go back there again, Mother?" she'd asked once, on a day when her mother seemed particularly sad.

"I shall never," Morna said, but then she'd smiled.

The child she'd been, perceptive and almost hurtfully honest, had known that her mother did not wish to discuss her home. So she hadn't mentioned it again, and it never occurred to her until now, when Morna seemed inches from death.

Had her mother ever wished to return to Scotland? Had she missed her own family, people Sarah had never met?

That question might never be answered.

The clouds, visible through the French windows, were swirling overhead, forming pendulous bellies darkening from soft gray to nearly black. As she watched, lightning flashed from one swollen cloud to another.

When she was a little girl, she was afraid

156

of thunderstorms, cowering in her bed whenever they came. A rainy spring only brought terror for her. Countless times, her mother had sat with her, trying to get her to smile. Morna told her one story after another, transforming the freakish sound of thunder to Thor's hammer, God laughing, or a dozen other futile analogies that didn't ease Sarah's fears one whit.

She had outgrown her childish fear and come to love storms, feeling curiously attuned to them, especially today, when the air hung heavy over Chavensworth, and the clouds dropped lower over the land.

Softly, she stroked the back of her mother's hand. Morna felt even colder today than she had the day before, as if she were dying by degrees.

Sarah took a deep breath, wondering what she could tell her mother that wouldn't worry her on the off chance that she truly could hear her. Chavensworth's finances? Never as grim in Morna's days of caring for the estate. Her marriage? What could she possibly divulge to her mother? That Douglas Eston was inciting her to abandon, and she'd never felt so depraved or excited. Perhaps it wasn't Douglas's fault at all but some flaw in her own nature. A flaw further magnified when she'd awakened this morning and been disappointed to find him gone.

She stood, walked to the French windows, opened them, and left the room, closing the doors behind her. Before she had this room transformed into her mother's sickroom, it had been the Summer Parlor, a room that looked out over the Greek Garden and a small brick patio just like the Duchess's Suite on the floor above.

She wrapped her arms around her waist and looked up at the sky. Did God truly live in the heavens? Or was He in every place and everything?

The wind tossed her hair, and threatened the care with which Florie had arranged it. She felt like pulling every pin from her hair, throwing them on the ground, heedless and reckless, as if daring God and the coming storm.

No one would call her feckless. No one would think of her as having a rebellious nature. If given an unattainable goal, she somehow attained it. If handed an unbearable circumstance, she nonetheless endured it. Lady Sarah coped.

She heard a sound behind her and turned to see Hester opening the door.

"Come in, Lady Sarah. It's dangerous out there with the storm."

She didn't want to go inside. She didn't

want to be safe. Besides, nothing was truly safe anywhere, was it? She had gone to London, to her father's home, and found herself married because of it. She had come home to Chavensworth, and her mother was dying within its walls. Where was the safety?

"I'll be fine," she said, but had to raise her voice over the sound of the wind. "I just need some air."

Hester looked doubtful, but she'd had enough of Hester's care. Let Hester dole out her compassion to her mother. The entire world should weep because this sweet and generous soul was dying.

She turned away and began to walk, leaving the patio and its hedge border, down past the rose garden and the intricate ornamental garden crafted from boxwoods. The clouds lowered still farther, the wind picked up, gusts drifting beneath her skirt, billowing the fabric into a perfect circle.

How immodest.

She didn't care. How very odd was that? She always cared. She was very decorous in her appearance at all times, even around Chavensworth, even when she was ill. At those infrequent times when she didn't leave her bed, she insisted that her face be washed and her hair brushed and arranged in a pleasing manner.

She had never been abandoned.

Nothing Douglas had done the night before had been without her willing participation. Still and all, it seemed so hideously decadent and improper that she warmed even now thinking of it. He had touched her with silken fingers and whispered words, and her entire body had curled around him like a new leaf. She was a virgin, but after last night she considered herself a little more knowledgeable. If not about passion itself, then about her reaction to it.

Sarah entered the Greek Garden. She'd learned more about the opposite sex studying those statues than in her two seasons in London. When she'd been a child, her mother had put skirts on two or three of them, but Sarah had waited until she was alone and raised the hem and looked underneath. Only later had she learned the skirts were kilts, and that discovery had led to learning that her mother was Scottish.

Douglas was more physically gifted than any of the young Greek statues in the garden. His thighs were more muscular, his calves better developed. His manhood, that curious appendage never covered by a fig leaf in the Greek Garden, was much longer and thicker.

They were boys, and he was a man.

160

His thick black hair was cut a little shorter than was fashionable. Clean-shaven, he had a carved, high-cheekboned face and blue-green eyes that showed what the Mediterranean must look like on a summer day. Each time he came into a room, the air seemed to hum, as if he were an important personage, a member of the royal family, a man of deep and consuming public interest.

She circled the statues like greeting old friends, making mental notes of their condition, and where some needed to be repaired. Perhaps it was time to move some of the older statues inside, at least during the more punishing winter months.

In the middle of the garden was a luckinbooth, a Scottish symbol of two hearts entwined and topped with a heart. The luckinbooth had been started when her mother had first come to Chavensworth. The gardeners had followed her plan, and now the intricate design was fully formed in mature boxwoods.

Sarah's hands fell to her sides, and she continued walking, past the lane that led to the sloping hill with its lone tree, the site of so many picnics. How many times had they gone there together, just she and her mother? The last time had been only two years ago, and already signs of weakness had slowed Morna's walk. She'd been winded by the time they reached the oak, and even though she had waved aside Sarah's concern, there had been shadows beneath her eyes and a slight bluish tint to her lips.

Sarah wished the heavens would open up and the air turn white with rain. No one would be able to tell her tears from the downpour then. Now, however, they chilled her face as they were blown away by the wind.

She found herself walking toward the stables, taking the gravel path to the right and, at the fork in the lane, abruptly changing directions and veering to the left. There was one place at Chavensworth where no one would disturb her. Only one place she could go and sob in solitude. Where neither footman nor maid or housekeeper or steward would dare open the door and intrude upon her privacy. From her childhood on, she'd always sought refuge in her grandfather's observatory. The same man who made life miserable for her now with his heritage of the Henley Gift had created a magical place from which to view the stars.

When her father had moved away from Chavensworth, taking up residence in London, she'd gone to the observatory. When her mother had first become ill, Sarah went there. When she fancied herself in love during her first season, only for the young man to offer for another's hand, she'd returned home from London and immediately gone to the observatory where she sat listening to the sough of the wind around the oddly shaped building.

How very foolish she had been, and how very foolish she felt right now. She was no longer a woman past the first blush of youth, but a child at this moment. She wanted comfort from the very woman who could not give it to her. She wanted her mother to tell her that things would be all right, but she was very much afraid they weren't going to be, ever again. Sarah wanted her to sit up in her bed and announce she was famished, that it was time she was up and about. Sarah knew, however, that as much as she wished for something, as much as she wanted it, wishes and wants did not make them happen.

A wagon sat in the middle of the path. As she watched, Douglas left the observatory, went to the side of the wagon, and grabbed another crate. As he lifted it, he looked up and saw her.

At least he was fully dressed.

But, really, should she be able to remember the sight of him naked so clearly?

CHAPTER 12

"What are you doing here?" she asked. Thunder rolled from cloud to cloud, deadening her words, tossing them into the wind as quickly as they were voiced.

He shook his head to indicate he didn't understand, and she shouted the question again. Once more, he shook his head, then glanced upward at the lowering storm before setting down the crate, circling the wagon, and grabbing her arm to pull her inside the observatory.

He had made changes here, changes that she hadn't authorized or approved. Changes that had forever altered the atmosphere of the observatory, her childhood sanctuary.

For long minutes, she remained silent, studying what he'd done. He'd wiped the dust from the shelves, loading them with his own possessions. Cylindrical glass vials sat next to an assortment of green-tinted bottles with cork stoppers. Wooden frames were propped on four of the shelves, each frame strung with a dozen or more filaments.

On one side of the room, Douglas had mounted a large sheet of paper with an arrangement of numbers and letters written on it. Not a foreign language but something she couldn't decipher. Two or three chests sat below each shelf. The worktable, made of wood and having lasted two generations, was now piled high with a series of trunks and crates.

"How did you get the roof open?" she asked, glancing over at him. "It hasn't worked in years."

His gaze traveled from the rounded top of the observatory to her face. "It just required a little oil," he said.

The observatory had ceased to be her sanctuary. Douglas had put his mark on it as adeptly as if he'd written his name everywhere.

"What are you doing here?" she asked one more time.

"Satisfying my bargain with your father."

She frowned, then remembered his words the night before about her waiting in judgment of others and smoothed the expression from her face.

"How?"

"By making diamonds," he said, smiling.

She stared at him, every thought flying out of her mind. "Only God can make diamonds."

"God has seen fit to share that knowledge with me," he said, his smile not altered one whit.

"How?"

"It's a process I've developed."

She sat down on a crate and stared up at him. "That's what my father was willing to invest in? A way to make diamonds?"

He nodded.

"And you've made diamonds before?"

He reached into his vest and withdrew a small black bag, then walked to where she sat.

"Put your hand out," he said, and she found herself doing exactly as he asked.

Slowly, he covered the bowl of her palm with diamonds.

The observatory was barely lit by the open door, but the diamonds still sparkled as if they were a source of light themselves. She stared at her hand in amazement.

Finally, she tore her gaze away from the diamonds to rest on his face. He was still smiling.

She didn't know what to say to him, so she only stretched out her hand, watching as he poured the diamonds back into the velvet bag.

"This place has a special significance to you, doesn't it?"

"How do you know that?" She didn't look at him when she asked. Instead, she examined the label on one interesting-looking crate. She didn't know the language printed on the side.

"Because you're angry."

She glanced at him. "I'm not, actually. I'm sad," she said, a bit of honesty she hadn't meant to give him. What was there about this man that compelled her to tell him the truth?

For long moments, they didn't speak, merely looked at each other. She was the first to glance away, uncomfortable with the intensity of his gaze or perhaps the compassion in it. She knew, without being told or without understanding truly how she knew it, that if she held out her hand, he would take it and hold it in his large warm grip. If she walked into his arms, he would embrace her, and perhaps bend his head down and lay his cheek against her windblown hair. If she wept, he would probably withdraw his handkerchief and blot her tears.

She stood and looked around the observatory one last time. She knew she would not come back here again.

"I think the observatory would serve your purposes well," she said. After all, she had all of Chavensworth. Granted, the estate felt overrun with people occasionally, but if she needed a place uniquely hers, then it was no doubt an emotion that Douglas experienced as well. She pasted a smile on her face. Let her be a gracious hostess of Chavensworth.

"You must let me know what else I can provide to make it a more hospitable place."

"Your presence, perhaps," he said, surprising her again.

She felt her brow furrow and deliberately smoothed it.

"I know nothing of making diamonds," she said.

"But you know a great deal about making conversation, and I find that I enjoy our conversations very much."

"You do?"

She couldn't prevent her lips from curving into a smile. And she had no idea how to forestall a sudden spurt of warmth at his words. How very kind he could be.

"I'll leave you to your work," she said.

"Must you? I would much rather unpack crates while you talk to me."

"Are you very certain you don't simply

want another helper?" she asked, smiling at him. "There might be some chicanery behind your nice words."

"Chicanery? Me?" he said. "No chicanery, I assure you. Only self-interest. It's a boring job. I'd much rather have the company of a beautiful woman."

She laughed. "Now you go too far," she said. "I almost colluded with you until that remark."

He frowned at her. "I don't think you're soliciting compliments, Sarah, but I find it almost impossible to believe that you don't know how lovely you are. Are you that modest?"

"On the contrary," she said. "I know all my assets as well as my liabilities, Douglas. My father insisted upon it. There is nothing you can tell me about myself that has not been pointed out to me on countless occasions."

She turned to leave, and he reached out one hand and grabbed her arm.

"Do you take everything your father says as the truth, Sarah?"

"What do you mean?"

"Do you hold him up as an oracle of wisdom? Do you value what he says about Chavensworth? For that matter, do you value what he says or does about your mother?"

"You, of all people, should know that I don't."

"Then why give what he says about you any credence?"

"It was not simply my father, Douglas. I have had two seasons. Two. Two very expensive seasons. I attended hundreds of events; I was fêted as only the daughter of a duke can be. I was introduced to every eligible male in all of the Commonwealth, I believe. I was presented to the Queen."

"And?"

He could not be that obtuse.

"I did not attract the attention of one man. Not one."

She was not going to tell him about the tendre she had for the young earl who'd danced so magnificently, and acted so attentive, only to ignore her the next time she saw him, as if she'd been rendered invisible. She'd learned, later, that he'd become engaged, to an heiress, of course, leaving Sarah feeling as if her heart had been badly bruised.

She did not wish to be more of an object of pity than she was.

"Then they were all blind," he said flatly.

"There is no need for kindness, I can assure you."

He would've responded had a knock on the door not interrupted them. She turned to find Hester standing there, her face twisted by grief, tears bathing her face.

Without a word, she knew. Her mother had died, and Sarah had not been there.

Sarah didn't remember returning to Chavensworth, only that it had begun to rain. The storm was as fierce as promised in the dark clouds and wind. She didn't care that she was sodden by the time she entered her mother's room. Someone — she didn't know whom — placed a towel around her shoulders and patted her face dry. She absently said, "Thank you," but was unaware of anything else.

She sat on the chair and wished herself alone, wishing that all the suddenly solicitous people would disappear and the world would be a sweeter and kinder place than it was proving to be on this dark and rainy day.

Behind her she could hear the sound of weeping and wondered if she were crying. She placed both palms against her cheeks to find them cold from the rain, but dry.

She pulled her chair closer to her mother. Hester had placed her hands outside the sheet on either side of her body so that it looked as if she were merely asleep. Her eyelids were closed and sunken, her skin as pale as the sheet. But unlike the past days, her chest did not rise with each tortured breath. There was nothing but silence, punctuated by the sound of sobs.

Sarah could not think. She was incapable of placing a thought in her mind and leaving it there. Someone was pressing a cup of tea into her hands, and she took it and stared down at the amber liquid. A moment later — or was it five minutes, she didn't know — someone blessedly took it from her.

Her hands felt as cold as her mother's. She placed her hands on her upper arms, trying to control her shivers. Did her mother's spirit linger in the room? Should she say something? Could her mother see that Sarah was here?

She wanted people to be gone, so that she could say her farewells privately.

"I think it would be best if you gave Sarah a few moments alone with her mother."

Douglas's voice. She would need to thank him later.

She felt his hand on her shoulder, his palm brushing against her neck, causing shivers. How strange that she could feel something, anything. His hand was so very warm, and she wanted his warmth, needed it.

"You can talk to her," he said softly. "Now is the time to tell her whatever you wish." He moved to the door and opened it, looked back at her, and said, "When you're ready, Sarah, come out. Until then, I'll make sure that people leave you alone."

She nodded in response, grateful beyond measure but unable to verbalize it.

The door shut behind him, and, finally, she was alone with her mother.

Tears welled in her eyes, and she bent her head, feeling lost. Her mother had been her friend, her confidante, the one person whose advice she valued, whose opinion she solicited. They'd spent hours in conversation, in laughter. Their shared jests would have to be abandoned now because no one else would understand. Her memories would have to be shuttered away because to remember them would be too difficult.

How could she endure such pain?

She brushed her fingers against her mother's cheek, then to her temple, smoothing her graying hair away from her face. Even in death, she was a beautiful woman.

There were so many things to do; there were so many arrangements she had to make. She had to notify her father, who wouldn't care. She would have to notify the solicitors. Arrangements would have to be made for her mother's funeral and burial in the family chapel.

Her mother would have died on the way to Scotland.

She had given her mother that, at least. She'd allowed the Duchess of Herridge to die in her own home.

Her father should be punished for what he'd almost done. God should cause lightning to strike his carriage while he was out on the London street. Let him die in screaming suffering or slowly, with pain eating his joints, so that each day was misery.

She took a few deep breaths, folded her hands palms together, and blew on the tips of her fingers. Her breath was hot, while the rest of her body felt so cold.

Hate would have to wait until she was done with the pain.

She bowed her head. What should she say? If her mother's spirit lingered in the room, what did she want her to hear?

"I miss you already," she said. "How am I supposed . . ." Her words abruptly stopped. *Dear God, give me the strength to do this. Give me the strength to endure this. No one should die without a struggle. A person shouldn't simply fade away like this.*

At last the tears came, hot and thick. She was a child again, and her mother hadn't

174

come back from London on the day she was expected. She felt like that lonely little girl now, looking vainly for a ducal carriage approaching Chavensworth. She was bewildered and defenseless, and the sudden agonizing grief cut her in two. Sarah rocked back and forth on the chair, holding her middle lest she break into a hundred pieces, her gaze on her mother's hand, the slim-fingered hand that lay there so still.

Her tears were hot and endless. She cried until there was nothing left but a feeling of emptiness inside her. Someone came and placed his arms around her, lifting her effortlessly. She made a token protest with a weak wave of hand, but buried her face against a masculine neck. Douglas. She could tell it was him by his smell, something earthy and tantalizing like sandalwood.

He took her to a chamber — she didn't know whether it was the Duke's Suite or her own room — and unfastened her dress. A woman helped him, a woman whose voice she knew — Hester? They removed her shoes and stockings, dressed her in a sturdy linen nightgown, and tucked her into bed as if she were five and had had a fright.

Even though she kept her eyes closed, she couldn't hold back her tears. When he would have left her, she simply stretched out her hand. She felt him sit on the side of the bed, then lie beside her, pulling her close until her head rested against his shoulder.

She gripped the front of his shirt, burrowed her hand between it and his shirt until she could feel his warmth. He was alive, and she desperately needed to feel alive at this moment.

"It's all right if you cry, Sarah," he said tenderly.

She clung to him as if he were the only solid object in the sea of her tears.

An hour later, they were still in the same position, but Douglas had drawn up the counterpane so that she was finally warm. She felt herself drifting off to sleep and clutched his shirt, afraid that he might leave her.

He brushed a kiss against her forehead, causing her to press closer.

A knock on the door was an intrusion, but not enough to pierce the haze that seemed to surround her.

Douglas murmured something to her, a caution, a reassurance, she wasn't sure which, before leaving the bed. She made a sound of protest, but it was so weak she might have only thought it.

"She cannot be bothered with that now," he said.

She should rouse, long enough to discover what was so important that someone had come to her chamber. She felt herself drifting off again.

When Douglas returned to the bed, he gathered her up in his arms, and she went without protest, surrendering to a grief-tinged sleep.

They wanted her to adjudicate some damn dispute among the maids.

He looked down into Sarah's tear-ravaged face and wanted to swear. She had just lost her mother, a woman to whom she was obviously devoted, and the damned house-keeper didn't have the sense — or the tact — God gave a gnat.

"You need to handle it yourself," he said, and the woman looked surprised.

He held Sarah tenderly, even though the position was an uncomfortable one. For now, she needed someone to care for her, to shelter her.

The next days and weeks would not be easy for her. The initial pain would eventually fade, but it would take its toll. There would be times when she couldn't bear it, and that was when he was going to be here for her.

He'd never believed in love at first sight. Perhaps lust, yes, that he could understand only too well. But love — that made no sense. Until, of course, Lady Sarah had walked into the Duke of Herridge's study like a gust of wind, and he'd been blown over in the same moment. He'd been unable to speak. He had simply studied her, unbelieving that anyone could be quite so lovely and be real.

With her flashing gray eyes, and her black hair, she was a Celtic princess, not simply a Duke's daughter. She was imperious, insistent, stubborn, self-deprecating, and she'd loved her mother like all mothers should be loved.

She'd agreed to marry him, sacrificing her future for a woman who'd lived only a matter of days and without knowledge of her daughter's gesture. She would not suffer for it. He would not allow Sarah to rue the agreement, to wish it had never happened. She would come to love him, of that he was certain — as certain as he was of his diamonds. He could not compel another person to fall in love with him, but he could charm. He could cozen; he could convince, and he intended to do all of those.

For now, however, he would hold Sarah and allow her to grieve.

CHAPTER 13

"Get that look off your face, man," Anthony, Duke of Herridge, said.

Simons stiffened, but his eyebrows leveled, and the pull to his mouth lessened.

Normally, the Duke of Herridge didn't pay any attention to his servants' moods, but Simons had the rare effect of irritating him today.

Morna was dead.

He held the black-bordered note from his daughter's husband in his left hand and a port glass in his right. He couldn't quite decide if he was toasting his late wife or celebrating her passage.

Thank God she'd finally died. There, the answer to that question.

"Tell the footman that you'll return with him to Chavensworth," he said, glancing at Simons again.

"Your Grace?" Simons said, his eyebrows elevating once more. "Will you not be attending Her Grace's funeral?"

He really should, shouldn't he?

However, he'd always prided himself on the fact that he wasn't an out-and-out hypocrite. He'd grown tired of Morna, and bored with her as well. Why should he now play the part of grieving widower?

The tongues would wag if he didn't attend Morna's funeral.

Who the hell cared about society gossip? He was the Duke of Herridge. Let them talk. A little spice merely meant that his name was mentioned more, his company sought out, his presence requested more often.

His search for an heiress might even be made easier if people talked about him.

"I think not, Simons," he said. "You'll stand in my stead."

He placed the note on the footstool in front of him, sat back in the high-backed chair, and savored first the color of the port, then its taste. Through it all, Simons stood tall as a tree and twice as proud. He'd often thought Simons had the demeanor to be a duke himself.

He waited a few moments before speaking again.

"While you're about it," he said, catching

Simons in midbow, "bring back her jewel chest."

"Your Grace?"

"She had some rubies left, I believe, in that ugly brooch her mother gave her. And a few sapphires here and there. Bring those to me."

"Your Grace," Simons said, completing his bow.

As Simons made his way from the room, Anthony called after him. "There's no need actually to *attend* the service, man. Just get the damn jewel chest."

Simons halted but didn't turn. He'd insulted the old boy, evidently. One of the few enjoyments he got from life.

"Yes, Your Grace," Simons said, and closed the door firmly behind him.

Anthony smiled and reached for the note from Douglas Eston once more before taking another appreciative sip of his port.

"Tell the steward I'll meet with him shortly," Douglas said, consulting his small notebook.

The footman nodded.

"And tell Mrs. Williams that she's to carry on as she always had. There are no new instructions at the moment."

Once again, the footman nodded.

"We should have a large post going out

this afternoon," Douglas added, closing his notebook.

"What time would you like me to return for the post, sir?" the footman asked.

"At two," Douglas said.

The footman clicked his heels together, turned, and walked down the corridor with the stiff bearing of a Chavensworth servant.

Douglas closed the door of the Duke's Suite and turned to face Hester.

"It's uncanny, isn't it, sir? First the mother, now the daughter." She looked at Sarah asleep in the middle of the bed on the dais.

He stared at the woman, wondering if he'd made a mistake soliciting her help. But he needed someone to watch over Sarah while he took care of a few details, and Hester had struck him as being exceedingly sensible as well as caring. But he'd banish her this moment if she coupled Sarah together in her mind with the duchess.

"They're nothing alike," he said. "Sarah is not dying. She's simply grieving."

Hester didn't argue with him, but the look she sent him was dispute enough. He had to admit, it was a little worrying. Sarah had slept for a whole day and didn't look as if she wanted to rouse yet.

"I'll return in a few hours," he said,

hesitating at the door.

Hester settled into the high-backed chair beside the window. "Go along now with you sir," she said, pulling out a crochet hook and a bit of thread. "I'll sit here 'til she wakes, you've no worries on that score. Do what needs to be done."

He closed the door behind him, surprised that the corridor leading to the Duke's Suite was empty. In the last day, he'd been assailed by at least six people, all of them intent on reaching Sarah and obtaining permissions, approvals, guidance, and direction for various projects. His answer to them had been the same, "Handle it yourself."

Beecher, however, had been insistent, standing outside the Duke's Suite with a tenacity in direct proportion to his frailty. Douglas had finally convinced the man to retire to his office and that he would follow shortly.

The journey to the steward's office required walking down three long passages and taking two staircases. At the end of his journey, Douglas could understand why the steward looked so frail.

He'd already discovered that Chavensworth had six wings in total. Four wings comprised the main, boxlike, structure while the remaining two wings formed an

H at the southernmost part of the box and were connected by a portico.

Just how many miles did Sarah walk each day?

He knocked on the door, hearing the shuffling footsteps of Chavensworth's aged steward. Beecher opened the door a few moments later, standing aside to allow him to enter the room.

Bookcases occupied three walls, each filled with ledgers. A large mullioned window overlooking the courtyard occupied the fourth wall. The majority of the space, however, was taken up by a large table, one more often seen in a dining room than a steward's office. Beecher evidently used it as a desk.

He waved Douglas into a chair on the other side of the table and sat as well.

The morning sun streaming in through the window did not favor the man. With the light behind him, Beecher looked even more frail — his hair appeared so light in color as if to be invisible, and the bones of his face seemed even more prominent.

Just how old was the man?

"You said there are matters that cannot wait, Beecher?" he asked.

"The draining of the upper fields must occur tomorrow, sir, and Lady Sarah always

185

supervises the event as well as the cleaning of the sluices."

"Why?"

Beecher's eyebrows drew together. "Why, sir? Because it is Chavensworth."

"Are you not the steward?"

"I am, but the Dukes of Herridge have always had an intimate knowledge of the estate, all the way back to the first duke."

"Lady Sarah is not the Duke of Herridge."

Beecher blinked several times while his mouth worked. Evidently, he was thinking of rejoinders and dismissing them as quickly. Finally, he fixed a lowering frown on Douglas and sighed heavily.

"Lady Sarah has always assumed those responsibilities that needed to be seen to, sir, in regard to Chavensworth."

"What you mean to say, Beecher, is that her father has abdicated his responsibility, and she has assumed it."

Once again, the steward seemed at a loss.

Finally, he reached behind him, and, with some effort, lifted a large ledger, one of the biggest books Douglas had ever seen. He laid it flat on the table between them and opened the cover, using his forearm to help turn the pages. Reaching a section midway in the book, he turned the volume a little so that Douglas could see.

"These are the plans laid out by her grandfather," he said, pointing to a map carefully drawn up of Chavensworth's many fields. "In addition to lavender, we here at Chavensworth grow a variety of crops. But in the larger farms, we rotate four crops in order to give the land a boost. It was Lady Sarah herself who suggested clover, following the recommendations of some men with whom she corresponded."

"Did she?"

"Indeed she has," Beecher said proudly. "She has always supervised the draining of the upper fields. The irrigation sluices must be seen to, and she has always approved the building of new connections." He looked over at Douglas. "The sluices themselves accumulate mud, you see, and the wood rots, no matter how much pitch is used."

"Is this not something you can handle, Beecher?"

The man looked startled. "Indeed no, sir."

He studied the man for a few minutes before finally saying, "Tell me where to be and what to do, and I shall oversee in Lady Sarah's stead."

The man evidently wasn't satisfied by Douglas's suggestion. "Lady Sarah has been present for the lambing, for the castrations, for the drilling of two new wells. She has trod every inch of Chavensworth land, sir, in foul weather and fair."

"And you saw nothing wrong with that?"

The man looked surprised. "I doubt I could have stopped her, sir. Lady Sarah is extraordinarily diligent when it comes to Chavensworth. She could not be more so if she were the Duke of Herridge herself."

"Thank you for your time, Mr. Beecher," Douglas said, standing.

"Shall I apply to you in the future, sir? Have you taken on the care of Chavensworth since your marriage to Lady Sarah?"

"Good God, no," Douglas said. "I have no knowledge in the running of properties."

"But you shall observe the drainage?"

"I'll do whatever needs to be done until you can find someone at Chavensworth with the energy and desire to take on the tasks Lady Sarah has assumed." He leveled a look at Beecher.

Beecher swallowed heavily. "My replacement, sir?"

"Let's say your apprentice, Beecher. Someone you can train in the running of Chavensworth so you don't rely on Lady Sarah to the same degree."

Beecher didn't speak, only slowly closed the book.

"I am to meet with the housekeeper,"

Douglas said, moving to the door. "Is there a shorter way back to the kitchens?"

"I'm afraid not, sir," Beecher said, his mouth curving in a rusty-looking smile. "Continue down the mirrored corridor, take a left at the main part of Chavensworth, and ask any footman for Mrs. Williams."

Douglas nodded. "I'll be at the upper fields tomorrow," he said.

Beecher put both hands on the table in front of him and pushed himself to a standing position.

"If you would convey my best wishes to Lady Sarah, sir. It is difficult to lose a parent, especially in Lady Sarah's case. She and her mother were devoted. There are arrangements pending?"

"Yes," Douglas said, but nothing further. He would let Mrs. Williams be his confidante.

He left Beecher then and found his way through the labyrinth of Chavensworth's back stairs. Twice, he asked directions, only to find that Mrs. Williams was nowhere in sight when reaching first her office, and secondly, the kitchen complex. He found her finally in the library, supervising the dusting of the volumes he'd admired only two days ago.

She glanced at him, frowned, then approached him. Although she appeared pleasant enough, her soft blue eyes looked capable of spearing a footman or maid in place.

She separated from the others and led him to an alcove evidently dedicated to a Herridge forbear. He wasn't interested in the words written on the glass-encased scroll mounted beside the bust of an elderly man.

"I need your assistance, Mrs. Williams," he said, pulling out his notebook. "Lady Sarah is indisposed," he said, wondering if that was the right description for what Sarah was enduring. "I need to make arrangements for a funeral."

The world was a gray, amorphous place, with no boundaries, no discernible markers. There were no doors, or windows, or stairs, or clouds, or stars. There was no heaven or hell. There was no sky or grass. The world, her world, was simply there, shrouded in a fog that Sarah was in no hurry to banish.

Please, let the fog last forever.

She roused to take care of her body's needs, to wash her face and hands, but then fatigue claimed her, forcing her to stumble back to the bed and rest. If six hours passed, that was all well and good — it was six hours she did not have to endure awake.

She knew it was nighttime only because she felt the mattress sag with the weight of her husband. She didn't even care that they shared a bed, or that he sometimes pulled her close so that she could feel his warmth. More than once she awoke in the middle of the night with her cheek pressed against his bare chest, wondering at the thudding sound, only to realize it was his heart beating in sleep.

Part of her was shocked that she was so close to an obviously naked man, but she silenced that concern by rolling over, clutching her pillow, and willing herself back to sleep.

The days passed smoothly, one into the other. If she kept her eyes shut, she eventually fell asleep again. She roused to eat when her stomach hurt, diligently focused upon her plate long enough to still the hunger pangs before returning to bed again. People asked her questions, and she just waved them away, or if that gesture became too much, she simply ignored them.

More than once her skin was dampened with a cold washrag, the soap itching when it was not removed quickly enough. She didn't want to be bathed, but a sound of protest only resulted in a brush covered in tooth powder being forced between her teeth.

Every night, Douglas came and removed her from the bed, placing her on his lap as he sat in one of the high-backed chairs by the window. He covered her with a blanket if she began to shiver. He held long conversations with himself, sometimes speaking of his diamonds and the formula he had discovered, in India, of all places.

When she sat on his lap, she always rested her head against his shoulder, her lips so close to his throat that if she leaned forward slightly, she could have kissed his neck.

One part of her, perhaps more lucid and logical, slowly began to rouse from her self-induced slumber, and began to notice her actions, shouting at her to pay attention, to cease being involved in her own grief. The inhabitants of Chavensworth depended on her. The yearly evaluations must be done. The fields had to be drained. The stables were to be painted. There were so many other chores that lay in abeyance, waiting for her to wake.

How long had she been asleep? Or, if not asleep, then how long had she retreated to her bed, unable to face the world? Had it been weeks? Days?

How very odd that she didn't know. How

very odd, too, that she was so very tired even now.

"You must come back to the world, Sarah," Douglas said, twirling a lock of her hair around his finger. "As difficult as it will be, you cannot avoid it." He shifted her in his arms, and her hand tightened on his neck.

"I shall be here to help you. You won't be alone."

The hand slackened.

"Shall I tell you of my visit to Africa?" he asked, not expecting an answer. "Or would you prefer to hear of China?"

Her breathing was soft and regular, and he suspected she wasn't asleep at all but listening to him intently.

"I envy you," he said, realizing it was true. "You remember your mother, and always will. I have only shadowy memories of my parents, adults who figured in my life and then were suddenly gone. I wish my mother could have been as kind as yours. I wish my own memories were as filled with love."

He decided not to continue in that vein.

"When my parents died, there were no other family members, so perhaps the Almighty brought me Alano, to ensure someone was watching out after me."

He arranged himself more comfortably in

the chair, shifting her weight. By the way she moved with him, he knew she wasn't asleep. He reached up where her hand rested against his neck and encircled her wrist with his fingers. Slowly, he drew her hand down, linked his fingers with hers, and kept them pressed against his chest.

He hesitated, allowing silence to drape them in a comfortable cocoon. "I think it's difficult when any parent dies, no matter your age."

"She shouldn't have died," came a hoarse response.

He glanced down at her. Sarah's eyes were determinedly closed.

She'd taken too much on herself — the running of Chavensworth, the well-being of its servants, her mother's health. Everyone around her cheerfully allowed her to assume all the responsibility, to the extent that they could not manage their own affairs without her approval.

He'd overseen the cleaning of the sluices, inspecting the painting of the stables, adjudicating a young girl's tearful confession of theft and the resultant punishment, in addition to solving a dispute between an upper maid and a scullery girl, approving the overage of the orchard harvest to market, settling a dozen or so monthly bills to tradesmen, approving the quarterly rotation of the silver into storage, and overseeing the funeral of the Duchess of Herridge.

That had just been the first day.

When had her mother relinquished the care of Chavensworth to Sarah? And when had Sarah begun to bear the responsibility for too much?

Instead of thinking Sarah superhuman, let the housekeeper assume more of her own authority, the land steward make decisions of his own, and others in positions of authority be responsible for the tasks under their command. Only if they could not manage would he allow them to seek out Sarah.

Those in positions of power would earn them, or they would no longer have them. He'd already made that point clear to the staff, and so far, there had been no hints of rebellion.

He hadn't continued to work on his diamonds. Nor had he uncrated the rest of his supplies. His only accomplishment in the last three days had been to send two of Chavensworth's stableboys to begin to dig out the foundations for the furnace.

"Nothing I said or did made any difference," Sarah said.

He felt like he was treading barefoot on broken glass.

"Just because the people at Chavensworth believe you responsible for everything does not mean you've the power of God as well, Sarah."

She stiffened in his arms.

"When it has been long enough, when enough time has passed, you'll begin to realize that you did everything you could. You'll think of your mother and, instead of pain, your memories will warm you. Until then, you can only walk through the days. But you must do that. You cannot escape the pain of your grief."

She put her hand flat on his shirt above his heart.

"The funeral is being held tomorrow, Sarah. I've delayed it as long as I can."

"My father?" Her fingers fluttered against his chest.

"I've sent word to him. I've not heard anything in response."

She sighed deeply.

"You need to attend, Sarah."

She nodded, moving her head against his shoulder.

"I will," she said, her voice so soft it was little more than a breath. "How long have I been asleep?"

"Five days," he said. Five very long and worrisome days.

CHAPTER 14

Dressing seemed to be a task alien to Sarah, as if she'd never before donned hoops, or placed her fingers on the tapes to hold them while Florie tied them around her waist. She dropped her hands when that task was done, obediently raising them again when Florie helped her on with her dress, one of her favorite garments dyed mourning black.

The service would be held in Chavensworth's chapel, a building on the other side of the estate. The first Duke of Herridge, the man who'd designed Chavensworth, had insisted on symmetry. If there was one building on the east side of the estate, then there must be a corresponding building on the west. The stables were balanced by the dairy, and the chapel by a rather patrician-looking barn. The only exception to his rule was the observatory, planted on a knoll in the middle of a field, no doubt considered an abomination had the designer of Chavensworth seen it. But he had been dead for hundreds of years before her grandfather had the structure erected.

Florie toiled with her hair for some time as Sarah stared in the mirror at herself. Her eyes were still gray, and her hair as black. But her face had paled, and there was not a spot of color on her cheeks. She looked ill, almost lifeless herself.

The angle of her jaw seemed too sharp, and she wondered if she'd lost weight. Her hair seemed dull and not as shiny as it normally was. She'd always taken great pride in her hair — it was something uniquely hers — as none of the other members of her family had black hair. Her mother's hair was auburn, with touches of the sun in it. That was what Sarah had told her when she was a little girl, fascinated with the glints and highlights.

"It's you who are the sun, dearling," her mother had said, and swung her up in a huge, warm hug.

Florie held out two veils, one that would only cover her forehead, nose, and mouth. The other would shield her entire face and reach to the middle of her chest. The seamstress attached to Chavensworth had been diligent in her task. Sarah selected the longer veil, and Florie helped her affix it to her hair.

"It's a windy day, Lady Sarah," she said, explanation for the extra pins she used. "It's a sunny one, in fact. The world is a bright and beautiful place. Do you think that God gives us such days to counter our sadness?"

She'd never known Florie to be so philosophical.

"Perhaps He does," she said, unwilling to venture the comment that she had no inkling as to the Almighty's thought processes.

Florie handed her the wrist-length gloves that would complete her mourning ensemble. Sarah walked to her bedside table and retrieved her Book of Common Prayer.

"I will see you in the chapel," she said, as if today were another Sunday.

"Do you wish me to accompany you, Lady Sarah?"

The offer was a kind one, and Sarah blessed the fact that the veil obscured her face. She needn't try to smile in response. "That's not necessary, Florie. Take your time with your own dressing."

According to the timetable she'd been given by Douglas, services were not due to begin for another hour. She intended to go to the chapel early, not to inspect arrangements, or to ensure that everything had been done in accordance with propriety. She simply wished time alone with her mother.

"Are you sure you're all right, Lady Sarah?"

Sarah hesitated before answering. She performed a quick inventory of herself. There was a pain behind her right eye, but that seemed linked to the tears she'd shed in the last week. Her lips felt dry and her voice scratchy. Inside her chest was a new, huge, hollowed-out cave. How did she handle that? But all she said to Florie was, "Yes, I'm fine, thank you."

She made her way to the chapel, walking with her head down, intent on the gravel path. Twice, someone passed her, their murmured words barely penetrating the heavy veil. She raised her hand in acknowledgment of their greeting but otherwise paid no attention.

She should have assisted in preparing her mother's body, rather than Hester supervising the task. She should have met with the minister herself to arrange for the funeral service. She should have overseen the refreshments to be served to the funeral guests. She should have met with the staff in order to give them a day off in honor of the Duchess of Herridge.

From what she'd been told, Douglas had

seen to all those duties. Not once had he mentioned anything to her. He'd simply done what needed to be done, seeming to expect no recognition for it.

The chapel entrance faced a small ornamental garden. Instead of continuing down the path, she turned and faced the garden. Someone — Douglas? — had seen to it that the hedges and grass were trimmed.

Only white roses had been planted in the beds here, her mother reasoning that red roses would convey the thought of blood. Today, lush, blowsy ivory blooms gently swayed in the morning breeze. She smelled their scent from here, as well as the earthy smell of new mown grass. For just a moment, Sarah was tempted to remove the veil and turn her face up to the sun, letting its heat warm her.

She didn't, of course, because it wouldn't be proper.

Slowly, she turned and continued down the path, nodding to a footman stationed there. He turned and pulled open one of the pair of doors.

She hesitated in the foyer, allowing her eyes to become accustomed to the change in light. Since she attended services here every Sunday, there was no hesitation in her

201

step as she walked down the broad main aisle.

Near the altar, at the end of the aisle, sat a catafalque. On it rested the Duchess of Herridge's coffin, half-draped beneath a length of greenish blue tartan.

At each of the four corners of the catafalque, a footman was stationed with his back to the coffin, each man so still and ramrod stiff he might have been one of the numerous life-size statues in the chapel. Beside each man was a candelabrum nearly as tall, filled with brightly burning candles.

Sarah bent her head back to see the stained-glass window her great-great-grandfather had installed, the scene one of Lazarus walking. Light splashed into the chapel interior, transformed to jewel-like colors: ruby, indigo, gold, and emerald. Bright white sunlight filtered through the floor-to-ceiling windows on the south side, freshened the gilt of the altar appointments, and brought summer and life into the chapel.

She moved closer to one of the footmen. "I would like to have some time alone," she said softly.

The young man lowered his gaze, nodded, and without a word turned and motioned to the other three. In moments, they were gone, their footsteps muffled by care and the thick red carpet of the chapel.

Sarah went to the pipe organ and moved the organist's bench next to the catafalque.

The carpenters had outdone themselves. The deep mirrorlike ebony glazing of the coffin was beautiful; the handles and appointments were brass, so highly polished that they reflected the light of the candles.

She sat on the bench and removed her veil, placing it beside her. Florie would fuss that she'd dislodged so many pins and no doubt destroyed the arrangement of her hair.

"It's a beautiful day today, Mother," she said, her voice sounding rough and unused. An effect of days of weeping?

Sarah removed the glove from her right hand and placed her palm against the casket. The surface was cool. Why had she thought it would be warm?

She'd always been able to talk to her mother. Why was it so difficult now? Because her mother wasn't here. She was forever laughing beneath an old oak tree, or sitting in front of the fire with a tender smile as Sarah shared stories of her first painful season. She was walking through Chavensworth with Sarah trailing behind her, a journal clutched tightly to her chest. She was a memory, a blink of an eye, a wish.

"I do not know what heaven is like, Mother. I hope that it is what you want it to be. I hope that you're not in pain, that you're able to feel happiness." She hesitated, lowering her head. "I shall miss you for the rest of my life."

Slowly, she put her glove back on before moving from the catafalque to the altar, kneeling on the padded kneeling bench.

"Dear God," she said, realizing that this was the first time she'd prayed since her mother had died. She'd not solicited God in any way. Would He fault her for that?

"Dear God," she began again. "Please bless my mother and keep her safe beside you. I would like to think that she's an angel. Perhaps if I need her from time to time, You would not mind sparing her."

She expected only silence in reply, but instead heard the sound of the chapel door opening and closing. Sarah turned to see a tall, broad-shouldered shadow walking toward her.

Douglas stopped at the other side of the catafalque and regarded her with that piercing blue-green gaze of his. His perusal took in the top of her hair to the veil she held clutched in her left hand, then returned to her face. Did he think to check for tears?

She had no more tears left.

She stood, took the two steps down from the altar, and slowly approached him, stopping only when her mother's coffin was between them.

"Thank you," she said softly. "For everything you've done, and all the arrangements you've made. Thank you for everything."

She, more than any other person, knew what was required to keep Chavensworth running smoothly, not to mention arrangements for a funeral of this magnitude.

"Mrs. Williams helped me with the notices," he said. "I trust that we've invited everyone you would have liked to attend."

She nodded. "My mother kept to herself in the last few years," she said. "Granted, there were one or two friends she had in the neighborhood, but for the most part, she remained at Chavensworth."

Her gaze veered away from him and focused on one of the statues mounted in the corner between the windows. Her great-grandfather had been a great believer in life-size statues. In addition to furnishing the Greek Garden, he'd peopled the chapel with five of them. These, unlike the ones in the Greek Garden, were at least garbed, but in robes reminding her of Roman togas.

"I'm glad to see you recovered."

"I don't feel recovered," she said.

"I don't mean your grieving is over," he said, walking around her mother's coffin to stand only a foot or two away. He reached out and placed his hand on her arm, and she could feel the warmth of his touch through the cloth of her dress. "But that you've begun to grieve. It's a journey, Sarah, and unfortunately, a solitary one."

She nodded.

"Have you eaten today?"

"Have I eaten?" she asked, feeling foolish for repeating the question. The change of subject was so jarring that it took her a moment to realize that no, she hadn't eaten anything. When she said as much, he shook his head.

"The services are not due to begin right away. Shall we go and find something in the pantry? We needn't disturb Cook or her helpers, but I'll wager we can find a plate of scones and some jam."

He crooked his arm, and she placed her hand on it before realizing she had to replace her veil.

Douglas moved to help her, settling the veil atop her hair and smoothing it down in the back while Sarah fitted it over her shoulders.

"What perfume are you wearing?" he

asked, so softly that the sound was barely a whisper.

"A scent made for me here at Chavensworth," she said. "Mostly lavender with some roses."

He was very close, so close, in fact, that if she stepped forward just an inch, she would collide with his chest. His arms were raised to reach the back of the veil, and it was almost an embrace. But they'd shared more than one embrace in the last week, hadn't they?

She'd awakened from sleep to find her head on his shoulder, or her hand pressed flat against his chest. He'd wrapped his arms around her, and held her when she wept. He had always been there, a companion in the midst of misery.

"You held me," she said. "While I slept, you held me."

"You needed comfort."

She nodded, grateful for the veil and its obscuring lace.

"Thank you," she whispered.

"Of all things you should thank me for, Sarah, that is not one of them."

She could feel her cheeks warm.

He crooked his arm again, and she placed her hand on it and allowed him to lead her from the chapel.

CHAPTER 15

The funeral was a restrained ceremony, befitting the Duchess of Herridge.

Her father didn't attend. Nor had he sent any word of explanation for his absence unless it was by way of Simons, whom she'd noticed in the congregation. She nodded to him, and he nodded back, his face creased into wrinkles she interpreted as compassionate.

Following the funeral, Sarah was directed to the crypt, to oversee the Duchess of Herridge's interment. Since her father had not deigned to attend his wife's funeral, Sarah was the only representative of the family present. When the time came for the mason to seal up the heavy stone slab, however, Douglas stepped forward and gave the order.

After the minister said the blessing and left the crypt, Douglas gently escorted Sarah back up to the chapel, now empty since the guests had been escorted to the funeral supper. As they left the chapel, instead of turning toward the east wing, Douglas took her arm and headed in the opposite direction, toward the family quarters.

"Where are we going?"

"You're going to rest," he said, his tone implacable.

"I've been resting, Douglas. I've had nearly a week of rest."

"You don't need to attend the supper. Everyone would excuse you."

Slowly, she raised her veil, then pulled it free, uncaring if her hair was mussed. She had to convince him.

"It's expected," she said. "My mother would expect it," she added softly.

"Your mother would want the best for you."

"My mother would want me to represent the family, especially since my father is not here. Chavensworth has guests and needs a hostess."

They reached the stairs. Only the family used this staircase, it not being as grand as the one leading from Chavensworth's main entrance but larger than the servants' stairs originating in the kitchen.

He stopped at the base of the steps, his gaze searching her face.

"I'm worried about you. Your fingers are shaking."

She made her hands into fists, so he couldn't tell whether they trembled or not.

"I must do this, Douglas. You've taken care of everything else, but I must do this." She forced a smile to her face. "Besides, the scones you found for us were not nearly enough."

"Are you hungry?"

How strange that he looked happy about that.

Before she could answer, his glance swept to a spot behind her. He stepped forward and would have placed himself in front of her had she not recognized the person in the shadows. She put her hand on his arm.

"I beg your pardon for disturbing you, Lady Sarah," Simons said.

"What do you want, Simons?" Douglas asked.

She shook her head at Douglas. Her really shouldn't be so protective of her.

"Simons, what is it?" she said, turning to her father's majordomo.

"Your father . . ."

"Was not in attendance at my mother's funeral," she said flatly.

Simons looked down at the floor, then up at the expanse of steps. "No, Lady Sarah, he wasn't." He took a deep breath and continued. "Lady Sarah, your father sent me for the jewel case. Your mother's jewelry."

"My father sent you for my mother's jewelry," she repeated, very calmly.

Douglas moved to stand behind her, so close she could feel the warmth of his body.

"Yes," Simons said.

To his credit, the man looked uncomfortable.

"By all means," she said, and turned to walk up the staircase. Halfway up the steps, she turned and looked back at Simons.

"I shan't wait on you, Simons. If you want my mother's jewelry, you'll have to come and get it."

Simons mounted the steps slowly, followed by Douglas. Sarah led the way down the corridor to the Duchess's Suite, and without waiting for either man, opened the door and swept inside. She'd not entered the room since her mother's death, and she was instantly assailed by dozens of memories, all of them of a happier time.

Deliberately, she pushed the memories away. She didn't have time for grief right at the moment. She walked to the armoire where her mother kept the small casket of jewelry, opened the door, and retrieved a small wooden box. The casket, with its rounded lid and ornate iron banding, was never kept locked. There was no reason to fear thievery at Chavensworth — unless it was from the duke himself.

As Sarah opened the rounded lid, she was prepared for the onslaught of memory and numbed herself to it. She withdrew a rectangular piece of vellum and slowly opened it, showing it to Simons. Inside was a chain of daisies, now desiccated and brown. Her mother had told her once that she'd considered it one of her prized jewels.

"I made this for my mother when I was six," she said. "It has no worth to my father, and I'd like to keep it."

Simons only nodded. She tucked the vellum packet into the pocket of her dress and handed the open casket to Simons.

"There," she said. "Take them all. Couldn't he at least wait until my mother was buried for a day?"

Simons looked as if he would like to say something, but then he merely shook his head. What could he say? His loyalty was reserved for the Duke of Herridge, not for her, and, regretfully, not for her mother.

He bowed, lower than was necessary. "Lady Sarah," he murmured.

"You mustn't look like you want to pummel the man, Douglas," she said after he'd gone. "It is not his fault. He is simply following the orders my father gave him."

Douglas, who had been silent during the exchange, moved to close the armoire doors behind her.

"Are you certain you don't wish to rest, Sarah?"

Her fingers traced the small vellum package in her pocket. "Perhaps I shall," she said. She didn't like confessing her own weakness, but perhaps it wasn't a failing to love someone, and to feel only a horrible sense of loss when they were gone.

"You needn't escort me," she said. "One of us must make an appearance for our guests."

He looked hesitant for a moment.

"Please, Douglas."

He finally nodded. They parted in the corridor, and he startled her by leaning down and placing a kiss on her cheek, near her temple.

"Promise me you'll rest," he said, almost as if he were a solicitous husband and truly cared for her.

Sarah closed her eyes, and in that next second, she pretended. "I will," she said. She felt the brush of his cheek against hers. He turned and was gone, striding down the corridor.

She walked slowly to her own chamber, entered, and closed the door behind her. Withdrawing the packet of flowers from her pocket, she placed it in her secretary.

Only then did she ring for a maid, and when one of the upstairs maids responded, Sarah said, "Don't bother Florie, you can do the job just as well. I need to be unlaced, please. And my hoops removed."

The girl was not as practiced as Florie, but Sarah didn't want to take her maid and her husband away from the funeral supper. The occasion might have been a somber one, and at the beginning there would be prayers and a great deal of conversation about Morna Herridge, as people remembered her. But as the hours wore on, less thought would be given to death and more to life, and the supper might well become an enjoyable social gathering.

Let people laugh. Let them enjoy the company of others. Let something come out of this, even if it was an evening filled with conviviality. She was tired of darkness, of despair, and this sickening feeling of emptiness.

Once the maid was gone and her clothing put away, Sarah lay on her bed in her chemise. She would rest for an hour, no more, then she would decide what to do. Right now she was incapable of any other decision.

Her hour must have stretched far longer, because it was dark when she awoke. There was no light coming in from the windows at all, only from the small lamp Douglas had lit. She would probably not have wakened at all if he hadn't bodily picked her up and was carrying her to the Duke's Suite.

"I am too sleepy to argue with you," she said.

"Good."

"But you must set aside some time for me tomorrow."

"I can spare an hour in the morning. Is that enough time to fuss at me?"

She thought about nodding but decided that the gesture was too strenuous. "Yes," she said, and wished her voice sounded more commanding. But it was difficult when he was holding her so close, and he was so warm and smelled of such luscious things like wine and tobacco, fresh air, and the bay rum he used. She turned her face so that it rubbed against his jacket and sniffed appreciatively.

All in all, it was rather comforting sleeping with another person. She knew that at any time she could reach out her hand to touch him, just to feel his warmth or his presence. She needn't fear for anything because he was a very tall, very strong, very able man. Yet for all that, he hadn't bothered her. Not once has he insisted upon his marital rights. Granted, it had been a time of sadness for her, but she doubted all men were as driven by honor or compassion.

Who was Douglas Eston? An explorer, she knew that from his comments. A scientist, a fact she discovered after he told her about his discovery. It would take a man well versed in science to create diamonds, wouldn't it? A man who obviously still missed his family.

More than that, she didn't know, but she wanted to discover more.

When he laid her beneath the counterpane, she curled toward him, tucked her hands beneath her pillow, and fell asleep again.

She awoke in the morning to find that her husband had gone once again. Did he wake at dawn? Was he at the observatory? She would much rather concentrate on what Douglas was doing rather than think about the dreaded chore in front of her. Today, she must send replies to calling cards and notes from those who'd not been able to attend her mother's funeral. Good manners dictated that she respond as quickly as possible.

Once seated at the desk in the library, resigned to her duty, she bent and opened the lower drawer. After retrieving her personal stationery, she took out her crystal pen and pulled the inkwell closer.

She sighed as she stared at the stack of correspondence and black-bordered calling cards. Each and every one of them would be a sincere expression of emotion, and each and every one of them would be difficult to read. Someone — Douglas? — had tied the stack tightly with string. She'd have to find a knife or a pair of scissors. Her hand rested on the stack, but she didn't move from her chair to locate either tool. She didn't want to read them. She drew her hand back, leaned her head against the chair, and closed her eyes.

On the way to the library, she'd caught herself walking to her mother's room to sit with her for a few minutes until she realized what she was doing. Morna Herridge would never require her presence again. Sarah should give orders to have the room transformed back into the Summer Parlor again, but she doubted if she'd ever sit there in the evening working on her needlework.

She found her scissors and cut the string,

beginning to read each letter. By the third, she was weeping again, but she didn't allow her grief to interfere with her duty. Toward the bottom of the stack, she realized that she'd stopped crying, intent on finishing her chore.

When she finished, she stared at a new sheet of stationery, knowing that she should begin to work on the most important letter, the one she'd not written, the one that hung over her head like the Sword of Damocles.

Suddenly, she knew that she couldn't write that letter because that letter should not be written.

She stood and made her way to the butler's pantry, where Thomas was polishing the silver in his work apron. At the sight of her, he stepped back and reached for his jacket.

Sarah raised one hand to forestall him. "Have you seen Mr. Eston?"

"Not this morning, Lady Sarah."

"Thank you, Thomas," she said, leaving him.

Douglas must be making his diamonds. She left Chavensworth, beginning to walk toward the observatory. The day was a breezy one, but the air felt heavy, as if rain was imminent. Sarah hadn't been back to the observatory since the day her mother had died, and she was shocked at the changes.

Empty crates were scattered about on the grass outside the observatory, and a huge hole had been gouged out of the knoll. Four stacks of bricks were placed on the side of the lane.

What on earth was Douglas building?

She knocked on the closed door of the observatory and, for a moment, wondered if he were inside. Finally, the door opened, so quickly that she was startled by it. Sarah pressed her hand her throat and subdued her gasp only by force of will.

"I don't need anything, thank you," he said, his tone sharp.

He wasn't even looking at her when he spoke, but at the doorframe. When his gaze finally did settle on her, his look of annoyance faded to surprise.

"Who were you talking to?" she asked, curious.

"Your staff," he said, once again annoyed. "You have a very diligent staff, Sarah. They call upon me three or four times a day to ensure I don't need anything. Cook sends luncheon and tea, and once a tankard of ale. I think they're afraid I'll waste away out here."

"But I do hope that you don't scare the

poor things with that tone of voice. It isn't the least bit friendly."

"I didn't know that one was supposed to be friendly to the staff."

"Well," she said, amending her comment, "if not friendly, then at least civil. You weren't at all civil, Douglas."

"My apologies," he said.

"I haven't come with any offerings," she said. "Does that mean I cannot come inside?"

She peered around his arm to see a selection of beakers and vials and curious round glass objects sitting on the work surface.

"It isn't safe," he said, placing his arm across the door like a barrier. "Or I would invite you inside."

"Not safe? If it's not safe for me, why is it safe for you?"

"I never said it was safe for me," Douglas said.

Her eyes widened as she stared at him. "You never said anything about it being a hazardous process, Douglas."

"We actually didn't discuss the process in detail, Sarah."

Well, that was certainly true. She'd barely discovered what it was her father was willing to bargain her for, let alone discussed the matter. Still, she was a little annoyed by his reticence. Was she supposed simply to ignore the fact that he might be in danger?

"Is there a reason why you're here, Sarah?" he asked.

She should definitely resent that tone of voice. Or the careful look in his eyes. And she should most assuredly not take notice that his white shirt was open at the throat, and his hair just a little bit mussed as if he'd threaded his fingers through it.

However many times Sarah saw him, however many times she told herself he was her husband — nothing prepared her for the shock she felt in the presence of his sheer physical perfection.

"Sarah?"

Startled, she stared up at him. What did she want? She blurted out the news.

"I have to go to Scotland," she said.

The words seemed to hang in the air between them until she wanted to prompt him to speak. For the longest time, he didn't say anything, merely propped his hand against the frame of the open door and regarded her the way he might one of the components of his dangerous process: with a great deal of care.

"Why do you have to go to Scotland? When I first met you, you were arguing *against* traveling to Scotland, I believe."

"My grandfather lives in Scotland. My mother's father. I have to tell him about my mother, and I cannot simply send word to him in a letter, Douglas. Besides, I've never met him."

His brows drew together. "Do you think now is an opportune moment to do so?"

"My mother and her father were estranged, and I know it always saddened my mother. Now, at least, I should make the effort to heal that rift. Besides, I cannot, in all good conscience, write that poor man and tell him the news that his daughter is dead in a letter. How cold and cruel would that be?"

"You couldn't be cruel, Sarah. You worry too much for those in your care."

She tucked that comment away to study later. For now, she needed his . . . consent? Surely not. No, she needed his company.

"Can you spare the time?" she asked.

"So you want me to go to Scotland with you?"

"Of course I do. You're my husband."

"And I'm Scottish," he said.

She stared at him in surprise. "You're not."

"Never tell a Scot he's not a Scot," he cautioned.

"You never said. Nor do you sound like one."

"I've lived all over the world since I was fourteen. I speak a number of languages. I haven't been home in some years."

"There," she announced. "All the better reason why you should return. I couldn't imagine being away from Chavensworth all that time."

He ignored that comment for a question. "Where does this unknown grandfather of yours live?"

"Outside of Perth."

He stared at her. "Perth, is it? That's a bit of a coincidence."

She frowned at him.

"I was born in Perth," he said.

Actually, she had no knowledge of Scotland, other than it was a rugged, mountainous land, peopled — according to her father — with barbarians. She'd dismissed that opinion since her mother was Scots and certainly not a savage.

He glanced back into the interior of the observatory, then back at her. "How soon are you set on leaving?"

"A day? Two days," she decided.

He nodded. "I'll need a week," he said.

"A week?" She thought of protesting, then kept silent.

"A week," he said. "Are you very sure this is something you're set on doing?"

"Very sure," she said. "How many days do you think it will take to reach Kilmarin?"

"Kilmarin?"

"My grandfather's home," she said.

For the first time since she had met him, Douglas seemed truly out of sorts. Not irritated exactly, as much as discomfited. If she didn't know better, she would think she'd given him a shock.

"Do you know Kilmarin?"

"I would venture to say that anyone in Scotland knows Kilmarin, Lady Sarah," he said.

She was startled at his vehemence.

They looked at each other for a few long moments, then Sarah left him, glancing back to find him still regarding her with that intent gaze of his.

Why did she feel as if she had just begun a significant journey, one a great deal more important than a simple visit to Scotland?

CHAPTER 16

Douglas walked out the door in the north façade, an entrance not in daily use by the inhabitants of Chavensworth. This view of the house was distinguished by five chimney stacks flanking a tall central clock tower, all of them in a beige brick that had mellowed over the centuries.

He waited until the carriage turned and stopped in front of the steps. This particular carriage had been his first purchase on arriving in London, and the coachman the first person Alano had hired. Both looked well cared for and perfectly at home in front of one of the grandest estates in England.

"Am I the Queen of England then?" Alano said, lowering the window of the coach. "Here you are to meet me. It makes me wonder if I shouldn't turn tail and run back to London." His gaze encompassed the façade of Chavensworth. "Though I can see why you haven't returned."

"I've been hoping you'd make it in time."

"In time for what?" Alano asked. "I'm thinking that you didn't ask me here simply to fawn at your new home."

"It's not mine," Douglas said. "I doubt I'd want the responsibility even if it were. It takes a great deal of time and effort to oversee Chavensworth."

Alano had never been known for his handsome appearance. He looked more like a pirate than a successful, well-traveled man, especially when he was annoyed, like now. His eyes narrowed, and the wrinkles around his nose deepened, and deep furrows on his brow appeared.

"Are you going to tell me, then? Or are we playing a game of guess the reason?"

Douglas reached for the door handle and pulled it open. "What's got you in such a bad mood? That new butler of yours?"

"He's a molly woggle," Alano said. "Always correcting me. I'd fire the fool, if I didn't think it would make him happy."

"In what way?" Douglas asked, stifling his smile.

"He'd know he got the best of me. I'll have him quit before I give him the satisfaction of firing him."

Douglas decided that any further conversation on the subject of Paulson would be fruitless, so he gave the driver directions to the stables before escorting Alano up the steps.

"Have you arranged that other matter?"

Alano pulled some papers out of his jacket and handed them to Douglas. "Done and ready for you," he said. "Cost you a pretty penny, though."

"Thank you," Douglas said. "I'm going to Scotland, Alano. To Perth."

Alano halted on the step and studied him. "Are you, now? Are you ready for that?"

"I am," Douglas said, certain of it. "But I need your help in another matter. The crystallization process has already begun, and the crystals will be ready in a day or two. I can't leave it unattended."

"When do you leave?"

"Within the hour," Douglas said.

"That's a bit of poor planning, isn't it?"

"Exceedingly," Douglas said.

Alano squinted at him. "You really do need my help, not to insult me back."

"I never insult you, Alano," Douglas said amiably, familiar with this long-standing verbal game. "I only tell the truth."

"Before you leave, you'd better tell me what else I need to do," Alano said, sighing loud enough that Douglas could hear.

This time, Douglas didn't bother to hide

his smile.

A week later, Sarah understood why Douglas required the time before they left for Scotland.

She'd expected that they would be driven to King's Cross Station. She'd not expected that the carriage would travel some distance beyond the station to the very end of the train.

They left the carriage, and walked to the siding. Douglas pointed the way to a railcar, nearly as long as the other passenger cars, built of wood, and painted a deep blue. No words or identification marred the outside, marking it immediately as privately owned.

"I dislike traveling with eighteen other people," Douglas said.

"Is this yours?" she asked, utterly surprised.

"Shall we say it's ours? I haven't time to furnish it the way I wish, but Alano assures me that it's as fine as I could obtain, given the time."

She turned and stared at him.

"You've purchased a railcar," she said.

He smiled and held out his arm. "Shall we go see what it looks like? I've not had time to inspect it myself."

Windows lined the car on both sides, each

window adorned with a shirred-ivory curtain, now closed to provide privacy. Mahogany cabinets lined the back of the car, several faced with glass and revealing a selection of books in one, and a decanter and glasses in another. A small square table sat in front of the windows on one side of the car, flanked by four straight-back chairs upholstered in the same blue shade as the outside of the car.

At the front of the car was a large sofa, facing two overstuffed chairs, this fabric a softer blue. The cabinets at this end of the car allowed for a door in the middle, the half window in it covered by the same ivory curtain fabric.

Both she and Florie were agog, especially when they discovered the small stove in one cabinet. Douglas, however, seemed to take the luxury in stride.

"We can only take the train to Perth," he said. "From there we'll have to take a carriage."

"Have you purchased a carriage as well?" she asked.

"We'll simply take the one that brought us to London, and have it lashed to a flatcar. Tim will accompany us," he said, naming their coachman and Florie's husband. He turned to her now. "If you'd like to be with him, Florie, I've arranged for first-class tickets for both of you."

Florie glanced from Douglas to Sarah, trying to restrain some of her enthusiasm and failing miserably.

"Go on," Sarah said. "We shall see each other in Scotland."

"I'll just put the hamper away first," Florie said.

Cook had prepared a hamper for that day, packing it with two salted hams, three jars of potted pork, at least a dozen jars of pickled vegetables, dried apricots, peaches, and quinces, along with a selection of breads.

"How long will it take to reach Perth?" she said, once Florie had left the car.

"Fifteen hours," he said. "Unless we spend the night at a siding." He moved to open one of the cabinets. He was exploring, just as she and Florie had done.

"That fast?" she asked, dropping onto the surprisingly comfortable sofa.

She shook her head, unable to comprehend the extravagance. Granted, Chavensworth was a beautiful home but it didn't belong to her, and everything within it — portable and sellable — had been stripped from it by her father. She had no ready funds, exchanging the income Chavensworth produced for necessities such as food and other commodities that the estate could not provide.

Turning to Douglas, she watched him. He was smiling, obviously delighted by his exploration.

"Did you do this for me?" she asked.

He turned to study her, his gaze intent. "Engines are extraordinarily loud," he said. "In addition, I dislike plumes of steam and smoke."

She'd dreaded her first time on a train, but this was almost magical. Had the circumstances been any different, she would have been as thoroughly delighted as Douglas appeared to be.

An hour later, when the train began to move, Sarah decided that the sofa was not a good choice and relocated to one of the chairs. Here, she at least could grip both arms as the speed began to increase. Douglas, who'd already spread his papers across the surface of the table, glanced over at her and smiled.

"It's a great deal faster than a carriage," he said, "but there's no need for alarm."

"I'm not afraid," she said, lying. "I'm simply being cautious."

He turned his chair to face her. "Is this the first time you've traveled by rail?"

She nodded. "I suppose you've done so many times before."

He smiled. "I have, but I felt the same as you at the beginning."

A very nice thing to say, but she wasn't at all certain Douglas had ever been afraid of anything.

They were soon out of London, through beautiful open country. Lowland hills began to swell up from the earth, gradually surrounding them. The weather was fair and the rails smooth, and gradually Sarah's discomfort gave way to acute boredom.

She looked through the books in the cabinet, found one on botanicals that looked interesting, and carried it back to the chair. She halted in the middle of the room, transfixed by the feeling beneath her feet.

"What is it, Sarah?"

She turned to smile at Douglas.

"The floor is vibrating. The speed of the train makes it very challenging to walk, doesn't it? However does one become accustomed to it?"

He smiled back at her. "I imagine it's a bit like getting your sea legs. It takes some time to learn how to walk aboard ship, especially in inclement weather."

She made it to the chair, sat, and turned to him. "Have you been all over the world,

Douglas? And traveled by whatever conveyance?"

"I've seen most of it," he said. "But my most impressive journeys were those on the back of an elephant, or riding a camel."

"While this is my very first occasion to travel by rail. How countrified you must think me."

He looked at her for a moment, as if he wished to say something, then changed his mind. Finally, he only smiled, devoting himself to his work again.

"I understand you will be staying with us for some time, Mr. McDonough," a woman said.

Alano looked up to find that an angel was speaking to him. Not an angel with long blond hair and ethereal wings, but an angel with soft blue eyes and a coronet of brunette braids upon her head.

He walked to the base of the stairs and placed one hand on the newel post. She still stood above him, making no move to equalize their positions. She might be considered Queen of the Angels, so regal did she appear. A thought he decided to keep to himself for the time being.

"I will," he said. "A fortuitous event, would you not agree?"

She raised one eyebrow and looked at him imperiously.

"Is there any food you do not like, Mr. McDonough?"

"I'll eat just about anything," he said. "Except for lamb. Dinner, however, was very tasty. If lonely."

She looked startled.

"How do you prefer your mattress made? I've had the maids mound it in the middle, but that can be changed."

"I'm of an age that anything other than the floor is fine with me," he said.

"Is there anything we need to know to make your visit with us as pleasant as possible?" The words were hospitable; the tone in which they were uttered was icy.

He found himself utterly fascinated.

"Have you been here long?" he asked.

She looked surprised at the question, but answered nonetheless.

"A number of years. Why do you ask?"

"No reason," he said.

He just wanted to keep her there talking. Any subject was acceptable, including the weather. But it was such a bucolic English night that he didn't think it would interest her for long.

"Have you ever known a Spaniard?" he asked.

Another lift of an eyebrow.

"Why do you ask?"

"No reason," he said.

She slowly descended the steps, still clutching that odd book with one arm. It looked heavy enough that she could use it as a weapon.

As she passed him, Mrs. Williams uttered a word that only someone well versed in colloquial Spanish would know. In fact, he was so startled by her whisper that he wondered if he'd misheard her.

She glanced over her shoulder at him, the smile playing around her mouth telling him he hadn't been mistaken after all.

He began to look at his stay at Chavensworth in a whole new light.

The movement of the train had lulled Sarah to sleep. Douglas reached into the cupboard and retrieved a blanket, then placed it across her lap before tenderly tucking it around her shoulders.

The train hadn't halted at a siding after all but continued on through the night. The moon shone through the window. A Scottish moon. For the first time in twenty years, he was home. In the time he'd been gone, he'd seen the world, experienced adventure, been in danger as well as financial peril.

He'd come to value friendship, honesty, honor, and courage. He'd also come to feel some degree of shame for those things he'd done, as a boy, to survive.

Coming home was easier than he'd thought it to be. Perhaps that was due to Sarah's presence beside him. Sarah, intense, duty-driven Sarah, who smiled so rarely that he'd come to look for it. Something about her smile seemed to lighten his heart.

Sarah made a sound in her sleep, and one hand brushed against her cheek. He bent and smoothed her hair free of her face.

Chavensworth was entailed, and the Duke of Herridge had not mentioned any other estates. Consequently, Douglas had believed the fortune he'd amassed to be substantially larger than anything she would inherit. But if she were to inherit Kilmarin, it meant his wife would probably become the wealthiest woman in Scotland.

Ever since he was a little boy, he'd heard of Kilmarin. The castle seemed to embody all that was great and wondrous about Scotland, its history, and the ferocity of its people. There were places at Kilmarin, he'd heard, that were seven hundred years old.

Not only was Sarah the Duke of Herridge's daughter, but she was a Tulloch of Kilmarin.

Was Providence throwing boulders in his path on purpose?

He settled into the chair beside her, willing himself to sleep as well. He missed holding her while she slept, which was ridiculous. He'd slept standing up in a mud hut once, during a monsoon that had nearly floated him away. He could damn well sleep on a reasonably comfortable chair in a private rail car.

His memories, and their attendant guilt and shame, could wait until they reached Perth.

CHAPTER 17

They arrived in the city midmorning of the next day. As they pulled slowly into the station, Douglas realized that this journey was one of the longest he'd ever taken. Not of distance, but of time.

Douglas Eston, world traveler, explorer, inventor, and man of wealth was visiting the past.

Perth sat at the head of an estuary of the River Tay. To the southwest were the Ochil Hills, and the Sidiaw Hills lay to the northeast. Across the river, to the east was Monereiffe Hill and nearer, Kinnoull Hill, each nearly a thousand feet high. He'd climbed both as a child, pretending to rule over all his domain.

Perth was not only the site of his history, but that of Scotland itself. Once known as St. Johnstown, the city lay between two broad meadows, and had been, sometime ago, the capital of Scotland. In its past, it had also been a Royal Burgh, and in the hands of the English more than once. There, in the Church of St. John, where services had been attended by Charles I as well as Charles II, John Knox had delivered a sermon against idolatry.

As they waited for the carriage to be removed from the flatcar, he noted the people congregating in the station. When he was a boy, he would have tried to steal from them, or conjure up enough tears to summon their pity. Yet even then, rouser that he was, he'd dreamed of becoming the man he was now. Oh, he'd no idea of the manners and the clothes, the carriages, horses, houses, and the like. All he'd thought of was the money. He'd wanted to have enough money that he could buy anything he wanted to eat, at any time. If he was hungry in the middle of the night, he wanted to be able to order up a meal.

He had come too close to starving too many times.

The first true meal he'd had in years had been when he was fourteen, in a small bistro in France. Alano had been so disgusted by his table manners that he'd turned away, but at the time Douglas hadn't cared. He'd eaten until he was nearly sick, unable to believe that he could have whatever he wanted. It had taken years to lose that panicked feeling, until he realized that he didn't have to stuff himself at every meal, that food was readily available to him.

When the carriage was finally off-loaded, the horses coaxed from their car and into their leads, they were nearly ready for the rest of their journey.

Sarah and Florie were taking advantage of the station's many shops. Douglas remained where he was, trapped by memory. Only when Tim signaled did he move to escort the two women to the carriage.

They traveled down South Street, past the older parts of Perth, to the walled enclosure that held the ruins of Balhousie Castle. He'd escaped there when he could, feasting on the apples from the orchard, sleeping in one of the small outbuildings with its roof still intact. When he was chased off, he went back to the alleys.

With its whiskey distilleries, linen, and bleaching industries, Perth was a thriving city, and almost as crowded as London. They were blocked in at one point, the carriage slowing to a crawl. From the window, Douglas could see the entrance to a dark, wet alley. Perth occasionally flooded, and it sometimes felt as if the city would never dry. There were places in it that smelled forever of salmon and rot. That alley looked familiar to him. He'd probably hidden behind a few barrels at the end of it, made it his home for however many days or weeks he could escape undetected.

The boy he'd been, eight years old and forever frightened, seemed to look out at him through the mists of time. Uneducated, illiterate, starving, almost animallike, he'd somehow survived for six years, until the day he'd stowed away aboard a ship, bound for the world and his fortune.

Douglas didn't have to enter the alley to experience it fully or even to remember. For the whole of his life, he'd be able to recall and be grateful that he'd somehow escaped.

The carriage was a lovely thing, equipped with soft blue velvet cushions, rolled shades, and brass appointments. There was even a clever little contraption between the seats that rose up, allowing her to put her feet a little higher.

Since the roads were so splendid and smooth, they decided to continue traveling and not stop for lunch. Instead, they would eat in the carriage.

"What about Tim?" Sarah asked, opening the hamper they'd purchased in the station at Perth. "We need to save him something."

"I've already given him his share, Lady Sarah," Florie said. "My Tim is always hungry."

Sarah handed out a selection of meat pies, fruit tarts with fresh berries, and ale from stoneware jugs.

"When will we reach Kilmarin?" Sarah asked, when their meal was done.

"Tomorrow," he said.

Four hours later, they stopped at a coaching inn. To her great surprise, Douglas gave the innkeeper orders to hold the four horses for their return, along with the payment to do so.

"The horses are better than most," he explained, before asking of the innkeeper, "Do you have two rooms available?" At his assent, Douglas turned to Sarah. "You and Florie can sleep in one," he said. "I'll take the other, and Tim will watch over the carriage."

Sarah didn't comment and kept her expression mild, so as not to betray her thoughts. He was simply being considerate. It would not have been safe for Florie to sleep alone, and Tim needed to watch over the carriage. She would accustom herself to sleeping without him. Heaven knows she had had years of practice at doing so.

Douglas thanked the innkeeper, and after

he'd shown them to their rooms, affixed a strange device to the edge of her door.

"What are you doing?" she asked.

He handed her a key.

"It's a traveler's lock," he said. "Keep it on the door and lock yourself in."

"You are much more experienced at traveling than I," she admitted. "I would be foolish not to take your advice."

"In this matter, I will not let you disregard it. Either the lock, or me."

For a moment they studied each other in the dimness of the hall. What would he say if she removed the lock and handed it to him? Would he understand that she wasn't inviting him to her bed as much as seeking his comfort? The past weeks had taught her that Douglas Eston could be a very great source of comfort.

"I haven't done anything today," she said, "but I'm remarkably tired. Why do you think that is?"

"Traveling for long distances in a confined space can wear you out as well as any tedious labor."

He bent down and before she could stop him, before she was even aware of what he was doing, kissed her.

Speechless, she could only stare after him as he walked across the hall and opened the door to his own room. He didn't turn to bid her good night. Nor did he fix one of those strange locks to his door. He only closed the door as she stood there watching.

She pressed two fingers against her lips and could almost feel the imprint of his mouth. He had kissed her. Such a soft and sweet kiss that it lingered on her lips.

An hour later, Sarah stood, rearranged her nightgown so it wasn't twisting around her, and lay back in bed, smoothing the sheet over her before folding it down at the top. She placed the pillow right in the middle of the bed, put her head in the middle of it, and closed her eyes, deliberately seeking sleep.

Five minutes later, her eyes popped open.

She wished she had a book to read. Something lurid, or even frightening, a plot that would banish all her thoughts. She would have written in her journal but she didn't want to wake Florie.

He had kissed her, and she'd wanted more.

She lay staring up at the ceiling, listening to the sound of Florie sleeping on the cot on the other side of the room. Her maid had not been happy to be separated from Tim, but he was sleeping in the stable, and there hadn't been any room for Florie.

Husbands and wives should probably always sleep together. Did they? How very odd that she didn't know. Her own parents' union was not usual; she was well aware of that. Her father utterly despised her mother and made no secret of it. But did normal husbands and wives sleep together?

Had her mother ever been lonely? That was another question she had never asked herself, had never thought until this moment. The Duchess of Herridge had seemed content enough with her flowers and gardens, her needlework and her love of the pianoforte. But had she ever lain awake like Sarah was now, listening to the sounds of night and wishing for something she couldn't name?

A soft knock sounded on the door.

She sat up, draped her legs over the mattress, and slid from the bed, padding barefoot to the door.

"Who is it?" she whispered.

"Douglas."

She pressed her hand flat against the painted wood.

"Just a moment."

She found the key on top of the bureau, returned, and opened the small lock. She turned the knob slowly and pulled the door open.

Douglas stood there attired in a white shirt half-unbuttoned and black trousers. His hair was mussed; his night beard gave his face a saturnine appearance, and he looked monumentally irritated.

"What is it?" she asked softly, conscious of her sleeping maid.

She opened the door farther so he could enter the room, put her finger to her lips, then pointed to Florie.

"Do you have a bottle of your scent?" he asked, his voice sounding gruff.

"My scent? Yes, of course. Why?"

"It's of no importance," he said. "May I have it? I'll return it in the morning."

"You want a bottle of my perfume?" she asked, not comprehending exactly what he needed.

He scowled at her, an expression of such animosity that she almost took a step back. Then her pride came to the forefront, and she frowned right back at him.

"I can't sleep," he said. "And I thought it might help if I smelled you."

She stared at him for a moment, then turned and walked to the bureau, clutching her hands into fists so that he couldn't see that her hands were trembling.

She returned with a bottle in her hand and held it out to him. "It has a screw top," she said. "You must be certain to close it tight, else it will spill everywhere."

He took the bottle from her, and looked as if he would like to say something but evidently thought better of it. With his mood as sour as it was, she had no idea what he might have said. He held the bottle in his hands, studying the triangular top and faceted crystal body as if it were the most important object in the world.

"You needn't use the perfume," she said. "If you would prefer to sleep in here, I would have no objections."

He glanced over to where Florie was sleeping.

"I don't believe I will," he said, looking at her. His gaze was so direct and unflinching that she felt speared by it.

A moment later, he simply whirled on his heel, turned the handle of the door, and was gone, leaving her staring after him.

CHAPTER 18

Sarah had evidently not slept well the night before, and the lulling motion of the carriage was too much of a lure. Douglas watched as she rested her head against the cushioned corner and closed her eyes. In moments, she was asleep.

Douglas hadn't slept any better, but he would rather watch Sarah than doze. They'd been married only a matter of weeks, and in that short amount of time, he'd seen her grieve for her mother, bristle at her father, care for those in her keeping, and engage in herculean tasks for the benefit of Chavensworth. She was passionate about those people and subjects that interested her, and too damned vulnerable.

She was also an eternal distraction, as if he carried a miniature of her in his mind.

After consulting his pocket watch, he decided to stop for lunch. They'd switched out the horses twice today and made excellent time. This afternoon, they'd be at Kilmarin.

"What do you say, Florie, that instead of eating in the carriage today, we make an adventure of it?"

She smiled brightly because his suggestion also meant that Tim would be able to relax as well, and the two of them would be able to share a meal.

"I would like that, sir." She glanced over at Sarah. "Shall I wake Lady Sarah?"

He shook his head. "Let her sleep," he said. "We'll set up our picnic, then wake her."

A quarter hour later, that was exactly what he did, entering the carriage after they'd set up a meal on a grassy brae. Tim and Florie had moved some distance away, and he'd not encouraged them closer. For one thing, they'd been married barely six months. For another, the class system in England wasn't as rigid as some societies he'd known; but all the same, Tim and Florie wouldn't have been comfortable eating with them.

He entered the carriage and sat beside Sarah. Her bonnet had come askew, and he reached over and slipped the bow free, carefully removing the bonnet from her head.

She started, her hand reaching up to touch her cheek, then her eyes opened, at first a little confused, and they filled with emotion.

"I was dreaming of my mother," she said softly.

"You will," he said. "For some months, I think. It's a way of saying good-bye."

She nodded and looked out the window.

"We've stopped," she said.

"I thought we deserved a relaxing interlude."

Douglas reached out with his hand, and after a quizzical look, she placed hers in it, allowing him to lead her from the carriage and up the hill. A red squirrel spotted them and danced in alarm back to the seclusion of the Scots pines woodland.

The skies above were a pale blue, nearly covered in fluffy white clouds with flat bottoms. The hills were indigo turning to gray when the clouds, racing like skiffs on a current of air, passed over them.

They climbed higher, the path running close to the edge of the cliff. As a precaution, Douglas put himself between Sarah and the overhang.

At the clearing, he halted, hearing her indrawn breath with satisfaction.

Below them was the River Tay, gleaming like a sterling snake through the emerald countryside. To the north were the Cairn-

gorm mountains, stretching into the Highlands. To the west were the Loch Earn hills.
The air seemed softer here, diffused, as
though seen through a fine mesh.

He was home, and his heart knew it,
seeming to expand with each mile.

"What is that?" Sarah asked, pulling her
hand free and pointing to their left.

"Tulloch's Folly," he said. "The tower on
it was built last century by one of your
ancestors."

"Does that mean we're close to Kilmarin?"

"A few hours, no more," he said.

"Does anyone live there?"

He shook his head.

"Then why build it?"

"I believe it's an homage to the castles on
the Rhine in Germany," he said. He pointed
down to the River Tay. "We have our own
version of the Rhine, but no castles."

She pointed to the right, to the ruins of
another structure on a hill below the one on
which they stood.

"What's that, then?"

"That's the castle of the White Lady," he
said, his smile beginning from somewhere
within him and spreading outward. "I heard
about it as a boy. I don't remember who it
belonged to, if I ever knew. But it's rumored

to be haunted by a girl who fell in love with a manservant and was banished to her third-floor bedroom. She threw herself from the window, evidently."

"Good heavens."

He reached for her hand again. "You mustn't be saddened by such an old tale, Sarah. Who knows if it's true?"

They walked several feet away from the path and the cliff, and only then did she see the blanket and the basket.

He released her hand, and she gracefully settled herself on the corner of the blanket.

"How do you do that?" he asked.

She looked up at him.

"With your skirts. You look like a flower sitting there, and you did it as gracefully as if you were curtsying."

She looked startled by the compliment.

"I've been trained to do it," she said.

"Do you go on many picnics?"

"I used to," she said. "My mother and I would take our noon meal beneath the oak to the south of Chavensworth. It's a lovely place to sit and read or talk."

"I'm surprised you allowed yourself a respite from all your duties," he said, sitting on the opposite corner.

"When I was six years old, I began my training. That's when it first was made clear to me that I was the daughter of the Duke of Herridge, and consequently different from other people."

He didn't comment.

"I was encouraged to act in a decorous manner at all times, and remember that people would look to me, the only child of the Duke of Herridge, for clues as to my father's character. I was never to shame him. Never to embarrass him. I was never to do anything untoward."

"A paragon of virtue, in other words."

She smiled faintly. "Perhaps.

"If I had any questions as to how I should act, my mother was my mainstay. She was a source of information for most things. In London, I had my aunt to consult."

"Your mother didn't accompany you to London?"

She shook her head. "No," she said. "My father didn't allow it."

With every conversation, he was beginning to understand her a little better, and as he did so, he realized how very insular a life she'd lived.

"I have no doubt that you were the perfect duke's daughter," he said.

"My life has been proscribed by my behavior." She hesitated for a moment, then continued, "By expectations of my behavior." She looked directly at him, her gray eyes unflinching. He was reminded of that afternoon in the Duke of Herridge's study. "But I don't know how you want me to act, Douglas."

She began to arrange the food, unwrap the cheese from the muslin and slice it thinly. He was unaccustomed to being waited on, but he found it a heady experience to have his wife serve him.

"You couldn't have said anything that pleased me more," he said.

Now she looked confused. Good.

"I want you to act like yourself, Sarah. Not as you think is proper. Not as you believe people would wish you to act, but the way you feel."

He reached out and grabbed one of her gloved hands between his. She was always covered up, always shielded, always protected from the gaze of others. He wanted to see her naked in the light of day, and although now was neither the time nor the place, he gave a moment or two of thought to it.

"I didn't have the chance to tell you how exquisite you looked, standing there in our bedroom. Your legs are magnificent, your waist and hips perfect. May I say, Lady

Sarah, that you have a magnificent derriere."

"You said that."

He was both amused and pleased to see
the flush on her cheeks.

"You smiled," she said.

"Is that why you went back to the cot,
because I smiled? I was delighted, enchanted, overjoyed. Why shouldn't I smile?
I'm surprised I didn't dance a jig."

She looked startled again.

Slowly, he began to remove the glove, one
finger at a time. She didn't protest, remaining compliant. His gaze was on their hands,
and when he glanced at her, it was to find
that she was doing the same.

The air around them was still, a summer
silence, as if nature itself were waiting. Not
even a cricket chirped.

He turned her hand over and unbuttoned
the button that stretched across her palm.
One by one, he extracted her fingers from
the silk. When her fingers were finally free,
he removed the glove from her wrist, tossing it to the other side of the blanket. Now
their hands were joined, palms touching.
Hers was warm, warmer than his, as if an
inferno burned inside her body, and it was
only expressed secretly like this.

"It's perhaps not fair," he said. "You, a

proper and virtuous duke's daughter engaged in a liaison with an adventurer."

"We aren't engaged in a liaison," she said. "We're married."

"Until the day we consummate this union, Lady Sarah," he said, "this is nothing but a dalliance."

"And once we have, you will treat me with the decorum I have come to expect of men in my presence?"

He lifted his head to look directly at her.

"Do you mean will I cease embarrassing you? Will I never speak of your breasts again? Or your bare back? Or the texture of your skin?"

"I really wish you wouldn't say such things," she said.

"Perhaps once we lie together, Lady Sarah, I will have other things to mention. The gasp of surprise as I enter you, for example. Or how your nails cling to my shoulders when you take your release. Or how your nipples harden into little pebbles as if they're seeking my tongue to soften and warm them."

"Did you not hear me?" she asked.

He leaned closer to her. "Understand this. You're free to say anything you wish to me. I'm as free to disregard it."

Slowly, she withdrew her hand from his

and clasped her two hands together. She stared down at them fixedly, not at him.

He put his fingers beneath her chin and tilted her head up.

"Instead of a dalliance, Lady Sarah," he said, "I think you and I shall have a love affair. If it goes no farther than my skin needing the touch of yours, and your body craving mine, then so be it."

She looked away, then back at him. He could feel her tremble beneath his fingers and wanted to smooth his hand over her cheek. In actuality, he wanted to do more, to pull her into his embrace and warm her as he placed both hands on her back, pressing her closer. He would croon to her, soft syllables that meant nothing other than to convey comfort. He would ease her into passion and away from fear, until passion became more commonplace and fear only rarely felt.

He sat back, reached for some cheese and a jar of ale, and smiled at Sarah, unsurprised when she looked away rather than smiling back at him.

"Tell me about your grandfather."

She prepared a plate for herself, then finally answered. "I don't know anything about him. Donald Tulloch. Is Tulloch a common Scottish name?"

"Around Perth it is," he said. "Was there a great deal of antipathy between your mother and her parents?"

"I'm not sure it was antipathy," she admitted. "Occasionally, I think my mother was very sad about their rift. She never commented upon it, but more than once she said that two people can make a family. She and I were as much a family as any large group."

"There's every possibility that your grandfather won't see you. Are you sure he's even alive?"

"He was as of a month ago," she said. She glanced at him. "I had my solicitor make inquiries."

"You knew this day might come."

"I was more concerned that my father would exile my mother to Scotland. I wasn't sure where we would go, so I wanted to ensure that my grandfather would take us in."

"Does he know you're coming?"

She shook her head. "No, I never communicated with him, and I asked that my solicitor not inform him of my interest. But from what he was able to understand, my grandfather is alive and the head of the family."

She fell silent. Was she wishing that Morna

Herridge had been as long-lived as her father?

"But you don't know anything else about him, or about Kilmarin?"

She shook her head again. "Do you?"

"Kilmarin is probably to the inhabitants of Perth what Buckingham Palace is to a Londoner. Parts of it are spectacularly ugly, and other parts are beautiful, a monument to what man can create."

"My mother never said. In all those years, she rarely mentioned Scotland at all. It's as if a door simply closed on that part of her life."

He didn't respond. What could he say? Sometimes, for the sake of survival, an individual had to wall off certain parts of his — or her — past.

"Is there no one you wished to see in Perth?"

"If there had been, I would have come home a long time ago."

"There's no one you would wish to see again?"

"Are you fishing for information, Lady Sarah?" he asked with a smile. "I was too young when I left Scotland to have broken many hearts."

"But you have broken some," she said. It

wasn't a question as much as it was a comment.

"Should I pretend to have been celibate since birth?"

She looked intrigued at the question, enough that he began to shake his head.

"I have your bottle of scent," he said, and watched, delighted, as her face began to bloom with color. "Shall I return it to you? Or keep it in case we are forced to sleep apart again?"

Perhaps the key to winning Sarah's heart was to keep her off-balance, long enough that she didn't realize she was being wooed.

CHAPTER 19

Scotland had welcomed them with sunny skies for the past two days, but by afternoon, the scuttling clouds changed their nature, turning dark. Even the air felt different, heavy and filled with moisture.

"It looks like we're in for a downpour," Douglas said, studying the clouds. Through the hatch in the roof, he signaled for Tim to stop and pull the coach over to the side of the road.

"What are you doing?" Sarah asked, the first comment she'd directed to him since their meal.

He glanced at her. "We need to make arrangements. The loose gravel and dirt on the roads could easily turn to mud. In a few minutes, the carriage could become mired in it."

"What do you suggest we do?"

"It all depends on what nature has in store for us," he said.

But beyond that cryptic remark, he didn't explain.

She glanced at Florie. Her maid didn't like storms, and her growing discomfort would have been evident even to a stranger.

Sarah reached over and patted her arm.

"I'm sure it's going to be fine, Florie. Tim is an excellent driver, and Mr. Eston seems to have a level head on his shoulders."

There, did she sound suitably wifely? Her own voice was calm, devoid of any anxiety whatsoever. But then, she'd had years to practice her skills at prevarication. If she was afraid, she doubted anyone in the carriage could have discerned it.

She opened the door and peeked her head out to see Tim and Douglas standing by the horses in earnest conversation. Were they making decisions about their safety and yet not involving them?

She closed the door and sat back on the seat.

"Sometimes men are very difficult," she said, a comment she should not have made under any circumstances.

Florie, bless her tactful heart, pretended she hadn't spoken.

"Do you think there's an inn nearby, Lady Sarah?" Florie asked a few minutes later.

"I sincerely hope not," Sarah said. "I had

planned on reaching Kilmarin today. I am not willing to spend another night at an inn."

Douglas entered the carriage again, turned to Florie, and spoke to her first. "Tim says that you mustn't worry. We'll find shelter before the storm hits."

Florie's complexion was as pale as plaster, but she forced a smile to her face as she nodded. "Thank you, sir. I worry about my Tim, too."

"As well you should," Douglas said, which earned him a frown from Sarah. The last thing he should do was commiserate with Florie; it would make her hysterical. But he continued on, oblivious to Sarah's censorious look. "It's the lightning we have to fear."

Finally, he turned to her. "We're not far from the main road," he said. "We're going to go ahead and meet up with it."

"Will we find an inn, sir?" Florie asked.

"We'll reach Kilmarin first," Douglas said.

They exchanged a long look, and she recognized that expression in his eyes. He was more than willing to be as implacable as a brick wall if it meant obtaining what he wanted. How very strange that she'd not recognized his stubbornness before they left Chavensworth.

He began to smile, a thoroughly charming

smile if one didn't notice the wickedness of it. His eyes, too, gave away his thoughts, and she was certain that if Florie weren't here, he would have begun to laugh. Or perhaps something even worse, like scoop her up from the seat, put her on his lap, and proceed to nuzzle at her breasts.

That was not a thought she should have. She reached into the convenience pocket of the carriage, withdrew a blank note card, and began to fan herself. When his smile looked to have no sign of abating, she frowned at him.

"Mr. Eston," she said. Just that, just his name, and it made his smile even broader.

"Stop it," she said, her teeth clenched.

"I am doing nothing, Lady Sarah," he said, still smiling. "Other than thinking first and foremost of your safety."

She couldn't dispute that remark although she wanted to find something to criticize. At least, openly. Heaven knew she had enough knowledge of his private behavior, but publicly he behaved like a perfect gentleman.

Not unlike those knights her mother had told her about, always concerned about their ladyloves. But those knights had sent flowers and composed poetry, and planted gardens. She doubted one of those knights would have whispered decadent suggestions in his lady's ear, nor teased her with fingers, lips, and wildly improvident words.

She looked away, concentrating on the scenery through the carriage window. Within moments, the air darkened, the grass rippled with the increasing wind, and Florie moved closer to her. Sarah glanced at her maid and smiled reassuringly, then looked back through the window, ignoring Douglas. Not that it was easy.

The explosive crack of thunder made her jump. Florie grabbed her arm and let out a little squeal. Sarah looked across the carriage at Douglas, and he smiled reassuringly. Without speaking a word, he held out his hand, and she took it, the three of them now linked by a touch.

"If we can't find shelter soon," Sarah said, "I think we should stop and let Tim join us. It can't be safe for him out there."

Douglas nodded.

"Who is Alano?"

He frowned. "You've met Alano."

"Yes, but who is he?"

"Why are you asking now?"

The carriage was beginning to be buffeted by the wind, and she could hear Tim yelling encouragement to the horses.

"Are horses frightened by the elements?"

she asked.

"I would imagine that all animals have an instinctive need to feel safe. Anything different might be perceived as being frightening."

She nodded, distracted by another crash of thunder.

"Do you really care about Alano, or is that your way of avoiding the storm?"

"I am not afraid of storms," she said. "I deal quite well with any natural occurrence." She frowned at him intently.

"Do you?"

The horses whinnied, and she closed her eyes, trying to ignore the fact that Florie was holding on to her arm with a talonlike grip.

"I met Alano in France. I was fourteen at the time. He rescued me from a situation I couldn't hope to escape on my own." His glance seemed to encompass the past. "He became a mentor to a very angry young man. Now he's my second-in-command, if you will."

"Like a majordomo?"

"More a friend," he said.

Thunder shook the carriage, followed instantaneously by the flash of lightning. Florie screamed, then immediately clamped both hands over her mouth. If Sarah hadn't been discomfited by the storm before, she was now.

Douglas squeezed her hand reassuringly, his attention on the landscape.

"It's not long now," he said, pointing with his free hand. "That's our destination."

She peered through the rain. "We're at Kilmarin?"

"We are," he said.

Sarah was not given to listening to portents or believing in omens. However, there was something about the stormy afternoon that scratched at her nerves. The rain fell in sheets, threatening to wash the carriage away as it climbed the hill leading to Kilmarin. She could hear Tim shouting to the horses. The carriage trembled in the force of the wind as Sarah tried to ease Florie's fears while appearing outwardly calm herself.

A quarter hour passed — a bad quarter hour in which Sarah was certain they were going to be washed away. Florie was still given to excited outbursts every few minutes, and Douglas glanced over at Sarah often enough with a concerned look in his eyes to let her know that she hadn't been quite successful at hiding her own anxiety.

"We'll be there in no time at all," he said.

She only nodded.

Through the rain-sheened window, she couldn't see much of Kilmarin. What she could see amazed her. Had Douglas felt the same upon viewing Chavensworth?

She'd always considered Chavensworth a magnificent estate, almost preening when people mentioned it in London gatherings. But from the glimpse of her mother's childhood home, she was quite certain that Chavensworth was much smaller in size.

The road on which they were traveling seem to wind around the mountain. When she mentioned as much to Douglas, he only nodded. Some moments later, he spoke.

"I imagine it was constructed that way for defense," he said. "Remember, Kilmarin was built seven hundred years ago."

"Chavensworth is quite old as well," she said, feeling an absurd desire need to defend her own home.

He only smiled faintly, his attention on the road.

She preferred to ignore their upward climb, as well as the fact that the higher they traveled, the narrower the road seemed. Another way of Kilmarin defending itself? At least she faced the side of the mountain, and not the cliff. She wasn't exceptionally fond of heights, especially in a storm of this magnitude.

A gust of wind pushed eagerly against the carriage, and the vehicle shivered in response. Perhaps they would be thrown off the road entirely, to plunge down the side of the mountain. Her compassionate errand would end in the deaths of four people.

She closed her eyes, patting Florie's hand reassuringly even as she wished her maid would simply hush.

A bolt of lightning struck too close for comfort, and her eyes flew open to meet Douglas's gaze.

"We are there," he said softly.

She knew, without a doubt, that if Florie had not been there, he would have taken her into his arms and held her there as he had so many nights after her mother died.

The road abruptly leveled so they were no longer climbing uphill. Instead, it seemed as if they had come to an entrance of sorts, the shadows in front of them becoming an iron gate.

"Just how many defenses does Kilmarin need?"

"You're talking about a country that has its share of ruined castles," he said. "Evidently, Kilmarin has just the right number of defenses."

She heard Tim shouting again, but this time his directions weren't for the horses.

The carriage slowed and stopped. Despite the fact that it was still raining hard, Douglas opened the door.

"Where are you going?"

"To gain admittance to Kilmarin. I doubt they welcome visitors."

Another difference from Chavensworth. They had never turned away a traveler. Yet she couldn't imagine anyone coming to Kilmarin's gates voluntarily.

"You'll get wet."

"Yes," he said, smiling. "I imagine I will. But I'll also dry. Nevertheless, thank you for your wifely concern."

"I'll not care for you if you become ill," she said.

"Nonsense. Of course you will. Despite your fierce looks and stern frowns, Lady Sarah, you've a generous heart and a loving nature."

What on earth should she say to that?

As he left the carriage, she reached out her hand and touched his shoulder.

"Be careful, Douglas."

A nod was his only response.

When Douglas stepped out of the carriage, it was to find three men encircling Tim. He approached them slowly, hands out, palms to them, so they would know he carried no weapons.

Ahead of them, shrouded in the dim light, was the approach to Kilmarin. On either side of the iron gates was a tall pedestal, each topped with a statue of a man holding a spear. The effect was not the least bit welcoming, but he didn't suppose the Tullochs really cared. They'd held power in this part of Scotland for generations.

"Is Donald Tulloch your laird?" Douglas asked.

The taller of the three men separated himself from the group around Tim and faced him. Given the other inequities in this situation, Douglas was happy to see that they were the same height.

"He is. And why would you be speaking of him?"

"His granddaughter is in the carriage, and has come from England to see him."

"He has no granddaughter," the man said with some certainty.

"He does. Lady Sarah Eston, of Chavensworth. Her mother was Morna Herridge. The Duchess of Herridge."

The man stared at him for several moments. Since the rain showed no sign of lessening, and since he was drenched anyway, Douglas was more than happy to stand there as long as the other man decreed. But when he showed no sign of moving or saying anything further, Douglas folded his arms and suggested a compromise.

"Why don't you send word to Donald himself, and have him make the decision whether or not to allow admittance to his granddaughter. Otherwise, I can't think him pleased with your decision to turn her away. Unless, of course, he defers to you in all things."

The other man surprised him by smiling. "Aye, we'll do that, then." He signaled to the two men who still stood by Tim, and within moments, they had disappeared from view.

Their leader walked some distance away before glancing over his shoulder at Douglas. "Do you like standing out in the rain, man? If you do, you're welcome to it. If not, come with me."

He and Tim followed, and when the man disappeared into a shadow, Douglas approached cautiously, only to find himself in a cave hewn from solid rock. A warm fire blazed in the brazier near a table and four chairs. A lamp sat on the table, along with a deck of cards. Evidently, guarding Kilmarin's gate wasn't strenuous work.

He motioned to Tim to take one of the chairs, and he took another, stretching out his sodden boots to the heat.

"I take it you're the gatekeeper of Kilmarin," Douglas said.

"You take it wrong, then," the man said. "I'm Robert Tulloch, grandnephew to Donald himself. We all take turns at the gate, just as we all take turns doing what needs to be done at Kilmarin."

Tulloch sat as well, focusing his attention on Douglas.

"You look familiar," he finally said.

"I was born and raised in Perth," Douglas said. "Perhaps we met there."

The man nodded. "Aye, perhaps we did."

The cave was evidently hewn from solid rock, but that hadn't stopped whoever had created it from adding a few comforts. Two deep and long ledges carved into the wall looked as if they could be made into pallets if necessary. A shelf on the far wall held a quaich, a wooden two-handled bowl, and a small barrel.

Tulloch stood, walked to the other side of the cave, and filled the quaich from the barrel.

"Tulloch whiskey," he said, returning to the table and placing the quaich between Douglas and Tom. "The best in Scotland. You'll know that if you're from Perth."

Douglas stifled his smile, as well as his

comment that every distillery in Perth made that pledge. Still, he wasn't averse to warming his insides since it was all too evident his outside was going to stay wet for a while.

By the time they finished their whiskey, the two men returned. They ignored Douglas and Tim, turning to Tulloch.

"He'll see them."

Douglas stood. "I thank you for your hospitality," he said. "And the whiskey."

Tulloch only nodded, following them out into the rain.

Douglas entered the carriage, keeping his distance as much as possible from Sarah and Florie. He was still sodden.

"Your grandfather has agreed to see you."

She sat back against the seat, adjusted her bonnet, then clasped her hands together primly.

He wondered if she knew how difficult the next few hours would be. Coming to Scotland was something she'd felt she had to do, and he knew her well enough to know that she would have come to see her grandfather either with him or without him. The least he could do was stand at her side.

The great black gates of Kilmarin swung slowly inward, almost as if giving them time to reconsider whether or not they truly wished to enter.

Four floors tall, Kilmarin was constructed of deep red stone. Few windows faced the drive, and only from the upper floors. Kilmarin was stolid and huge, dwarfing the countryside but possessing none of the aesthetic beauty of Chavensworth. Douglas had thought, from the first moment of seeing Chavensworth, that it resembled a French château. Kilmarin was defiantly Scottish.

Tim drove the horses through the gates and up the sweeping drive to the castle. On a fair day, in the morning light, the gravel might have sparkled, the flower beds with their nodding blooms would have seemed a pleasant precursor to this meeting. In the afternoon, the sun would have lightened the deep red stone of Kilmarin, weathered it to a dusky pink. In a Scottish storm, however, there were only beds of blackened flowers, and shadowy fingers of darkness stretching onto the gravel drive, as if trying to snare a carriage wheel. Kilmarin's brick was the color of blood.

None of them spoke; the only sound was the drumming pattern of rain on the carriage roof.

They didn't reach Kilmarin as much as they were enveloped by the structure. As they drove beneath the porte cochere, the silence was sudden and as loud as the rain. The carriage rolled back and was still. Seconds later, the door opened.

Douglas looked over at Sarah.

"Are you ready?" he asked, more than willing to turn the carriage around and leave Kilmarin if she changed her mind.

She straightened her shoulders, tilted her chin up, and smiled. He'd studied her avidly over the last few days and knew pretense from genuine emotion. She was terrified, but he doubted anyone else could tell.

He reached over and placed his hand on top of hers.

"I'll be with you," he said.

She bit her bottom lip but didn't comment. A swift nod was the only acknowledgment she gave him. But there was a momentary look in her eyes, a glance of surprise and gratitude that would have to suffice.

Douglas left the carriage first, nodding to the man who'd opened the carriage door. Unlike the servants of Chavensworth, he was not dressed in livery and, also unlike the servants of Chavensworth, he stared back. There was no subservient lowering of the eyes here. The man was as curious about Douglas as Douglas was about Kilmarin.

He turned and held his hand out to Sarah. She placed hers on top of it and allowed him to help her down the steps. She spent some time fluffing up her skirts, but he could tell that she was also using the moments to look around and get her bearings. Kilmarin was awe-inspiring from a distance. Up close, it was even more amazing.

He had never been here himself, had only heard about Kilmarin as a boy — how there was a dungeon rumored to be below the main structure, and how a young boy ghost haunted the Great Hall.

Kilmarin was proving to be the equal of his childhood stories.

Shields were displayed on all four pillars of the porte cochere. Not baronial shields that might reveal a man's coat of arms, but shields that looked as if they had been used in actual battles, round, thickly plated, and dented in several areas.

An arched door led to what was evidently the interior of the castle. As he turned, extended his arm to Sarah, the door opened.

By Douglas's calculations, Donald Tulloch must have been in his seventies. He'd thought to find him ailing, a man near death. The man who greeted them held a cane in his right hand, but he brandished it more like a weapon than an aid for walking.

Once, he'd probably been taller than Douglas, but age had shrunk him. His shoulders curved toward his chest, and his knees were bent as if unable to support his weight, skeletal though it was. A thick mass of white hair hung to his shoulders, and his face, long and narrow, was lined and weathered. The blue eyes that peered out from beneath bushy white eyebrows, however, were surprisingly alert.

For several long minutes, he and Sarah stared at each other, neither speaking.

Finally, Douglas stepped forward and because Sarah had taken his arm, she was forced to either drop it or come with him. They approached her grandfather with slow, measured steps, stopping a few feet from Donald.

"Thank you for agreeing to see us," he said.

"Who are you?" he asked in a voice that sounded scratchy and unused.

"Douglas Eston," he said.

Before he could introduce Sarah, she stepped forward.

"I am Lady Sarah Eston," she said, in the most regal tone he'd ever heard her use. "My mother was the Duchess of Herridge."

Donald was quicker than his gatekeeper. He tapped the end of the cane against the flagstone floor. As if it were a signal, everyone around them fell silent.

"My daughter is dead?" he asked.

Sarah straightened, facing down the old man.

"My mother is dead," Sarah replied.

Donald Tulloch nodded. A moment later, he turned, and slowly walked into Kilmarin.

Douglas put his hand on Sarah's arm as her grandfather vanished into the interior of Kilmarin. As a strategy, it was a fine one. They didn't know if they'd been dismissed or welcomed.

The storm had not abated; the day was advanced, and he was damned if he was going to allow Donald Tulloch to banish them so summarily.

Like it or not, Kilmarin had some visitors.

Douglas turned to the young man who'd opened the carriage door. "Have our trunks directed to our room and find someone who can show us our accommodations." Before the young man could speak, Douglas held up his hand. "I will also need arrangements for my coachman, and my wife's maid."

"I'll see that it's done. They'll be treated with Scottish hospitality."

Douglas turned to find that Robert had followed them.

He nodded to the other man, then glanced over at Tim. "Send me word if you need anything," he said.

Tim nodded. "I will, sir." He looked around at the gathering of people under the porte cochere. From his expression, Tim was feeling a little overwhelmed by all the Scots.

"We haven't fought a battle with the English for a good hundred years, Tim," Douglas said, both as a reassurance to Tim and a reminder to the Tullochs who surrounded them.

A young girl stood at the doorway, her arrival evidently a signal for the others to disperse. One by one, they melted away into the storm.

"Will you come with me?" she asked, stepping aside so they could enter Kilmarin.

Sarah stroked her hand across his arm.

"Your jacket is soaking. You need to get warm and dry."

"I do enjoy a solicitous wife," he said with a smile.

She frowned at him, but the expression was only surface deep. Pain still lingered in her eyes.

"Shall we enter?" he asked.

Her gaze encompassed the open door, the shadowed interior.

"If we absolutely must," she said, her smile fixed and determined. Sarah turned at the door. "Florie, after you and Tim are settled, have someone direct you to my room."

Until that moment, Douglas hadn't realized how close to tears she was.

Oh, love.

He reached out, took her hand gently in his, and led her through the door.

CHAPTER 20

The young girl — Sarah was uncertain as to her actual position in the household — led them to a grand marble staircase that would have dominated any other structure, even Chavensworth. Kilmarin, however, was like a giant beast, and this marble-and-mahogany staircase seemed its spine.

Sarah kept her hand firmly in Douglas's, telling herself it was only for balance. Unfortunately, she had to release his grip when she needed to pull her skirts up slightly in order to navigate the stairs.

"The family sleeps in that wing," the girl said, pointing to a corridor lit by candelabra. Instead of heading to the left, toward the family wing, she turned right, to the rooms evidently set aside for visitors.

Very well, let Donald Tulloch consider her a visitor. She wouldn't be remaining at Kilmarin long enough to feel slighted.

The girl stopped halfway down the corridor, opened the door, waiting for them to enter. Douglas stepped to one side so she could precede him, and for once she wished he wasn't so chivalrous. As if he knew how loath she was to enter the room, he grabbed her hand again, and smiled at her, such a tender smile that her heart ached.

"I'll have the lamp lit in a moment," the girl said. "It's a fine and dreary day, isn't it?"

True to her word, the space was illuminated in only minutes. Had she not been trained so assiduously in decorum, Sarah might have gasped aloud at the sight that met her eyes.

This was a suite, not merely a bedchamber. The sitting room was predominantly blue, the silk of the walls matching the upholstery of the two sofas arranged in front of the fireplace. Between them was a low mahogany table with carved legs ending in lions' paws. A lamp sat at the end of each sofa, and another on the table beside the window, next to a high-backed chair and footstool. A small bookcase next to the chair was filled with gilt-edged books.

"It's the Queen's Room," the girl said. "One of our finest chambers."

Perhaps she'd misjudged her grandfather after all. If Kilmarin showed its unwelcome visitors this beauty and comfort, she could only wonder at the rest of the castle.

She walked to the entrance to the bed-chamber. The bed was massive, oversized, as was all the furniture in the room. Each piece of furniture was heavily carved, the relief stained a deep greenish blue, nearly the shade of Douglas's eyes. Gold curtains hung at the bed and the skirt of the vanity. An intricately detailed gold screen sat half in front of a closed door — a bathing chamber?

The counterpane was white, but in the center, heavily embroidered in gold thread, was an unusual crest, dominated by the figure of a wolf, stalking, its nose low, its jaws agape. Hardly amenable to dreamless sleep.

"Does Tulloch mean wolf in Gaelic?" she asked.

"Actually, it means hill," Douglas said from behind her.

"Shall I give you an hour, miss?"

She turned to face the young girl.

"An hour?"

"Donald eats supper early," the girl said. "I'll be back in an hour to take you to the dining hall."

Before Sarah could think of a reason to refuse, she was gone, and Sarah was left staring helplessly at Douglas.

"It's only a meal, Sarah," he said, his tone absurdly kind.

She nodded.

"It's only a meal," she repeated, but that didn't make her feel appreciably better.

Douglas began to change out of his wet clothing. Not behind the gold screen, or in the room behind it, which did turn out to be a bathing chamber. Instead, he simply peeled off his clothing, acquired a towel, and wrapped it around his waist. All done with the unselfconscious actions of a human who knows he's quite attractive.

"Have you always been that way?" she asked, grateful to have a subject to discuss other than her mother or grandfather.

"What way?"

"Comfortable with being naked. Especially in front of a stranger."

He folded his arms and regarded her, the expression in his blue-green eyes one she couldn't decipher.

"I wouldn't consider you a stranger, Sarah. It concerns me that *you* do."

Perhaps this wasn't a good topic of conversation after all.

She turned and walked to the bureau, removing her bonnet with its lone wilted feather. It had begun the journey so perky, and now it looked so bedraggled. While she couldn't have said that the journey was begun with any perkiness on her part, she felt the same.

Those blasted tears were back. She blinked them away furiously, wishing that she'd been given her own chamber. If she had, she would probably have succumbed to a bout of weeping and felt better for it.

"You will get through this," Douglas said, coming up behind her and placing his hands on her shoulders. Slowly, he drew her back. She closed her eyes and allowed herself to rest against him.

"You will get through this, Sarah. But you won't get past it. You will always grieve, in your way, for your mother. You will always miss her. If I had the power of God, I would take away your grief, but in doing so I would have to take away your memories. Would you want that?"

"No," she said softly. "It's just so hard. How did you bear it?"

He pressed his cheek against her hair and didn't quite answer her. "One day you'll smile, then you'll find yourself laughing. But the moments will always come when you remember. You'll feel her loss forever, all the while you'll know you were blessed by being loved."

She was so tired, tired of fighting the pain, tired of being strong. Douglas wrapped his arms around her, and she turned her head, laying her cheek against his chest. For long moments they stood simply and quietly together.

Finally, Sarah pulled away, conscious of two things. Douglas was nearly naked, and she liked touching him.

She busied herself by investigating the bathing chamber. The copper tub was a beautiful piece of art, deeply embossed with thistles and roses along the edge. Two sets of taps sat on the edge, and when she opened one, she was shocked to find that hot water ran through it. Evidently, Kilmarin had a boiler — more than Chavensworth could boast.

The drain in the bottom of the tub led to a series of pipes, and she could immediately see that the system was the same as at Chavensworth. She couldn't help but wonder if they had the same problem of the drains occasionally becoming clogged, but when she mentioned it to Douglas, he only laughed.

"You are not the chatelaine here," he said, "and you needn't worry."

"I know," she said, "but habits die hard."

He smiled at her, and she looked away.

That was another thing she should caution herself about — she was becoming habituated to his smiles. She had even grown to anticipate them, if not to encourage them. She'd never been overly adept at womanly wiles, at least those practiced in her two London seasons. She couldn't flirt coyly, and she was abysmal with a fan — she kept knocking it against objects and people, or dropping the silly thing. She didn't bat her eyelashes prettily, and she really wasn't interested in playing to a man's vanity.

But Douglas brought out something in her that she'd never before identified, a certain wantonness of spirit. She'd begun to think errant thoughts, improper thoughts, but that wasn't the only sign that she was skirting impropriety. Her body seemed to know when he was near, as if attuned to him in some odd way. Her pulse raced, her breath tightened, and her heart beat louder.

Even in the midst of her grief, there was another component to it, something new and different and almost overwhelming.

Perhaps her life would have been so much easier if she'd remained unmarried, but then, what would have happened in the last weeks? Once, she would have been confident enough to say that she could handle almost any situation, but now she knew there were some circumstances beyond her. Sometimes, she needed other people's assistance, and this time had proven that fact only too well. What would she have done without Douglas? Had she even thanked him adequately? Had she told him of her certainty that Chavensworth was a better place for his presence there? Or had she simply assumed that he would know?

She walked into the sitting room, where he stood in front of a now-roaring fire, still clad only in a towel.

"Thank you," she said.

"For what?" He turned to face her.

She kept her gaze on his face. "For being here," she said. "For being at Chavensworth. For being kind."

"I'd be a poor husband if I wasn't at least kind to my wife."

She didn't know what to say to that.

He walked back into the bedroom, and she followed.

Although her trunks had not yet been delivered, his solitary trunk had been, and he opened it now, gathering up his clothing.

"You really need a valet," she said.

"You say that because you don't like to see me naked."

On the contrary, she was becoming quite

used to it. Perhaps even anticipating it, actually.

He went behind the screen to dress, and when he returned, he wore a formal white shirt adorned with pins and tucks down the front, black trousers, and black leather shoes with silver buckles. He withdrew a jacket from the trunk and laid it on the rounded top before taking out a leather case.

"Are you going to work again?" she asked, as he walked into the sitting room and placed the case on the table between the sofas.

"Chavensworth has taken a great deal of my time during this last week," he said. "I need to be about my own business."

"Not diamonds," she said.

"Not diamonds. I'm involved in a great many businesses."

He sat on the sofa, withdrew a sheaf of papers from the case, and began to arrange them into stacks. In no time at all, he had created three stacks, one larger than the other two. From the leather case, he extracted a set of quills, a small vial of sand, and a curious cubic object.

She walked to the table, curious despite herself. She picked up the small ivory square and examined it from all angles. Although it was a lovely thing, heavily incised with flowers and birds, she couldn't see its purpose.

"What is it?"

He reached out and took the ivory cube from her, set it down on the table, and pressed two spots at once. The top slid back to reveal a cork-topped bottle, cunningly concealed.

"It's a traveling inkwell," she said, delighted.

"I've tried more than one apparatus for carrying ink, and this is the best I've found."

"Do you always work when you travel?"

He glanced up at her again. "I don't like wasting time."

"And this journey is a waste of time?"

"I think you're deliberately misinterpreting what I said, Sarah." He pulled one stack of paper toward him. "I can't help but wonder why."

She didn't answer, annoyed at him. True, she wanted to know what he examined so assiduously, but to do so would be to advance a curiosity that probably wasn't wise. Yet, they had few common bonds between them: a shared afternoon in her father's study, her mother's death, a knowledge of Chavensworth, perhaps.

She abruptly sat down on the sofa.

"Tell me about your businesses," she said.

He glanced over at her.

"Are you commanding me, Lady Sarah? I don't deal well with commands, especially uttered in that tone of voice."

"You can be very irritating, Douglas. There, is that tone better?"

"Not appreciably," he said. "Perhaps if you work on it, I'm sure you can manage to sound somewhat amiable."

He turned back to his work, evidently finished with the discussion.

She stared at him for several long minutes.

"Do you always dismiss people when they question you?"

"When they treat me as if I'm their footman, yes." He glanced over at her. "You're not angry at me, Sarah. You're angry at your grandfather."

What an absurd time to want to cry, she thought.

"I truly am interested," she said. "Forgive me if I sounded imperious."

"No doubt it comes from being a duke's daughter," he said, not turning his attention from his papers.

"I think it comes from being the Duke of Herridge's daughter," she confessed. "You dare not show an ounce of weakness with my father. I think he would have been a great military genius had he been so inclined. I do believe that he sees conversations with people as battles to be fought and confrontations as wars to be won. I think he has a tally in his mind of winners and losers, and he is determined not to lose."

Her attention was directed to the hills and valleys of the fabric of her skirt, and when she looked up it was to find that he was looking at her.

"How old were you when you realized this?" he asked.

"I think I was nine," she said.

"Was it a confrontation with your father, or did you witness a battle between him and your mother?"

"My mother was always submissive to him," she said, again feeling that awful urge to weep. "Once, she said it was keeping peace, that a wife had to acknowledge her husband as the head of the household."

She looked over at him again. "I have no problem with allowing someone to be the head of the household other than myself," she said. "But I don't see why my spirit has to be dulled in doing it."

"It doesn't," he said.

"Other than being a creator of diamonds, what business do you have?"

A knock on the door interrupted Douglas's answer. When Douglas opened it, two

293

young men entered, carrying her trunks. Florie trailed behind, with a small valise in hand, directing them where to put them, and adding for good measure, "See that you don't scratch them. That's fine Florentine leather."

Where had the frightened girl gone? In the last hour, Florie had gained her composure. Evidently, the continuing storm held no terror for her as long as she was out of the carriage.

Florie looked around the room, took in the bedchamber, and stood in the doorway of the bedroom.

"I'll be doing your hair now, Lady Sarah," she said, in a no-nonsense tone Sarah had never heard from her.

She'd come to Scotland, and the world had gone mad.

Alano knocked on the door of the house-keeper's room. He waited patiently, which was a surprise given that he was not a patient man.

When she finally opened the door, he smiled at her, undeterred when she frowned back.

"You can be very off-putting," he said. "I imagine that serves you quite well being the housekeeper. However, I am a guest at

Chavensworth, and such behavior doesn't put me off. I could even mention to Lady Sarah that you've been brusque with me."

She looked unimpressed at his threat.

His smile broadened. In addition to being incredibly lovely, she was also intelligent.

"Is there anything I can do for you, Mr. McDonough?" Her look dared him to say something improper.

"I would like some tea," he said.

"There is a bellpull in your room, sir. If you will but ring it, the maid will serve you anything that you desire."

"I'm afraid that will not do, Mrs. Williams," he said. "I am desirous of your company. Besides, you owe me an explanation."

She folded her arms in front of her, and he could almost hear her toe tapping.

"I have no intention of partaking of tea with you, sir. And what explanation do I owe you?"

"How do you know Spanish?" he asked.

A flush transformed her face, rendering it younger.

"Let us just say I have some knowledge of Spanish, Mr. McDonough."

She moved to close the door, and he inserted his foot between it and the frame.

"Mrs. Williams, I am here on behalf of

Mr. Eston, who is my friend. Mr. Eston is married to Lady Sarah, who is responsible for everything at Chavensworth. Do you not think that the two of us have significant interests in common that we could become cordial acquaintances?"

He held up his hand before she could speak, and added, "I'm not saying friends, Mrs. Williams. I am merely saying that it is a very large house, and I have no one with whom to speak. Your Thomas is a very nice young man, but I do not feel that he is as schooled as you in certain matters."

"Perhaps, Mr. McDonough. I shall think about it."

He removed his foot from the door, and she immediately closed it in his face.

He really shouldn't have felt like laughing.

CHAPTER 21

A knock on the door made Sarah roll her eyes.

"Can you get that, Florie?" she asked. "There have been more people in this suite in the last hour than I've seen in days."

Florie went to the door. Sarah heard two female voices, then Florie appeared once more.

"Linda Tulloch is here, Lady Sarah, to take you into dinner."

Who was Linda Tulloch?

Sarah walked into the sitting room to find a woman standing there, attired in a dark blue dress with a full hoop, drawn up at the bottom in two places to reveal an underskirt of white lace. A delicate cameo at her throat was her only ornament. Her hair, a shade between brunette and blond, was parted in the middle and drawn into a severe bun at the nape of her neck.

She was lovely but gave the appearance of

either being bored with her looks or uncaring for them. Winged brows arched over deeply brown and thickly lashed eyes. Her cheekbones were high, almost as if she were an exotic creature from the Far East and not Scotland at all. A mouth, perfectly formed, was pulled into a thinner line than nature had designed, however, giving Sarah the impression that Linda Tulloch did not often smile.

"I'm your cousin," she announced. "My father was your mother's brother."

Until this moment, she'd not even known she had an uncle.

"I'm here to take you to dinner, but we must hurry." Linda turned, and glanced behind her impatiently. "Grandfather does not allow for any tardiness. If you're late for dinner, you simply won't be served."

Sarah nodded to Florie. "Don't wait up for me," she said.

As they descended the stairs, Sarah noticed what she hadn't seen earlier. Shields and claymores, broadswords and dirks were mounted on the walls, above the arches, and sweeping into a large, spacious room where three people stood waiting.

Douglas was there, and beside him the man she recognized from the porte cochere, and her grandfather, Donald Tulloch, who was frowning in her direction.

If he thought to unsettle her, he was doomed to disappointment. Ever since childhood, she'd been forced to stand in front of her father's desk and wait until he raised his head to acknowledge her, all the while praying that she wouldn't cry when he spoke. After those childhood experiences, Sarah doubted she was capable of being intimidated.

The two of them approached the others, Donald reaching out to take Linda's arm, as Sarah went to stand beside Douglas.

"She's my cousin," she told him.

"You'll find that a great many of us are related." The man to the side of Douglas stepped forward. "Robert Tulloch," he said, introducing himself. "Another cousin. Third or fourth or more, I believe."

Donald turned, and began what Sarah could only call a procession. Linda and Robert next. Douglas offered Sarah his arm, and they followed.

"He's not an adversary," he said in a whisper. "He's at least seventy, and deserves some respect. For survival if no other reason."

She frowned at Douglas, but he only shook his head and escorted her into the adjoining room. The dining hall was as cavernous as the room they'd just left, with an arched ceiling reminding Sarah of a cathedral. The sound seemed magnified here too, as Douglas pulled out a thronelike wooden chair for her and walked around the table and took his place. Legs grated against the pitted stone flooring, and for a few minutes that was all she could hear.

The table where they sat was pocked and scarred, at least twenty feet long and made from rough planks nailed together at irregular intervals. In places, the lacquer was darker than in others. The chairs were upholstered, seat and back, in cracked brown leather. Did this table, did all the furnishings in the Great Hall, date from Kilmarin's beginnings? Everything was rustic and oversized, built for Scottish warriors, a definite contrast from the furniture in the Queen's Suite.

The settings looked oddly out of place, as they seemed like something she'd find at Chavensworth. She immediately identified the Spode china, with its distinctive crimson-and-black pattern. The napkin was well-pressed linen, with a wolf's head embroidered in the corner. The silverware was sterling, as were the serving pieces.

Sarah sat opposite Douglas in the middle of the table. Linda sat next to Douglas, and

Robert sat to Sarah's right. At the head of the table was Donald, while the foot of the table was left empty.

Donald waved his hand, a signal, evidently, because a parade of young girls came through the door at the far end of the room bearing trays of food.

"Move the cattle tomorrow," Donald abruptly said in the silence.

"I've already moved them," Robert said.

Donald stared at him. "Did I give you leave to do so?"

"Yes," he said, an answer that evidently surprised the older man. "The minute you put the herds under my control, you gave me leave to do so."

Donald sat back and regarded Robert for a minute, then surprised Sarah by repeating: "Move the cattle tomorrow."

Robert only smiled.

Evidently, this was a game of long standing, and the only conversation at the table.

Dinner consisted of two types of fish, neither one of which Sarah could identify, slices of beef, a selection of ripe cheeses, and a dessert made from strawberries and tayberries atop a round of cake and topped with cream.

The fish was flaky and delicate; the beef was succulent, and each selection of cheese seemed more pungent and aromatic than the next. But it was the dessert that almost made her moan aloud, and more than once she caught Douglas looking at her as she savored her portion.

Her dessert finished, Sarah placed her spoon on the edge of the dish and blotted her mouth with the napkin.

Was she supposed to remain silent? Did everyone at Kilmarin treat Donald as they would a king? Was he as much a despot as her father? Was he as cruel? She had stood up to the Duke of Herridge; she would not cower before Donald Tulloch.

"My mother never talked about you," Sarah said, lobbing a comment into the silence. She glanced at Linda. "I didn't know that she had a brother, let alone that he had children. I thought, until tonight, that I had no family other than my father. And you."

"Did she not tell you of Kilmarin?" Donald asked.

"She mentioned the name once or twice in stories she told me, but nothing of her family."

Donald closed his eyes, as if Morna's silence was a sorrow greater than her death.

"You've not asked about her. Don't you want to know? If she was happy? Or even how she died?"

Linda looked aghast. Robert only wore a small smile as if he was applauding her rebellion. As for Douglas, she didn't dare look across the table to see his reaction.

"Would you like me to assist you from the table, Grandfather?" Linda asked.

Donald focused a stern look at her, and Linda subsided without a word.

The silence in the cavernous room was loud enough that it was an occupant. Thunder rolled across the roof, and Sarah was grateful for the sound of the renewed storm. In those minutes, when Donald placed his napkin on the table and folded his hands on top of his lap, Sarah discovered that she was capable of being intimidated after all.

However, Douglas was here, and she knew he would protect her.

Donald still didn't speak, and it was a silence left uninterrupted by the other occupants of the dining hall.

"Your mother chose to leave Kilmarin," Donald finally said. His voice was eerily calm, his Scottish accent adding a sweetness to the raspy tone. "On that day, she stated that nothing would ever bring her back. Nothing did. Not her mother's death. Not her brother's death. Nothing."

For long moments, he didn't speak, as if

composing himself.

"They grieved for her until the day they died, her mother especially. She spoke of her as she lay dying, but Morna never came. She delivered to them a cruel blow."

Sarah glanced across the table to find that Douglas was watching her grandfather with a curious expression, one she could almost interpret as compassion.

Yes, Donald was old, and yes, he might be frail, but he couldn't be permitted to say such things about her mother.

"My mother was the kindest and the gentlest person I've ever known," Sarah said. "Everyone loved her. If she never returned to Kilmarin, if she never wished to return, there had to be a good reason. Perhaps it was something *you* did that kept her away."

Linda glanced at her, wide-eyed.

For some time, Donald studied Sarah's face with great deliberation. Finally, and with great difficulty, he stood, but when Linda moved to help him, he waved her away. "Leave me be, child," he said. "I'm old, and I move like I'm old."

"Grandfather, you aren't old at all."

Donald ignored her. He took a deep breath, leaned on his cane for just a moment, then straightened to his full height.

He left the room slowly, all four of them watching him depart. Neither Linda nor Robert spoke.

Douglas glanced at her, and she nodded, understanding his unspoken question. He came around the table and pulled out her chair. When she stood, Douglas placed his hand at her back, guiding her down the hall to the grand staircase. She didn't shake off his touch or move away.

She couldn't go to her mother and ask why she'd left Kilmarin and never returned. All she had were her grandfather's words, and an ever-present feeling of loss.

Anger was an acceptable haven, but even in that she was frustrated. Who was the worthy object of her anger? Her mother, for hiding secrets? Her grandfather, for his bitterness? Or even herself, for thinking only of reaching Scotland and not about her reception?

"Are you all right?"

Douglas hesitated on the landing, turning to her.

She looked away rather than face his intrusive glance.

"Sarah."

She nodded. Why must he always see her weep?

"I'm fine," she said, forcing the words past

the lump in her throat. "I'm fine, really."

He didn't speak, leading her to their suite in silence.

Once there, he lit the lamp in the sitting room and led her to the sofa in front of the fireplace. She didn't demur when he bent and renewed the fire. Although it was summer, it was chilly in the room. Or perhaps she was the one who was cold.

She closed her eyes and wished herself away from Kilmarin.

"I'll draw you a bath."

She opened her eyes to find him standing over her.

"You needn't be my servant," she said, remembering his earlier words. "Not my footman."

He smiled. "I don't mind serving you occasionally, Sarah. I'm not constrained to certain behavior by a title. I just won't be addressed as a servant."

"I frankly doubt you would have been constrained even as a footman."

She took his hand and stood, but instead of stepping back, he stepped closer, the tips of his shoes disappearing beneath the fullness of her skirts. He was so close that she could feel his breath on her forehead.

Suddenly, she couldn't breathe again, but it wasn't tears that held her silent. Instead, some other emotion, something startling bright, flooded into her mind as if he were sunlight, and just by standing so close to him, he illuminated all the dark corners inside her.

"Oh, Douglas. I made a mistake coming here," she said, so softly that he had to bend his head to hers in order to hear. His cheek, growing more bristly with his night beard by the hour, gently abraded hers, and she shivered at the touch. When he would have drawn away, she raised her left hand and placed it against his face, keeping him in place just for a moment.

"Why haven't you made me your wife?" she said, and a second later pulled back, horrified. What had compelled her to ask such a question? She looked up at him, dropping her hand to her side.

He smiled. "Should I have seduced you while you wept? The time was not appropriate, Sarah," he said. "But my desire hasn't vanished."

She really shouldn't have brought up the issue at all.

"Doesn't it say something to you, that I cannot sleep without your scent?"

She didn't answer.

"Or that my dreams, like it or not, are filled with you?"

"Why wouldn't I like it?"

"Because man was not designed to be a celibate animal, Lady Sarah," he answered. "And I hurt for you."

He pulled back. "What else can I do for you?" he asked. "Besides your bath, I mean," he added. His expression was somber, his eyes intent.

Do not look at me as if you find me wanting. Do not judge me by your standards of honor, higher than any I could hope to achieve. Do not undress before me as if I'm so cold and unfeeling that I'm unaffected by it.

"Nothing," she said. "And you don't even have to do that."

He held up one hand as if to forestall her objections.

She answered with a smile.

Douglas turned the cold-water tap, then the hot, thinking that he could easily become accustomed to this degree of convenience. He needn't ring for the upstairs maid or summon any servants to their suite.

He walked back into the sitting room where Sarah still sat in front of the fire, her gaze pensive and focused on the flames.

"Your bath is ready," he said, rolling down one sleeve.

She looked up at him.

"I found some bath salts and put them in as well."

"You're quite well versed in a lady's bath," she said.

"It doesn't seem that difficult," he said. "Put some water in the tub, sprinkle in something that smells good. You're done."

She smiled and stood. "You're right. It does sound simple enough. But thank you for your trouble all the same."

"Go take your bath," he said. "Do you want me to find a nightgown and wrapper among your things?"

She looked so horrified that he smiled. "I'll do it," she said quickly, and stepped aside, intent on her trunk. After selecting the top two garments, she held them close to her chest and slipped behind the screen and into the bathing chamber.

"Can I wash your back?"

Silence met his question, then Sarah's laughing response, "No!"

He walked back into the sitting room, banked the fire, and sat on the sofa. The sounds of water splashing made him smile. Preparing her bath had been such a simple act, and one she'd found difficult to accept.

Why haven't you made me your wife? Now there was a question, wasn't it? *Because, my lovely virgin, I wanted to seduce you, but Providence has thrown just about everything between us.*

With that thought, he went in search of a jot of whiskey.

CHAPTER 22

Sarah emerged from the bathing chamber to find that Douglas had disappeared. He wasn't in the bedroom or the sitting room. By the time she'd braided her hair, cleaned her teeth, and finished folding her clothing and placing it in the trunk, he was still missing.

Disappointed, she sat on the edge of the bed. She hadn't slept beside her husband since Chavensworth. How foolish she was to anticipate it tonight.

The bed was incredibly soft, and also so large that it felt as if she had entered an island. The mattress sagged slightly in the middle. She made a mental note to speak to the housekeeper about how that could be avoided with a few judiciously placed additional straps before catching herself. This was not Chavensworth, and she doubted the staff would welcome her advice.

She closed her eyes and willed herself to

sleep, even though she'd left the light on for Douglas's use. She would think of something pleasing, something without memory, something that only offered up a picture to her mind. Perhaps she'd recall an illustration in a book, a sunset over the hills, the swirl of storm clouds. Douglas, naked.

Douglas, naked. That was a sight, but hardly conducive to sleep. More to examination perhaps. She closed her eyes and focused on the memory of him. His feet were long and narrow, and his toes, surprisingly, bore tufts of hair. His legs, too, had hair, but not so much that touching him had been unpleasant. His chest — her fingers had often threaded through the light dusting of hair there.

There were at least a hundred things she could think of right now that would be more proper, but she doubted that any of them would be as interesting.

His chest was quite lovely, actually, with all its muscles. His arms well-defined, almost as if he had once been a laborer. She'd never thought of a man's shoulders being so masculine-looking, but his certainly were, as was the way his neck tapered down to his shoulders.

His buttocks were surprising, too, and she clenched her eyes tighter as if to keep her thoughts hidden. Should she even be thinking of a man's buttocks? Possibly not, but this wasn't any man, this was her husband. Surely a wife had the right to think about a husband's form?

Even if it was vastly improper, she couldn't stop thinking about it, and that was something she didn't want to consider at the moment. His buttocks were round, yet taut, and she had the feeling that if she patted one cheek, that her hand would bounce. She rolled to her side, hiked up her nightgown, and ran her hand over her own derriere. She was much softer there.

She untwisted her nightgown, lay on her back, and opened her eyes. The ceilings at Kilmarin were lovely, decorated as they were with murals and rosettes. Had any other bride lain here and contemplated her husband's body? Or was she the first?

All in all, it wasn't a shocking inventory she'd performed. She'd studiously avoided thinking of a certain location that was even more fascinating than the sum of all his perfection.

She was no stranger to desire, having felt a tingling in her midsection when a handsome man smiled at her, or a rush of heat when a man touched her bare hand with his. She'd accepted that such was normal and natural, that these sensations would be harnessed until she was married, then set free within the proscribed boundaries of the marital bed.

What were the societal rules about passion during mourning? Was she to refuse her husband for six months simply because she was observing mourning for her mother during that period of time? She stared at the ceiling. Surely not.

Douglas didn't seem the type of man who would countenance waiting six months to claim his husbandly rights. But then, he didn't seem the type of man who would be without female companionship for long. Look how the maids at Chavensworth sought to serve him.

She really shouldn't have started thinking about him. Sleep would have to wait. Sarah lay on her side, stretching her hand over to the area where Douglas would sleep. The sheets were cold, and she was instantly chilled.

Their relationship was so very odd, almost tenuous. She had never thought to have a marriage like this one.

She rolled over on her back, then sat up, thumping her pillow into a more comfortable shape. The housekeeper at Kilmarin could do well to mix a little lavender among

314

the down in the pillows.

Kilmarin was a very quiet place at night. The only sound in the entire suite was her breathing. She should go to sleep and not be curious about Douglas's whereabouts. He was not required to stay by her side at all times.

Sliding to the edge of the bed, she draped her legs over the side, bouncing her feet back and forth in the air. She'd been lonely so rarely in her life that it was a curious sensation to realize that she was lonely now. The only time she could remember being feeling this way was when she went to London. No, even in London there had been a sense of hope because she'd be going home soon, and that knowledge always colored her reactions.

Here, however, at Kilmarin, there was no sense of an eventual homecoming. Granted, she would return to Chavensworth, but nothing would be the same again. The words spoken at dinner would forever be in the back of her mind. Why had her mother never corresponded with her family? Why had Morna simply turned her back on Scotland?

Rather than remain in the bed, Sarah slid from the mattress, grabbed her wrapper, walked into the sitting room, and sat on the sofa. The fire had long since died, but she was not in the mood to light another. Nor did she want to rouse a maid to do it for her. Her father would not have hesitated. Douglas would not have disturbed someone else to do a task he could perform. Two men, both of whom had a profound effect on her life. One she couldn't tolerate; the other she respected more each day.

Where was he?

The day she'd gone to London had turned out to be an excessively fortunate one for her, that was something she was just beginning to understand. What would the past few weeks have been like without Douglas at her side? The staff at Chavensworth might have stepped in to make arrangements for her mother, but no one would have held her in the night and let her weep. No one would have been there to warm her when she felt so chilled. No one would have sat with her in his arms and rocked her until she slept. Who would have accompanied her on this journey? Who would have protected her and defended her?

What had he asked for in return?

Her observatory and the time to make his diamonds. The first she'd begrudgingly surrendered; but he'd hardly had the latter, had he? First, with her mother's death, and secondly, with this journey to Scotland.

She'd not been a very good wife, had she?

Had he sought comfort from someone else?

She stood, uncomfortable with that thought.

Returning to the bedchamber, she removed the wrapper and climbed into bed. Somehow, it felt even colder, larger, and emptier than earlier.

She lay on her back, staring up at the ceiling again.

Would she know? If he'd been with someone else, would she be able to tell? What would she do if he had been? What did wives do in such situations?

The door opened, so softly that she wouldn't have heard the noise if she'd been sleeping. A figure hesitated in the doorway.

"I'm awake," she said. "It's no use trying to sound like a mouse."

"Aw, Sarah darlin', you missed me," Douglas said.

She sat up.

"Are you foxed?" she asked.

"Only the faintest bit. The world seems an extraordinarily friendly place with a few drams of Scots whiskey."

"Is that what you were doing? Drinking?"

"I was mending fences," he said, smiling

faintly. "Your cousin twice or three times removed and a few other men. They wanted to know all about Lady Sarah."

"They did? What did you tell them?"

He came closer to the edge of the bed.

"Behold, the presence of a great lady, a most magnificent woman. I also told them that you were as strong-willed as Donald, as charming as a brownie, and as beautiful as a fairy princess."

"You did?" Warmth coursed through her.

"I didn't tell them you were still a virgin bride, or that it was my great fear you might be as cold as a Highland morning."

She stared at him, wishing she'd extinguished the light. If they had been in darkness, she wouldn't have been able to see his boyish grin or that suddenly intent look in his eyes.

What did he expect her to say? That she didn't know, wholly, what he meant? That she had an inkling, but she was too inexperienced to know for certain?

"Thank you for honoring me," she said. What a weak and ineffectual response.

But it seemed that he didn't think so, because his grin disappeared as he reached out and cupped her face with one very large, very warm, hand.

"Sarah darlin', I honor you from the bottom of your feet to the top of your head," he said, sounding like a Scot for the first time since she'd met him.

"Oh."

He dropped his hand and turned, before she could say anything further. He continued talking as he walked into the bathing chamber.

"I'll take a bath," he said, glancing over his shoulder at her. "I smell of smoke and whiskey, I'm afraid."

He sang well, she realized a few minutes later, and evidently he thought it necessary to continue singing as he bathed. The taps gurgled in accompaniment, and she found herself smiling.

She reached over and extinguished the lamp, just in case he decided to come out of the bath naked. Did he have any toweling? Wasn't there a cabinet in there? If she were a good wife, she'd take him a towel.

Instead, she pulled the sheet up past her nose and closed her eyes. She should feign sleep. Resolutely, she turned to her side, away from the empty side of the bed.

She knew the minute he left the bathing chamber. Rapid footsteps heralded his approach, and the mattress suddenly sank as he bounced onto it.

"God's knees," he said, burrowing under

the covers. "That Scottish water was damnably cold!"

"Scottish water is no colder than English water," she said, smiling into her pillow. "You're the silly one who wanted to bathe tonight. Did you not use the hot-water tap?"

"I thought a cold bath might suit me best," he said, nuzzling against her, his cheek pressed against her back. Even through the nightgown, she could feel how cold he was.

She turned and held out her arms below the covers.

"You are a foolish man, Douglas Eston," she said, pulling him into her embrace.

"You have no idea, Sarah darlin'," he said softly.

"And you're cold as ice."

"I really thought it would help," he said. "But I'm very much afraid I'm past that."

His knee was suddenly pressing against her, his leg insinuating between hers. Her nightgown was twisted, leaving her legs bare, and she could feel every inch of his skin. Somehow, in the last minute or two, he'd embraced her as well, and now they were a tangle of arms and legs and very, very close.

He seemed to be warmer. So much warmer, as a matter of fact, that she really should pull away. But she didn't move. At this moment, it was impossible to force herself to the other side of the bed.

Douglas bent his head and kissed her cheek, his lips soft and chilled, but all too soon turning warmer. She didn't turn away. Instead, it felt almost necessary to press closer, to turn her head just so, and lift her chin.

Finally, he was kissing her.

"I want you naked," he said, some moments later.

She shivered, and with some rational part of her mind, she wondered if he'd transferred his chill to her. That thought abruptly disappeared when he deepened the kiss.

A sound escaped her lips, and was then swallowed by his mouth, coaxing hers open. She held on to his shoulders, as if needing a reference in a world suddenly strange and more than a little exciting.

With each kiss, her breath grew tighter, and when his hand slid to the hem of her nightgown, she gasped.

She really should protest. She really should pull away. No proper woman would have unbuttoned the placket of her garment so that he could ease the garment over her head. But it didn't seem important to be proper at this moment, while it was vital that she feel him.

"Unbraid your hair," he said, his voice sounding ragged. He sat up and helped her off with the nightgown, pulling it over her head.

She didn't fight him, didn't even think of protesting. The time for that had come and gone weeks ago. This moment was what they'd both been wanting, why he'd touched her in exploration and tenderness, why he'd teased and tormented her.

She was about to be made a wife, and she didn't know if she should be terrified or as excited as she felt.

Please, God, let it be all right for her to feel what she was feeling, whatever it was called. Rapaciousness, wantonness, passion, or even desire — she'd never considered that she might be in the throes of it. No, what she had not considered was that she might enjoy it so thoroughly.

Her hands shook as she fumbled with the end of her braid, then his fingers were there to help her, threading through her hair and spreading it loose.

"God, you're beautiful," he murmured, and because he said it, because his voice shook when he did, she felt beautiful.

His hand cupped her breast as he laid her down on the mattress, his thumb playing over her nipple. A streak of lightning ran from her breast to deep inside. She made a restless movement of her legs, turning to him, and placing her hand on his face.

"Douglas," she said, speaking his name because she had to say something.

He pulled away from her touch, bent over her, and placed his mouth on her breast.

She jerked, startled, amazed as a sensation traveled from the deepest core of her to center at her nipple. Her fingers trailed across the nape of his neck, over his ear, then threaded through his hair. At another time, perhaps, she might have noted how soft it was, how thick, but now she was concentrating on other feelings: her breath, captured around an exclamation of wonder; her stomach tightening involuntarily from surprise; the fact that her body rose in an arch as if to offer herself to him more fully.

Shockingly, she wished she'd left the lamp burning. She heard herself moan and clamped one hand across her mouth. Proper women did not enjoy their subjugation, surely?

Why, then, did it feel less like she was being overpowered than being led to another place, one she'd never before dreamed existed. One whose halls she'd never walked, whose windows she'd never seen. Yet she was not wholly alone in this place. Douglas was here, a smiling Douglas, who held out his hand and beckoned her closer.

His hand stroked across her stomach as if to ease the sudden tension there, traveled down one leg, fingers splayed. He measured her knee, softly touched the back of it, almost inciting a smile from her, before her attention was engaged by the touch of his mouth. His tongue flicked her nipple before his lips soothed it, then he drew it between his lips, the action increasing the jolt of sensation in the core of her.

She did not whimper. Such a sound did not come from her.

He turned his attention to her other breast, and her hand, still softly stroking his hair, trailed to his back. His beautiful naked back with its definition of muscles, with its bronzed skin that so tempted her to touch it. Once again, she wished she'd not extinguished the lamp.

Sarah allowed her hand to travel downward, as if she had no will to direct it elsewhere. Her fingers strayed to the end of his spine, halted at the base, then traveled to the top of one buttock. She would like to cup it in her hand, wasn't that shocking?

He rose over her, looking down at her. Did he smile? Was that a flash of his teeth in the darkness? She really should ask, but he was kissing her again. His tongue urged her to open her mouth, and she did so without hesitation. His tongue mated with hers, and all she did was grip his shoulders and hold on to him in a world suddenly turned heated and strange.

Abruptly, he was on his back and she was rolling atop him, so surprised to be in that position that she braced her hands on either side of his waist and sat up. In front of her was something very stiff and very hot. Immediately, she knew it was his masculine appendage.

"Douglas?"

He didn't answer her, only slowly raised his knees so that she slid slightly forward.

She reached out and gripped him with both hands. Not to steady herself, which she could certainly claim if he quizzed her. Nor to orient herself, because even in the darkness she knew exactly where she was. If she touched him, if she slid her hands down the length of him, amazed at the girth and the size, it was due to curiosity alone.

The surface was soft and heated; the instrument itself was quite stiff. She had the curious thought that it was not unlike a branch. In this case, a well-developed branch of an oak. It most certainly did not bend; could it break?

"Am I hurting you?" she asked, concerned.

"God no," he said, but his voice had a note in it that she'd never before heard.

"Are you certain? It seems to be getting stiffer."

A startled laugh was her answer.

"That's in response to you, Sarah."

"Oh."

Her fingers traveled up its length and back down, fascinated with its size and the fact that it seemed like a separate sensate creature, responding to her touch with a quiver.

"I think I've made a huge mistake," he said, rolling over again and depositing her flat on the bed.

He loomed over her and she waited for his kiss, but when it didn't come she opened her eyes.

"I wish the first time could be painless for you, Sarah."

"Painless?"

"It will not be. There will be some discomfort," he said.

"Will there?"

How hideous that she'd not known that. Were men the only ones versed in the act of copulation? If so, how unfair.

"Will it be painful after the first time?"

she asked.

"No, it will not," he said softly.

She began to breathe again.

"Then we should quickly be about the business of dispensing with the first time, don't you think?"

He laughed again. "No," he said, "I don't think we shall."

Just what did that mean?

Before she could ask, he bent and kissed her again, spending several long minutes — or was it hours — on that delicious kiss. When he ended it, she almost moaned. Darkness and stars exploded behind her eyelids, and her breath was so tight she felt as if she'd just raced up four flights of steep stairs.

A second later, all the magic evaporated as her eyes flew open.

"Douglas!"

"Relax, Sarah."

"How can I relax when you're doing that?"

He was kissing her stomach, soft little sucking kisses that made her stomach flutter. That was not, however, the worst of it. His fingers were trailing from below her knee up to her thigh, and to the hair there. Nor was he stopping there.

"Douglas," she said, attempting to roll toward him.

He rose, bent over her, and kissed her cheek softly and sweetly. The embrace one might give a friend, or a relative not long seen. Not a kiss one would give a wife while trailing a finger through a place fingers were not supposed to travel.

"Douglas!"

"Sarah," he said, kissing her mouth now, attempting, futilely to direct her attention some place other than where his hand was and what his fingers were doing.

Dear heavens, her legs were opening.

Her body wanted to arch upward, into his touch. As if her body was as separate an entity as his instrument. As if she had no will to direct it to behave.

"Douglas," she said.

"Lady Sarah," he answered. "Relax and enjoy."

How could she possibly enjoy something as invasive and intrusive? How could she enjoy something so hideously embarrassing?

Her hands clutched at his shoulders as he deepened the kiss. It was not enough for him to lead her somewhere forbidden and exotic. He had to send her there as well, catapulting her through a starlit sky or rainbows, or the mist of a waterfall — all places with which she had no familiarity except in dreams.

His fingers stroked forbidden places; her body warmed and seemed to swell. Her heartbeat raced, and every sensation, every thought, every feeling was centered on where his hand was and the action of every separate finger.

He stroked through her swollen folds, played with the dampness there, pressing on one certain spot that summoned a gasp, followed by a moan.

He smiled against her lips and did it again, teaching her that he hadn't been repulsed by her earthiness, but delighted, instead.

Her hands gripped him tighter as the rhythm of his fingers increased. Slow, at first, then faster, and just when she had anticipated the quickness of his touch, he slowed again, leaving her wanting more.

Her legs spread, her body opened, even as his kiss deepened.

She was a novice and he the expert, and she could only hold on to him, helpless.

Sarah placed her hands against the back of his head. In an effort to halt him? Or in an entreaty for him to continue, only quicker, please? She wanted to be done with this innocence of hers, as if it were a cloak enveloping her, shielding her from him. She wanted to know everything, to have done everything, to have felt it all before only for the joy of feeling it again.

He was suddenly over her, his body warming hers, settling onto hers so perfectly it was as if he could see in the dark. He was braced on his forearms, his fingers playing with her hair, his chest pressing against her breasts, his back arched so that his instrument was at the opening of her body.

"I'm ready," she said in a voice too breathless to be hers.

"Are you?"

She nodded.

He bent and kissed her, and entered her at that moment.

She braced herself for the pain. He was large, his sheer size causing her to gasp aloud. But there was no pain as he entered her inch by inch. Just a feeling of being invaded, and a curious feeling of being stretched. Her hands grasped him at the waist, slid to his hips, before curving to hold his buttocks. Her legs widened as if her body instinctively knew how to welcome him.

He pressed against her, and a shiver traveled through her body.

"Are you ready?"

She could only nod.

Now the pain would come. Would she scream? Would the inhabitants of Kilmarin know that she'd been made wife? Was that why everyone tried to ply a bride with spirits on the occasion of her wedding? To numb her for what must surely happen?

He pulled out of her slowly, and she lost her grip on his buttocks. Her hands fell to the sheet before she placed them back on his hips. His skin was soft and hot, as if a furnace burned just below the surface.

When he entered her again, it was as slow. Nor would he speed up the pace no matter how fiercely she pulled him to her.

She really couldn't tolerate this. The tension in her body was nearly unbearable.

"Douglas, please."

He drew back. "Am I hurting you?"

"No, not yet. Please hurry though. I don't like waiting for pain."

"In my own time, Lady Sarah," he said, and she could swear he was smiling.

Should he be so amused?

He slowly withdrew again, and this time, her body recognized the pattern. She arched up as if to follow his withdrawal, then subsided when he entered her again.

She couldn't think, all her mind's ability pinned to his movements. He kissed her and licked her. She followed him when he pulled back, as if he had somehow linked them with the power of his mouth.

She wasn't feeling as stretched as before. Instead, she felt as if she fit him perfectly. Sarah flattened her hands on his buttocks, and when he would have left her, she pulled him closer and wiggled beneath him.

Should he really be swearing at this moment?

She forgot about his manners a second later, because he entered her faster this time and the next. Every time he pressed up against her at the ending of his strokes, the sensation of lightning traveling through her almost ripped her in two.

His skin was growing damp, his breath as ragged as hers, and she couldn't help but wonder if his heart was also racing frantically.

He held himself nearly out of her, supporting his weight on his hands.

"No pain, Sarah?"

"No," she said. Had she failed in some elemental way? "And you?"

"More than you could imagine," he said.

Had he somehow taken her pain?

He lowered his body and began stroking again, faster and faster, increasing the pace until she had no choice but to grip his waist and allow her body to do as it wanted. Her mind was left to make some sense of copulation.

He made a sound between his teeth and suddenly collapsed atop her, his head on the pillow next to hers.

A few minutes later, he turned his head. His breath fanned across her cheek. If she moved just so, she would be within kissing range of him. He didn't seem in a kissing mood, however, since he rolled to his side and propped his head up on his hand.

"How do you feel?" he asked softly.

"Well, thank you."

Should it be this difficult to converse with him? She couldn't help but remember that his hands had been everywhere on her body, not to mention his member deep inside.

"No pain?"

She shook her head before realizing he probably couldn't see her. "No, no pain. Just a little discomfort," she said. "You're very large, you know."

He didn't answer her, just bent closer and nipped at her ear with his teeth — such a surprising gesture that she jumped.

"What else do you feel?"

"I don't know what you mean."

"A feeling as if you can't quite catch your breath?"

"I seem to be a little out of sorts," she finally admitted.

"Are you?"

She nodded, then substituted a word for the gesture. "Yes."

One hand stroked over a breast, hovered just lightly over a stiff nipple, then moved to her stomach.

She was not prepared for the invasion of his fingers, especially since he chose that moment to nip at her ear again.

"Douglas."

"Hush, Sarah," he said, a smile in his voice. "I'd use my mouth, but I think it's a little early for that."

His mouth?

While she was adjusting to that startling bit of information, he slowly inserted a finger inside her. She was so shocked by his actions that she turned to him just in time for him to lower his mouth over hers.

His kisses really were intoxicating.

He started that rhythmic movement with his fingers again, stroking over her swollen flesh so delicately, then moving quicker.

The strangest feeling was beginning to overwhelm her, almost as if she were melting, as if she were turning into honey. Her skin was on fire, beginning where he was stroking and stretching outward to all her limbs. Even her toes curled as pleasure traveled through her. She turned toward him, her hands flailing against him.

She would have whispered his name had any coherent thought been left to her. Her skin, slick and wet, felt hot and tight as if fire burned inside her.

She moaned into his mouth. He broke off the kiss, nuzzled at the nape of her neck, then kissed his way up her throat while she was desperate for breath.

"It's all right, Sarah," he said softly against her ear. "I've got you. You can soar."

And she did. Just when she thought the pleasure couldn't get any stronger, it ended, stopped in full motion by a burst of exhilarating sensation through her body. A sound escaped her, softer than a scream, louder than a moan, but she didn't care.

Her thoughts, her mind, her body was centered on the extraordinary pleasure she felt and the man who'd brought it to her.

CHAPTER 23

Douglas awakened to the feeling of Sarah's skin against his. His right hand lay on her hip, as if claiming her even in sleep. He lay still, listening to her breathe, the curve of her derriere against his cock coaxing him stiff without one movement on her part.

Raising himself on one elbow, he studied her as she slept. Were all women as beautiful? Despite a wealth of experience with women, he'd never been captivated by the sight of one asleep.

But then, Sarah had been a first for him in a great many ways. He'd never before been taken by a woman so instantaneously, to the degree he'd married a stranger. He'd been astonished by the sheer amount of work she performed, by her judgment and persistence. His heart had been touched by her grief, and by the depth of her courage.

A touch of pink colored her cheek; a smile curved her lips. He fought a battle with himself — to kiss her or to leave her in peace?

She'd been a virgin the night before. He needed to restrain himself, not a common response around a beautiful woman, especially the one who was his wife. She had the ability to arouse him simply by walking into a room, but he doubted she was aware of his reaction. Or the fact that he'd been in love with her from the very moment he'd seen her — he, Douglas Eston, scientist, adventurer, explorer, a man with a single-minded focus on his own pursuits.

Her hair was strewn across the pillow. She would fuss at him this morning for the time it took to comb out the tangles. He smiled. Perhaps she would allow him to be her maid.

Watching her sleep made him melancholy for some odd reason. Was it because he felt closer to her now than he would when she was awake? She'd become the duke's daughter then, a woman born to privilege, unlike him.

He left the bed, grabbed his clothes, and dressed in the sitting room. A quick glance at the mantel clock assured him he had plenty of time before his meeting.

Douglas left the chamber without disturbing Sarah, almost immediately regretting his chivalry and the fact that he hadn't kissed her.

When she awoke, Douglas was gone. Sarah sat up on the edge of the bed, realizing she was sore in places she'd never before felt. This matter of being a wife was a great deal more complicated than she'd believed. It wasn't simply losing her virginity. She was not prepared for the emotions, either. She felt absurdly joyous, then just as oddly filled with sorrow, as if consummating her marriage had set her on a journey from one emotion to its extreme counterpart.

Perhaps her confusion was due to her mother's death and the fact that tears were never far away. Her grief was almost like a black miasma hanging over her head, surrounding her like a veil. Even in the midst of it, however, she'd smiled and felt amusement, and the layering of that emotion on top of her sorrow seemed to give it a different dimension.

So did passion.

He'd put his mouth on her. He'd kissed her just below her shoulder on the upper curve of her breast. He'd kissed her everywhere tenderly and lingeringly, then delivered her delight, offering it up to her with the knowledge that her body was capable of bliss.

She stared down at her feet. How strange that they didn't seem like her feet. But then, her body didn't feel quite hers either. Nothing felt the same. Even the morning air was a little different, as if she'd never before noticed what it was like to feel chilled.

She didn't know what to do, how to behave, and in a lifetime of being told how to act, how to comport herself, she was left floundering. She wasn't certain that what had happened last night was proper at all, but there was no one to ask, of course. There were some questions, evidently, that were destined never to be voiced.

Perhaps she should simply ask Douglas. She would frame the question in a very desultory manner, as if she were not even interested, then pay great attention to his answer.

"Does everyone do this?" There, that seemed like a proper enough question.

"Does every woman want to do this?" A less proper question, but closer to what she truly wished to know.

"How do you make me want to do this?" That question was devoid of pretense entirely.

Why did she feel warm every time he

came close to her? Why did her breath feel tight and her heart begin to pound so relentlessly even when looking at him?

Slipping from the bed, she went into the bathing chamber and took care of those necessary morning ablutions. She really should ring for Florie, but she wanted a few more minutes to herself. Standing at the foot of the bed, she looked up at the mussed pillows. The sheets were tangled, and there was an impression on the side of the mattress where Douglas had slept.

Why hadn't he awakened her? Or had he been as strangely sensitive this morning as she felt? But then, he wasn't a virgin, was he?

After last night, almost any question should be acceptable to ask.

Evidently, she wasn't expected to observe a mourning period for her marital duties. Was it entirely proper to feel so delighted at that prospect?

A knock on the door made her sigh, and she grabbed her wrapper and answered it. A young maid stood there, nearly bent over with a heavy tray, and standing next to her was her cousin, exquisitely gowned in a lovely emerald day dress Sarah recognized as French.

She directed the maid to the sitting room

and greeted Linda.

"Grandfather says you should be shown Kilmarin," Linda said. "Shall we meet in the Great Hall? In an hour?"

Sarah nodded, and her cousin turned and walked down the corridor without another word. Did Linda resent her presence at Kilmarin? Or was she just short with everyone? The lamentable fact was that her cousin was not entirely likeable.

Anthony, Duke of Herridge, surveyed himself in the mirror. He was not a vain man, yet for the first time in his life he was conscious of the fact that while he might possess an acceptable appearance, he was not handsome. However, he was the Duke of Herridge. A heritage of twelve generations preceded him. Chavensworth accompanied him.

Soon, he would have to begin looking for a bride, one with a fortune to bring to their marriage. A fertile girl, as well, one who would give him a son.

He went to the bureau, withdrew the jewelry box, and overturned it on the top of the bed. The pieces were small, inconsequential. Hadn't he given Morna anything better over the years?

He'd hardly had the money, had he? He'd

married her thinking that her wealth would solve his dilemma. Instead, her family had disowned her, and he'd been left with a wife and the same problem: no funds.

If he were a yokel, he could live well at Chavensworth. The family estate had always paid its way. But he was destined for better things, for cosmopolitan life in London, for entertainments. For that he needed money. An heiress was the answer. First, however, he had to bolster his bargaining position. What the hell had Eston been doing all this time?

He walked to the door, opened it, and shouted for Simons.

A half an hour later Sarah was dressed, her hair set to rights, and she was waiting in the Great Hall. Being perennially early was a fault, perhaps, but she'd been taught that it was rude to be late to any meeting.

When she'd agreed to meet in this room, she'd not realized that the chamber would be so oppressive, even on a sunny day. Its dark shadows and weapons of death did not lend itself to pleasant thoughts. She was very much filled with pleasant thoughts this morning. In an attempt to retain her good mood, she wandered out a door she'd not seen the night before and into a portico that led, surprisingly, to a garden.

Flowers blossomed along the path, their full-bodied heads bowing beneath the brush of her skirt. Sarah halted, taking in the wonders of this unexpected oasis of beauty: the birdbath in the shape of a giant lily pad, the gurgling fountain with a wolf's head, the graveled walks adjacent to the walls and cutting through the internal square in an X. Lining the walks were hedges and more plants, left to grow as high as they wished. The whole of Kilmarin's walled garden was a hodgepodge of types and heights of flowers, in abundant and glorious profusion.

The sound of the birds was comforting although she couldn't see them. Had they been rendered invisible in this enchanted garden? Or simply perched high in the branches of the trees? Sarah could also feel a soft breeze and suspected it came from another hidden corridor.

Benches were placed against each of the four walls, as if to encourage the examination of the garden. Sarah sat, drawing her skirts around her. Dancing light filtered through the fully leafed branches of the trees and played on the stone path. This was a lovely place to be alone, and she reveled in the peace and silence.

She needed the solitary moment.

Even in the midst of the quiet, with the sound of the birds and the fountain to keep her company, her mind was occupied with recollections of last night.

"You're the Englishwoman."

Sarah looked up to find that the garden wasn't solitary after all. A man dressed in dark brown trousers and a white shirt stood at the corner of the garden staring at her.

Slowly, he advanced, stopping until he was only feet away.

His eyes were the same shade as hers, and his hair the same color. His nose was not unlike hers as well. In fact, his features were so similar, it was almost like looking into a mirror, if the mirror had been a masculine one.

"Aren't you?" he asked.

"I'm Sarah Eston," she said. "Who are you?"

"Brendan Tulloch." He hesitated, then spoke again. "You're Morna's daughter," he said, studying her intently.

Was he experiencing the same bewilderment she felt?

"Did you know my mother?" she asked, moving aside so he could sit on the bench beside her.

He chose to stand, instead, never moving his gaze from her face. His scrutiny was so intense that she felt herself begin to warm with embarrassment.

"I didn't know her," he said, finally speaking. "My father did, though. He spoke of her often before his death."

"I'm sorry. It's difficult to lose your parent," she said. "I know."

He nodded. "Did she ever mention him? Michael Tulloch."

"She rarely spoke of Scotland," Sarah said. "And never of him, I'm sorry."

He stared off into the distance, as if he were trying to decide on something. Finally, he directed his attention to her once more.

"Are you going to be staying here, then?"

"No," she said. "We're leaving soon."

"Back to England?"

She nodded.

"You're Scots, you know."

Half, she almost said, but didn't get the chance.

He turned to leave. "If you were staying, we might be friends, you and I."

It was such a strange thing to say that she watched him as he walked away. When he was almost to the archway, he encountered her grandfather. They spoke, but they were too far away for Sarah to hear the words. Her grandfather leaned against his cane, looked first at Brendan, then at Sarah, and she wondered if he, too, were marveling at the resemblance.

A moment later, Brendan disappeared, and her grandfather walked toward her. She stood, hands folded in front of her, a calm, pleasant aspect to her face — the same appearance she wore when summoned to her father.

Donald stood in front of her, then sat on the bench, lowering his body with a sigh of relief.

She sat beside him.

"Dratted knees," he said, folding his hands atop his cane. "Age is a series of failures. Failures of joints, and eyesight, and hearing." He stared off into the distance, much in the way Brendan had done only minutes earlier. "Other failures." He sighed.

He glanced over at her, leaned heavily on his cane, then angled out one leg.

Sarah looked away, glancing at the fountain with its wolf's head.

"Why do I see a wolf everywhere? Is it a family motto?"

Donald smiled faintly. "You were telling the truth when you said you knew little of Kilmarin."

Sarah nodded.

"Wolves travel in packs, hunt in packs, live in packs. Wolves are a reminder to the

Tullochs that we're a clan, as fierce and loyal as any found in the Highlands."

"Except for my mother," Sarah said. "Why did she leave Kilmarin?"

Donald looked down at the stone beneath his feet.

"It's my fault she left," he said. "Mine, and I've taken the brunt of that decision for all these years."

He didn't look at her. Instead, it seemed as if his gaze was turned inward.

Should she leave him to his memories?

He looked over at her, his wrinkled face set in uncompromising lines, the face of a man who was not happy with his life but accepted it nonetheless.

"Your grandmother loved this garden," he said. "It was my greatest gift to her." Several moments passed. "One of my few gifts to her," he added.

She glanced over at him, then at the pattern of sunlight on the flagstones.

"I've got only a short time left on this earth," he said, his lips curving in what might, possibly, be considered a smile. "I shouldn't be lying in the face of the Almighty."

"Why is it your fault?"

She wondered if he was going to answer her, and he finally did.

"She was in love with a clansman," he said. "A proper match, but I wanted more for my only daughter."

He turned his head and studied her. She wanted, suddenly, to pat her hair into place, or ensure that her face was not too flushed, but finally the intense scrutiny ended.

"I told her she was destined for greater things." He looked toward the wall, where a stone urn sat cradled in an embrasure. "I was a fool back then, thinking of only wealth and power. I arranged for the young man to marry." He glanced back at her. "I can't lie about that, either. It was a good match, but it was not well-done of me. I gave him a bit of land, and a dowry, of sorts." He hesitated for a few minutes before continuing. "But I also gave him lies. It took me nearly twenty years and a promise to my wife on her deathbed to tell him the truth. He thought Morna wanted him gone because that was what I told him."

She waited in the silence, determined not to be the first to speak.

"I told him that Morna had fallen in love with another." He sighed. "After he married, she never mentioned him again. If her heart was broken, she never spoke of it." He straightened his left leg. "But she was like that, with her pride and her stubbornness."

348

He sighed. "She showed me both when she came to me with her duke.

"They'd met in Edinburgh. He was a rooster sort of man. I'd seen his type before, ridiculing the very society he meant to impress. This duke of hers thought we should be very happy to have him enter our family."

He glanced over at Sarah. "The man knew your mother was an heiress to the wealth of Kilmarin. As a Tulloch, she was well provided for."

Sarah remained silent.

He folded his hands on top of his cane. "He only wanted her money. I knew that. Just as I knew he cared nothing for her. But we cared nothing for his title. Morna would not listen to me. When my words failed, I disowned her. My only daughter."

Was that why her father disliked her so?

"And I almost did it again, God help me," Donald said. "Maybe the Almighty sent you to me for that very reason."

She frowned, not understanding.

"Did you ever ask that she return? Or did you order her back to Kilmarin? My mother had a great deal of pride." Sarah knew that only too well, having observed her mother's staunch silence in the face of her husband's desertion.

"I didn't order her," he said. "I begged her." He smiled. "All these years, I thought it was Morna and her pride against me and mine. Until you came yesterday, I believed it true."

"Now it's not?" she asked. A curious stillness passed over her.

"Have you given no thought to the resemblance between you and Brendan, girl? If his father was still alive, I'd parade you in front of him and dare him not to see his face in yours."

Stunned, she could only stare at her grandfather.

"Morna never came home because the world would see who you were, just as I've known ever since last night." He took a deep breath. "Perhaps she married her duke for pride's sake," he said. "But she did it to give you a name as well."

CHAPTER 24

Donald Tulloch, Laird of Kilmarin, had arranged for this meeting to take place in Kilmarin's chapel. Perhaps the atmosphere was meant to act as an impetus to any confession Douglas might wish to make. Or perhaps Donald thought himself God.

The chapel had been recently constructed, which in Kilmarin terms, meant in the last hundred years. Evidently, the Tullochs had only recently come to an understanding with God. Plain and unadorned, the chapel was Calvinist in nature. Not one statue, like those found at Chavensworth, deflected the penitent's attention from his pleas to God. Not one brilliant stained-glass window colored the air. Even the pews were rough-hewn, no doubt leaving splinters in the behinds of any supplicant.

Douglas stood straight and tall, his hands clasped at his back. He knew, only too well, that this meeting was an inspection of sorts, and he was damned if he was going to fail it.

The Laird of Kilmarin was a crusty old demon, one who knew how to intimidate those who might challenge his command. But there was also a glint of humor in his eye, as if he knew only too well that he was being an ass about this meeting.

Donald sat at a table in the front of the chapel, not far from the altar itself. Douglas wouldn't have been surprised if the laird had chosen to use the altar as a desk. Again, the comparison to God occurred to him, and he knew it was one Donald encouraged.

"Sit," he finally said.

Douglas slid a chair forward by hooking it with his foot, and sat, resting one ankle on the opposite knee and loosely clasping his hands in his lap.

"Does Sarah know you're here?" Donald asked.

"She doesn't. It was your request to keep our meeting secret."

"Not secret," Donald said, "just not something to be gossiped about. Women always speculate, have to whisper about everything." He sat back in his throne-like chair, one similar to those in the dining hall, and studied him from beneath bushy white brows.

"It's my opinion that woman are similar to men in that regard," Douglas said. "Give a person enough information, and he will not have to speculate."

"Are you given to sharing your opinion all that often?"

"Relatively often," Douglas said. "It depends, of course, if I find myself in a friendly country or one ruled by a despot."

Donald snorted and leaned back, pushing himself up on one side, as if the hip pained him.

"Robert tells me you're from Perth."

"I am."

"Who's your family?" Donald asked, eyes narrowing.

"No one you would know," Douglas said. "They died from cholera when I was eight. Any family they had is scattered."

"Yet you somehow managed to marry the daughter of a duke."

"An event I will forever treasure," Douglas said, looking straight at the older man. He had no intention of telling the old demon of the circumstances of his marriage.

Donald didn't say anything for a long while, but if it was a test, Douglas was more than ready for it. He'd stayed some months at a monastery, where the rules of silence were rigorously obeyed. He had no difficulty with the Laird of Kilmarin's petty tyranny.

"You're as arrogant as any duke," Donald finally said.

"Am I?" Douglas smiled.

"It wasn't a damned compliment." Donald rearranged himself on the chair again.

A few more minutes passed while Donald looked him over.

"Did you know my daughter?" he finally asked.

"I didn't have that pleasure," Douglas said.

"Is she happy? My granddaughter?"

Douglas stared at the altar, stymied as to how to answer that question. Sarah had everything a woman would need to be happy — a magnificent estate in which to live, adequate food, and clothing. Someone to love her? Someone to love? He'd have offered himself up to her had he been certain she'd be willing to have him. Last night, perhaps, but passion died with the dawn and was sometimes replaced by regret.

Did she regret her wedding night?

"I don't know," he said finally. Perhaps his honesty would prove to be too blunt an answer.

The old man levered himself up from his chair.

"I've asked Linda to take Sarah on a tour

of Kilmarin," he said. "I'll have Robert do the same for you."

"It's not necessary," Douglas said. "I doubt I'll be this way again."

"Do you know your Gaelic, Douglas, or have you forgotten it like the fact you're a Scot?"

"I've never forgotten I'm a Scot, Donald," he said, calm in the face of the older man's gibe. "It's in my blood. As to my Gaelic, I've probably forgotten most of what I knew."

"Then here's a Gaelic word you should know," he said. "*Sealbh.* It means fortune or luck. Providence. Some things are meant to be. Some are not."

Douglas couldn't help but wonder why the old man's words sounded like a warning.

Sarah would have liked to spend some time thinking about her grandfather's revelation, or at least his supposition as to why Morna had never returned to Scotland. Unfortunately, her cousin was intractable, insisting upon showing her Kilmarin, because, of course, Donald Tulloch requested it.

After only a few minutes, however, she found herself enthralled by the tour of her mother's family home.

Kilmarin was easily four times the size of

Chavensworth, a complex of ten buildings all linked by porticos. The first castle had been built atop a circular mound, but now fingers of buildings stretched outward over the hills and toward the River Tay. In the last hundred years, the walls of the oldest courtyard had been rebuilt, emplacements for ten guns had been added, and a new courtyard added to the area north of the towers.

Linda led her to one of the ancient towers of Kilmarin. The circular space was saved from total darkness by the narrow arrow slits high in the six-foot-thick walls. Sloping, treacherous looking steps, their centers worn down by generations of Tullochs, led to the top of the tower.

"Shall we?" Linda asked, moving to the base of the steps.

"I would rather not," Sarah said. "It's not important that I explore everything, is it?" She waved her hand in the air when Linda would have spoken. "Grandfather will just have to be satisfied with what I've seen."

Linda's face froze into lines of distress, but she didn't comment.

The Tullochs made their own cloth, weaving wool from the sheep that grazed on the sides of the hills adjacent to Kilmarin, and milled their own flour from the power of the River Tay. Kilmarin even had a dungeon, although she'd chosen not to explore it, either.

At the beginning of their tour, Sarah had managed to restrain her reaction to all the wonders of her mother's ancestral home, but at their noon meal, taken on a small terrace overlooking the River Tay, Sarah finally asked, "How on earth do you manage it all?"

For the first time, Linda seemed a little less confident than she'd acted all morning. "I don't," she said. "I've nothing to do with Kilmarin. I *want* nothing to do with Kilmarin."

Perhaps that was why, when Sarah had begun to contribute what she'd done at Chavensworth to control mice, Linda had cut her off with the comment, "You need to tell Grandfather." When she'd dared to tell her cousin how she'd rid the rooms of a wet smell after a storm, Linda had said the same thing. By the time Linda complained about the shortages in the larder or the problem of the warped floors in the east wing, Sarah had learned her lesson and remained silent.

Their meal had been pleasant enough, consisting of a hearty lamb stew. The terrace on which they sat was adjacent to the dining hall and built to give a visitor a view of the River Tay through the balustrade.

The small square table where they'd taken their meal was as rough-hewn as the dining table, but its surface was not as dark, and the pine scent it gave off was an indication that it had been recently constructed.

At the conclusion of their meal, Linda remained silent, staring at the river for so many minutes that Sarah was left without knowing what to say or do.

Her cousin turned finally and, with an apologetic smile, addressed her. "All your suggestions were good ones, cousin. But Grandfather is the one who dictates what happens at Kilmarin," she said. "The rest of us simply obey."

Sarah raised her hand, as if to push the words away. "I'm sorry," she said. "I didn't mean to cause any discord by coming here."

Linda smiled. "You haven't. We've been at odds for months, he and I. Your presence has given me a respite, if you must know. I've been excused from lectures for two days."

They sat in silence for a moment before Linda spoke again. "Do you like being married?"

Sarah looked at her cousin. It was such a strange question that she wasn't sure how to answer.

"I should think," Linda said, before Sarah could formulate a response, "that being married to the man you love is the most wonderful feeling in the world."

Sarah didn't quite know how to respond to that remark, either, especially after last night.

"Perhaps some people are simply luckier than others." Linda drew herself up and smiled at Sarah.

The expression didn't look the least bit sincere.

She didn't know her cousin well enough, wasn't certain if she would be rebuffed, but Sarah asked the question anyway. "Whom would you marry, Linda?"

The other woman didn't answer for a moment. When she did respond, it was in a tone that warned Sarah that confidences wouldn't be forthcoming. "Does it matter, cousin? What Grandfather wants is what will happen."

Douglas left his meeting with Donald Tulloch, and, while waiting for Robert, took advantage of the fair day to explore more of Kilmarin. The whole of Kilmarin was less beautiful, perhaps, than Chavensworth, but built for the rugged land on which it sat.

He began to climb, feeling a need to find

the highest point of land, a feeling he'd known as a boy desperate to escape the filth and despair of his surroundings.

At the top of a small hill, scarcely taller than a knoll and nowhere near the mountain he'd wished for, Douglas stopped, planted his feet apart, and surveyed Kilmarin and the surrounding countryside.

This was Scotland, his land, his home. Here, he'd played as a boy, dreamed of being more than he was even when he was hungry and cold. He looked to the left, where grayish blue hills gave way to rolling glens, the braes carpeted with lush green grass. To the right was the River Tay, sparkling in the morning sunlight, the sight of it bringing a lump to his throat.

He'd wanted so much as that small boy — to be bigger and stronger, to be able to protect himself. He'd achieved every one of his dreams and even more.

He loved.

That single emotion seemed a miracle in itself. Having never felt it from his parents, he hadn't known how to accept it from others. Alano's kindness to an angry young man had been initially rebuffed. Only later, many months later, had Douglas realized that some people didn't need to hit the defenseless to prove they were stronger.

He'd begun by respecting Alano, and from that respect had come friendship. Because he'd been able to feel friendship for another person, he'd learned to love.

A frightening emotion, love. Far more frightening and powerful than anything he'd ever experienced, including fear. Perhaps love was what made heroes of simple men.

He would do anything for Sarah. He would climb mountains and swim the River Tay for her. He would lay bare his soul, and stand in wait, naked and defenseless, for her scorn.

Perhaps he could become someone braver than he was, someone magnificent and capable of great and wondrous acts. All for love.

He would open the envelope of time and show her who he'd been, reveal the boy filled with rage and determination and the man overflowing with curiosity and passion.

For her, and in deference to what he felt for her.

Toward the end of the day, Sarah and her cousin were walking through the corridor belonging to the family rooms when Linda suddenly stopped in front of one of the doors.

"This was your mother's chamber when

she was a girl. Would you like to see it?"

Surprised, Sarah turned toward the door. Kilmarin was evidently so large bedrooms could be set aside and never used again. She nodded, and Linda withdrew a key from the ring she carried, inserted it into the lock, and stepped back.

Sarah walked forward, turned the latch, and entered the room.

The curtains were shut against an afternoon sun, but light streamed between the panels.

She'd thought her mother's chamber at Chavensworth was lovely, but it was nothing compared to this room. A four-poster bed decorated with stunning ivory and red panels sat against one wall. Adjacent to it was a large armoire, and on the opposite side of the room were both a vanity and a small desk. There was no dust anywhere. Neither was there a musty scent, as if the room had often been aired.

As if the room were readied for Morna's return.

"Do you know how to get back to your own room?" Linda asked softly.

She nodded.

"Then I shall leave you." She came to Sarah's side and pressed a key into her hands. "If you would lock the door when you're finished. Grandfather does not like the room disturbed. He keeps it just as it was before your mother went to England."

"Like a shrine," Sarah said softly.

Linda didn't answer, only turned and left the room, closing the door behind her.

Sarah stood motionless, wondering at the scent in the air. Something that smelled of roses, or perhaps lilies. Something lighter than the perfume her mother had worn at Chavensworth. A girl's perfume, perhaps.

Slowly, Sarah walked toward the vanity. On the wooden top was an array of crystal bottles, some of them still revealing traces of perfume. A long silver comb sat beside a silver-backed brush. To the left of the vanity, and reflected in the oval mirror, was a small oil lamp.

Had her mother sat here as a girl, wondering about her future? Dreaming about it, in the way that young girls are wont to do?

Sarah thought her heart would break.

Sarah opened the right-hand drawer of the vanity, startled to find that it was filled with jars and bottles, some of whose contents had long since evaporated. One or two, she was surprised to find, were still full, like the container of talc, and the jar of pomade. Had Morna left for England, then, without any of her personal possessions?

Instead of feeling as if she were a trespasser, someone rifling through her mother's things, Sarah felt as if her mother would approve. Even more than that, she felt as if her mother were in the room here and now, the first time she'd truly felt Morna's presence at Kilmarin.

Here was the girl Sarah had never known. A child who'd evidently been cherished and treated as a princess. Had it been difficult for her, leaving Kilmarin and never once returning?

She thought about what it would be like for her if she had to leave Chavensworth. What if circumstances decreed that she live somewhere far away? For now, her father was content to have her manage the estate, but perhaps he would remarry and bring another woman home. Would she grieve?

Sarah looked at her reflection in the oval mirror of the vanity. She'd never before thought of leaving Chavensworth, and as Sarah did so now, she felt no sense of deep pain. The memories she had of her home were those involving people. Her early recollections of her father before she'd learned to avoid his presence. The joy of her days with her mother, her governess, the servants she'd grown to love. Without its inhabitants, a house was just a structure, however

364

beautiful it might be.

Was that what her mother had felt about Kilmarin?

All these years, she'd thought she knew her mother, not strictly as a parent, but as a friend, a confidante. As she stared at herself in the mirror, Sarah realized that she didn't know Morna Tulloch Herridge at all.

She opened the left-hand door, deeper than the one on the right-hand side. Here, the drawer was nearly empty, except for an ornate inlaid box, the dark wood hinting at its age. She placed it on top of the vanity and opened the top.

Inside was a hand mirror, crafted of gold, its handle heavily incised with trailing roses. She turned it over to see that the glass was brown with age.

Something was written on the back, in a language she thought at first was Gaelic, but then recognized as Latin. Her governess had insisted she learn Latin, but it had been years since she'd done any declinations of verbs.

Animadverto vestri, visum posterus. Either the words meant to see the truth of the future, or to view your future, she wasn't sure which.

Slowly, she turned the mirror and held the brown glass up in front of her face, raising her eyes to her own reflection. The dark surface of the mirror was no doubt due to its age. Behind her, she could see nothing. The only reflection was her face, and it was her but not her at the same time.

The eyes of the woman who faced her were filled with grief, but not the sorrow she still felt, and would probably always feel, for her mother. This was a living, clawing emotion comprised of rage, denial, torment, and loss. As she watched, clouds boiled around her, as if her reflection were in the middle of a storm. Her eyes seemed to be windows into a pain she could not bear to witness.

She lowered the mirror to the dressing table's surface and placed both hands over the back of it, as if to keep the reflection within the glass.

If such anguish was truly her fate, she didn't want to know the future.

CHAPTER 25

Douglas wasn't at dinner.

When Sarah inquired about his absence, neither Linda nor her grandfather knew of his whereabouts. But Robert was also missing, which made her think the two men were together.

Dinner consisted of a Kilmarin version of kedegeree, a dish consisting of flaked fish, rice, and greens. Served with Kilmarin venison sausages and black pudding, it was a very filling meal. Unfortunately, she didn't have much of an appetite.

"You spent the entire day with Linda?" her grandfather asked.

Linda nodded. "She did, Grandfather."

"You've shown her all of Kilmarin?"

Sarah spoke. "She has. I'm surprised my shoes have not lost their soles. Kilmarin is larger than it appears."

"Tullochs have been here seven hundred years," Donald said. "Each generation has left its legacy. Sometimes that meant more building."

Sarah stifled her smile. From what she'd seen, Donald was more than willing to continue that legacy. Scaffolding over the exterior of the east wing had been erected for workers to add a two-story conservatory built to Donald's specifications.

"I found something in my mother's room," she said.

"I thought she would like to see Morna's room," Linda hurriedly explained when Donald Tulloch turned an angry glance on her.

"And I did," Sarah said. "Thank you, cousin."

"What did you find?" her grandfather asked.

"A mirror. A hand mirror in a box. It looks to be quite old, and bears a Latin inscription about the future."

She waited for one of them to explain what she'd seen in the mirror, but both of them appeared confused.

"I know of no mirror," he said. "It might have been a gift to Morna, but it was not from me."

Her grandfather didn't mention her mother again, and the dinner was a pleasant one, as if they'd never spoken in the garden, as if he'd never hinted that she might be a bastard.

She excused herself finally, returning to the suite she shared with Douglas, only to find it empty.

Where was he? She sat on the bench at the end of the bed. If they had been at Chavensworth, she would have gone to the observatory, but where did she seek him out at Kilmarin?

At the sound of water she jerked her head around. She stood, walked behind the screen and opened the bathing room door, only to discover her husband standing there, once again naked.

Two faint scratches marred the perfection of his left shoulder. Had she done that?

"Where have you been?"

A large oval mirror was mounted on the wall above the basin. He stared into it rather than look at her.

"If I walked in on you, Lady Sarah, I'd be chastised, if not commanded, to leave the chamber."

She felt her cheeks warm. He was absolutely correct. She would not have tolerated such behavior from him. She turned to leave, her hand on the doorframe.

"Forgive me," she said.

"I didn't command you to leave," he said.

She warmed even further.

"I've been exploring Kilmarin land," he said. "And Kilmarin. I've been told that you received a similar tour."

She nodded. "Not of the land."

"Or the sheep," he added.

"Or the sheep."

"How about the cattle?"

She shook her head, smiling. "No cattle."

"You education is lacking, I can see," he said.

"You weren't at dinner," she said.

"I would have made it to dinner if I could have."

"Are you hungry?"

He shook his head. "We entered through the kitchens. I've been fed by an assortment of females."

"Oh?" Her eyebrows rose.

"All aged, with missing teeth and hairy moles," he said.

"I cannot remember encountering anyone of that description."

"Surely you're not jealous."

The fact was unavoidable — she was. How idiotic of her. She was feeling jealous and unsettled, and a dozen other emotions.

He came out from behind the basin. "What is it, Sarah?" He reached for a towel, wrapped it around his waist, and led her into the sitting room, to the sofa. Instead of sitting opposite her, he sat next to her, so close that she could feel the heat from his body.

Was this entirely proper?

"Are you glad you came to Scotland?"

"I don't know," she said, finally. "I met my grandfather, but I know when we leave here I'll probably never see him again. I don't want to find someone only to lose him."

His smile surprised her.

"Have I said something amusing?" she asked.

"What you've just described is life itself, Sarah. Not very much about life is permanent. We find friends only to lose them. We find lovers only for them to prove inconstant. We assume we'll always be young and healthy, and yet time delivers its own blow."

"That sounds horribly dour, Mr. Eston."

His smile deepened at the use of his surname.

"Not at all, Lady Sarah. The lesson is to celebrate what we have, when we have it. Love as if you will never love again. Share each moment with a friend. Never take your life for granted or your health. Wring from each day all the laughter that's in it, all the adventure you can stomach, all the emotion your heart can hold."

She listened to him in silence, then glanced away. "I think it's easier to hide yourself away rather than to be hurt repeatedly," she said.

"I never said it was easy living in the moment, Sarah. It takes courage."

"I am not certain I'm that brave," she said.

"While I'm absolutely certain you are." He picked up her hand and studied it in silence. "Do you regret last night?" he asked finally.

She looked at him, shocked. "No."

"Are you certain?"

"Is that horrible of me?" she asked. Her own voice sounded small and tiny and frightened. She cleared her throat. "Is it wrong to want to feel joy and pleasure?"

"That's called life, Sarah," he said, smiling.

What had he said? *You and I shall have a love affair.* At the moment, that was exactly what it felt like. He smiled at her, and her heart felt absurdly light, as if he were capable of washing away grief with an expression.

He stood. As he stretched out his hand to her, the towel dropped to the floor.

Oh my.

What a truly mesmerizing sight, especially

the way his manhood seemed to grow as she stared at it, as if it were a giant waking and stretching.

She took his hand and stood, reaching up to touch his shoulder below the scratches.

"Did I do that?"

He glanced at the mark and smiled. "I'm more than willing to be wounded in the art of love, Sarah."

With that, she allowed him to lead her to their bed.

She looked as if she were torn between running away and pulling him after her, propriety vying with decadence. She bumped against him, her skirts enveloping him, her breasts against his chest.

A gasp escaped her.

"Are you well, Sarah?"

She nodded, her hair brushing against his bare chest. He tried not to shiver at the feel of her breath against his skin.

"I didn't hurt you last night?"

She shook her head, tossing her hair against him again.

How did he ask his wife if she would couple with him again? There was nothing in his journal addressing the situation.

He was hot and hard and heavy, breathing with great difficulty as if the room were an oven and not the chilly place it was. He wanted to be inside her, and surrounding her, keeping her warm and loving her. He wanted it all, all the feelings of her, the smells, the silkiness of her skin, the sighs she gave when her body pleased her.

In the most carnal and atavistic way, he wanted to mate with her, place her legs over his shoulders and bury himself in her.

He walked into the bedroom and halted at the side of the bed. He turned his back to the bed and pulled her into his arms. Not to kiss her; kissing Sarah was an occupation in itself. No, right now he needed to rid her of all those clothes.

He began unbuttoning the buttons of her black dress. Should he tell her that she looked beautiful in her mourning, or would that be considered loutish behavior?

"Why are you even wearing a corset?" he asked, annoyed with the laces that stood between him and her skin.

"Would you have me act the harlot?" she asked breathlessly. "Dear heavens, I am, aren't I?"

He raised his head. By the lamplight her eyes were bright, her hair tumbled, color suffusing her cheeks and a smile curving her lips. She had never looked lovelier. His wife, waiting to be ravished.

"If you are, then I'm . . ." He hesitated. "What is the male equivalent of harlot?" he asked.

"Pan?" she suggested.

He didn't know who or what Pan was, and made a mental note to write the name down in his journal and learn about it later. For now, he concentrated on unlacing her corset.

"Why do women wear these infernal things?" he asked, fumbling with the long cords.

"To produce the right curves of the female frame," she said.

He stared down at her upturned face. "You have to be jesting. You have the perfect form."

Her color deepened.

She bent her head, removing first one sleeve, then the other. Finally, she pulled off the bodice of her dress and her unlaced corset, tossing both to the bench at the end of the bed. She was left with a shift, he thought it was called, and her skirt, round and plumped by more confusing womanly garments.

"It's a hoop," she said, brushing away his impatient hands so she could untie the tapes herself.

"I know nothing of fashion," he said.

"A hoop is to shield the female frame."

"The same one the corset is trying to form?"

She laughed, one of the first times he'd ever heard her laugh so freely.

He stilled, his hands on his hips, feeling his heart turn over.

"I know well enough where all your parts are," he said softly. "Do you not realize I think about you all the time, Sarah? Or that my hands can feel the shape of you even when you're not around?"

She didn't speak, concentrating on untying the tapes, both hands at the task. But her face was flaming red, and her fingers trembled. Finally, the tapes were untied, and the hoops dropped to the floor, along with the skirt, leaving her attired in her shift and the cutest ruffled garment he'd ever seen.

He realized he'd never before seen her undress. She'd always been in her night-gown, or had disrobed behind a screen.

"There's a lot to this getting you naked, Sarah," he said, smiling.

She looked as if she wanted to admonish him, but she smiled instead, slowly dropping the lacy drawers to the floor.

"Could we extinguish the lamp?" she asked softly. She was still dressed in her shift, but the garment was so sheer that he could see enticing shadows and her breasts pressing against the thin linen.

Darkness would ease her, even though it would strip him of the pleasure of looking at her. He walked to the bedside table and extinguished the lamp, then returned to her side.

A rustle of fabric alerted him to the fact that she was now naked.

He reached out and pulled her into his arms, holding her against his body for a moment until she gripped his shoulders. A moment later, he effortlessly lifted her to the bed, joining her there.

His fingers swept from beneath her arm, along the swell of her breast then down to her waist and stomach. The palms of his hands pressed against the side of each breast until the plump curves met. He bent his head and kissed both of them at the same time.

"You've beautiful breasts, Sarah," he said. "Not only are they lovely in shape and form, but they're very sensitive." He bent and licked one nipple.

"Douglas," she whispered.

"My dearest Sarah. My lovely Sarah." My beloved.

He cradled her in his arms, whispered in

her ear, crooned to her in a soft, entreating voice. She turned to him, her face nestled in the space between his neck and shoulder, her breath hot, her heart racing.

"Oh, Douglas."

His fingers knew her, stroked across her skin, explored her, seeking out places that made her sigh, that made her clutch him with urgent fingers. She repeated his name, her voice sighing. His palms tenderly stroked across her skin, his lips followed, and when he kissed her, his mind quieted and found peace.

His open lips touched hers, and in that kiss was all the reserve he used, all the tenderness he'd ever shown her, and just a hint of the passion he felt.

His body was simply an extension of his mind, or a wick to his soul. Slowly, gently, carefully, so as to cause her no harm or discomfort, he entered her, centered himself, seated himself, and felt in that instant that in her heat, dampness, and mystery, he'd found himself home at last.

"Sarah," he whispered, nearly done in by the pleasure coursing through his body, by the astonishing joy lightening his spirit. "Sarah," he said, and her name became a benediction, and a way of expressing the inexpressible.

CHAPTER 26

Leaving Kilmarin was more difficult than Sarah had anticipated.

She hugged her grandfather, who suffered her embrace in silence. When she drew away, he reached out to touch her cheek, and she was surprised to feel his hand tremble.

"I'll not see you again, child," he said. "But I'll be sure and tell your mother that you're doing well."

Without giving her time to respond, he turned to Douglas.

"You need to come home to Scotland," he said. "Bring my granddaughter back to her home."

They exchanged a look, and Donald finally nodded, as if satisfied with what he saw. He turned, and without another word, walked back inside Kilmarin, leaving Sarah and Douglas standing beside the carriage in the porte cochere.

Douglas smiled, helped her inside, where she sat next to Florie. Her maid yawned discreetly behind a gloved hand, then smiled a greeting.

Before they could pull away, the carriage door opened again, and Linda peered inside. Her face was radiant; the girl had gone from lovely to exquisite. Her eyes filled with tears, and she reached out one hand to Sarah.

"I don't know how you did it, cousin, but thank you. Thank you!"

"What did I do?" Sarah asked, confused.

"Grandfather has said that I can marry Brendan, after months of refusing. Months!" Her smile was tremulous but joyous all the same. "Thank you."

Sarah grabbed her hand and squeezed, wishing that she could have met this version of her cousin earlier.

"Be happy," she said, knowing that they would probably never see each other again.

Linda startled her again, by reaching behind her and then handing her the box she'd found in her mother's room.

"Grandfather wanted you to have this, since you found it. Something of your mother's, to remember your visit to Kilmarin."

She smiled again, and withdrew, closing the carriage door.

When Douglas opened the box, she glanced at the mirror and then away.

"It's very old and very ugly," she said, careful not to look into the mirror. She wasn't certain of what she'd seen, but she didn't want to view it again.

"But you'll cherish it all the same," he said, returning the mirror to the box, "because it belonged to your mother."

He placed the box on the floor of the carriage, in the clever little well designed to store small articles, and she smiled her thanks.

She glanced at Kilmarin only once as they pulled away, then concentrated on her clasped hands.

Douglas handed her a handkerchief.

She glanced over at him and smiled, even as a tear fell down each cheek. His look was compassionate, and much too intimate to be witnessed by Florie. A glance at her maid, however, proved that Florie was as tactful as she was talented. Florie was staring out the window as if the view were fascinating.

In the circumstances, it was all too natural for Douglas to lean forward and place a kiss on Sarah's forehead. She pulled back, blotting her face with his handkerchief and holding on to it as a talisman for most of the day.

The journey back to Chavensworth was, thankfully, quickly done. Or perhaps it had taken the same time as traveling north and just seemed faster to Douglas. The weather was fair; the stops to change the horses and stretch their own legs were the only punctuation to the days.

The same inn at which they'd stayed on the way north had only one room available, and he gave it up to Sarah and Florie. Sarah had slipped her bottle of scent into his hand when he'd escorted them to the room. They'd exchanged a look that had warmed him through the night.

The train was as comfortable; the only difficulty was waiting for their car to be attached and the carriage lashed to an available flatcar.

When Chavensworth was sighted, he almost sighed in relief. Even the horses seemed ecstatic to have reached the end of their journey. Their pace sped up, as if Tim couldn't control them, and all of them had to hold on to the straps mounted above the windows in order not to be tossed to the side of the seats.

Tim pulled to the front of Chavensworth, and Douglas exited first, holding out his hand for Sarah, then Florie. Thomas was coming down the steps, two footmen behind him.

"Have our trunks taken to the Duke's Suite," he directed, before turning again to Sarah. "I'll go with Tim to the stables," he said. "I need to check on the diamonds."

She patted his lapel with one gloved hand, the brim of her bonnet shielding her face.

He reached out and touched her cheek, his fingers sliding over the smoothness of her skin, resurrecting other memories, creating a yearning in him for a proper kiss.

She tilted her head back and smiled at him, as if she knew exactly what he was thinking.

"I shall see you later?" she asked. "Not much later, I hope."

Did she ache for him as much as he ached for her?

"If it weren't necessary to see to the diamonds," he said, too softly for Thomas or Florie to hear, "I'd accompany you to our room right this moment."

She flushed, the perfect response, and one that summoned his smile. With that, he bent and kissed her, ignoring the presence of the others. Sarah must have forgotten them as well, because she placed both hands on his shoulders and stood on tiptoe to deepen the kiss.

Finally, he pulled back, smiling at her. She picked up her skirts with both hands, turned, and ascended the steps.

He watched her all the way.

At the top, she turned and glanced down at him, her smile a sign that she was well aware of his perusal.

He entered the carriage again, and when they reached the stables, left Tim, heading for the observatory. Alano had been busy in his absence.

Two dozen square wooden frames were scattered throughout the observatory, propped on ledges and resting against walls. Each frame held more than a dozen twisted silk fibers. On each strand were dozens of viscous droplets now glittering in the faint light from a dwindling sun. Interspersed between the droplets were translucent granules, some no larger than clumps of sand. He began inspecting the diamond threads. Growing diamonds was successful only if the area was pristine. Anything in the air, such as dust or dirt particles, could be transmitted to the granules themselves, resulting in dirty diamonds. Diamonds with flaws wouldn't fetch a good enough price to satisfy the Duke of Herridge.

Alano had been fastidious, as usual.

Douglas had replaced the dirt floor with long planks of wood nailed together and sealed with a marine varnish. Alano had covered the floor with linen to catch any dust seeping up into the observatory. Likewise, he'd covered the dome ceiling with a canopy of linen, another preventative measure. Every shelf was carefully dusted and covered, every surface in the observatory was as clean as they could make it.

The clusters fed on the droplets, growing quickly over a period of days. After they dried, the final part of the process was heating the clusters, the most dangerous part of the process, simply because the formula used to grow the diamonds was volatile.

Satisfied with the results inside the observatory, he left the building to inspect the construction of the furnace. Hearing a noise behind him, he turned, expecting to see Alano, and faced, instead, Simons, the Duke of Herridge's ubiquitous majordomo.

"Simons," he said. "What the hell are you doing here?"

"His Grace is very displeased, sir. It's been some time, sir, and you've not reported to him. Nor have you produced any diamonds. He's done his part of the bargain, Mr. Eston; he is most impatient to see that you perform your part."

"There have been a few mitigating factors, Simons, or has His Grace forgotten the death of his wife?"

Simons had the good sense to look a little embarrassed.

"I understand that you've been to Scotland. Is that another mitigating factor, sir?"

He didn't answer that comment. "His Grace is going to have to be patient, Simons."

Simons allowed himself a small smile. "Patience is not one of His Grace's better qualities. You must give me your co-operation, Mr. Eston. I implore you."

"And if I don't?"

"The Duke of Herridge is not a man to take lightly, Mr. Eston. He is capable of a great many actions."

"I'm not worried about what your duke can do to me, Simons."

"Then are you concerned about what he can do to Lady Sarah?"

Douglas stilled. "What could he do?" he asked.

"You have been out of England for some time, Mr. Eston. Have you heard of the Matrimonial Causes Act?"

Douglas shook his head.

"What His Grace has made happen, he can ensure is undone. If you will not cooperate with the agreement, if you will not furnish the diamonds as quickly as he wants them, he will ensure your marriage ends."

"You're jesting," Douglas said, even though it was all too obvious that Simons wasn't. "Wouldn't that require Sarah's cooperation?"

Simons' look was pitying. "Do you think she would refuse to cooperate if commanded by her father?"

Unfortunately, Douglas wasn't all that certain what Sarah was feeling. Passion was one thing, but was that enough to keep her linked to him? Was it enough to turn her back on her past, her upbringing?

"She would have to prove your adultery, Mr. Eston, but trust me, a number of women could be persuaded to come forward with tearful renditions of how you misled them. While it's true there are a number of other conditions, please be assured that His Grace could provide them."

"He would do that? Wouldn't divorce ruin Sarah's reputation?"

Simons smiled. "Do you think he cares, Mr. Eston? Sarah had one duty, to marry for money. She failed in that."

"Tell him he'll have his diamonds in less than a week."

Simons bowed carefully and respectfully.

"I hope, Mr. Eston, that nothing interferes with your delivery of the diamonds. His Grace, as I said, is not a patient man."

Simons melted away, the perfect servant.

Douglas unclenched his fists and turned to the furnace. The structure looked a little like a pyramid, broad at the bottom and tapering to a triangular top. The large base would provide for a deep firebox; the blaze must be equal to that a blacksmith would use to forge iron. He'd experimented for months before determining exactly the right range of temperature to cure the diamonds. Even that process had taken a considerable amount of time.

He'd not lied to the Duke of Herridge about making the diamonds larger. However, he'd not correctly gauged the duke's impatience or desperation. The man wanted results, and he wanted them immediately, and he didn't seem the type to listen to rational discourse on the subject.

As for the other, could he actually persuade Sarah to divorce him? Would she? Could the Duke of Herridge actually destroy his marriage?

Douglas had walked into the lion's den himself, convincing himself that the lion was no more fearsome than a tabby cat. Unfortunately, the Duke of Herridge was a lion in truth. If Douglas was devoured, the only person who should be blamed was himself, for not knowing enough about the ruthlessness of the nobility.

"Well, was your journey to Scotland successful?" Alano asked from behind him.

Douglas turned.

"Kilmarin is quite a sight," Douglas said. "I'm sorry you weren't with us."

"I had my own share of discovery right here," Alano said, sitting on the stack of bricks next to the furnace. "That Mrs. Williams of yours is a firebrand all right. Ignores me as if I'm a wall."

"That can't have pleased you," Douglas said. "Given your reputation with the ladies."

"She just needs a little extra persuasion."

"I'd rather you didn't try to seduce the female staff at Chavensworth."

"It's not the staff. It's that one annoying woman," Alano said, frowning.

Douglas bit back his smile. He knew only too well what it was like to be at the mercy of one lone woman. Women might act defenseless, but they had their own kind of armament. A hesitant glance, a tremulous smile. And tears. Good God, but he could handle anything but tears.

"Perhaps you could tell Mrs. Williams that

we've returned," Douglas said, giving Alano a reason to seek out the housekeeper. "Ask her to prepare an early dinner for us."

He glanced toward the west, where the sun was beginning to set, orange streaks heralding its passing.

Alano stood. "I could do that." He eyed Douglas carefully. "What's got you snarling mad?"

Douglas shook his head, deciding not to confide the Duke of Herridge's threats. "I'm going to need to see my solicitor," he said. "I think I've gotten myself into a spot of trouble."

Alano didn't speak for a long moment. "Is there anything I can do?"

He glanced at Alano. "You've always been a friend, Alano, and I'm grateful for that."

Alano smiled, but his eyes were worried. "You'll let me know if I can help?"

Douglas nodded, then looked back at the observatory. "You've done plenty. Thanks to you, we'll have hundreds of diamonds for the Duke of Herridge."

Alano's mouth twisted at that thought, but his expression soon turned to a smile when he remembered his errand, and his excuse to see Mrs. Williams.

Douglas watched him follow the path toward Chavensworth, his hands thrust deep in his pockets, and his passage accompanied by a whistled tune.

He occupied himself in the observatory, removing the silk fibers from the mature frames and feeding the smaller diamonds. An hour later, Douglas closed up the observatory and went back to the house using his own path.

The moon was an opalescent disc hanging among the scattered diamonds of the night sky. He was attuned to night, in a way he'd never understood, finding it friendlier, somehow, than stark daylight. Yet night had never been his friend, at least not as a child. Night meant hunger and cold, and being afraid.

He was no longer a child but a man who'd made his own way. He'd learned to think deeper thoughts than those focused simply on how to survive. He'd learned to ponder the imponderables of his existence.

What is the meaning of life?

He didn't know the answer, but he was closer today than he had been years earlier.

What did he want from life?

To matter to someone. To scratch his name on the rock of existence and have some traveler a hundred years hence marvel that he'd been there. To care, and to love, and to experience all that he could know, see, do, taste, feel, and be.

Philosophy, now that was something to twist a man's mind. Not as much as love, but it would do in a pinch.

CHAPTER 27

Sarah stood, walked to the pier glass, and surveyed herself in the mirror. She looked like a walking shadow. Her nightgown was black, her wrapper was black. Her hair was black. Her face, neck, and décolletage were stark white, causing her lips to appear even more brightly hued than usual. Slowly, she removed the pins from her hair, watching her reflection the whole time. There was no sign of the woman she'd been a month ago. Yes, the physical form was the same, but the look in her eyes had changed. There was sorrow there, and something else, knowledge that hadn't been there before Scotland.

Time would heal all wounds. That was what everyone said, wasn't it? That, and she should simply remember the good times and not dwell on death. She didn't want to go through her life with this hole in her heart, but she was all too afraid that it would be with her forever.

But so would Douglas.

She fluffed up her hair, then went to her vanity, where she sat and began to brush the tresses free. Finally, she pushed her hair back so that it fell off her shoulders. Did she look too young to be having thoughts of seducing her husband?

She stood and faced the door, dared herself to walk through it. Even more, to travel the short distance to the Duke's Suite and her husband.

She must have been truly courageous after all, because she opened the door without hesitation.

He removed his boots, then his shirt, and finally his trousers and undergarments, walking into the bathing chamber barefooted. This room was more luxurious than the chamber at Kilmarin. He was surprised at how quickly he'd come to enjoy — and perhaps expect — luxury.

He stared at his image in the pier glass. Tonight, he looked like a workman with streaks of black across his forehead and cheeks. He washed with icy water and dried with a length of toweling, scrubbing at his head until his hair was nearly dry.

He left the bathing chamber to find Sarah standing in the middle of the Duke's Suite.

For the longest moment, she simply stared at him, her gray eyes widening.

He looked away, not to avoid the intensity of her stare, but to mitigate its effect on him. He walked toward the bed. The maid had pulled down the counterpane and turned down the sheets.

"Are your diamonds all right?"

"Everything is fine," he said, sitting on the mattress and draping the sheet over his lap, feeling curiously like an untried boy with randy thoughts. Or a bridegroom.

"What is this?" she asked, picking up the slender notebook he'd left on the table beside the chair.

He stilled, keeping himself from racing across the room and pulling it from her grasp. Sooner or later, she was bound to discover it. Sooner or later, she was going to find out. Better now. Better when their marriage teetered on the brink of dissolution.

She smiled at him quizzically, but he didn't say a word. Nor did he speak when she opened the book and began to read its contents. At first she frowned, but then she started glancing at him repeatedly, as if seeking either his reassurance or his confirmation.

"What is this, Douglas?" she asked, as

prettily as if she were noticing a button loose on his shirt or inquiring as to part of the process of making diamonds.

He clasped one hand to the back of his neck and tilted his head back, his gaze on the ceiling. He breathed deeply once, then again, letting the second breath out slowly, gaining time.

"It's where I write those things I learn. So that I don't forget."

"Is it so important to know how to address a duchess?" Her brow furrowed.

"I know little of the nobility," he said.

At her silence, he knew she was waiting for more of an explanation. "I was born without anything to call my own," he said. "I didn't have a house like Chavensworth. I had only heard of Kilmarin in tones of awe. I made myself what I am. And I'm proud of that, but I don't have a lineage like yours. I'm not a Tulloch of Kilmarin, and I'm not the offspring of a noble. I am simply Douglas Eston."

She didn't answer him. Instead, she sat and studied her hands with great deliberation, as if surprised to see them attached to her wrists.

"Chavensworth has never been mine," she said. "It's been my burden, my responsibility, perhaps. But I can't inherit it because

I'm a woman. I've always known that."

"But you've also been a Herridge from Chavensworth. You grew up knowing that everything around you belonged to a family that could trace its lineage back six hundred years. You have a title that you can never lose because of your birth. Or marriage."

She looked at him, but he didn't allow her to speak.

"I lied to you once, when I told you I had a happy childhood. I didn't. I was made an orphan at the age of eight. I stole and begged for enough food to eat. I was hungry as a child, for food, for knowledge, for something better than I had." He smiled. "Do you know how I met Alano?" he asked. "I was robbing him." He looked down at the floor. "Alano was determined to rescue me." He glanced at her. "And he did. He taught me to read and bought me books. I couldn't get enough of it. It's as if someone gave me whiskey and I was drunk on learning."

He studied the ceiling. "You think I don't sound like a Scot? You should have heard me then. No one could understand a word I said. Alano was all for making something of me, so he taught me manners, first, then how to dress, how to act properly."

He folded his arms, leaned one shoulder

397

against the carved headboard. "I learned Spanish first, from Alano, then French, and a few other languages as well. The more I traveled, the less I sounded like myself, until I could talk without an accent — or much of one."

"Why are you telling me this? Do you think I'll be repulsed?"

He smiled again. "It's not a repulsive story, for all that, Sarah," he said. "It's proof that a man can make of himself what he wants.

"I decided that I wanted to be more than an alley rat, stinking of salmon. I wagered at first, finding that my luck at the tables was better than it should have been. The first time I lost all my money, I learned that I could be as much a fool as anyone. So I began to buy from one town and sell to the next, becoming little more than a peddler, with my wagon and my wares. I learned what people wanted and gave it to them. I learned that I was fascinated with all things odd and unusual. I learned that I was better suited to the role of merchant than adventurer."

"Is that why you hesitate when you speak, sometimes, as if you're searching for the right word?"

"You rob the words from me, Sarah," he

said softly.

Her hands were folded on her lap, and she studied him with solemn gray eyes.

"I've been advised that there's something called the Matrimonial Causes Act. That it's possible to have a marriage dissolved."

"Is that what you want, Douglas?" she asked in a very small, very composed voice.

A knock on the door interrupted his answer.

Sarah stood, opened the door, and remained motionless as two maids and a footman delivered their dinner. She waved them away when the footman would have set up a table, and closed the door after them.

Slowly, she turned to face him.

"Was what happened in Scotland all a ruse, then? Did you feel nothing for me?"

Did she have any idea how sensuous she looked, standing there attired all in black? Black was the color of mourning, true, but it was also the color of night, of sin, of secrets whispered by lovers, and soft, moaning sighs. She was exquisite in black, a creature with a creamy complexion and a mouth that hinted at bruising kisses.

"That's an absurd question," he said, pulling back the sheet to reveal his growing erection.

"But you don't want to be married."

His wishes weren't important here, but hers. Before he could say that, his queen of the night, his specter of darkness, his enchantress, fled the Duke's Suite without another word.

She'd failed dismally at seduction. She'd failed so horribly that she was almost in tears when she'd reached her room. She didn't run back to her chamber, exactly, but the journey was certainly quickly done. She closed the door behind her and sagged against it.

She should begin a mental inventory of Chavensworth's linens. Keeping a proper tally of the sheets, pillowcases, mattress covers, lengths of toweling, cloths, and rags was an ever-present problem. After so many months of checking and rechecking the numbers, before and after laundry day, she knew exactly how many of each item she should have. Or if that didn't suffice to take her mind from Douglas, perhaps she should simply scour her memory for anything her mother might have said about Kilmarin and about a man named Michael.

Anything but think of how hideously she'd just shamed herself, just when he was thinking of ending their marriage.

Dear God, what did she do now?

■ ■ ■ ■

Perhaps it was just as well he'd hurt her. It was a lesson for him, was it not? He should begin to tamp out any feelings he had for her. Lady Sarah could accede to her father's demands and find herself without a husband without any appreciable loss of dignity. Would such an act ruin her in polite society? He doubted it. She was, after all, a duke's daughter, and society seemed created for such people.

He doubted she'd even miss him.

She'd lain in his arms and welcomed him into her body.

The act of a woman who knew what was expected in marriage.

She'd wept in front of him and clutched at him as if she'd be bereft if he were gone.

The act of a woman lost in a fog of grief.

This marriage had been a gift. A present, perhaps, from a suddenly beneficent Almighty. Remember that time on the Nile when you nearly drowned in the floods? Or the bite from the spider in the Africa savannah? Do you recall when you were certain you'd lose a toe or two from frostbite in the Alps? And when you were robbed by pirates in the Caribbean? For all those adventures, for all your suffering, I'm granting you a boon, a precious one at that. Here, into your keeping, is the daughter of a duke, a sweet lass with eyes the color of fog and a nature just as impenetrable. She's a beauty, she is, but she's also her own woman. She'll not take lightly to being given as a gift. You'll have to woo her until you've won her.

She'd been dressed for seduction, and he'd been frozen by his pride.

Just what sort of idiot was he?

"Open the door, Sarah."

She stood in front of the door and stared at the pane. He sounded angry.

"Sarah."

"I think we should both retire for the night," she said.

"Exactly my thoughts. Open the door."

She jerked it open, but the words she was about to say vanished when she saw him. He only wore a shirt, nothing more, and the shirt was left unbuttoned.

"Come in," she said, throwing open the door. "Quickly, before any of the staff sees you."

"I've worn my shirt," he said, beginning to smile.

"Yes, but your derriere is quite visible, Douglas, not to mention . . ."

"Other parts?"

She frowned at him, but that didn't dim his smile.

Pulling her wrapper closed, she turned around and walked in the opposite direction. The terrace was as good a place as any to retreat, and she did so, waiting for him to join her. He didn't.

Finally, she returned to the bedroom to find that he had dispensed with the shirt and was standing there as unadorned as one of the statues in the Greek Garden.

Oh, he was fascinating, and so much better constructed. His body was warm and alive, and tanned in places that shouldn't be tanned.

"Douglas, you really have to start wearing clothes more often."

"Really?"

He allowed her to stare for several moments, his only response a growing smile and something else growing as well.

"Come here, Sarah," he said gently.

She shook her head. It was better if she was on the other side of the room.

He began to walk toward her, and she would have been wiser if she'd gone back out to the terrace and closed the door between them. But he was so beautiful and she was so transfixed by that hard and jutting part of him.

"How can you think I'd want to dissolve our marriage?"

She looked up at him. "I thought you didn't want to couple with me anymore. That what happened in Scotland wouldn't happen at Chavensworth."

"Where in hell did you get that idea? I want you every hour of every day, Sarah."

Her eyes widened.

"Shall I show you what I learned as an adventurer?"

"From all your women?" She frowned at him.

"From the pleasure palaces," he said. "From books and drawings."

A wiser woman would have held up her hand to forestall him, or left the room, perhaps. But a wiser woman would have had to be blind not to be captivated by the sight of Douglas, naked. Douglas, with what made him male rigid and reddened, and altogether fascinating.

She turned again, forced herself to breathe deeply.

He moved to stand behind her, so close that she could feel his instrument against the curve of her bottom. His hands slid around her waist and pressed against her stomach, pulling her back against him as if he wanted to impale her.

He bent his head and whispered in her ear. "My mouth could bring you indescribable delight, Lady Sarah."

She shivered.

"Shall I show you?"

"You already have," she said.

"I don't mean on your beautiful breasts," he said, stroking his thumb against a nipple, barely covered by the sheer fabric of her nightgown.

"Douglas."

"It's all right, Sarah. Passion isn't forbidden."

She sighed. She'd never be able to explain. Even if it had been forbidden, she wouldn't have been able to prevent it. Being around him was magic. She trembled inside. She quaked with it.

She turned and reached up, pulled his head down for a kiss.

When she pulled away, she was breathless, and delighted to see that Douglas was as well. She walked toward her bed, dropping her wrapper on the floor. She'd never had the freedom to be as naked as he. She'd never had the confidence or the courage. Tonight, with the lamplight spreading through the room with a golden glow, she would simply have to be brave.

She grabbed her nightgown with both hands and pulled it over her head.

He didn't say a word as his gaze traveled over her body. She straightened her shoulders, kept her hands flat against her thighs, then without a word, turned and climbed onto her bed.

He was suddenly there beside her.

She laughed, excitement racing through her blood.

They were tumbling among the sheets, tangled in heat and desperation. Turning, hands sliding over skin, palms curving over shoulders, elbows, buttocks, knees. Her fingernails gently trailed across the skin of his back, and he responded by curving over her.

She was the one to deepen their next kiss, tasting the contours of his lips, rubbing her palms over the bristles on his cheeks.

His skin was hot, and she warmed herself on it, exposing herself to the air when her own heat threatened to engulf her. She rose onto her knees, brushing her hair back from her shoulders, swooping down on him like a siren of need and want, nipping at his chest, the muscles of his arms, hearing his laughter and knowing it was in praise of her boldness.

She was mad for him.

She sat astride him, pressing both hands against his instrument, holding it possessively against her palms, She loved the feel of it, soft, and hot and hard. Her fingers measured its length, burrowed in the nest of hair at its base, and palmed the sac there.

Even when he rose and strained against her, even when he made a low, groaning sound in the back of his throat, she wouldn't let him inside. Instead, she placed both hands on the mattress behind her and arched back, exposing herself to the cooling air, to his hands, to his glittering gaze. He touched her everywhere, fingers trailing along her neck, thumbs brushing against her nipples, and there, where he sought out her swollen folds, playing amid the dampness, causing delight with his talented fingers.

She reached for him again, needing the touch of his manhood like it was a lodestone for her hands. The head at the end of this magical instrument wept for her, and when she circled it with tender, fascinated fingers, he emitted a low, mirthless chuckle. Raising himself again, he offered himself to her. A pagan sacrifice, and one that she received with exultation.

He was hers.

He would not leave her. He couldn't.

She'd lost her mother, and possibly her identity. She wouldn't lose him as well.

Suddenly, she was on her back and he was atop her, his knee at the apex of her thighs. She widened her legs in invitation, and he smiled at her, the lamplight giving him the appearance of a reiver, a Scottish invader.

She placed one hand on his cheek and the other behind his neck, pulling his head down for a kiss.

She hurt for him, a pulse beating deep in her core that could only be satisfied by him. Her body was damp, swollen. She needed him in her.

Her fingers trembled, her breath was too tight, and her heart raced. She gripped him, but instead of being reticent and ladylike, instead of being restrained, she gripped his shoulders and pulled him to her.

"Douglas," she whispered, in a voice too demanding, too harsh.

Now.

He was suddenly in her, blocking out every thought but how he felt, how he moved. She held him by his hips, setting him in motion, the rhythm hard, strong, and fluid. He pulled one of her hands free, then the other, holding them clasped with each of his so that they were joined in all ways, in all places.

She was making little sounds, but she didn't care.

He slid in and out of her, increasing his pace, pushing against the mattress as if to bury himself in her. She held on, wrapped her feet around his calves, shuddering when the pleasure overwhelmed her. A moment, an instant, a lifetime later, she watched as his head tilted back, his eyes closed, and the muscles of his throat pulled taut. His face, that wonderfully handsome face of his, stiffened and held, then relaxed in lines of pleasure.

How had she lived without passion? How had she ever lived without *him?*

CHAPTER 28

Rain had fallen throughout the night, pinging against the oak leaves, falling in a gurgling melody through the downspouts of Chavensworth's roof. A few times during the night, Sarah awakened from the sound and curled against Douglas. More than once, she'd registered that his hand was flat on her naked hip, his fingers splayed as if he claimed her in his sleep. When she awoke the last time, it was to find that it was morning, and Douglas was once again gone from their bed.

She rang for Florie, pulled out the dress she wanted to wear, and began to comb the tangles from her hair. Dressing took less time than usual because she resolutely refused to look in the mirror. She didn't want to see that her eyes were bloodshot, and dark circles below them made the rest of her face look much paler than usual.

She probably looked, in the words of one

very snippy young thing during her first season — like an overly powdered ghoul. Of course, the girl hadn't been speaking of her at the time, but of a famous widow who, after discovering that her beauty was enhanced by widow's weeds, insisted upon dressing all in black even as she rouged her lips and cheeks.

"Just do what you can with it, Florie," she said of her hair, not caring a whit.

Finally, she glanced at herself in the mirror, only to see a stranger staring back at her.

Her eyes were wide and not red at all. Her cheeks were the palest shade of pink, and her lips, well, they looked well kissed. A little swollen, perhaps, but the effect was charming. Her complexion wasn't ashen but creamy, and her hair looked glossy and lovely in the way Florie arranged it.

How very odd. Passion had made her beautiful.

She tied on a serviceable apron — Florie delivered a fresh one every morning — grabbed her journal, and began her rounds.

Passing the wing that housed the Duke's Suite, she turned and glanced down the corridor, but only to ensure that the carpet was in good repair and the candelabra had been recently dusted. If she happened to look toward the double doors, it was only to verify that the brass handles had been polished.

She was not checking to see if Douglas was inside; she knew only too well where he was.

Diamonds captured his attention the way Douglas captured hers.

All the way to the steward's office, she made little mental notes of things to discuss with Mr. Beecher before realizing that she'd not done so since before her mother's death.

Awareness came, as slowly as her footsteps at first, then in a rushing flood. Two weeks had passed. Two weeks, and in all that time, Chavensworth had subsisted without her. No servants, anxious for direction, had camped at her door. No one whispered to Florie, "When will she awake? We need answers." No one seemed to know or notice that she'd returned from Scotland, and yet Chavensworth was being tended to, cared for, and seemed to run like a well-maintained clock.

She clutched the journal close to her chest with both arms and walked the rest of the way to the steward's office, trying to determine whether it was pride she felt or some sort of offense.

As she knocked on Jeremy Beecher's door,

she decided that she would not make up her mind yet, and when he called out, she stepped into the room, a determined smile on her face.

Jeremy stood, extending a large ledger out to her.

"Good morning, Lady Sarah. How was your journey to Scotland?"

"Interesting," she said, and hoped that would end Scotland as a topic of conversation. She put her book down on the table and took Mr. Beecher's ledger with both hands.

Mr. Beecher had excellent instincts. He no longer referred to Scotland, but what he did say surprised her.

"I've done the quarterly inventory, Lady Sarah. And, as you'll see from the ledger, so has Mrs. Williams. I've received the report on the home farms, and that's included for your perusal as well."

"You did all this when I was in Scotland?" she asked, amazed.

"Indeed, Lady Sarah. With the help of my assistant."

She frowned. "Your assistant?"

He nodded. "I've promoted one of the footmen, Lady Sarah. A smart lad with a head on his shoulders. He ciphers well, and can read better than the others."

As she was digesting this startling information, he continued. "It was Mr. Eston's decree, Lady Sarah, and I must admit I was doubtful at first. But it's proven to be a godsend."

"Has it?"

"Mr. Eston made it very clear that we were responsible for our areas of expertise, and that you were to be consulted only when Chavensworth was in jeopardy."

"He did?"

He nodded.

"May I tell you, Lady Sarah, that your trust in us has had a remarkable salubrious effect. And the rekindling of the Henley Gift is a magnanimous gesture."

"It is?"

Dear heavens, was she doomed to ask insipid questions for the whole of this conversation?

"Mr. Eston has given me to understand that the Gift would be reinstated," he said, a small frown marring the shiny radiance of his features.

"Of course," she said.

Smiling brightly at Jeremy Beecher, she picked up her journal, took one step back, and managed to remember her manners.

"Thank you, Mr. Beecher. If I have any further questions, I shall ring for you."

"Of course, Lady Sarah," he said, half bowing.

Sarah left his chamber, intent on escape. Instead of retracing her steps, she descended the steps hidden by the false wall and entered the portico that led to the garden.

Before her mother had become ill, Morna used to spend her mornings here, tending to the roses she'd loved so much. Sarah sat on the bench near the multicolored blooms, feeling the sun on her head. She couldn't remember the names of the roses, but she could almost hear her mother's voice. "You must always care for those who cannot care for themselves, dearling. The strong must protect the weak."

Who had protected Morna? For that matter, about whom was she speaking? Had she considered herself strong? Strong enough to ignore the family that had reached out to her?

So many things Sarah had thought were real were only real when viewed from a certain angle. If she stepped back, or to the side, another picture emerged. Her memories of her mother, how necessary she was to Chavensworth, even Sarah's marriage, her own propriety — each of these had changed in the last weeks. She felt as if her foundations had been shaken, as if everything she knew wasn't certain anymore.

She stood and began walking, nodding to the occasional gardener. Once, Chavensworth had employed a staff of twelve to see to the grounds, but in the last year, they could only afford four. Each man was overworked, and there were times when she regretted the necessity for economy, especially now, when the boxwoods needed trimming, and the rosebushes needed to be replanted.

She clutched her journal tighter. People weren't always what they seemed. Look at her mother, for example. She would never have known, for all the Duchess of Herridge's propriety, that she had been with child outside of marriage. Although it was not a situation all that uncommon, it didn't seem right that the oh-so-proper Morna would be one of those women. But Scotland had taught her that she hadn't known her mother as well as she'd thought.

Suddenly, she realized that there was nothing she needed to do. She had no duties in the next several hours. No appointments needed to be kept. For the first time in a very long time, she had the freedom to do as she wished, and she owed that to Douglas.

She left the garden, heading for her favorite place at Chavensworth, the tall and spreading oak atop a small knoll. Here, her earliest memories of her mother had been formed. She could remember countless afternoons resting against the trunk, listening while her mother read from *Ivanhoe* or another of her favorite books.

For years, she'd trailed after her mother as Morna had attended to Chavensworth. Sarah had her own set of keys, for unimportant locks. Their conversation had been about necessary things: candles and lamp oil, bootblack and livery, the proper recipes for furniture wax and silver polish. They had rarely spoken of Morna's past or, for that matter, Sarah's future. While it was also true that her mother had made her childhood magical with tales of knights and princesses and hoary dragons, it struck Sarah as she sat there that her mother had told stories more than she had ever truly conversed.

What secrets had she hidden with such skill?

The truth was that she would never know.

Sarah settled her skirts, spreading them out in an almost perfect circle around her. She opened the journal and, after retrieving the pencil from her pocket, began to write.

When she finished, she sat back against the old trunk, thinking of Douglas.

What had life been like for him as child growing up in Perth? For that matter, what kind of man leaves his home and changes himself to that degree? Had he expected her to repudiate him? Instead, she could only admire him.

Her father would be horrified.

How strange that she'd not thought of her father until now. Even though the marriage was his decision, and due to his manipulation, he would not be pleased that his only child was married to a man who'd once been poor and destitute. But was the Duke of Herridge even her father?

There was one person at Chavensworth to whom she could tell the story of Morna and Michael, and up until now she'd not done so. One person would listen and give her advice if she asked. Besides, she needed to thank him for funding the Henley Gift.

Smiling, she stood and went in search of her husband.

The morning was a bright, sunny one, with not a cloud in the sky. Nothing would interfere with the progress of curing the diamonds.

Douglas caught a glimpse of Sarah as he turned to put more wood into the fire. He watched her walk along the graveled path, her skirts swinging.

"Good morning," he said pleasantly, spearing the shovel into the ground, clasping both hands on the end of the handle and leaning against it.

She looked straight at him, then smiled slowly, sending heat straight to his groin. She took in his appearance from the top of his head to his toes. The fact that he'd shed his shirt earlier hadn't meant much to him at the time, but it did now. He was — conveniently — halfway to undressed.

"We have servants, Mr. Eston," she said, her tone very measured. There was, however, a twinkle in her eye, and her voice trembled slightly.

"Not for this, we don't," he said. "No one works on my diamonds."

She nodded, fixing her gaze on his chest. Suddenly, most of the heat he was experiencing was being generated by his body and not the furnace.

"Can Alano not assist you?"

"Do you think I need assistance, Sarah?" He almost flexed his muscles, then, but restrained himself.

"I should think you would want help," she said.

Her gaze had not moved from his chest. She was really making this difficult.

"Blame Mrs. Williams," he said.

At that, her gaze lifted to his face. "Mrs. Williams?" she asked, clearly confused.

"I believe Alano is smitten," Douglas said. "At least that's my thought after seeing them together this morning."

"Mrs. Williams?"

"Do you object?" Surely she wasn't that much of a snob. In fact, he hadn't thought her a snob at all despite the fact she was the daughter of the Duke of Herridge, a man very much impressed with his status in life. Look at how easily she'd taken the news of Douglas's past. "Alano is a good man."

"I'm sure he is," she said quickly, "but Mrs. Williams is not in the first flush of youth."

He began to smile, understanding. "She's not dead, either, Sarah. She has a right to love and lust along with younger people. So does Alano. Or do you think such feelings disappear after a certain age?"

She looked wide-eyed at him, as if she'd never given it any thought.

He left the shovel speared into the earth and walked slowly toward her.

"Lust doesn't just disappear, Sarah. It might go to ground a bit, but it never truly goes away."

"Really?"

How very proper she sounded. How very English. But her stormy gray eyes were now as soft as dandelion down, and her cheeks were colored pastel pink. She was biting her bottom lip, and he wanted to ask her to let him do that, instead.

"Truly," he said, reaching her. "And lust has another enormously interesting component. It renews itself. Constantly."

"Really?" She was evidently so lost in that thought that she didn't seem to notice he was steering her toward the observatory.

"Most assuredly. I can guarantee it, as a matter of fact. Before seeing you, I was basking in the warmth of my thoughts of last night. Now that memory isn't at all sufficient."

"It isn't?"

He knew that he would fall apart if he didn't have her. Now. He would cease to live, and the man he'd known himself to be — resilient, intractable, focused — would simply falter. Or he would crumble to dust.

When they reached the doorway, she looked up at him, her features aware and alert, as if she were trembling on the edge of a great discovery.

"Oh, Douglas, it's the same with me," she said softly, almost unmanning him.

He hesitated, needing to be with her, but

holding himself away at that last little bit of moment. His mind, forever urging caution and prudence, was not silent on this occasion, but his body overruled his sense, reacting silently and powerfully in a burst of heat that filled his cock and made it rock hard.

"Let me show you how it can be," he said, and led her into the darkness of the observatory.

It was the sound like pebbles Sarah heard first, a clink, ping, clink against the tile sides of the observatory.

She pressed her palm against Douglas's bare chest as he raised his head from their kiss.

They looked at each other.

"What is that?" she asked.

She could suddenly *feel* the silence, as if the absence of sound had created a hollow space around her. She looked toward the slightly open door. Suddenly, a whoosh of heated air flung them both against the curved wall.

The air was suddenly black. Chunks of bricks thudded against the side of the building as loud as if God Himself were hammering the observatory.

Douglas swore, and pulled her deeper into the building, but the explosion wasn't the only danger. A fireball scorched through the grass and licked at the doorway. He reached up, tore the linen from the ceiling, then stood on one of the shelves and began opening the roof. The wheel had evidently been oiled, and it swung open easily.

He reached down for her. "Come on, Sarah."

In a moment of sickening clarity, she understood. They were in grave danger and must escape the observatory.

However, she was never going to fit in the opening with her hoops. Reaching below her waistband, she tore the tapes of her hoops, pulling at them until they were free. She stepped out of her hoops, grabbed the material of her skirts, and scrambled up beside him.

He made a step out of his interlinked hands, and she put her right foot against his palms, holding on to his shoulders as he gave her a boost. The opening wasn't large, but she could fit. Could he?

"I'm not leaving until you promise to be right behind me," she said.

"Not only right behind you," he said, "but right next to you."

She peered out the top of the observatory. The fire was racing through the fields to the west, but they could still escape to the rear of the building.

A moment later, he boosted her up even farther. She pulled herself up with both arms, elbows striking the copper of the roof.

The tile was rough on the side of the building, abrading her fingers as she grappled for a handhold. The small iron ladder built into the curve of the roof was a godsend, however, and she managed to hold on to it, lower her legs, and fall into the grass, thankful that it had grown so high.

Douglas was right behind her, and she hugged him when he landed next to her. He stood and caught her up in his arms a second later.

She didn't have a chance to protest, because he bent his head and kissed her, silencing her as he carried her from the flames.

CHAPTER 29

Douglas carried her through the crowd of servants as she pressed her face against his bare chest. Each of her separate breaths, heated and soft, seemed to burrow beneath his flesh, into where the essence of him lived, and brand him for all time as hers.

"She's fine," he murmured to Thomas, and pushed himself past Jeremy Beecher and Mrs. Williams. He nodded to Cook, and with an aside only a few heard, said, "Can you send a tray to the Duke's Suite? A bit of fruit, perhaps. Maybe some tea?"

She nodded and turned, disappearing into the crowd so sleekly she might have been an eel.

He made it to the rear of Chavensworth, caring hands brushing against him like palm fronds. Sarah was not light, but neither was she a burden he had any intention of releasing.

Two young men stood beside the door,

and when he gestured to it with a lift of his chin, they hurried to open it.

Once inside Chavensworth, he set Sarah down on her feet, gathering her into his arms and pressing his cheek against the top of her head.

"Are you certain you're all right?"

One hand came up to rest against his bare chest.

"Yes," she said softly. "I think so. I also think I shall never be able to face anyone again."

He pulled back and tilted up her face with one hand. "Yes you will. You're Lady Sarah Eston."

"I've never appeared nearly undressed in front of my staff, however."

"You're only missing your hoops," he said, smiling. "Not your corset. Brazen it through," he said, bending to kiss her. He didn't mention that her lips were swollen and pink, or that her cheeks were delightfully flushed. Anyone with any experience would be able to look into her beautiful gray eyes and know that she'd recently been kissed, and well.

They began walking up the stairs to their chamber, Sarah careful to keep her skirts, which trailed without their underlying hoops, from tripping her up.

The Duke of Herridge was not going to be happy about the explosion.

Douglas found it absurd that he slept in the man's bed, all the while loathing the arrogant peer. Despite the poverty he'd been born to, and the privilege the duke enjoyed, Douglas would have easily chosen his life over His Grace's. There was nothing about the duke that he would emulate, least of all the way he treated his daughter. Sarah was simply a commodity to him, and the Duke of Herridge had rid himself of the problem of his only child in exchange for the promise of diamonds.

As if Sarah were only worth a mere purse of diamonds.

If he'd been married for months, instead of only weeks, he'd have felt a little more secure in explaining to Sarah exactly what her father had planned. Not only was their marriage tenuous because of how it had occurred, but Sarah had been through enough in the past month. She didn't need to know the extent of her father's perfidy.

These past weeks had only accentuated what he'd felt for her from the beginning. He wanted to protect her and keep her safe. He wanted to give her pleasure more than he wanted it for himself. In the night, when he couldn't sleep, when dreams beckoned yet couldn't capture him, he wanted to speak to her in hushed tones in the shadows. He wanted to tell her what it was truly like being Douglas Eston from Perth, Scotland. He wanted to share with her feelings he'd never shared with another living soul, not even Alano.

If he left now, he could make it to London in two hours, speak to his solicitor, and at least ease his mind about the duke's ability to end his marriage. In addition, there must be some way to get out of his agreement with His Grace. No money had exchanged hands, only the very precious hand of the duke's daughter.

The best view of the observatory and the western fields was from the Duchess's Suite. Sarah stood on the terrace, watching the footmen douse the grass around the building and where the furnace had been. The fire had been extinguished, but Douglas had returned and was now directing people and equipment. Alano and a few of the other men dragged the diamond frames from the observatory, while still others removed the jars and jugs.

Could anything be salvaged?

The explosion could have killed them both.

If he hadn't entered the observatory, Douglas would have been right there in the midst of the explosion.

She glanced down at the garden, her mother's garden with the luckinbooth. Perhaps it was because she was standing at this angle, but the luckinbooth didn't look like two hearts intertwined and topped with a crown. She walked to the other side of the terrace and looked at the hedges again.

A moment later, Sarah left the room, intent on her own chamber. Grabbing her journal and her pencil, she returned to the Duchess's Suite, slowly sketching what she saw both from the doorway and from the far end of the terrace. Only when she was finished was she certain — the luckinbooth wasn't two hearts, but two entwined initials. Two Ms — for Michael and Morna?

Douglas went to the stables and gave orders for the carriage to be readied.

"I'll be happy to drive you, sir," Tim said from behind him.

Douglas turned. "I'm going to London, Tim, and I've a mind to be back before nightfall."

Tim nodded. "That suits me well enough, sir. Are you ready to leave now?"

Douglas looked over to where two boys

stood laughing at the corner of one stall. He motioned one of them over, gave him an errand to perform, before turning to Tim.

"I'll be ready in a quarter hour," he said.

In actuality, it was less than that. Alano came walking through the stable doors ten minutes later, his valise in his hand and Douglas's jacket slung over his arm.

"Time was," Alano said, "I'd have to remind you to be proper dressed. It's good I don't have to train you anymore." He handed Douglas his jacket with a smile. "If you're going to London, I'll follow you."

Douglas glanced down at the valise in his friend's hand.

"There's no need for you to leave, Alano."

"Yes, there is," Alano said. "I'll not howl at her door like a lovesick puppy."

Douglas raised an eyebrow but didn't make a comment. He'd never before seen his friend in such a mood over a woman. Perhaps it was something about Chavensworth, but he didn't think so. The two of them had simply found the only two women in the world capable of twisting their guts into frenzied snakes.

"Then I'll be glad of the company," Douglas said.

Alano gave orders for the second carriage, the one he'd arrived at Chavensworth in, to follow them. The coachman looked ecstatic to be returning to London.

Douglas signaled to Tim, and he and Alano climbed inside the first carriage. They were on their way to London less than an hour after he had made his decision.

Sarah walked back into her mother's room. The tall windows had heavy burgundy drapes shut against the bright summer day, but she didn't open them.

Slowly, she walked toward the secretary her mother had used until she'd become too ill. Sitting on the high-backed chair in front of the desk, she pulled open the bottom right drawer. She could remember the first time her mother had shown her the secret compartment.

"What's in there, Mama?"

"Mama's jewels, dearling."

Although she'd been a little girl, she'd known her mother kept her rings and brooches in the small casket in the bottom of the armoire, but she'd not argued. She'd been old enough to know that a good daughter never questioned.

The drawer held unremarkable items — a porcelain potpourri container that still managed to scent the drawer with roses after all this time, another small jar that had once held ink, now dry. A silver rocker blotter, and a selection of nibs. One by one, she removed all the items, placing them on the surface of the secretary. Once the drawer was empty, she reached toward the back and, using her nail, slid the false bottom toward her and lifted it.

Inside the secret compartment was a stack of letters, tightly tied in yellow ribbon.

She withdrew the letters, holding them in both hands. She had no right. Curiosity was not enough. Morna was a woman with secrets, some of them confusing, true, but they were her secrets.

Sarah studied the handwriting on the envelope. Large and sprawling, it seemed to be written in a masculine hand. If she opened this letter, she would read words that weren't meant for her. Perhaps the words would be commonplace, the correspondence of acquaintances, friends. Or perhaps they were more, words of love, of devotion, and of sorrow.

God forgive her, but she couldn't go for the rest of her life without knowing.

She replaced the false bottom and loaded the items back into the drawer before returning to her room. Once back in her chamber, she sat on the chair beside the window, resting for a moment with the letters on her lap as if to give herself another chance to do the proper thing.

She began with the oldest letter, one that seemed much read if the fragile folds were any indication. The letter was dated five years earlier.

Dearling,

Her eyes widened at the endearment, but she continued reading.

Forgive me for writing you, but your father has told me the truth he kept hidden all these years. Forgive me for once believing that you would love another.

I have no right to be in your life, now, but I want you to know that you have been forever in mine. I have never forgotten you, dearling, and every day that passes does so with my earnest prayers for your joy and health.

There was no name at the bottom of the letter. The second letter, however, was signed with a bold M. This time, there was no salutation.

You say that it's wrong, that we cannot love each other. I say, how do we stop? By words? By actions? What more can be done to us, dearling, than to marry us to other people?

The third letter of the thirteen covered three pages, detailing his life, his children, his loneliness for the woman he called dearling. At the end of it, he signed his name, and she knew. Michael.

She skipped the remainder of the letters, hesitating over the last one. Finally, she opened it to find that it was dated only a few months earlier. Slowly, she began to read, thinking that her own heart would break.

I shall not write you again, dearling, nor shall I see you, I fear.

My heart is tired, and the beating of it has been of great concern to my family of late. My eldest son is posting this letter for me, and I hope it reaches you soon. Perhaps my soul will visit you at your English castle to say farewell before my letter arrives.

I shall love you into eternity. I shall wait for you there.

Tears blurred Sarah's vision, stinging her eyes.

Morna Tulloch had found herself with child, just when her lover had been tricked into marriage. To protect her unborn child, she'd married an English duke desperate for an heiress. She'd managed to have a life away from Scotland.

Her memories of her mother, wrapped in the gauze of time, now saw a smile less happy than bittersweet and a faraway look less contemplative as simply longing.

Perhaps her mother had never told Michael that she'd borne his child, hiding that secret from everyone, everyone but Sarah, to whom she showed the false bottom of the secretary and whom she called dearling.

Had she wanted Sarah to know, in the end? For that matter, had her mother simply willed herself to death? Could one die of a broken heart?

Sarah stood, walked to the fireplace and knelt, building a fire. Once it was caught, she fed the letters to the flames, hiding the secret of her mother's love and sorrow.

Douglas left his solicitor's office feeling a little more heartened. The Duke of Herridge could not dissolve his marriage without his consent. Even if Sarah wanted their marriage to end, she would have to prove he'd been an adulterer, as well as guilty of several other sins. As long as he drew breath, he would contest any such action.

There was still time to court his wife.

Unfortunately, there was one task still remaining to do first.

The carriage stopped, and he exited, striding up the steps to the Duke of Herridge's house.

Simons opened the door.

"I'm surprised you're not out doing your master's bidding," Douglas said.

"This is my master's bidding, Mr. Eston." There was a small smile playing around Simons's lips, an expression so irritating that Douglas gave some thought to knocking it from his face.

"Is he here?" Douglas asked.

"What shall I tell His Grace is the purpose for this meeting?" Simons asked.

"His Grace's impatience, Simons."

"I doubt His Grace will want to discuss that, Mr. Eston. Instead, I believe that he will want to see the results of your labors. I trust you have diamonds with you, Mr. Eston."

"Where is he?"

Simons bowed, then turned on his heel, leading the way to the duke's library. At the door, Simons rapped lightly on the wood, waited one moment and turned the handle. Once the door was open, he stepped aside and announced Douglas.

The Duke of Herridge didn't stand at his arrival. Nor did he even bother looking up from the papers he was signing. Instead, he waited until Douglas walked to the middle of the room and came to stand in front of his desk. Only then did he look up, replacing the quill in its stand.

"You said it would be only a short time until you had results, Eston."

"I said it was a matter of weeks, Your Grace. Not days. Threats will not accelerate the process."

"Threats?"

"To dissolve my marriage?"

The Duke smiled. "I wondered if that would work. You are quite taken with my daughter, aren't you?"

The Duke of Herridge was one of those creatures that, once scenting vulnerability, used the knowledge as a weapon. He wasn't about to give him any information, especially about Sarah.

"There was an explosion at Chavensworth," he said.

Herridge sat back and regarded him steadily, his smile fading.

"All of the diamonds that were being harvested were destroyed in the fire," he said.

The duke's expression didn't change.

"You'll have to wait even longer than I originally estimated," Douglas said.

"Why did this explosion occur?" Herridge asked, staring down at the blotter on his desk. "Is there a flaw in your formula?"

"There is no flaw. Perhaps the mortar for the furnace didn't cure long enough. Perhaps I tried to fire too many diamonds at once."

"Can you prevent such a disaster from happening in the future?"

Douglas frowned. The Duke of Herridge had begun to smile, which was not a good sign. Anything that pleased the older man was probably not in anyone else's best interests.

"I believe so, yes," he said cautiously.

"Then you will have to prove that," Herridge said.

He stretched out his hand, grabbed a brass bell from the corner of his desk, and rang it twice.

Simons opened the door so quickly that Douglas wondered if he'd been standing on the other side all this time.

"See Mr. Eston to the third floor," he said. "Make sure he has suitable accommodations and all the equipment he needs to make his diamonds."

"I'm not staying here, Herridge," Douglas said.

"Oh, but you are, Mr. Eston."

Simons stepped aside. Two burly men who looked more like fighters than footmen entered the room. Each man grabbed one of his arms, and although he struggled, he was no match for the two of them.

"I do apologize for the necessity of this," Herridge said. "But I truly need those diamonds, Mr. Eston." He turned to Simons. "See to it, Simons," he said, pulling open the drawer and retrieving a pistol from the interior. He handed the pistol to his majordomo. "Shoot him if necessary."

Simons took the pistol wordlessly and pointed it at Douglas as the two men dragged him out the door and up the stairs.

Sarah dressed in a very simple black gown. For the occasion, she wore jet earrings and a small jet brooch. She dispensed with large hoops, only wearing two petticoats, but one of those was lace-edged taffeta that made a slithery sound when she walked.

Although she hadn't seen Douglas since the morning, she'd given Cook orders that dinner was to include all of those foods that Douglas had requested in the last few weeks. Consequently, they had a variety of meats and puddings — Douglas had a liking for sweets — some fruits, and two wines.

Unfortunately, all of her plans were for naught when she was informed that Douglas had left Chavensworth hours earlier.

She stared at Mrs. Williams, hoping that the woman could not discern her shock.

"He's left?"

"I understand Mr. Eston has business in London."

"Who told you this?" she asked, very calmly.

"The stable master," Mrs. Williams said.

Sarah managed to eat her dinner, remembering her manners at the end of it. She called Cook and her staff into the dining room.

"I only wish that we had more visitors," she said to all three of them. "Other people deserve to eat your food. As it is, I consider myself very fortunate to live at Chavensworth. Thank you for a wonderful meal."

She was beyond humiliated. Cook and her staff had labored for hours to produce a feast that only one person had eaten.

"Please distribute the food among the staff."

"And we'll save a bit for Mr. Eston," Cook said, smiling brightly.

Could he do no wrong in their eyes? A

smile from him, and the silly women beamed for the rest of the day. If he jested with them, they blushed and simpered. This meal had been for him, and he'd missed it. So what did they do? Simply accepted it, put some food back for him, and eagerly awaited his arrival.

Douglas didn't arrive in the next hour, when she paced through the public rooms. Nor any hour after that when she made a point of walking in the corridor near the Duke's Suite. Finally, she gave up and returned to her own room to find Florie sitting on the bench at the end of the bed, looking undeniably fatigued.

"Go to bed, Florie," she said. "I won't need you anymore tonight."

"Let me help you with your dress," she said.

The unfastening done, she waved Florie off. "You're the one who looks like she needs her bed," she said. "Go and get some rest."

Night was a whisper, a soft entreaty to sleep. Sarah stood on the terrace outside her chamber, staring off toward the eastern sky. Tonight she could see the heavens in all their glory, marveled at the clear summer night, feeling small, insignificant, and yet part of all the majesty that God had created.

A breeze, scented with lavender and roses, swept over her, tenting her nightgown.

I've been advised that there's something called the Matrimonial Causes Act. That it's possible to have a marriage dissolved.

Dear God, was that what his business was in London? Surely not. Not after her spending hours in his arms, weeping in bliss against his chest. Not after last night. Or even this morning, when he'd carried her back to Chavensworth and treated her as if she were precious and rare.

She walked to her escritoire, took out her journal, and began to write, putting into words all her heartache, all the sudden and inexplicable sense of loss she felt. When she was done, she put her pen down, watching as the ink was wicked from the tip to the blotter.

When she began to cry, she told herself that her tears were for her mother.

CHAPTER 30

The next morning, Sarah sent Florie back to her own room, with instructions for her maid to take as much time as she needed to recuperate from the journey to Scotland. Florie looked drained and exhausted, and if she weren't better in a few days, Sarah would insist upon her visiting the physician.

She next went in search of Alano, discovering that finding their guest was almost as difficult as locating her husband. Alano wasn't in the chamber assigned to him, or helping clean up the area around the observatory. When Sarah inquired as to his whereabouts in the kitchen, one of the cook's helpers volunteered, "I'd ask Mrs. Williams about that man," she said, then looked away.

Chavensworth had not been the same since she married. Some of the changes were long overdue, but some of them were very odd. She opened the door to the kitchen garden and stepped outside.

Instead of diligently inspecting the planting of the new herbs, Mrs. Williams was seated on the garden bench, her face in her hands.

Sarah halted, shocked beyond measure. She'd never before seen the inimitable Mrs. Williams cry. She didn't know whether to continue onward or slip back into the kitchen. Finally, her need to talk to Alano was greater than her reticence about disturbing Mrs. Williams, and she stepped forward.

"My dear Mrs. Williams, are you all right?"

The other woman dropped her hands and hastily retrieved a handkerchief from her apron pocket. She wiped her face dry, while nodding, all the while looking away from Sarah. A few minutes later, she'd gathered her composure.

"I'm fine, Lady Sarah," she said, standing and facing her. "Is there something you wanted?"

"My mother wouldn't want for you to grieve overmuch, Mrs. Williams."

The look of surprise on the other woman's face was response enough.

"But you aren't grieving for my mother, are you?" she said.

Mrs. Williams blotted her eyes with the handkerchief and pointedly ignored the question. "Is there something I can do for you, Lady Sarah?"

"Do you know where Mr. McDonough is? One of your helpers thought you might know."

The statues in the garden couldn't be any more frozen than Mrs. Williams's face.

"He has returned to London."

"With Mr. Eston?"

"I'm sure I don't know, Lady Sarah. All I do know is that Mr. McDonough is no longer in residence at Chavensworth."

And Mrs. Williams missed him a very great deal, a supposition that could be entirely incorrect, but Sarah didn't think so.

"I have his address in London," Mrs. Williams said, "if you would like to correspond with him."

"I would appreciate having the address," Sarah said, not asking how the other woman came to have it, suspecting that the question would result in one of two reactions: a cold stare or Mrs. Williams's tears. Neither one was welcome.

"I shall bring it to you."

Sarah nodded her agreement and left the kitchen garden. What was she supposed to do now? Pretend that Douglas was not gone? Ignore his absence? Evince no curiosity? Remain patient, keeping a vigil for his return? That might be easier if she knew where he'd gone.

A high, screeching wind howled through the branches of the trees, audible even through the walls of Chavensworth. Her shoulders rose as if to protect her neck from the sudden, unseasonable cold.

At the double doors to the Duke's Suite she hesitated, then continued on to her own chamber. Her pristine childhood room, and the bed where Douglas had slept the night before last.

She carefully and slowly unfastened her dress, her corset, and her undergarments. She told herself that she was as tired as Florie. And her nakedness? A matter of defiance, or simply a way to remind herself of her husband. Despite the fact that it was barely noon, Sarah drew the curtains shut and crawled into bed, smelling the scent of him, and wishing him there.

He was damned if he was going to make diamonds for a man who was holding him prisoner. All the same, he'd given Simons a list of the equipment and solutions he needed, and Simons, like the good little toady he was, asked him some questions about where he could obtain the various materials.

"Figure it out yourself," Douglas said.

"We have taken the precaution of putting your coachman in a safe place," Simons said. "I would hate for anything to happen to him, Mr. Eston."

"Just how badly do you need a position, Simons?"

"I beg your pardon, sir?"

"When does becoming a perfect servant pale in comparison to being a halfway-decent human being? Do you not ever have any problems with your conscience?"

"Where can I obtain these materials, Mr. Eston?"

Douglas told him and watched as Simons shut and locked the door behind him. He'd been outmaneuvered, but not for long.

He hadn't lied to the Duke. He had figured out what had caused the explosion. The curing process required fire. However, because the crystals were much larger than usual, and because there was more of the volatile chemical present, the result had been an explosion. Either he needed to make the crystals smaller, resulting in smaller diamonds, or he needed to cure them one by one.

Douglas opened the window and peered

out, but there wasn't a roof overhang to support his weight, only the ground three floors below. He looked up. The eaves were too sharply angled for him to lever himself up and onto the roof, which meant he'd have to find another way out of the room.

The door was securely bolted, and he didn't have a doubt that one of the duke's mastiffs was sitting outside the door armed with a pistol. There was only one way to get around that fact, either overpower the guard or surprise him. But he couldn't overpower a guard he couldn't reach.

He wanted out of here, now. Longing for Sarah exploded like his diamonds, a thousand smaller bursts that lodged in his heart, his mind, and his body. He was not going to allow the Duke of Herridge to dictate the course of his life, and he was certainly not going to let His Grace keep him from his wife.

Only one thing would work, and the more he thought about it, the better the idea seemed.

All he had to do was wait for Simons.

Two days later, Douglas had not yet returned. Sarah attempted to go about her duties as she normally would, but she found herself without much to do. Even when she should have been relieved to have time to write in her journal, she spent the time staring off into the distance, wondering about Douglas.

Twice, she wrote to Alano at the address Mrs. Williams had furnished. Twice, she tore up the letter, knowing that it revealed too much of their circumstances and her personal fears.

She knew, however, as each hour passed, and Douglas still didn't appear, that something would need to be done. She could not go on like she was, pretending that nothing was wrong, pretending that life at Chavensworth was as serene as it had been prior to her mother's death.

No one mentioned Douglas's name. Not one person remarked on his absence. Did each person employed at Chavensworth think that Douglas had left her? She suspected they did from the pitying looks she was receiving.

On the evening of the second day, she entered her room, opened up her writing desk, and wrote a third letter to Alano. Regardless of how much she revealed of herself, she needed to know where Douglas was, and she hoped Alano would know. Whether or not he told her was another problem entirely. The letter done, she sealed it and propped it up against the inkwell. In the morning, she would send it to Alano via a footman and request that the young man wait for a reply.

She stared at the bed, viewing it as an enemy rather than a simple piece of furniture. She hadn't been able to sleep well since Douglas had left Chavensworth. Tonight, she would not go to bed until she was sufficiently exhausted. If she needed to remain awake the whole night, then so be it.

She smoothed her hand over the top of her bureau, feeling the silken wood, well dusted and waxed. The mantel had been dusted; none of the bric-a-brac had a speck of dust. The brass of the andirons and the screen was perfectly polished. On her dressing table, the crystal atomizers were perfectly aligned. The silver tray on which they sat had been buffed to a gleaming shine.

Everything was perfect, and nothing was right.

The knock on the door proved a welcome respite from her own company. She walked to the door, opened it and smiled at Florie.

"Are you feeling better?" Sarah asked.

Florie ignored that question for one of her own.

"Lady Sarah," Florie said. "I wouldn't

bother you, Lady Sarah, but I wonder if you know when Tim might be coming home?"

She gestured her maid into the room with one hand and closed the door behind her. "I didn't know he was gone," she said.

"He took Mr. Eston to London, two days ago. But he told me that he'd be home that night. It's been two days, Lady Sarah, and I've heard nothing."

Sarah felt both foolish and selfish. She'd never even thought about Tim. "You've had no word since then?"

"No, Lady Sarah. Nothing."

"Do you know why they were going to London?"

"No, Lady Sarah. I don't think Tim knew," Florie said, beginning to weep.

She led Florie to a chair and sat beside her. Despite her tears, there was a glow about the girl, a beauty Sarah had never before noticed. A suspicion slipped into her mind.

"Florie, are you with child?"

Her maid beamed through her tears, a smile of such joy that Sarah almost reeled from its brightness.

"Yes, Lady Sarah, I am. But I haven't even told Tim," Florie said, her smile fading to tears once again. "I was going to tell him Tuesday, but he never returned home."

Sarah glanced at the note on the secretary. "I'll see to it myself, Florie," she said. "Tomorrow I'll go to London and see what has happened to Tim."

"Can I go with you, Lady Sarah?"

"You must take care of yourself now, Florie."

Florie smiled. "A smooth carriage ride will not hurt me, Lady Sarah. My mam had seven of us and worked the whole time."

"She didn't work for me," Sarah said. "If she had, she'd have taken better care of herself."

A shadow flitted over Florie's face. "It wouldn't be proper for you to go off on your own, Lady Sarah."

"Nonsense," Sarah said, smiling. "I'm a married woman now. I can do as I choose."

That statement wasn't entirely true, but she kept a smile on her face as she hustled Florie from the room with hopeful words and cautions not to overdo it. She watched as her maid walked to the servants' stair. Where would they live? In their snug little apartment above the stable? With a child? Chavensworth's accommodations for its staff did not run to cottages, but perhaps it was something she could arrange. Or a suite of rooms, perhaps, on the fourth floor. But Chavensworth wasn't hers, and any arrangements Sarah made could be easily over-turned by the Duke of Herridge.

She sat on the edge of the bed, knowing that sleep would come late tonight, if at all. Yet she needed to be rested for the journey, for the meeting with Alano, and for the news she might receive, however terrible it might be.

When had she fallen in love? Was that what she felt? This horrible, yawning cavern inside her chest, what was that? Not the same kind of grief she felt for her mother, but something different. As if her heart had begun to shrivel or turn to stone.

She lay back on the bed, staring up at the tester.

In less than a month, Douglas had changed her life. Yes, he'd brought her passion, but he'd also brought her tenderness. He'd amused her, and touched her heart, and held her when she'd cried. He'd been loyal to her, and at her side, accompanying her on her errand to Scotland. He'd demanded that each member of her staff work on his own, in a way she'd never before considered, but only to spare her tasks she sometimes found onerous.

He was stubborn, intelligent, and given to striding around naked more often than not. Yet he'd let her see his vulnerability. *It's where I write those things I learn. So that I don't forget.* He'd seen the world, but she had the feeling that he'd never be complacent with past deeds. Douglas would want to learn more and do more throughout the whole of his life. Living with him would be a passionate, tumultuous adventure.

And living without him? What would that be like?

CHAPTER 31

On Friday, Sarah dressed in one of her favorite ensembles, along with her newest set of gloves, and one of her mother's favorite hats, all of which had been dyed black for her mourning.

The journey to London marked the first time Sarah had traveled to the city and been so acutely aware of every aspect of the journey and the time it took. Normally, her interest was captivated by a conversation, a book, her journal, or even the passing of the scenery. Now, however, nothing seemed to make the trip faster or ease the uncomfortable knot in the middle of her stomach.

She'd given the coachman, a very capable young man named Edmunds, Alano's address in London. He'd promised to find it, and she'd only nodded, knowing that it was common to become lost in London more often than not. To her surprise, however, he drove straight to the square located not far from her father's home.

"It's a very fashionable place, Lady Sarah," he said, helping her from the carriage.

His comment only spurred more questions, but she had a more important task at the moment than to inquire of her coachman's past.

Edmunds preceded her up the stairs and knocked forcefully on the door.

Sarah looked around the square surreptitiously, surprised at the prosperity of the place. A small square park sat in front of the house, enticing a visitor to sit on the wooden benches or take a walk beside the blooming flower beds. An ornate iron fence enclosed the park. If this was like the Duke of Herridge's home, the occupants of the adjoining houses had keys to the gate.

Alano was wealthier than she'd imagined.

The door was opened by a young blond man attired in a leather apron and smelling of vinegar.

"Yes?" he asked, looking down his not-inconsiderable nose at them. "Who are you?"

He looked first at Edmunds, then at Sarah, and finally at the coach with the ducal crest sitting in front of the steps to the town house. If anything changed his mind on how to address them, it was not politeness as much as the carriage. He whipped off the apron and bowed too deeply.

"May I assist you?"

"I have come to see Alano McDonough," Sarah said. "Is he at home?"

"May I announce you?"

Contrary to Douglas's comments, she didn't often tout her title. But something about this young man made her want to do so. If she'd been a duchess, so much the better. The daughter of one would have to suffice.

"Lady Sarah Eston," she said. "Of Chavensworth."

Again, she had the impression it was not so much her person as what accompanied her — in this instance, the mention of Chavensworth — that impressed the young man.

He managed to step back, open the door, and bow, all in one effortless movement. If he hadn't annoyed her, she would've commended him on the poetry of his movements. As it was, she was determined to ignore him.

"I shall summon him forthwith," he said, and disappeared into the interior of the house, making no provisions for where they were to wait, or taking her gloves and bonnet, or even her card. He just disappeared.

Thomas, for all his inexperience in his position, would not have erred so abysmally.

A few minutes later, long enough for Sarah to become even more irritated, Alano appeared out of the shadows.

"I'm sorry, Lady Sarah, that the buffoon left you standing there," he said, motioning to a door set in a far wall.

She was always a little disconcerted to hear his Spanish accent, but she smiled and turned to her driver. "If you wish to return to the coach, Edmunds, I shall be fine," she said.

"If you're certain, Lady Sarah."

She nodded and watched him leave the house, opening and closing the door behind him.

"Where did your majordomo disappear to?" she asked.

"I've set him to polishing the silver. It's the only way to rid myself of him for a while. But he's not mine. He's Douglas's." He grinned. "Although I do admit to having hired Paulson, a fact Douglas will not allow me to forget. Staff the place, he said, and for my sins, I thought Paulson was versed in manners."

Alano looked around the room. Crates and barrels littered the space.

He led her to a sofa, and she sat.

"If the damn fool knew anything, he'd have offered you refreshments," Alano said. "But then, it doesn't appear we're up to any kind of standard."

She turned to face him, schooling her features so as not to betray her surprise.

"This house belongs to Douglas?"

"Your husband is a very wealthy man, Lady Sarah. More wealthy, I'd say than your father could ever hope to be."

She knew that, from his purchase of a rail car. But there was one question for which she needed an answer.

"Why did he enter into an agreement with him, Alano?"

"Are you talking the agreement to make diamonds for him? A man would be a fool ever to use all his own money to finance a venture, Lady Sarah. As to the wedding, you will have to ask him that yourself." He smiled kindly at her.

"But you didn't come here to talk about your wedding. Did you?" He peered into her face. "Because I couldn't speak ill of Douglas, Lady Sarah. He's almost like a son to me."

She folded her hands in her lap, took a few deep breaths to compose herself, and looked up at Alano, who was still standing beside her.

"I've come to ask if you know where he is. Is he here, since this is his house?"

"He's not here, Lady Sarah," Alano said, frowning. "I haven't seen him since he and I shared a carriage from Chavensworth a few days ago."

She took another deep breath, but perhaps one of the whalebone stays had come loose in her corset, because a sharp pain seemed to go through her stomach at Alano's comment. She was gripping her hands so tightly they resembled fists, and she forced them open.

"Did he mention to you any errands he might have? Or where he might have gone?"

Alano sat beside her.

"There was one thing," he said slowly, his gaze not on her but the floor. "He was set on seeing his solicitor. He wouldn't tell me why." He faced her finally. "That's all I know, Lady Sarah."

"Why have you come back to London, Alano?"

"Douglas and I have never lived in each other's pockets, Lady Sarah. London's close enough to Chavensworth that I won't lose touch with him. Besides, London tolerates me more than Chavensworth."

"A house does not have the capacity for

tolerance, Alano," she said gently. "Only the people within it."

His look changed, became as frozen as that worn by Mrs. Williams.

"Do you know the address of Douglas's solicitor?" she asked.

He nodded. "I'll tell your driver and give him directions," he said.

She didn't say anything until she reached the door, then she turned to him. "Mrs. Williams seems to miss you a great deal," she said. "She was weeping the last time I saw her."

He didn't respond, merely descended the steps to speak to Edmunds. Once he'd done so, he turned to Sarah again. "It's not like Douglas to disappear, Lady Sarah. If he isn't at Chavensworth, there's a reason for it. If there's something he had to face, he'd do so. The man is not a coward."

She didn't know what to say to that, so she opted for the truth. "I need to know why he left."

"Let me come with you," he said. "I might be of some use."

Surprised, she nodded. "I would be grateful for the company," she said.

The solicitor's office was located in an area of the city unfamiliar to her. Edmunds waited with the horses while she and Alano entered the small office. After a flurry of introductions and some stuttering responses from his clerk, she and Alano were shown into an inner office and introduced to Peter Smythe, her husband's solicitor.

The man was the antithesis of what she'd imagined. Instead of being stoop-shouldered, he was tall. When he stood and came around the desk to greet her, he did so with a smile. He was also younger than she'd thought he'd be — not much older than Douglas. He wasn't as attractive a man as her husband, but she had to admit, sitting there, that if she'd never seen Douglas, she would have thought the solicitor handsome.

A thought that lasted only until she'd come face-to-face with Mr. Smythe's incredible recalcitrance. Her husband's solicitor was even more stubborn than Douglas, and more obstinate than her most intractable Scottish relative.

"I'm afraid, Lady Sarah," he said, "that I cannot divulge the information you seek Perhaps if you sought the answers from your husband, he could tell you why he came to see me."

She didn't like feeling powerless, but she kept her smile anchored in place, all too conscious of Mr. Smythe's watchful glance and Alano's presence at her side.

"Are you being confidential because that is what every client deserves, Mr. Smythe? Or is there a particular reason you might be keeping that information from me?"

"I beg your pardon?"

She took a deep breath. "If I left the room, would you give Mr. McDonough the information I need?"

He drew himself up in his chair, a quite impressive performance, actually.

"I would not, Lady Sarah," he said. "On the contrary, I would probably interrogate Mr. McDonough with a great deal more severity than I'm questioning you. I might ask him, for example, why he is so desirous to know? Why has he come to me? Is there a reason why he thinks I might give him the answer he seeks?"

She applauded Mr. Smythe's honor, yet at the same time, it played havoc with her intent to learn where Douglas was.

"But you can verify that my husband was here on Tuesday," she said.

"I will do that much, Lady Sarah." He stood, a rather impolite way of ending the meeting.

She stood as well, catching Alano's glance, and wishing she could tell him that she would deal quite well with this setback. She would not be an object of pity. She bent her head, playing with the catch on her reticule to give her some time to frame her words.

"Mr. Smythe," she said, looking up at the man, "can you at least tell me if my husband sought your counsel in the matter of the dissolution of our marriage?"

Was there compassion in his gaze? Perhaps so, but she couldn't retreat now. Nor did she shake off Alano's hand on her arm. Sitting in her bedroom and wondering at the future was so much worse than being faced with the truth.

She tilted back her chin, and faced him resolutely.

"I cannot say, Lady Sarah."

She bit her bottom lip, clenched her jaw, and was determined not to cry.

Turning, she glanced at Alano and only nodded at him. Would he understand that it was her way of saying that she was fine?

"If he had, however," Mr. Smythe said from behind her, "I would have advised him of the details of the Matrimonial Causes Act."

She glanced over her shoulder at him.

"If I had spoken to him about such a matter, I would have told him that it requires him to prove that his wife had been unfaithful."

"I see." She forced a smile to her face. "Even if it's false?"

There was definitely pity now, and she was not going to fade in the face of it.

"Lady Sarah, if a man truly wishes to divorce his wife, there are ways to do it. Or, if the man is an adventurer, he can simply leave the country."

She turned and faced him.

"Mr. Eston would not have done such a thing. Instead, I believe him to be an honest man with honorable principles."

"As do I, Lady Sarah."

Wordlessly, they faced each other.

"I am trying to find my husband, Mr. Smythe," she said, her pride falling beneath a greater need, that of locating Douglas. "He seems to be missing."

His expression changed, became more cautious.

"When was this?"

"Immediately after visiting you, sir. Do you have any idea where he might have gone from here?"

He shook his head.

"Are you certain?"

"Lady Sarah, if I had any additional information that I could pass along to you, I would do so. Unfortunately, there is nothing more I can say."

She caught the inference in his words. "So, my husband did seek your advice on another matter as well."

"I have said enough, Lady Sarah," he said, walking to the door. He opened it, held it open, and smiled, a perfectly genuine smile if she hadn't looked in his eyes. He appeared as worried as she felt. "Good luck with your search. Please let me know what transpires."

She wasn't willing to leave quite yet.

"You have no idea where he might have gone, Mr. Smythe?"

"Give my good wishes to your father, Lady Sarah. He is the Duke of Herridge, isn't he?"

She was almost through the door when she turned and looked back at him. There was a solemn expression on his face, one he'd not worn in all the time she'd been in his office.

"How do you know my husband, Mr. Smythe?"

He smiled. "He saved my life, Lady Sarah. I was aboard a ship that sank off the coast of France. Your husband was aboard the rescue vessel. He kept me afloat until I could be rescued."

"If I told you that I was going to visit the Duke of Herridge right now, what would you say?"

"I would wish you the best of luck, Lady Sarah. I would also tell you to be careful."

She nodded and left him without another word.

Edmunds was standing outside, guarding the carriage.

"You're going to see him, then?" Alano asked. "He's not a nice man, your father."

"You're right," she said. "He's not a nice man." In addition, there was every possibility that he wasn't her father after all.

"Does your father have a stable?" Alano asked.

"Yes, of course," Sarah said. "Why?"

"Where's the carriage?"

She stared at him. "And the coachman? Where's Tim?"

Edmunds drove them to the front of her father's home.

"You go inside," Alano said, "and I'll do some snooping out here."

She nodded, left her reticule in the carriage, and stared up at the façade of the Duke of Herridge's town house. He'd ceased to be Father to her, even in her mind. Even if no one actually came to her and told her that Michael Tulloch was her father, she knew it in her heart.

As she stood there, gathering up her courage, she knew that what happened next might well change her life.

Alano watched Sarah enter the house.

The approach of night was greeted by the lighting of lamps. Next door, a footman exited the house, lit a lamp at the base of the steps, then disappeared inside.

Alano walked around the end of the block and back up the alley to a small courtyard leading to the stables. Here, too, there were lights burning brightly against the darkness. All in all, the place was relatively spacious for a London home, with eight stalls for horses and three bays for carriages.

All eight stalls were occupied by fine-looking horses, all more than acceptable for pulling the two carriages located there. Each of them was ebony, heavily lacquered, but only one boasted a small ducal crest on the door. The other was brand-new, and belonged to Douglas.

He approached the stable complex warily, hearing whistling but being unable to pinpoint the source. A young man suddenly emerged from one of the stalls, pitchfork in hand.

Alano took a few steps forward. He flexed his hands, and began to smile, wondering if he'd get a chance to practice his boxing. It had been a long time, but he was more than

willing to test his skills.
He began to grin.

CHAPTER 32

"The Duke of Herridge is an excessively greedy man, Simons," Sarah said, probably the most personal remark she'd ever made to the majordomo.

From his expression, he wasn't exactly certain how to answer her.

"I believe that he would do anything to acquire wealth," she added.

She removed her bonnet, and handed it to him. Slowly, she divested herself of the gloves as well.

"I am sorry for my part in that, Lady Sarah," he said, placing her garments on the sideboard.

"I am not speaking of my mother's jewels, Simons," she said. "But of other deeds. Are you involved in those as well?"

She eyed Simons. This man probably knew more about the duke than any other living individual.

"I am not certain, Lady Sarah," Simons

said, his voice a mere whisper, "whether it is greed or desperation that compels your father's actions. He is, after all, a duke, and expected to live a certain way and to demonstrate a certain style of living."

"He has no money." She'd occasionally wondered about her father's income, about his insistence in taking from Chavensworth anything worth selling, but she'd put it down to her father's lavish spending. She'd never thought that he was completely without funds.

"Is that it, Simons?"

The man didn't answer, but his silence was assent enough.

"When the opportunity came along to get me married without any expense on his part, it must have seemed heaven-sent."

Simons allowed himself a small smile. "As you say, Lady Sarah."

"He could not have been happy about the delay in Douglas's diamond process."

He looked directly at her. "He was not, Lady Sarah."

"Enough to do something foolish, Simons?"

He moved to the sideboard and rearranged the placement of her bonnet and gloves. A few moments later, he gave a half shrug, a curiously self-deprecating gesture.

"His Grace is what he is, Lady Sarah, but I have been with him for more than a decade."

She remained silent, waiting.

"In all that time, Lady Sarah, he has done good deeds, and those which I regretted."

He looked up at the ceiling.

"I very much fear that this deed shall be ranked among those I regret."

She folded her hands in front of her and faced Simons, willing her expression to reveal nothing of what she felt.

"Is my husband here, Simons?"

The majordomo looked down at the intricate marble flooring. "He is, Lady Sarah."

"Of his own volition, Simons?"

He took a deep breath, exhaled it. "No, Lady Sarah."

She reached out and gripped his jacketed arm with her bare hand, the very first time she could ever remember touching the man.

"Can you release him, Simons?"

"It would mean my position, Lady Sarah."

She nodded. "I know. But there are other places that need you, Simons," she said. "Chavensworth, for one."

"I doubt His Grace would allow me to be employed at Chavensworth, Lady Sarah," Simons said with a small smile.

He was right. Chavensworth would not be

a haven for Simons.

"Then I shall have to convince the duke to release him myself," she said. "Is His Grace at home?"

"Yes, Lady Sarah, but I believe he's dressing for his entertainments this evening."

"Tell him that I'm here, Simons," she said. Would her appearance change his plans?

She walked down the hallway to the duke's study. Several weeks had passed since she'd been here. Weeks in which she'd been married, buried her mother, discovered family in Scotland, and surprisingly, and delightfully, found love.

And all this had happened in a matter of weeks.

She took one of the high-backed chairs in front of the fireplace. How odd that she'd never been invited to sit here, but always stood like a penitent before her father's desk.

As she sat and waited, it occurred to her that Douglas's freedom could be accomplished effortlessly. After all, there was no need for brute force, when she, herself, held the perfect weapon.

Sarah began to smile.

"They only hire me to clean up!" the young man said, his voice choked for the simple reason that Alano had him up against the side of a stall, his hands around the younger man's throat. The horse inside was spooked by the two men, his eyes almost as wide as the stableboy's. "I only work in the stables. I don't know anything about what goes on in there." His frantic eyes darted toward the town house.

"Have there always been two carriages here?" Alano asked calmly.

The boy shook his head. "The other one was here one morning when I came in. Never saw it before." The hand that had held the pitchfork, now tossed several feet away, shakily pointed to the bay where the carriage rested.

"And the driver?"

If anything, the young man's eyes bulged out even more. Alano released his grip somewhat.

"I don't have anything to do with that. I don't. I see the trays, and I hear the noises, but I only sweep up here. That, and shovel out manure." He glanced at the restive horse next to him. "Prince, here, needs a lot of shoveling. A lot."

Alano dropped his hands. "Where's the coachman?"

The young man looked up at the loft above the stable. A set of stairs angled up from the side of the stable. At the head of the stairs was an old door, now closed, and probably locked.

"How many people guard him?"

The stableboy didn't hesitate. "Just one. Sometimes, he leaves, but he comes back."

"Is he there now?"

The boy nodded.

What was there about this boy that reminded him a little of Douglas? Douglas's eyes had been filled with intelligence. Douglas was also more pugnacious — Alano doubted he would have allowed himself to be overpowered so easily. Perhaps they shared one trait — both had the same aura of desperation, the same panicked look. Douglas had grown out of it.

This boy was dressed in little more than rags, and his hands were richly callused. His hair needed a trim and a good wash, and it wouldn't be a bad thing for him to have a bath. But Alano had watched him for several minutes before sneaking up on the lad, and he'd diligently performed his job, even though it was apparent no one had been watching.

"Ever want to be a hero, boy?" Alano asked, grinning.

"I've never been a hero, sir." He clenched his fists, all the while eyeing Alano with some caution.

"Well, it's about time you started, don't you think?"

Alano bent and retrieved the pitchfork before turning and striding to the other side of the stable. As he began to climb the steep steps, he glanced back to find, to his surprise and satisfaction, the stableboy following him, having taken the precaution of arming himself with a shovel.

One way or another, they were going to rescue Tim, then Douglas.

Everything was in readiness. A brazier of sorts had been built in the fireplace. The crystals were growing on their frames, and although they weren't as large as he would have liked, he had no intention of remaining a guest of the Duke of Herridge for a few weeks. They would simply have to be large enough for his purposes.

The normal process was to remove each filament from its frame and set the filament into the fire. Within moments, the filament burned away, allowing the crystals to drop to the base of the fire. After a matter of hours, the flames were extinguished, and what emerged were diamonds.

As he'd learned at Chavensworth, however, the larger the crystals, the more unstable the process. He was going to duplicate what he'd done then, not by using larger crystals but by dropping three or four filaments into the flames at the same time.

The resultant explosion should be powerful enough to startle the guard somewhat and cause him to come running. His fists would do the rest. He grinned and felt substantially better for the first time in three days.

He removed the filaments from the first and second frames, draped them across the flames, and waited.

The door suddenly opened to reveal Simons standing there.

"His Grace will not approve, Mr. Eston, but then, I can't say I approve of his actions, either." Simons opened the door wide. "You're free to go. Please do so in the next five minutes. I've sent the guard on an errand."

Douglas looked down at the brazier and shook his head. "Damn it, Simons, you might have let me know you were getting a backbone. I'm afraid it's too late!"

Alano traded his pitchfork for the boy's shovel, slamming it into the door. It flew open, hitting the wall at the same time the man seated on the other side of the room stood.

Tim was lying on a cot, held there by ropes around his ankles and wrists, a cloth stuffed into his mouth.

The guard advanced on Alano with an oath. The boy at his side rushed the man, the pitchfork wielded like a spear. He was really taking his new role as hero seriously. Alano reached out and grabbed his arm at the last moment.

"We're here to free Tim," he said. "Not kill anyone."

But he wasn't about to be pummeled by a muscular oaf, so Alano released the boy and hit the guard over the head with the shovel. The man fell to the floor with a thud.

"Are you sure you didn't kill him, sir?" the boy asked.

Alano shrugged, strode to the other side of the room, and pulled the rag from Tim's mouth.

"Where's Douglas?" Alano asked, as he began working on the knots on the ropes binding Tim to the cot.

"Don't know, sir. I was waiting for him by the carriage when two men grabbed me."

"Are you up to a rescue mission?" he asked. "I suspect the Duke of Herridge is keeping Douglas as another unwilling guest."

The boy at his side spoke up. "We're being heroes, sir."

Tim and Alano shared a wry look.

"Care to join us?" Alano asked, as Tim cautiously sat up, rubbing his ankles, then his wrists.

Tim's response was quick, profane, and more than satisfying.

Alano glanced at the boy. "What's your name?"

"Jason, sir."

Alano smiled. "A good hero's name, Jason. Shall we?"

He stepped over the prone body of the guard, heading for the Duke of Herridge's town house, Tim and Jason behind him.

The Duke of Herridge entered his library with an affable expression on his face, as if he were remembering something particularly pleasant.

Sarah didn't particularly want the Duke of Herridge to be happy. She stood and turned in his direction.

"Let Douglas go," she said, then added the one comment that would ensure Douglas's release. "If you do not, I will let all of London know what you've done, and why.

I'll tell everyone you're penniless. You pride yourself on your heritage and your name. I'll make you a laughingstock."

His face changed. His eyes narrowed, and his expression stiffened.

She knew him so well, and knew herself even better. Countless times, she'd stood before his desk, either here in London or Chavensworth on his rare appearances there. She'd been called upon to explain each infraction, each character trait, and each defect of her nature.

How very odd that he couldn't affect her now, not as long as there was a doubt they were even related. Did he know? Is that why he'd felt nothing but contempt for her the whole of her life?

Until this moment, she'd not realized how much she was like the Tullochs of Kilmarin. Proud, determined, and not about to back down in the face of a bully.

"I will do it," she said. "And take great pleasure in doing so. But I'll never say a word if you release Douglas."

"Do you think I care what the world thinks of me?"

She didn't get a chance to respond. A great rumbling roar began in the sky and rolled around and through the house. Sarah had this sudden, horrifying thought that a giant had taken his balled fist and thrust it through the roof all the way to the wine cellar. Shards of wood and plaster rained down on them. All she could do was put her arms over her head and curl into as small a ball as she could, wishing that women's fashions had some contingency for emergencies such as this one. A full hoop was no assistance to survival.

The sounds, raucous and grating, continued for what seemed like hours. She couldn't breathe, and dust filled the air in huge, billowing clouds. She was suddenly being pressed against a chest, hearing Alano's voice from far away. His words made no sense, and she repeated them again in her own mind in order to decipher them.

"The damn fool blew himself up."

She said it again, and this time she sat up, pushing herself away from Alano with both hands. Horrified, she stared at him, but he was in darkness. Everything was dark.

There was a flickering light somewhere behind him, and she suddenly realized it was fire. The two of them began to crawl toward what had once been the door.

Were they the only ones to survive?

She looked up. Part of the ceiling was gone and the floor above that as well. The night sky shone crystal clear and black and beautiful.

He was beside her, pushing against her shoulder to guide her. At least his touch proved he was alive, and so was she.

"The damn fool blew himself up."

She began to scream, but the scream was in her mind. She rose to her knees, but the fire behind them silenced her. Slowly, she stood and held her hand out to him.

"Don't say that," she said.

His figure was coated in white, his face covered in dust. Did she look as hideous? How very odd that she didn't care.

They stared at each other for long moments, the roar of the fire behind them the only sound. That, and the bells of the fire brigade ringing in the distance.

"It's true." Alano's voice was calm, compassionate, the tone of it gentle, as if by saying the words softly she wouldn't be affected by them.

"No."

Alano glanced behind him and said something. She turned and headed for the street, uncaring whom he addressed or why. The fire was spreading, pushing her from the house. At what was once the front door, and was now only long pieces of shardlike wood, she hesitated, looking back over her shoulder. Alano was on one side of the Duke of

Herridge, Tim on the other. The sudden elation she felt at seeing Tim was instantly balanced by the thought that Douglas had been here.

The damn fool blew himself up.

Oh, dear God.

She almost fell, her legs suddenly so weak she didn't think she could make it out of the house. Alano was suddenly there, holding on to her, supporting her.

"Step over this now," he said as if he were coaxing an infant to walk. The smell of a fire was growing closer, and she knew she should be afraid, but it didn't seem real.

That was it. *This* was a nightmare. She was home at Chavensworth, and she was missing Douglas. If she awoke, stretched out her hand, she would find him beside her. Naked and manly and shockingly attractive.

She needed to tell him how beautiful he was. She needed to say the words. He should know that every time she saw him, her heart beat a little faster.

"We must find Douglas," she said. The words were almost impossible to say.

"She's been hurt," someone said.

"No," Alano said, "she's grieving. She just doesn't know it yet."

She tried to pull away, but Alano was gripping her so tightly that she couldn't free herself.

With every step there was an answering crunch as she trod on glass and slivers of wood. Debris still fell on them occasionally, and everyone was shouting.

The steps were there, finally, and she stumbled down them, hands outstretched as she headed for the carriage. Edmunds was standing there, staring at the destruction, his mouth open.

Alano was still beside her, and now he shouted something to Edmunds. He jerked to attention and sprinted to the door of the carriage.

"We'll get you out of here, Lady Sarah," Edmunds said.

"No." She turned to face Alano. She knew that the fire had begun to spread because she could see his shadowed features limned in orange light.

"Don't you see," she said, far more calmly than she thought possible. "He can't be dead."

"I'm not altogether sure anything could have survived, Lady Sarah," Alano said. "The top floor is gone," he added.

She turned to face the ruin of what had been the Duke of Herridge's town house. Alano was right. The top floor was gone, not to mention there was now a large hole in the middle of the second floor. Half of the front of the house had also disintegrated in the blast.

"Come now, Lady Sarah," Alano said, leading her to the door of the carriage.

Someone shouted, a woman screamed, and suddenly the rest of the roof caved in, a billowing cloud of dust, dirt, and ash swirling toward them.

"The damn fool blew himself up," Alano repeated.

She hated Alano at that moment. Hated him because he'd had years with Douglas while she'd only had weeks. She hated him because he said aloud what no one else had the courage to say, and in doing so had solidified Douglas's fate. She hated him because there were tears rolling down his face, and she had nothing inside — not heart or soul. Even her mind was numb, unable to make sense of what had happened.

"Lady Sarah, please, the safest place is in the carriage."

"I won't leave," she said.

Edmunds came and stood beside her.

She glanced up at him, and repeated, "I won't leave," she said. "I will not."

He nodded. "Let me pull the carriage up

the street, Lady Sarah. Away from the fire."

She nodded but refused to enter until the carriage was parked a little distance away.

Alano and Tim were pressed into service to help extinguish the blaze. Edmunds stood by the horses. "Go and help. I know you want to. I'll sit in the carriage."

"I'd rather take you home, Lady Sarah."

How very odd that the image of Kilmarin came to her at that moment. Kilmarin, with its jutting towers and sprawling mass.

"There is time enough for that," she said, not wanting to admit that she really didn't want to see Chavensworth at the moment.

She would have to sleep where Douglas had slept, gripping his pillow. When she cried, it would be silently and alone, where no one could try to give her comfort.

There was no comfort to be found.

"If you're certain, Lady Sarah," he said.

"I am," she replied, wishing he would just leave her. "Go."

She glanced over her shoulder to see an otherworldly scene: black shadows and licking orange flames, clouds of great white dust, and above it all, a clear ebony sky.

She reached up and opened the carriage door, taking great care when folding the steps down. Slowly, she placed her foot on the bottom step, then the next, reaching out to pull herself into the carriage. Once there, she rearranged her skirts with the decorum she'd always been taught. Her dress was ruined, of course. The fabric was torn in two places and the whole of it covered in that odd gray dust.

Nevertheless, she sat with ankles crossed below her skirts and hands folded atop them. Somewhere, in the night, she had lost her bonnet. But then, she'd also lost her husband. All in all, a bonnet wasn't that important. Not like a husband.

She closed her eyes and willed herself not to cry. There would be time for tears for years and years into the future. For now, all she had to do was get through this night. How many more hours were there until it was morning? She needed to know so that she could count them off in her mind. If she had some goal to strive for, she might be able to make it without screaming.

The door to the carriage abruptly opened.

"What in the name of all bloody hell are you doing here? I nearly killed you, you daft woman! Have you no sense?"

She stared at Douglas, incapable of responding. All she could do was take in the sight of him, covered in soot, his black hair sticking up in spikes, his face covered by dust. His white shirt was ripped, and there was a bloody scratch on his right cheek.

Her heart was beginning to beat again, expanding from the shrunken, shriveled little mass it had been for the past thirty minutes.

She flew out of the carriage and advanced on him like a demon, beating him with her hands, hitting that beautiful chest with her clenched fists, so furious, so enraged that she didn't care what she was saying. Nor did she give a flying farthing that people's attention was no longer on the blaze but on her — Lady Sarah Eston having a fit.

"You blew yourself up, you bloody daft man," she screamed.

"Sarah!"

He grabbed her wrists with both hands and held them away from him.

"You could have died! You could have died!"

"I had all I could think of without you being in the mix," he shouted. "I could have killed you, Sarah Eston. Did you never think of that?"

She lowered her head, her rage passing, but slowly. Several long minutes passed while she strained to regain her composure. He released her wrists, and she stepped back, still breathing heavily.

"Ah, love, I could have hurt you," he said softly.

She looked up at him. "You sound very Scottish," she said. "Why is that?"

He didn't answer. Instead, in full view of anyone who chose to look in their direction, he pinned her up against the side of the carriage and kissed her — gloriously, wondrously. All she could do was hold on to him and moan when he deepened the kiss.

She slid her hands across his chest, reached out to grab his shoulders, then smoothed her palms down his arms. She wanted to feel all of him, to reassure herself that he was actually there. He wasn't a figment of her desperate imagination. This wasn't a dream in which she was given her greatest desire. He was actually there, holding her, kissing her.

"Bloody daft woman," he murmured against her lips.

"Bloody daft man," she said. "You blew yourself up."

"Well, I wouldn't have if I'd known you were coming."

She pulled back and looked at him, her hands flat against his chest. He was so precious to her and so very angry. She was just as angry. Let him be enraged. Let them both be furious, as long as he was alive.

"I could have hurt you, Sarah," he said softly, both hands touching her face. His fingers danced along her cheekbones, then threaded into the hair at her temples. His palms were rough against her cheeks, but she wouldn't have moved for anything.

"You were in danger, and I never knew," he said.

Her hands reached out and clasped his wrists. "I couldn't just let him keep you there, Douglas. I had to do something."

He shook his head. "You're a Tulloch," he said. "For all that you're the daughter of a duke."

The duke. She'd completely forgotten. She remembered seeing him being carried between Tim and Alano, then couldn't recall anything about him.

"Did he survive?"

"The blast? He did. Unfortunately, part of the wall fell on him. I believe he has a broken arm, from what Alano says."

"And Simons?"

"He and I both made it to the second floor before the explosion."

At that moment, Douglas decided to kiss her again, so she couldn't possibly concentrate on Simons's fate.

A kiss or two later, she remembered something else and pulled back, staring into his shadowed face intently.

"Why do you want to end our marriage?" she asked.

Instead of answering her, he entered the carriage and pulled her in behind him. On another day, she would tell him that such actions were not those of a gentleman, and he would write the information in his journal. For now, she tumbled onto his lap and wrapped her arms around his neck.

He chuckled and pulled her closer, hugging her so tightly that she could feel his heart beat against her breast.

He spoke softly against her temple. "I would never let you go, Sarah," he said. "It was your father who threatened me with the dissolution of the marriage if I didn't produce his diamonds."

She slapped against his shoulder, pushing back so she could stare into his face.

"He has no right! How dare he even threaten such a thing!"

"He has no rights," Douglas said, "but I didn't discover that until I inquired of my solicitor." It was his turn to study her face. "Did you follow me?"

"I was trying to find where you disappeared. I thought you'd decided not to be married anymore."

He pulled her closer as if to admonish her

for such a thought.

"I actually went to try to negotiate with your father. I was going to give him all the small diamonds I had in return for the agreement we signed. I wanted him out of our lives. Unfortunately, I never got the chance."

She stared at him. "I don't think he's my father," she said, realizing that she hadn't told him. "I may not even be Lady Sarah." She explained what she knew about her mother and Michael Tulloch.

He was quiet when she finished.

"Would your life change all that much?" he finally said. "If you discovered it was true, and you were Michael's daughter?"

She glanced at him, surprised. "It would explain why the duke has always disliked me. But I wouldn't feel right living at Chavensworth."

"You, of all people, have earned Chavensworth. I've never seen anyone work so hard or be responsible for so much."

She sat back, a little overwhelmed by his praise. She'd never known he felt that way about her.

Perhaps it was the lateness of the hour, or the grief she'd already endured, but she looked at him, hiding nothing. "My dearest love, will you please give up those horrible diamonds? I cannot endure another hour of thinking you gone."

He didn't speak, only placed his hand against her cheek, searching her face.

"I didn't think you would ever say that to me," he said softly. "Dearest love?"

"My very dearest," she said softly. "Dearling."

He brushed her chin with his fingers, traced the line of her jaw, trailed them over her lips. "I fell in love with you the moment I saw you. The moment you leveled that disdainful glance in my direction, and I saw the fear in your eyes. I thought you brave before, but now I know how much courage is in your heart."

He leaned over and kissed her and, for a delightful few moments, conversation was simply unnecessary.

When he drew back, she slid her hands up to link them behind his neck and leaned forward, placing her cheek gently against his wounded cheek.

"I was so worried," she said. She'd been grief-stricken, like the woman in the mirror. She pushed that thought from her mind, in favor of curiosity. She pulled back. "Did you cause the explosion on purpose?"

He smiled. "Actually? I planned to blow off the door, not the entire house. If Simons hadn't decided to release me, I might have been scattered from here to Scotland."

"Good for Simons," she said. "Perhaps we can find a position for him somewhere."

"I think I'll offer him a position as major-domo," he said, surprising her. "He can either educate Paulson or replace him. Either way, Alano will be happy."

She chuckled and placed her hand against his chest, over his heart, feeling it beat strongly. At this moment, this perfect moment covered in soot and dust, and breathing the scent of fire, Lady Sarah Eston was the happiest she'd ever been.

CHAPTER 33

Sarah was in the library, in a special area she'd created on the second floor behind the book stacks, when Douglas entered and called out her name.

She stood and came to the railing, looking down at Douglas. His hair was windblown, his jacket askew. It must have been raining; his hair was damp and his shirt dotted with moisture.

Dear God, please don't let the Duke of Herridge have issued another edict. He'd been driving everyone mad with his demands. He wanted his toast in a certain way; he demanded to know the name of the young girl who was nearly rude to him this morning. His mattress needed to be shifted, he wanted the Duke's Suite painted, and he hadn't liked anything Cook had prepared during the last month.

He had even grumbled about the distribution of the Henley Gift, funded entirely by

Douglas, of course. He'd been such a disruptive presence that most of the staff had turned and frowned at him. Blessedly, he'd left shortly thereafter, and the gathering had turned into a well-deserved celebration.

The Duke of Herridge had not been in residence for a great many years, and from what she'd witnessed, the staff of Chavensworth wished he'd remained in London. But with his house destroyed, there was no other place for him to go, and he'd been living there for the past twenty-seven days.

Twenty-seven miserable days.

Regrettably, there were no funds to rebuild his house in London. However, Douglas had offered Sarah to do just that one night when the Duke of Herridge was being particularly difficult. They were sitting in the Chinese Parlor, one of Douglas's favorite rooms.

"It was my fault the house burned down," he said.

"It was *his* fault for imprisoning you! And Tim!"

In the end, he'd agreed not to begin construction.

She'd not forgotten that her husband was stubborn and Scottish. When she said as much to him, Douglas had only smiled, and said, "Your being wholly Scottish would explain your degree of stubbornness, my dear wife," he said.

She stared at him. "You've never said that before."

"Called you stubborn? I think I have."

"No, called me wife."

He smiled. "Yes, I did," he said. "Our wedding day, as I remember."

That comment had led to a kiss, which had led to even more delightful occupations. In fact, it was difficult to be in the same room with Douglas. Either the urge to touch him was too great, or his kisses were too intoxicating.

Now, she looked at him with a smile, thinking that it was a rainy afternoon, there were occupations other than being in the library to intrigue her.

"Are you writing?" he asked, beginning to ascend the curved iron staircase.

She felt warmth flow through her at his words.

"What do you know about my writing?" she asked.

He held up one hand, palm toward her. "After your mother died," he said gently. "I thought to find records of how many aprons were washed, or the number of soup bowls at Chavensworth."

"There are records like that. Mrs. Williams keeps them," she said. "But you read my journal?"

He nodded. "I didn't mean to pry," he said, "but I must confess, it wasn't easy to put the story down. You tell a very good tale of adventure."

"Really?" She searched his face, but there was nothing in his expression but interest. No derision. No amusement. Had he seen himself portrayed in her journal? He'd featured prominently in the pages. "I like losing myself in telling a story," she said, a confession she'd made only to one other person — her mother. "I would love to write about the Tullochs of Kilmarin," she added.

"Which reminds me," he said, pulling something out from behind his back. He extended a drawstring bag to her.

She looked at him quizzically and reached for the bag, opening it slowly, revealing the mirror she'd brought from Scotland.

"The Tulloch Sgàthán," he said, and when she glanced at him, he explained. "The Tulloch Sgàthán — Gaelic for mirror. I've altered it a little, and given it a bit of beauty."

Ever since the day at Kilmarin when she'd seen her reflection in the mirror, she'd not looked at it again. Her caution might be foolish. But what she'd seen in the mirror had come to pass. Had the mirror the ability to foretell the future? Or was that a foolish thought? It might well be, but she didn't want to look at her reflection and see anything other than the bliss she'd enjoyed in the past weeks.

Douglas had, indeed, given the mirror a bit of beauty. Around its circular back were a hundred tiny diamonds. She smiled, enchanted at the sight.

"It's lovely," she said. "But where did you find all the diamonds?" She lowered the mirror and looked at him in concern. "You're not making diamonds again, are you? Isn't the chance of explosion too great?"

He shook his head. "I found them," he said. "Alano and I lifted the observatory door, and they were in the grass. I think they were shot out of the furnace before the explosion."

"How is Alano?" she asked, smiling.

"Determined. He's taken on Jason's education." He smiled. "Jason reminds him of me, two decades ago, of course. Alano has him reciting the capitals of Europe while we rebuild the observatory. And Mrs. Williams has deigned to unbend long enough to send him lunch from time to time, so I suppose his campaign is working on that front."

She chuckled, retreating to the table, where she put down the mirror and picked up a letter before returning to his side.

"A trade," she said, handing him an envelope. "I have something for you, as well."

"A letter?" He glanced at the envelope but made no effort to take it. "Who would be writing me?"

She smiled. "You won't know until you open it," she said. "A messenger delivered it, but he wouldn't say from where or why."

He opened the envelope and read the contents of the letter, glancing at her when he finished.

"I'm sorry, love," he said softly. "I'm sorry. It's your grandfather."

"He has died," she said.

He nodded.

Donald Tulloch had been, essentially, a stranger to her. Perhaps later she would weep, for the death of the man she'd never known. Now, however, she could only feel the loss in a detached sort of way.

"There's something else," he said.

His eyes were glittering, and the flush on his cheeks wasn't just from the weather.

There were two letters, one that Douglas had already opened, and one inside, addressed to her with the seal intact. Her name had been written in a delicate script, so lightly on the page that it was barely there, like the filament Douglas used in making his diamonds.

She broke the seal, tilted the page toward the light, and read:

Granddaughter,
I have deeded Kilmarin to your husband, another Scot who needs to return to his homeland. The house will shelter you, give you protection, and within its walls you can find family.

That was all, just two short sentences, but the implication was staggering.

She glanced over at Douglas. "He left you Kilmarin."

He nodded. "I know."

On his face was the shadow of the boy he had been, poor and hungry, hearing of the great castle near Perth.

She approached him. "You're the laird of Kilmarin," she said softly.

"I am." He smiled. "Are you coming to Scotland with me?"

"Of course I'm going with you. I'm not about to let you desert me for Scotland." She smiled. "Wherever you go, Douglas.

Scotland, Spain, France, Queensland. To the ends of the earth, if necessary. I'll go with you anywhere."

He studied her for several long moments, his gaze sweeping over her face.

She stepped forward and wrapped her arms around his neck.

"If you can remake yourself, Douglas Eston, then so can I. You give me the power to be anyone I choose to be," she said. "I think I shall like being a new person."

"Not the duke's daughter?"

She pulled back and looked into his eyes. "Would you mind if I chose to be Sarah Eston of Kilmarin, instead?"

"As long as you don't forget your true role," he said, smiling.

"The laird's wife?"

"The laird's love," he said.

"The laird's love," she agreed, and stood on tiptoe to kiss him.

EPILOGUE

The Duke of Herridge stood at the door and watched as Douglas Eston's carriage, followed by two wagons laden with trunks, set off for Scotland. The wagons were, unfortunately, followed by another carriage, this one containing his cook, his underbutler, and his stable master, in addition to a few other highly capable servants. He'd already lost his housekeeper, who'd elected to move to London and marry some Spaniard. The other disloyal fools had evidently decided that Scotland offered them more than Chavensworth. Let them go. Let them all go, including the woman he'd brought up as his own child.

Bastard. The word seemed more fitting for a male than a female. Scottish bitch — that title he reserved for her mother. Six months after their marriage, she'd whelped that child and didn't even bother to pretend it was his. His pride had demanded a lie, so he'd pretended as well. What did it matter? She was a girl. No other children had been born alive, however, and after a while, he'd given up trying.

He withdrew the mirror from the concealment of his sling. He'd found it in the library one day, a gift for the taking. Besides, Eston still owed him some diamonds. The casing of the mirror was fine, with its heavily etched gold and diamond adornment. The glass of the mirror, however, needed to be replaced. Still, it would serve as an adequate bridal gift.

As luck would have it, he already had a girl in mind. A charming, lovely creature with a laugh that made him want to smile and a voice as enchanting as a forest brook.

Anthony, Duke of Herridge, smiled, and anticipated becoming a bridegroom.

AUTHOR'S NOTE

Not long ago, I read a fascinating article about artificial diamonds. One of the paragraphs sparked my curiosity, because it told of a process invented in 1850 to make artificial diamonds. Unfortunately, the formula has subsequently been lost. From that, the plot of *Sold to a Laird* was born.

The Matrimonial Causes Act of 1857 provided the first secular divorce. A man could divorce his wife for adultery. A woman could divorce her husband as well, but in addition to adultery, she *also* had to prove either incest, bigamy, cruelty, or desertion.

Kilmarin is based on a variety of castles, one located at the mouth of the River Tay.

The legend of the White Lady is taken from a castle near Perth.

Tulloch's Folly is based on a tower on Kinnoull Hill outside of Perth, built by Lord Gray in 1829 in imitation of the castles on the Rhine. It still stands.

Architect David Smart began to renovate Balhousie Castle in 1862. The castle was, essentially, rebuilt in the baronial style, since the only original feature to survive is a rubble wall on the east side.